PRAISE FOR SUZANNE BROCKMANN

"With its realistically complex and conflicted char-acters, intense sexual tension, and edgy humor, this is Brockmann at her best."
—*Booklist,* on *Breaking Point*

"Brockmann's characters volley badinage like gre-nades, keeping [the story] moving at breakneck speed. . . . Readers will be on the edge of their seats."
—*Library Journal,* on *Breaking Point*

"The plot really is riveting, with unpredictable twists, turns, and thrills along the way. . . . A good old-fashioned page-turner."
—*OutSmart,* on *Hot Target*

"A heady mix of tension, romance, and interna-tional intrigue."
—*Publishers Weekly,* on *Flashpoint*

BREAKING
POINT

A NOVEL

SUZANNE
BROCKMANN

BALLANTINE BOOKS • NEW YORK

2006 Ballantine Books Mass Market Edition

Copyright © 2005 by Suzanne Brockmann
Excerpt from *Into the Storm* copyright © 2006 by Suzanne Brockmann

Published in the United States by Ballantine Books, an imprint of The Random House Publishing Group, a division of Random House, Inc., New York.

BALLANTINE and colophon are registered trademarks of Random House, Inc.

Originally published in hardcover in the United States by Ballantine Books, an imprint of The Random House Publishing Group, a division of Random House, Inc., in 2005.

ISBN 0-345-48013-9

Cover illustration: © H & T

Printed in the United States of America

www.ballantinebooks.com

OPM 9 8 7 6 5 4 3 2 1

For all of the readers who spent the weekend with me in Tampa—and for those who were there in spirit, too.

ACKNOWLEDGMENTS

Thank you, first and foremost, to my early draft readers, Lee Brockmann and Ed Gaffney. (Thanks, also, to Deede Bergeron and Patricia McMahon, who were standing by, ready to help!)

Thank you to the wonderful people at Ballantine Books, who work hard to put the latest installment of my ongoing series featuring SEAL Team Sixteen, Troubleshooters Inc., and Max Bhagat's FBI Counterterrorist team into readers' hands as quickly as humanly possible: Gina Centrello, Linda Marrow, Arielle Zibrak, and Signe Pike. Thank you, also, to my wonderful editor, Shauna Summers.

Thanks to Gail LeBlanc for lending me her name!

Thanks to Vivian Tönnies for helping with German translations, to Erika Schutte for standing ready with information on Kenya, and to Major Michelle Gomez USAF, Retired, for too many things to list!

Thanks to the home team: Ed, Jason and Melanie Gaffney, and Sugar and Spice, the world's greatest schnauzers.

Thanks, as always, to Eric Ruben, Steve Axelrod, and Tina Trevaskis.

Thanks to everyone involved in my *Target: Tampa* weekend: Maya Stosskopf of EMA, Gilly Hailparn and the publicity team at Ballantine Books, and my wonderful guest authors: Catherine Mann, Alesia Holliday, and Chuck Pfarrer.

A shout out to the *Target: Tampa* volunteer coordinators—

Suzie Bernhardt, Karen Metheny, and Sue Smallwood—who made this weekend-long gathering of readers possible, as well as all of the wonderful volunteers: Elizabeth and Lee Benjamin, Lee Brockmann, Jeanne Glynn, Michelle Gomez, Kim Harkins, Stephanie Hyacinth, Beki & Jim Keene, Regina LaMonica, Kay Luecke, Laura Luke, Jeanne Mangano, Heather McHugh, Peggy Mitchell, Barbara Mize, Dorbert Ogle, Gail Reddin, Marla Snead, Shannon Short, Erika Shutte, and Melissa Thompson. You rock!

An extra thanks to Maya for coming up with the promotional line "The war is within" for the (fictional!) movie *American Hero,* and to Kathy Lague for letting Max borrow her Giant Forks from Outer Space nightmare.

Check my website at www.SuzanneBrockmann.com/Appearances.htm for information about my next readers weekend.

Last but certainly not least, thank you to my readers. I love hearing from you via e-mail and letters, chatting with you on my bulletin board, and meeting you at book signings.

As always, any mistakes I've made or liberties I've taken are completely my own.

PROLOGUE

NORTH OF WASHINGTON, D.C.
SEPTEMBER, 1986
NINETEEN YEARS AGO

Max had five minutes.

Tops.

Five minutes before the SWAT team snipers were in place.

Five minutes before Leonard D'Angelo became little more than an unpleasant job for a strong-stomached cleaning team to mop from the marble-tiled bank floor.

Okay, yeah, Lenny *was* guilty of some seriously screwed-up judgment. He *had* walked into this suburban branch of the Westfield National Bank with a pistol in his pocket.

And that whole taking of hostages thing was another very, *very* bad idea.

But even if FBI agent Max Bhagat hadn't spent the past fifteen minutes in the surveillance van watching footage from the bank's security cameras and listening in to the drama now unfolding in that bank via one extremely high-tech long-range microphone, he still wouldn't have believed Lenny deserved to die for his mistakes.

Apparently Lenny had gone into the bank with a note, demanding that the teller withdraw $47,873.12 from one specific account. Problem was, he didn't have the correct ID to access those funds, so after some conversation, complete with lots of gesturing, the teller had signaled the security guard. At which point Lenny pulled out his little hand-gun.

And, as he took it out of his pocket, he blew a neat little hole into the soundproof ceiling tiles overhead.

It was an event that had made nearly everyone in the bank burst into tears—including Bankrobber Lenny, who still continued to sob.

The so-called security guard had immediately handed over his own weapon—without making any attempt whatsoever to talk the gun out of Lenny's hand. After his full surrender, the guard then led the hostages safely down onto the floor, hands on their heads. Everyone except two very young children who were being held by their mother.

They huddled against the wall.

The head teller had hurried to make Lenny's withdrawal, but by then her cooperation was too little too late.

Because the noise of the gunshot had drawn first the local, then the state police, and then—because one of the tellers was related to a federal judge—finally this FBI team, of which Max was a junior member. The bank was now surrounded by dozens of cop cars: lights spinning, doors open as both uniformed and plainclothes officers stood in the street, well outside the range of the gunman's little weapon.

It soon became clear to the entire task force that their hostage-taker had no designs on the VIP teller and that he was, in fact, a total amateur. This was a fact which brought with it both the good news and the bad.

The good news was that Lenny was so criminally inept that he continued to stand smack in the middle of the bank. He was directly in front of big plate-glass windows—a clean, clear target for the SWAT team snipers.

The bad news was that, until the SWAT team got into place, he was a potential loose cannon. The man hadn't spoken a single coherent sentence since Max had started listening in. He just continued to cry, making oddly animal-like keening sounds as he now awkwardly held both his and the security guard's guns.

"Let me go in there, sir," Max had requested of his team leader, Ronald Shaw, who was also the agent in charge.

But Shaw shook his head, not even taking the time to answer the junior agent. Max had been working with the team for several weeks and he was pretty certain Shaw didn't know his name.

Still, he persisted. "Sir. Something's up with this guy. I'd like to try to talk to him."

Leonard D'Angelo had no record, no priors. He wasn't in the system for so much as a parking ticket. Desperate for information about the hostage-taker, Max had called a friend in the IRS, who'd told him that Lenny D. was a hard-working, taxpaying construction worker. He was also the married father of a young son.

He was Joe Average—or at least he had been before something had made him go postal.

Loss of job, loss of home, loss of wife and child through divorce. . . ? It could have been any number of things.

Max had tried calling Lenny's wife at their home number—only to be greeted by an automated message. "This number has been disconnected."

Not a good sign.

Following procedure, Max requested the local police pay a visit to the D'Angelo's tiny apartment—the morbid thought being that Len may have snuffed his entire family before setting out on this crime spree.

But Max didn't believe that scenario.

If this guy was homicidal, he already would've used his weapon.

And what about his request for an exact sum, down to the penny—what had he asked for. . . ? Twelve freakin' cents.

Max didn't have a whole lot of experience, but this

smelled to him like some kind of crime of passion. Retribution for money misspent or unwisely invested, perhaps?

Something was up, that was for sure. Because why, for the love of God, wouldn't Lenny pick up the bank telephone and talk to them?

He had to know they were out here. Fourteen police cars weren't something that could be overlooked by anyone but a blind man.

And okay, yes. Max could have it totally wrong. Maybe Lenny *had* killed his entire family. But even if he had, it was beyond obvious that his homicidal rage had faded. He was currently incapable of doing more than standing in the middle of the bank and crying.

Max was willing to bet his very life that he could walk right through those doors, right up to Lenny, and simply take the weapons from his limp-fish hands.

"I'd like to try," Max said to Shaw again.

"It's too dangerous," Shaw responded as they stood outside the van, watching a television monitor that showed the gunman crying in the middle of the bank. The camera responsible for that picture had a state-of-the-art zoom lens. Even shot through the reflective glass of the window, it provided a sharp close-up of Lenny's tear-streaked face. "Do whatever you have to do to get him to pick up that phone."

Ronald Shaw was weeks from retirement. Was it possible that he was afraid of smearing his record by giving one of his newest, greenest negotiators permission to get himself killed?

Even if it meant shooting Leonard D'Angelo without a single word of negotiation?

Goddamn it. Max had thought a man like Ronald Shaw would do better than that.

"Sir, we've got every phone line ringing in there," Max informed his boss. "He's not picking up."

"Keep trying, Matt," Shaw ordered curtly as he walked away from the van.

"It's Max," he shouted after Shaw. "And keep trying until when? Until the SWAT team snipers put a bullet through Lenny's head?"

But Shaw was gone.

Smitty Durkin was in the street, manning the bullhorn. "Mr. D'Angelo, you must pick up the phone immediately! Leonard D'Angelo, pick up the telephone!" As Smit's finger left the button, the bullhorn let out an ungodly squeal.

On camera, in full close-up on that TV monitor, Leonard D'Angelo didn't so much as blink.

Sure he was inside the bank, but still, that sound was freaking loud.

Grit-your-teeth-and-flinch loud.

And suddenly Max knew.

Okay, *knew* was perhaps too strong a word for it. *Strongly suspected* was more accurate.

Leonard D'Angelo hadn't picked up the telephone because he didn't hear it ringing. Max strongly suspected that Leonard D'Angelo, although not blind, was most likely deaf.

And Jesus, there was nothing to write on except a yellow legal pad in Max's briefcase. It wasn't half as big as he needed, but it would have to do.

There was a marker—one of those indelible Sharpies—attached to the inside panel of the van by a string. Max grabbed and pulled.

He wrote as he ran, pushing his way through the uniformed officers, moving outside of the protective circle of police cars and into the street directly in front of the bank's glass door.

I AM UNARMED. Max held up the sign with one hand as he shrugged off his jacket. He unclipped his shoulder holster, putting it onto the street along with the secondary weapon that he wore at the small of his back.

Inside the bank, Lenny had spotted him. Max could see the man shaking his head, his weapon now halfheartedly aimed directly at the door Max would have to pass through to get inside that building.

Max turned the page of his pad. I'M COMING INSIDE TO TALK. He held up that sign.

But Lenny still shook his head.

Max took off his tie and crisply starched white dress shirt, then used the marker to underline the words, holding up his first sign again. I AM UNARMED.

As Lenny kept shaking his head, Max could hear Ron Shaw's voice. Shouting. "What does that motherfucker think he's doing?"

Max was, of course, the motherfucker to whom Shaw was referring.

He kicked off his shoes, pulled off his socks, rolled up the bottoms of his pants. Nothing up these pant legs, Lenny. See? He held up the sign again. I AM UNARMED.

No, Lenny told him, still shaking his head.

"Get out of there, Bhagat," Shaw shouted. How about that? He'd finally learned Max's name. "The snipers are in place and you're in the goddamn way!"

The entire local police force and a whole lot of civilian spectators watched as Max unfastened his pants. But, oh *shit*. Look what he was wearing today.

Max Bhagat was the proud owner of fifty-seven pairs of utilitarian white briefs—all of which had been in the laundry when he'd gotten dressed this morning. He'd been forced to dig into the back of his underwear drawer and, when faced with a choice between a pair of boxers with pink hearts or black bikini briefs with the word *Stud* across the front in red sequins—both gifts from Elisabeth, a seriously misguided ex-girlfriend—he'd gone with the red sequins.

Right now, Max had no choice. He was not going to stand by and let Leonard D'Angelo get a bullet to the brain.

On the other hand, the idea of being known forevermore

throughout the Federal Bureau of Investigations as "Mr. Sequins" or, God help him, "Stud-Boy," was equally unbearable.

Which left him with option three.

As Max pushed down his pants, he hooked his fingers in his briefs and took them off, too.

And this time when he held up his sign, it was very clear to everyone within a solid two block radius that he was, indeed, completely and totally unarmed.

Inside the bank, Lenny's mouth had dropped open. He was no longer shaking his head and his gun hand had drooped significantly, so Max held up his second sign.

And walked, stark naked, into that bank.

Max stood in front of Ronald Shaw's desk, waiting for the noise to stop, mentally making a note to keep a change of underwear in his locker from now on.

It was possible he was slightly allergic to wool.

"You're not even listening, are you?" Shaw roared even louder.

Whoops. "To be honest, sir," Max admitted at a far lower decibel level, "when you started repeating yourself for the third time, yes, I did tune out. Was there something you wanted to add?"

Shaw laughed. And sat down. "You're pretty sure of yourself, aren't you, Bhagat?"

Max considered that. "I think it's safe to say I have a God-given talent when it comes to reading people, sir."

After walking into that bank it had taken him all of four seconds to gain possession of both of Leonard D'Angelo's weapons.

Max had been right—the man was no criminal, let alone capable of shooting anyone.

Leonard D'Angelo was a grief-stricken father who had made a whole series of flat-out stupid mistakes.

The man's two-year-old son had been born with a defective heart. He and his wife had sold their house and scraped together all of their savings to pay for an operation to repair the boy's faulty valve. But their son had died on the operating table.

With the wild irrationality of the deeply grieving, Lenny had gone to the doctor and demanded their money back—seeing as how the operation hadn't saved their boy's life.

When the doctor refused, Lenny somehow found out where the man did his banking, and went to get the cash that he felt should be returned to him.

Cash he needed in order to find his wife, who had taken off with their only car, inconsolable over the loss of their child.

"I told you not to go into the bank," Shaw reminded Max now. "I specifically ordered—"

"With all due respect, sir," Max interrupted, "you told me to do whatever I had to do to get D'Angelo to pick up the phone. But how was he going to pick it up if he couldn't hear it ringing?"

Max's intention had been to go in—sans clothing and therefore unarmed—and start a dialogue with D'Angelo. If the gunman had been willing, Max would then have picked up the phone. And, since the hearing-impaired hostage-taker also obviously couldn't hold a conversation using a conventional telephone, it had been Max's intention to act as a go-between—using pen and that legal pad to communicate between D'Angelo and the FBI negotiator out on the street.

And hopefully, somewhere during the negotiation, someone would have sent in his pants.

But Max had told Shaw all this already. Several times, in fact. In writing, as well.

Max had also stated that before he offered to act as D'Angelo's go-between, it had seemed something of a no-brainer simply to ask the hostage-taker to hand over his weapons.

Which the man had done. With a great deal of relief.

Max had been relieved, too. At which point he'd held his legal pad up like an office supply loincloth as the hostages had rushed outside and the police and FBI rushed in.

Smitty Durkin brought Max's things into the bank—except his underwear wasn't with the rest of his clothes. Max could only hope that they'd fallen out of the leg of his pants, and that a strong wind had pushed them underneath some car, and into a puddle still standing from last night's rain.

"I admire you, sir," Max told Shaw now. "Very much. Your record as a team leader is remarkable. And I would never say this outside the privacy of your office, but it's my opinion that you made the wrong call out there today. You should have given me permission to go to that bank. I think you know that, sir."

If Leonard D'Angelo had died today, it would have been on Shaw. Completely. And Shaw had Max to thank for preventing that tragedy.

But Shaw didn't say a word. He just sat back in his seat, gazing up at Max. His eyes were icy cold, and, if he hadn't had the reputation for being a fair-minded leader, or if he hadn't given himself away with that bark of laughter, Max might've been worried that he'd said too much.

As it was, Max used the lengthening silence to study the subtle way Shaw made himself completely unreadable, totally unapproachable. It was more than a flat lack of emotion in the man's eyes, more than the stony stillness of his facial expression. It was in his body language, too. He held himself open, elbows on the arms of his chair.

Interesting. That nondefensive pose actually added much to the hardass flavor of Shaw's entire unspoken message: "Quake in your shoes, underling, for you have no idea what I'm going to say or do next."

Except Max did know. Despite all the shouting, Shaw had finally noticed him.

It was a solid three minutes before Shaw spoke, but Max just stood there, holding the man's gaze, fighting his swallow reflex by sheer force of will.

"My replacement is Kurt Herdson," Shaw finally said.

Max didn't let himself so much as blink at the change of subject. "Yes, sir. I'm aware of that."

"Do you know him?"

"No, sir."

"He's a number cruncher." The smile Shaw gave him wasn't particularly nice. "You seem to like balls-out honesty, Bhagat, so I'll put it to you plain: He's going to hate your fucking guts."

"Yes, sir, he probably will," Max agreed evenly. He smiled, too. "I'm looking forward to the challenge."

Shaw laughed again. And again changed directions. "You married, son?"

"No, sir."

"Some unsolicited advice? Get married. Soon. When you make team leader you won't have time to chase women. Hell, you won't have time to breathe. If there's someone out there that you can't live without, leg shackle yourself to her before she gets away. You know the old saying? Wives wait but ladyfriends leave? It's true. Especially in our line of work."

Max shook his head. "I'm not . . . I don't . . . I appreciate the advice, sir." If there was someone out there that he couldn't live without, he hadn't met her yet.

"Even if you're a player, *stud* . . ." Shaw leaned on the word. *Oh, Christ.* "You're better off having one than none, especially when that one is waiting for you at home, doing your laundry and cooking your dinner."

Now Max was internally wincing for a different reason. He was glad that one of the women who worked in the office hadn't overheard. "I'm pretty good at doing my own laundry, sir. And, uh, speaking of laundry . . ."

But Shaw was waving him away. "Your secret's safe with me. Get out of here, I have work to do."

Max headed for the door, but Shaw stopped him before he closed it behind him.

"Bhagat."

"Yes, sir?"

"Thanks."

Max nodded. Leonard D'Angelo's unnecessary death would've been a hell of a thing for Shaw to carry around for the rest of his life. "You're welcome, sir. Thank you, too," he said, and shut the door behind him.

He was halfway to his desk before he realized what Shaw had said. *When you make team leader . . .*

When, not *if.*

Hot damn. Max smiled. He was well on his way.

Four days later, in East Meadow, Long Island—a post–World War II tract house 'burb of New York City—Gina Vitagliano started the first grade.

CHAPTER ONE

It was a fabulous day. Blue sky. Low humidity. Not a lot of traffic this time of morning. Green lights at every intersection. A parking spot within javelin-throwing distance of the office building.

The elevator opened at the touch of the button and he rode it, express, all the way up to his floor. The doors opened again, and he got a good look at himself in the foyer mirror.

Dressed to shine in his favorite black suit, with a new shirt he'd bought himself as a present, Jules Cassidy was not your average, run-of-the-mill FBI agent, that was for sure. He pocketed his sunglasses and adjusted his tie, then headed down the hallway with a spring in his step.

When you look good, you feel good. No doubt about them apples.

Laronda's reception desk sat empty, but Max Bhagat's office door was tightly closed.

As early as Jules had come in today, his boss, the legendary FBI team leader known as "the Max" to his younger, more irreverent, and slightly less original junior subordinates—but never, ever called that to his face—had come in even earlier.

Although, to be honest, it was equally likely that Max had merely stayed extremely late.

Not that anyone would ever be able to tell the difference. Max didn't do rumpled, even when staying up for seventy-two hours straight. In fact, he could be sat on by a hippopotamus in a bizarre zookeeping accident and the first thing he would say after regaining consciousness would be, "Somebody get me a clean shirt."

The man kept at least two complete changes of clothing in his office, not to mention a series of electric razors in his desk drawer, his briefcase, his car's glove compartment, and probably one or two places Jules didn't know about.

Hey now, ho now! Max wasn't the only one in early today. That was definitely gourmet coffee that Jules smelled brewing. Max may have been a brilliant negotiator, but the man was severely coffee-making challenged.

French vanilla. Lordy, lordy, Jules loved the French vanilla. Even though he hadn't gotten into the office before Max or the mysterious coffee brewer, it remained, indeed, a glorious, promise-filled day.

Jules stopped at the kitchen cubby and—thank you, baby Jesus!—found his favorite mug already squeaky clean in the drying rack. The container that held the ground coffee beans was empty, but there was enough for one more generous cup in the pot on the warmer.

The TV was set to CNN Headline News, but the volume was muted. As Jules filled his Mighty Mouse mug with the last of the coffee, the too-handsome anchor smiled sunnily at him, as if to say, "Good morning, sweetie-cakes! Something very good is coming your way today!"

At which point the station cut to a commercial break.

An olive-drab and sepia-tinted World War II battle scene—no doubt an ad for the History Channel—filled the screen. But then the fighting dissolved into a full color close-up of a helmeted young man, his perfect cheekbones streaked with dirt.

Holy GI! Those were Robin Chadwick's perfect cheek-bones. This was no History Channel ad, Batman, it was a movie trailer. Shit, it was *the* movie trailer.

In his haste to reach the remote control, Jules damn near scalded his hand, and the mug slipped with a crash into the sink. The coffee splashed—no!—right up onto his new shirt.

He ran his burned fingers under the cool water as he used his other hand to turn up the volume on the TV. He knew he shouldn't. He absolutely should've turned the damn thing off but he couldn't help himself.

Thundering choral music played while the picture dissolved again, this time to a close-up of another young actor as darkly handsome as Robin was fair.

It was Adam Wyndham.

Jules's lying, cheating, son-of-a-bitch ex.

God, he looked good.

As an actor.

He looked good *on film,* with the flattering lights and makeup. That's what Jules had meant. That was not some kind of masochistic, longing-for-reconciliation, *he-looked-good* thought that had popped into his head.

No, no, no, he was securely in the been-there-done-that phase as far as Adam was concerned.

But as Jules continued to cool his fingers, the picture dissolved again, this time to both actors as they sat shoulder to shoulder, dressed in World War II battle gear, gorgeous and giddy with silent laughter as the thunderous music played on—movie trailer code signaling that this was a meaningful epic drama.

Then a cut to another scene as, still side by side, the two men ran, weapons locked and loaded, up a beach into battle.

The picture froze with them both midstride, and faded back to that same earlier sepia tone as the voiceover announced, "*American Hero*. The war is within . . . Starts Friday in select theaters."

Jules's expensive new shirt was stained, his favorite mug had cracked, the French vanilla coffee was gone, and the movie starring his cheating ex–significant other, the movie he'd stayed out of theaters for the past two months to avoid seeing, the movie that had made him toss his subscription copies of *Entertainment Weekly* to avoid reading about, didn't even open until this Friday.

Fuck a duck.

But okay. That sky outside the window was still blue. And Deb Erlanger, one of his fellow FBI teammates, appeared like an angel of mercy bringing tidings of hope and caffeine. "Hey, Jules. We're going to Starbucks. Want something?"

Her partner, Joe Hirabayashi, was right behind her. What was this? National Come-In-Early day?

Jules muted the TV's volume again. "Any chance they've started selling business attire?" Like Max, he kept an extra shirt in his office. But unlike Max, he'd used his two days ago and had forgotten to replace it.

Yashi surveyed the damage and summed it up concisely, as was his zenlike way. "Shit, man. That shirt's ruined."

"Aren't you having some kind of review today?" Deb asked. "With Peggy Ryan?"

Yes, Deb. Yes, he was. In fact, his review today wasn't merely "some kind of." Instead, it fell into the subcategory of "review, comma, extremely important."

Jules was up for a promotion. So far he'd sat down with all of the team leaders—except for Peggy Ryan, to whom he was going to talk today.

Peggy was one of those people who dealt with her homophobia by pretending Jules simply didn't exist. In the past, Jules had cooperated by staying out of Peggy's way as much as possible.

But this was one meeting neither of them could avoid. It was going to make for an interesting afternoon, that was for durn sure.

"Maybe that's a good thing," Yashi said, gesturing with his chin toward the dark blotch that Jules was now half-heartedly blotting with a paper towel. "Coffee stain on your shirt. Kinda makes you look straight." He scrunched up his face. "If, you know, you squint . . ."

"You definitely need a gingerbread latte, extra whipped cream," Deb decided for Jules. "We'll be right back."

But it was then that George Faulkner appeared, blocking their route. He was out of breath, which was somewhat novel. Jules hadn't been aware that George even knew how to run.

"Where's Laronda?" George asked, his tone broadcasting all kinds of grim.

"She's not coming in," Deb told him.

"What? Why not?" Jules hadn't known it was a Laronda-less day.

Laronda was Max's administrative assistant. A day without Laronda was about as productive and as much fun as a day spent hitting one's thumb with a hammer. Over and over and over. Ouch, ouch, ouch.

"Her son's debate club made it to the national finals," Deb explained. "Just out of the blue—total long shot. The Max told her to take a few days and go to Boston with the kid. She won't be back until Friday."

Pain. Pain!

"Max needs to see this." George was ultrafocused and one-track this morning, holding up some sort of e-mail that he'd printed out.

"Temp should be here in an hour," Yashi said. "Put it on Laronda's desk, let her deal."

"No," Jules said. "Nuh-uh." Last time a temp came in to replace Laronda, it was twice as awful. "We want to get anything done today, we need to take shifts."

Deb and Yashi both started making noise, but Jules stopped them.

"An hour at a time at Laronda's desk," he said, in his

take-no-arguments voice. "We can all survive being Max's AA for one hour at a time. You know we can." But, shit, shit, shit. So much for running out to get a new shirt before his meeting with Peggy Ryan. "I'll go first, then Yashi, then George, then you, Deb . . ."

"I'll get lots of extra coffee," Deb decided.

"Good. Yash, call Fran and Manny, give them a heads up," Jules ordered. "Tell them to get in, ASAP."

"George, what do you want from Starbucks?" Deb asked.

"Max really needs to see this," George persisted, talking directly to Jules now. "Right away."

Shit. Jules took the e-mail and skimmed it, while Deb leaned in and read over his shoulder. It was a list of names under the morbid heading *Civilians Killed in Hamburg Cafe Blast.* This latest terrorist attack had occurred in Germany just yesterday morning, and the focus of most of the media's reporting had been on the fact that the casualties had been low—that the car bombing could have been much more devastating.

Seeing these names in a list, however, brought home the fact that quite a few people had died.

"We aren't handling this," Jules reminded George. "Frisk's team is. I know Max wants to keep in the loop, but there's no urgency to this particular—"

"Oh, yes, there is," George interrupted.

"Aw shit," Deb breathed, pointing at the very bottom of the list. Yashi leaned closer to look, too, and . . .

Jules followed her finger, and saw two words that made his heart stop.

Gina.

And Vitagliano.

He double-checked the heading. *Civilians Killed . . .*

"Oh, God, no," he said. Not Gina Vitagliano.

The only woman who had ever truly captured Max Bhagat's teflon-coated heart. A woman Max had not only let get away, but a woman he had pushed and shoved until she'd finally up and left.

Which didn't mean he hadn't loved her; that he didn't love her still.

Dear sweet Jesus . . .

"Someone's got to tell him," Deb whispered.

Jules looked up to find them all watching him. As if he were their team leader or something. No fair—he hadn't been promoted yet.

"Yeah, I'll do it," he said, in a voice that he couldn't quite make sound like his own. "Gina was my friend, too." Jesus—Gina *was*. He hated having to say that. God, how could this have happened?

Outside the window, the cloudless sky now seemed mockingly blue. Jules wished he could jump back in time to earlier this morning, when his clock radio had first burst into song. This time around he'd shut it off, turn over, and go back to sleep.

But really, that would've just put off the inevitable.

Somehow, someway, they were all going to make it through this awful, terrible day.

Jules cleared his aching throat. "Yashi, find out what Gina was doing in Germany. Last I knew, she was still in Kenya with . . ." Damn it, what was it? He pulled it out of his ass. "AAI—AIDS Awareness International. Get in touch with them—find out what you can. George, contact Walter Frisk. We'll want to know everything he knows about the blast, and we'll want to know it *now*." He turned to Deb. "Get that coffee, then assist George. Go."

They scattered.

When Max saw this e-mail, he was going to have a crapload of questions, none of which Jules could answer.

At least not yet.

Jules wiped his eyes, straightened his tie, and with a heavy heart beneath a ruined shirt that *so* didn't matter anymore, he began the long walk to Max's office.

ARLINGTON, VIRGINIA
JANUARY 12, 2004
SEVENTEEN MONTHS AGO

Max forced himself to relax. He kept his shoulders from tightening, his fists from clenching, and—hardest of all—the muscles in his jaw from jumping as he made certain he didn't grind his teeth.

He managed to cross his legs and slightly raise one eyebrow. He knew that this, in combination with the half-smile that he let flicker about the edges of his lips, made him look friendly and open to any and all conversation.

He'd been an FBI negotiator—no, he'd been *the* FBI negotiator—for more years than he could count on all his fingers and the toes of one foot. He'd worked his magic on hardened criminals and desperate terrorists—men and women who far too often were ready and willing to die.

This should be a cakewalk, this civil discussion between three rational, clear-thinking adults. Max. Gina. And Rita Hennimen, the couples counselor Gina had found in the Yellow Pages.

No doubt under the heading, "Max's Worst Nightmare."

Max had never been so terrified in his entire life.

Gina was watching him from the other side of the sofa. She'd purposely dressed like a teenager today in a snug-fitting T-shirt that didn't meet the low-cut waistband of her jeans. It was impossible to look at her and not think about sex, about her wrapping her legs around him and sending him into outer space.

Max cleared his throat, shifting in his seat—which made him lift his left arm just a little too high—zinging himself in the process.

Christ, would the pain in his shoulder ever go away? He'd been shot in the chest. There'd been a freaking hole in his lung, but it was the end result of that bullet ricocheting up and smashing his collarbone that continued to bother him the most.

As Rita finished reading through the forms they'd both filled out in the waiting room, Gina leaned closer. "You okay?" she asked Max.

"I'm fine," he lied.

She gazed at him for a moment before she spoke again. "One of the important rules of therapy is that you have to be honest. When we come into this room, we absolutely have to tell the truth. Otherwise, it's all just more bullshit."

When he'd first sat down, he'd hooked his cane on the arm of the sofa, and it now fell onto the floor with a clatter. Thank God. He bent to pick it up. After he straightened up, Rita was smiling at them, ready to begin.

"So," the counselor said. "Where shall we start?"

Gina was still watching him. "Good question. What do *you* want to talk about, Max?"

"Basketball?" he answered, and she laughed as he'd hoped she would.

"I suppose that's my fault for telling you to be honest." She turned to Rita. "Here's the deal. According to Max's definition, we shouldn't really be here, because we're not a couple. We're not together—we're friends. Only there's this thing between us. History. Chemistry. Oh, yeah, and the fact that I'm in love with him probably plays a part in there somewhere. Although Max will tell you that I don't really love him, that after years and years and years, what I feel is still partly 'transference.' As I told you on the phone, I was on this plane that got hijacked, and Max saved my life—"

"You saved your own life," Max interrupted.

"Apparently that part's subject to interpretation, too," Gina told the therapist. "I know he saved my life. He, no doubt, can argue that he didn't. Factor in the age difference thing—which frankly, *I* don't have a problem with . . ."

Rita glanced down at her clipboard, obviously checking their dates of birth. It wouldn't take long for her to figure out that Gina was almost twenty-four, and Max was nearly twenty years older. But the woman was a highly trained professional, so she didn't so much as blink. She *did* smile when she looked up and met his gaze.

"Love doesn't always stop to do the math," she pointed out.

Yeah, but everybody else did and most of them passed judgment, too. Debra, one of the nurses in the physical rehab facility, for example, sure as hell disapproved. If she could have, she would've turned Max into a smoldering pile of ashes weeks ago. But right now he just kept his mouth shut and let Gina go on talking.

"I can't get him to talk to me," Gina told the therapist. "Every time I try, we end up . . ."

Oh no, she couldn't—

". . . having sex instead."

Oh yes, she did.

"I figured if we came here . . ." Gina continued. "Well, with you in the room, I thought we might actually be able to have a conversation, instead of, you know."

As far as nightmares went, this could have been worse. He could have been transported back into his scrawny, undersized sixteen-year-old body, forced to wander the halls of his high school, naked, while searching for his locker.

No doubt about it, it was time for him to wake up. He grabbed for his cane. "I'm sorry. I can't do this."

He pushed himself up off the couch, even as he realized how ridiculous it was to run away. He could leave the room, sure, but he'd never outrun the chaos that clamored inside his head.

Gina stood, too, and blocked his route to the door. "Max. Please. There's so much that we just never talk about, that we just pretend never happened." She took a deep breath. "Like Alyssa."

Oh, Christ. Max laughed because laughing saved him the hundreds of dollars in dental work he'd surely need after damaging his teeth from excessive grinding. And even he, the teeth-grinding master—couldn't manage to grind his teeth while laughing. He turned to Rita. "Will you excuse us for a minute?"

But Gina crossed her arms. She clearly wasn't going anywhere. "This is the point of therapy, Max. To talk about things we can't otherwise seem to talk about. Right here, in front of Rita."

So okay. Now he was actually longing for the naked locker scenario. Or that doozy of a recurring nightmare he'd had as a child. Giant forks from outer space. He'd slept on his side for years, so as to slip between the tines and avoid death by impalement.

"Why don't we come back to this a little later?" Rita suggested. "This seems like a particularly sensitive topic."

"Okay, no," Max said. "You're wrong. It's not." He turned to Gina. "Alyssa Locke doesn't work for me anymore. You know that. I haven't spoken to her in . . ." Weeks, he was going to say, but that wasn't quite true.

"I know she came to see you at the physical rehab center," Gina said. "Don't you think it's odd that you didn't so much as mention that to me?"

What was *odd* was talking about this in front of an audience, like participants in some horrible reality TV show. True, Rita was only one person, but it still felt as if she were somehow keeping score on that notepad. At the end of their fifty minutes, she was going to lean toward Max with a sympathetic smile and tell him, "Your journey ends here. You're going home."

God, he wanted to go home.

Not to the rehab center. Not to his pathetic excuse of an apartment. Certainly not to his parents' homes—one on each coast.

So where did that leave him?

Gina was waiting for his answer. Didn't he think it was odd . . . ?

"There was nothing to mention," he told her. "Alyssa's visit was work related. I didn't want to . . ." He exhaled hard. "She's a non-topic. I suppose we could make her one if you really want to turn this into a soap opera—" Gina flinched at that, and he cut himself off, hating himself even more than usual. "Gina, please," he said quietly, "I can't do this."

"What, talk?" she countered, not trying to hide the hurt in her eyes. Hurt she usually was so careful not to let him see. It broke his heart.

"We talk," he said.

"You know, I pick up your mail from your apartment every other day. You don't think I could tell that the fancy envelope from Alyssa and what's-his-name was a wedding invitation?"

Alyssa again. "Sam," Max said. Alyssa's fiancé's name was Sam.

Gina turned to Rita. "It was really only a few months ago that Max asked Alyssa to marry him. She worked for him, and he fell in love with her, only he had this rule about getting involved with his subordinates, so he made sure they were just friends—at least that's what Jules told me. Just friends—right up until the day he asked her to marry him." She laughed, but he suspected she was laughing for reasons similar to his own, pertaining to dental care. "Here's something I've never dared to ask you, Max. Were you *just friends* with Alyssa the way you and I are *just friends*?"

"No," Max told her. "Alyssa and I never . . ." He shook his head. "She worked for me . . ."

"That wouldn't have stopped some men," Rita pointed out.

"It stopped me," he told her flatly.

"So acting honorably is important to you." Rita made a note on her notepad, which pissed him off even more.

Max turned to Gina. "Look, I'm sorry, but this is too personal. Let's go somewhere private where we can—"

"Have sex?" she asked.

Max briefly closed his eyes. "Talk."

"Like the way we talked after you got Alyssa's wedding invitation?" she asked him.

God. "What did you want me to say to you? 'Hey, guess what I got in the mail today'?"

"Considering we hadn't so much as spoken her name since before you were shot and nearly died," she retorted hotly, "it seemed to merit at least a mention, yes. But you said nothing. I came in and I gave you every opportunity to talk to me, and you remember what we did instead?"

Yes, Max most certainly did remember. Gina, naked and in his bed, was damn hard to forget. He glanced at Rita, who was smart enough not to need it spelled out for her.

Except, that night, Gina had seduced him. As she so often did. It was usually always Gina who made the first move. Although, to be fair, he never stopped her. Yeah, he tried, but it was never heartfelt. And he never succeeded.

Because if she was willing to give so freely of herself, who was he to turn her down?

And wasn't he the biggest freaking liar in the world? The real truth was that he burned for this girl. Day and night. Their relationship was all kinds of wrong for all kinds of reasons, and he knew he had to stay away from her, but he goddamn couldn't. So whatever she offered, he took. Greedily. Like an addict who knew that, sooner or later, he'd be cut off cold.

"Let's back up a bit," the counselor said. "This history you mentioned." She looked at Gina. "May I recap for Max some of what you told me over the phone?"

"Please."

"Correct me if I got it wrong," Rita said, "but you met four years ago, when Gina was a passenger on a hijacked airliner. This was pre-9/11—the plane was on the ground in . . ." She searched her notes.

"Kazbekistan," Max said.

"You were the . . . FBI negotiator? I thought the United States didn't negotiate with terrorists."

"We don't," he explained. "But we do talk to them. Try to convince them to surrender. Worst case, we stall. We listen to their complaints, pretend to negotiate, while rescuers—in this case a SEAL team—prepared to take down—take control of—the plane using force."

Rita nodded. "I see."

"The actual takedown happens in, like, thirty seconds," Gina told the therapist. "But it's intricately choreographed. They have to blow open the doors and kill the hijackers, while trying not to injure any of the passengers. It takes time to prepare for that."

Rita focused on Gina. "And you were on that plane for all that time. All those . . . hours?"

"Days," Max corrected her grimly. He sat back down. This was something that Gina needed to talk about, to work through—her harrowing experience of being held hostage. As much as he hated therapy, he would have stuck needles under his fingernails if it would help her find closure. "The terrorists who hijacked the plane got hold of a passenger list that said Senator Crawford's daughter, Karen, was on that flight."

"Except her ticket was stolen," Gina interjected.

"The hijackers demanded she step forward. Of course, she didn't, she wasn't there. The gunmen threatened to start killing everyone on board so Gina stood up and pretended to be this girl." Max had to stop and clear his throat. Her incredible, selfless bravery still impressed the crap out of him. "They brought her up into the cockpit of the plane, away from the other passengers."

"Held at gunpoint, all that time." Rita exhaled hard. "All alone?"

But Gina shook her head. "I wasn't alone. Max was with me."

Damn it, she always said this. "I was in the airport terminal," he told the therapist. "I used a radio to maintain contact with the plane. Gina acted as the go-between, because the terrorists didn't want to talk directly to me. So I talked to her, knowing they were listening in."

"That's not the only reason you talked to me," Gina said.

She was right. He had been inappropriately attracted to her right from the start.

"Did she give you a list of the injuries she received while I was *with her* on that plane?" Max asked the therapist. He ticked them off on his fingers. "Broken wrist, broken ribs, black eye, a variety of cuts and contusions—"

"She mentioned the attack," Rita said. "Of course."

"No, no, we don't use that word," Max said. "We prefer brutal honesty. We call it what it was—rape."

The word seemed to ring in the silence that followed, and he felt his throat tightened, his stomach knot. Ah, God . . .

"That must have been terrible, Max," Rita said quietly. "To be able to listen in, to witness that violence as it happened. Gina said there were surveillance cameras. It must have been devastating to watch that."

Why was she talking to him? "More so to Gina, don't you think?"

"I've finally started to forgive myself for it, Max," Gina said. "God, you were the one who told me it wasn't my fault, that I didn't provoke them. Why can't you do the same?"

The therapist turned to him. "Let's explore this. Do you remember what you felt, what you—"

"What, are you kidding?" Of course she wasn't kidding. Therapists didn't kid. In fact, kidding with clients was in the therapist rule book's Giant List of Don'ts, along with excessive use of whoopee cushions and plastic vomit, and wearing white coats after Labor Day.

But Max finally understood. They weren't here today for Gina, they were here for *him*.

As if this would help. As if digging and poking at his anger and guilt would do anything other than make him howl in frustration and pain.

He used his cane to pull himself back to his feet. "I'm done. I'm sorry. I can't . . ."

"Then what are we doing?" Gina asked softly. "Is our relationship really just temporary? You know, I keep making deals with myself. I'll only stay another week, until you're out of the hospital. I'll only stay until you get settled into the physical rehab center. I'll only stay until you can walk without your cane. But really, I'm lying to myself. I just keep waiting, hoping that, I don't know . . ." She laughed, a pain-filled exhale of air. "Maybe, I think if we keep making love you'll wake up one morning and say 'I can't live without you . . .' "

Jesus. "What I can't do is give you what you want," Max whispered.

"Even when all I want is for you to talk to me?" Her eyes filled with tears. "There was a time when. . . . You used to tell me everything."

Max couldn't answer that. What could he possibly say? *Actually, no, I left out quite a bit . . .*

Silence seemed to surround them both, stretching on and on.

Rita interrupted it. "Gina, if you could say anything to Max right now, anything at all, what would you say?"

"Stop treating me as if I might break. Even when we make love, you're so . . . *careful*. Like you bring that entire 747 into bed with us every single time. . . . Aren't you ever going to just . . . let it all go?"

Max couldn't begin to put it into speech—his anger, his rage over what she'd lived through. Let it go? Let it *go*? How could he let go of something that had him by the balls? There were no words, and if he so much as tried, he'd just howl and howl and howl. Instead, he cleared his throat. "I can't do this," he said again.

He started for the door.

But Gina beat him over there. "I can't believe I was stupid enough to think this would help. I'm sorry I wasted your time," she told the therapist.

"Gina, wait," Rita got to her feet. Now they were all standing. Wasn't this fun?

But Gina closed the door behind her. Quietly. Firmly. In Max's face.

Well, that went about as well as could be expected. Max reached for the doorknob. And wasn't this going to be one grim, silence-filled ride back to the physical rehab center?

"Have you ever told her how much you love her?" Rita asked him.

He managed to hide his surprise. The answer to that question was none of her goddamn business. He also didn't ask why in God's name would he tell Gina that, when what he really wanted, really *needed* was for her to find happiness and peace? Which she'd never do until she'd succeeded in leaving him behind.

"Although, to be honest," Rita added, "she certainly seems to know, doesn't she?"

"Sometimes all the love in the world just isn't enough," Max said.

She made a face. "Oh, dear. If you've allowed that to be one of your defining beliefs, that world of yours must be a terribly dark place."

Christ. Spare him from psychoanalysis by people who didn't even know him.

She didn't let up. "What are you so afraid of, Max?"

Leaning heavily on his cane, Max just shook his head and followed Gina more slowly out the door.

FBI HEADQUARTERS, WASHINGTON, D.C.
JUNE 20, 2005
PRESENT DAY

Peggy Ryan was in talking to Max. Jules could hear her, laughing at something their boss had said, even as Max shouted, "Come in."

They both looked up as Jules opened the office door, as he stepped halfway inside. "Excuse me, sir."

And just like that, Max knew.

It was a little freaky, but Jules saw it happen. Max looked at him, glanced down at the document Jules was carrying, then looked back, hard, into Jules's eyes, and he somehow *knew*.

He'd been leaning back in his chair, but now he sat up, holding out his hand for the news that he already knew was coming, his face oddly expressionless. "Gina?" he asked, and Jules nodded.

There was no way Max could have known that Gina was in Germany, let alone anywhere near that car-bombed cafe.

And although Jules admired the hell out of his boss and thought the man brilliant, highly skilled, and capable of outrageous acts of bravery as he employed his frontline method of leadership, Jules was firmly grounded in reality. Despite popular belief, he *knew* that Max was not capable of mind reading.

Which meant that Max had been waiting for this.

It meant that every single day since Gina had left, he'd been waiting for—fearing and dreading—this very news.

What a hell of a way to live.

Peggy Ryan was oblivious. In fact, she was rattling on about some case she was working on, even as Jules handed Max the dreaded list of civilians killed.

Jules turned to her and cut her off mid-utterance. "Ma'am. You need to leave."

She blinked up at him in shock, her expression rapidly morphing to outrage. "Excuse *me*—"

"Now." Jules grabbed her and lifted her out of her seat.

"What are you *doing*? Get your hands off me, you . . . you freak," she squawked as he pushed her out the door.

George was out there, by Laronda's desk, waiting to flag him down, cell phone to his ear. "Her body's in Hamburg," he told Jules.

"Thanks. Fill Peggy in," Jules tossed the order past the woman and shut the door in her angry face.

But then he wondered if he himself weren't on the wrong side of that door. God, but he couldn't bring himself to turn around and look at Max.

Who was stone-cold dead silent.

It would have been better if he were shouting and breaking things. Punching a hole in the wall. Max rarely lost his temper, rarely lost control, but when he did, it was an earthshaking event.

"Can I help you, sir?" Jules whispered, still facing the door.

"Has her family been contacted yet?" Max asked, sounding remarkably normal, as if he were inquiring about nothing more troublesome than the usual morning traffic on the Capital Beltway.

"I don't know, sir." He slowly turned around.

Max was sitting behind his desk. Just sitting. Jules could read nothing on his face, nothing in his eyes. It was as if Max had shut himself down, made his heart stop beating.

"But I'll find out," Jules continued. "We're also making inquiries as to why Gina was in Hamburg, why she left Kenya, what she was doing, where she was staying . . . I'll get you that information as soon as I have it. George just told me that her body is . . ."

His voice broke. He couldn't help it. Her body. Gina's *body*. God.

"Still in Hamburg," Jules forced the words out.

"Have Laronda get me a seat on the next flight to Germany," Max said, still so evenly, so calmly. But then he realized what he'd said, and for a moment, Jules caught the briefest flash of the emotion the man was hiding. "*Fuck!*" But Max just as quickly caught himself and was back to calm. Smooth. "Laronda's not coming in today."

"I'll do it, sir." Jesus, what a day for this. Max's assistant Laronda would know exactly what to do, what to say . . . Such as, *Sir, are you going to Hamburg to identify Gina's body and bring her home, or to locate and decimate the terrorist cell responsible for that bombing? Because that second thing might not be such a good idea unless you're looking to end your career.*

Jules cleared his throat. "Although, maybe you shouldn't go there by yourself—"

"Get me Walter Frisk," Max ordered. "And find Gina's parents' phone number. Laronda's got it somewhere on her computer."

Still Jules hesitated, his hand on the doorknob. "Max, God, I'm so, *so* sorry for your loss." His voice broke again. "Our loss. The whole world's loss."

Max looked up, and it was eerie to be stared at with such soulless, empty eyes. "I want that plane reservation on my desk in two minutes."

"Yes, sir." Jules closed the door behind him and got to work.

CHAPTER TWO

KENYA, AFRICA
FEBRUARY 18, 2005
FOUR MONTHS AGO

"Where," Gina asked, "are we going to put them?"

"The tents?" Molly replied as she dipped the first of the bedpans into the pot of boiling water.

"Mol, you're not listening." Gina did the same with the next one, careful not to burn her fingers as she took it out. "There are no tents. The tents won't arrive until *after* the busload of volunteers."

Molly stopped, pushing her unruly reddish hair from her damp face with the ungloved part of her arm. "We're getting a *busload* of volunteers? That's wonderful!"

"Most of them will only be here for a few days. Only two are permanent," Gina told her. Again. She loved Molly Anderson dearly, but when her tentmate's attention was focused on something important, it could be difficult to pull her away from the task.

And in this case, Molly's attention was focused on four thirteen-year-old girls who had been brought to their camp hospital with terrible, life-threatening infections.

They would, Sister Maria-Margarit had told them in her dour German accent, consider themselves lucky if just one of the girls survived the coming night.

To which Molly had muttered, "Over my dead body."

She'd then set to work sterilizing everything that would come into contact with their newest patients.

"When does the bus arrive?" she asked Gina now.

"In a few hours," Gina said, adding "Shit!" as she burned her fingers.

"Sugar!" Molly spoke over her, giving Gina a look that said *robot nun at five o'clock*.

The camp had two types of nuns. Human nuns, who laughed and sang and warmly embraced the diversity of the villagers and the volunteers, who saw life's glass as half full; and the nuns that Molly had nicknamed "robots," who looked out over a congregation and saw only sinners. Anything less than perfection was to be frowned upon. These robot nuns could, Molly had told Gina, find the problem with a glass that was too full. After all, it might spill, don't you know?

This sister frowned at them both.

Probably because, in the three-million-degree heat here in the kitchen, both Molly and Gina had had the audacity to roll up their sleeves.

"I think it would be a good idea if we made sure the two permanents were comfortable," Gina said as she helped Molly lift the pot and empty the hot water down the sink. The volunteer turnover rate here was bad enough as it was. If conditions in the camp were even more primitive than usual . . . "We don't want Sister Grace and Leslie Pollard changing their minds and leaving on the next bus out."

"The sister can bunk in with the other nuns," Molly said, leading the way into the hospital tent. She grabbed a surgical face mask from the pile by the door.

Gina did, too, reaching up to slip it on past her ponytail— except her ponytail was gone. She encountered only shockingly short waves. God, Max would so hate that. Not that he'd ever admit it, but he'd loved her long hair.

Except what he loved no longer mattered. The man wasn't in her life anymore. If he hadn't shown up looking for her by now, over a year after Gina had left D.C., then face it, he was never coming.

And she would not, could not be like Molly—who was waiting, waiting, still waiting for her so-called friend Jones to magically reappear. Oh, Molly swore up and down that she no longer spent much time thinking about the guy, but Gina knew better.

It happened mostly in the evenings, after their work was done. Molly would pretend to read a book, but she'd get that far-away look in her eyes, and . . .

It had been nearly three years since Molly had last seen the bastard. In all that time, he hadn't so much as sent her a postcard.

Of course, she should talk. Postcards from Max were also under the zero column in the file marked "in short supply."

But three years of pining was ridiculous. Shoot, one year was bad enough—and Gina had passed that particularly dark anniversary months ago. It was definitely time to stop hoping for things that would never be. It was absolutely time to stop wallowing in What-ifs-ville and move the heck on.

Maybe one of the men coming in on this afternoon's bus would be Mr. Wonderful. Maybe he'd meet Gina, fall head over heels in love, and volunteer to stay in camp for the rest of her time here.

It wasn't completely impossible. Miracles sometimes happened.

Of course, if the busload of volunteers all turned out to be elderly, or monks, or—the most likely possibility— elderly monks, then maybe it was time to reconsider that offer from Paul Kibathi Jimmo, who wasn't completely kidding when he told Father Ben he'd trade four pregnant goats in exchange for Gina's hand in marriage.

Paul was an outrageously good-looking, well-educated, and extremely kind young man who'd won a scholarship to Purdue University in Indiana. He'd returned to Kenya halfway through his junior year when his older brother died, probably of AIDS, although they didn't speak of it. He'd been needed to run his family's farm.

Which was located another hundred miles out in the wilderness. Gina couldn't know for certain, but she would be willing to bet the entire contents of her bank account, plus her parents' house on Long Island, that Paul's kitchen was without a microwave.

It was, quite possibly, without a roof.

Not quite Gina's style, even without taking into consideration the fact that Paul was already married to a Kenyan woman named Ruth.

"What's-her-name can stay in our tent," Molly told Gina now, as she checked Winnie's pulse, lifting the sheet to check the bandage over the girl's hideously inflamed wound.

Gina had to squint, looking out through her eyelashes, praying that . . . No, it wasn't bleeding through, thank God. Of course, that wasn't saying all that much since Gina had helped Sister Maura change it a mere hour or so ago. Still, out here, even the smallest of blessings was counted and appreciated with full fervor.

Molly looked up at Gina. "What was her name?"

"Leslie Pollard," Gina told her. "She's British. She's probably eighty years old and will expect tea upon arrival." As opposed to a sleeping bag on a rotting tent floor. "Even if we could find an extra cot, we'd never fit it into—"

"We can hot bunk," Molly said, moving on to Narari, as Gina helped little Patrice take a sip of water through lips that were cracked and dry. "You and me. One of us will be here with the girls all night anyway. Although . . . Are we absolutely sure Leslie's not a man?"

God, what a thought. But Leslie *was* one of those names that could swing both ways. "The message from AAI referred to her as *Ms.* Leslie Pollard," Gina reported. "So unless they've got it wrong . . ."

"Which isn't entirely impossible," Molly pointed out. She soothed Narari with a hand against her damp forehead. "Shhh, sweetheart, shhh. Lie still. You're with friends now."

But Narari was in pain. Her wound had reopened, too. There was so much blood.

"Nurse!" Molly shouted, and the sister came running.

It took a healthy dose of morphine to calm the girl down.

Gina had to go outside for air while Molly helped Sister Maria-Margarit reapply the bandage.

Not that the air out there was any less hot and heavy. Still, being outside the confines of the hospital gave the illusion of relief.

Gina sat on the bench that was right by the door—probably placed there for weak-kneed people.

Her mother, a trauma nurse, would smile to see her sitting there. But she'd hug Gina, too, and say what she always said. "The ER's not for everyone."

What was she doing here? Gina wondered that every single day.

It wasn't more than a few minutes before the screen door opened with a creak and Molly stepped outside. "You all right?"

"Compared to Narari . . ." Gina laughed as she wiped her eyes. She hadn't even realized she was crying. "Yeah." She shook her head. "No." She looked up at Molly. "What kind of parents would do that to their own child?"

"Last year at this time, there were nine of 'em," Molly told her quietly. "Of course, they weren't as sick—not like these girls. The knife they used this year must've been filthy." She ruffled Gina's short hair. "Why don't you go get the tent ready. Do me a favor, will ya, and put my Hunks of the NYPD calendar into my trunk? I don't think Lady Leslie will appreciate Mr. February as much as you and I do."

Gina laughed. Molly could always make her laugh. "When I grow up, I want to be you."

"Oh, and while you're in my trunk, find the last of the Earl Grey, will you? Maybe if we go all out with the welcome reception, this one will stay more than a month."

"Are you sure you don't need a break?" Gina asked. "Because I could—"

"I'm fine. You're better at cleaning, anyway," Molly lied. She opened the screen door and went back inside. "Bake some chocolate chip cookies for our distinguished guest while you're at it."

Gina laughed. They ran out of chocolate within forty-eight hours after the arrival of each package from home. She *did* have a few Fig Newtons left. "In your dreams," she called after Molly.

"Every single night," Molly called back. "Without fail."

But Gina knew that wasn't true. Molly sometimes cried out in her sleep, but it wasn't for chocolate.

Unless there was a brand of chocolate called *Jones* sold in Molly's home state of Iowa.

Gina had recently started praying at night. *Dear God, please don't let me still be dreaming about Max years from now . . .*

Of course, when she first left D.C., she'd thought about Max nearly all the time. Now she was down to, oh, only three, four times.

An hour.

Yeah, at this rate, she'd be over him just shy of her ninetieth birthday.

Of course, maybe that was all going to change in just a few hours. Maybe Mr. Wonderful really was on that bus. She'd take one look at him and fall madly in love.

And two months from now, she would be hard pressed to remember Max's last name.

It wasn't likely, sure, but it was also not entirely impossible. One thing Gina had learned from her time here was that miracles did sometimes happen.

Although she wasn't going to sit back and wait for a miracle to come to her. No, if need be, she'd get out there and hunt one down.

She was going to find happiness and meaning to her life, damn it, even if it killed her.

SARASOTA HOSPITAL, SARASOTA, FLORIDA
AUGUST 1, 2003
TWENTY-TWO MONTHS AGO

Max considered dying.

It probably would've hurt a whole lot less.

Problem was, every time he opened his eyes, even just a little, he saw Gina looking back at him with such concern on her face.

It was entirely possible that, during the excruciating haze of pain-drenched eternity since he was brought out of surgery, she hadn't left his side for more than a moment or two.

Unless it was all just a dream, and she wasn't really there.

But when he couldn't find the strength to open his eyes, he heard her voice. Talking to him. "Stay with me, Max. Don't you leave me. I need you to fight . . ."

Sometimes she didn't talk. Sometimes she cried. Softly, so he wouldn't hear her.

But he always did. The sound of her crying cut through this fog far more easily than anything else.

Maybe this wasn't a dream. Maybe it was hell.

Except sometimes he could feel her holding his hand, feel the softness of her lips, her cheek beneath his fingers. Hell would never include such pleasures.

But he couldn't find his voice to tell her so, couldn't do more than keep breathing, keep his heart beating.

And instead of dying, he lived. Even though it meant that he had to redefine pain. Because the pain he'd experienced prior to getting shot in the chest didn't come close to this torture.

But it was a torture that didn't hurt nearly as much as listening to Gina cry.

Then, one evening, he woke up.

Really woke up. Eyes fully open. Voice able to work. "Gina." Voice able to work a little too well, because he hadn't meant to wake her.

But wake her he did. She'd been sleeping, long legs tucked up beneath her, curled up in a chair beside his bed. Now she sat up, pushing her hair back from her face, then reaching for the nurse's call button. "Max!"

He knew he'd forever remember that moment, even if he lived to be five hundred years old. That look on her face. She lit up from within, yet tears brimmed instantly in her eyes.

It was joy he saw there on her face—a mix of love and hope and sheer shining happiness. It scared the living shit out of him.

How could anyone possibly be that happy?

And yet, somehow he was responsible—simply by saying her name.

"Oh, my God," she said. "Oh, my God! Don't go back to sleep. Don't . . ."

"Thirsty," he said, but she'd gone over to the door.

"Diana! Diana, he's awake!" She was crying, she was so happy.

It sure beat her crying because she was unhappy, the way she had in his car . . . When? Christ, was it just last night? Gina had been terribly upset, and he'd made the mistake of going with her into her motel room. To talk. Just to talk. Only, after she'd stopped crying, she'd kissed him, and he'd kissed her and . . .

Jesus H. Christ.

What had he gone and done?

Max had fallen asleep after they'd made love—first time

in years that he'd gotten a good night's rest. He remembered that.

Only there he was when he woke up—in Gina's bed. The one place he swore he'd never go. He remembered that all too clearly, too.

Still, he'd wanted to stay right there. Forever.

So of course he'd run away. As hard and as fast as humanly possible. And he'd hurt her badly in the process and—

Wait a sec.

He may have been woozy and viewing the world through a considerable amount of blear and that still relentless pain, but there were coffee cups and soda cans scattered around this hospital room. A couple of floral arrangements that were looking somewhat worse for wear sat on the few available surfaces. Along with a pile of books and magazines. Not to mention the fact that Gina apparently knew the nursing staff by name . . .

Woozy or not, it didn't take Max's extensive training and years of experience with the FBI to know that he'd been lying in this bed for more than just a day or two.

"How long . . . ?" he asked as Gina smoothed his hair back from his face, her fingers cool against his forehead.

She knew what he meant. "Weeks," she said. "I'm sorry, I can't give you anything to drink until the nurse comes in."

"Weeks?" No way.

"You were doing so well when you first came out of surgery," she told him, lacing his fingers with hers. "But then, a few days later your temperature spiked and . . . God, Max, you were so sick. The doctors actually gave me the prepare-yourself-for-the-worst talk."

Weeks. She'd stayed with him for weeks. "Thought you were," he labored to say, "going to . . . Kenya."

"I called AAI," she told him, "and postponed my trip again."

Postponed wasn't as good as cancelled. The thought of

Gina going to Kenya made him crazy. Of course so did the thought of her going anywhere more dangerous than Iceland, where the locals still didn't lock their doors at night. "Til when?"

"Indefinitely." She kissed his hand, pressed it against her cheek. "Don't worry, I'll stay as long as you need me."

"Need you," he said, before he could stop himself. They were the two most honest words he'd ever said to her—pushed out of him perhaps because of the drugs or the pain or the humanizing news that he'd cheated death—again. Or maybe Gina's glow of happiness had a hypnotizing effect, rather like a truth serum.

But luck was on his side, because the nurse chose that exact moment to come into the room, and the woman was energy incarnate, drowning him out with her cheerful hello. Gina had turned away to greet her, but now turned back. "I'm sorry, Max—what was that?"

He may have been temporarily too human, or woozy from drugs and pain, but he hadn't gotten to where he was in his career, in his life, by making the same mistake twice.

"Need water," he said, and with the nurse's permission, Gina helped him take a cool drink.

KENYA, AFRICA
FEBRUARY 18, 2005
FOUR MONTHS AGO

There *was* one incredible hottie among the crew that descended from the bus.

He had blond hair, a cute German accent, and really terrific knees, but as Gina got closer, she realized that he was the leader of the Temporaries—the volunteers who would only be staying for a few short days.

Which meant that his name was Father Dieter.

And *that* meant her chances of him falling in love with her at first sight were slim to none, with heavy on the none.

Other breaking news was that the bus was a real bus— not one of the nine-passenger rinky-dink VW vans that kicked up dust as they bounced along the so-called roads from village to village.

There were twenty-four volunteers in Father Dieter's party—ten more than were on the list of names Gina had seen. Father Dieter's tentless, luggageless party of twenty-four celibate priests, thank you very much.

Most of whom had the region's version of Montezuma's revenge, and were sicker than dogs.

Father Ben and Sister Maria-Margarit were running around, organizing workers to—shit!—dig more latrines, as well as forming a sort of triage to get those of their guests who were the most desperately ill into the shade.

They didn't want to bring them into the hospital building until they knew for sure what had caused the sickness, in case it was contagious.

God help them all if this was contagious.

Count on AAI to turn the arrival of a busload of volunteers into *more* work for the home team.

Gina spotted Paul Jimmo in the chaos. He must've been riding shotgun on the bus, a deadly looking weapon still slung across his broad back as he helped Sister Helen set up the mess tent as temporary living quarters.

He waved to her and smiled—a flash of white teeth in that too-handsome face—trying to flag her down. But Gina's job one was to find Her Majesty Leslie Pollard, and make sure that she didn't run screaming back to Nairobi to catch the next flight home to Heathrow.

Except, aside from the new nun in town, Sister Gracie, there didn't seem to be another woman in the crowd.

Gina approached Father Dieter, who looked to be the kind of guy who would know all. "Excuse me," she said.

And the holy man—not quite as handsome up close thanks to a severe sunburn—booted his lunch on her feet.

"Oh dear, *that's* quite the little problem," a crisply English-accented voice spoke from directly behind her.

But Gina couldn't turn to see who was talking to her because the priest just slowly keeled over, crumpling, as if to kiss the dusty ground. He was too sick to be mortified—which was a good thing. It was far better that he just became instantly unconscious, rather than attempting to apologize or even clean up the mess.

Sister Maria-Margarit rushed up to take the priest from her, thank you God, leaving Gina to deal with hosing off her feet.

Aw, gross.

"I'm afraid Father Dieter didn't partake of the goat stew that's being blamed as the source of food poisoning," the BBC *Masterpiece Theater*–wannabe voice continued. It was, of course, a very non-female voice.

Gina turned to find her expression of dismay reflected in a pair of dark sunglasses.

"Please tell me you're not Leslie Pollard," she said. But of course he was. She had vomit between her toes. Why shouldn't this day get even worse?

He sighed. "The powers that be listed me as a Miss again, did they?"

"No," she told him. "They had you as a Miz."

"Ah. And somehow that's . . . better?" He flipped up his sunglasses—they were the kind that attached to regular glasses—and blinked at her from behind the lenses. His eyes were a nondescript shade of brown in a face that was coated, literally white in places, with sun block. Obviously he was a Type B volunteer.

"I'm an American," Gina said, holding out her hand to shake, "so yes, it's better. But in this case, only marginally. Gina Vitagliano. I'm from New York." It was usually all she had to say.

Leslie Pollard gave her a dead-fish handshake—yeesh. He was definitely a Type B.

As if she couldn't tell from the virulently ugly plaid shirt that hung on his skinny British frame. Yes, this was a man who had rarely left his London flat dressed in anything other then a tweed jacket and slacks, stains from last week's tea on his tie.

He was taller than she was. Not that anyone would know it, because he, of course—in the grand tradition of Type Bs—slouched. Beneath his floppy hat, his graying hair was lank and unwashed. It was hard to tell if that was the result of the long bus ride or merely a poor decision in terms of personal hygiene, brought on by that common Type B malady—severe depression.

Gina was guessing number two.

Type Bs usually came to them after enduring some terrible personal tragedy. Like volunteers Type A, C, and D, they were looking to jumpstart their lives, to find meaning, to "make a difference." But unlike the others, they had never done a day of camping in their entire lives. They meant well, yes, but oh my God, they were ill-equipped and unprepared for this nonluxurious lifestyle.

They usually asked, within their first week, for the location of the nearest laundromat. Sometimes the nuns—the human nuns—even got a betting pool started. The sister who picked the date closest to when the Type B resigned would win the pot.

Yeah, this one wasn't going to be here for very long.

The good news was that despite the gray in his hair, dude was still somewhat young. During the two to three weeks he would spend here, he'd actually accomplish something. For example, he could help Father Ben dig that new well.

But then, as she watched, Leslie Pollard shouldered his duffle bag and picked up a cane that had been lying on the ground, next to it. Great. It was similar to the cane that Max had used while in the physical rehab facility.

Perfect. A Type B volunteer who not only couldn't walk without assistance, but would remind her, every time she saw him, of the one man she was trying most to forget.

Gina forced a smile. "Well, welcome. Will you excuse me for a sec while I go find some water, to, you know, de-puke?"

He smiled somewhat vaguely, distracted by the camp's activity. Still, Gina was grateful for small miracles. Type Bs sometimes didn't come with an ability to access their senses of humor, and a vague smile was way better than nothing.

"Actually," he said, "if you'll just point me to my tent . . . ?"

"Um, yeah," Gina said. "About that. See, we're waiting on a shipment of supplies, and until then, well, I'm afraid you'll have to share living quarters."

He nodded, barely listening as he looked around. "Of course. Believe me, after that bus trip, I can sleep anywhere."

Gina would believe it only when she saw it. Still, she managed another smile. "Good. Because I cleared some space for your things in the tent that I share with my friend Molly Anderson—"

"Excuse me?"

And just like that, she had Leslie Pollard's fully focused attention. His gaze was suddenly so sharp, it was a little alarming. She took a step back, for a second wondering if maybe she'd read him completely wrong and that he was a Type A instead of a B.

But then he blinked rapidly, almost as if he were doing a bad Hugh Grant imitation as he said, "I'm sorry? You cleared a spot in *your* tent? That won't do. No, I'm afraid that won't do at all. Doesn't AAI have rules about that—comingling, cohabitation? Do you open your tent to strangers—strange men—all the time?"

He was serious. Apparently, Leslie Pollard was even more of a prude than Sister Double-M.

"If you'd have let me finish," Gina said, "then you would've heard me say that my tentmate and I will be spending most of our time in the hospital for the next few days. Even without the invasion of the puke monsters, we have a few patients—little girls—who need round-the-clock care. You'll have the tent completely to yourself at night. And if you need to get something from your bag during the day, just make sure you knock before you come in. I cleared out a storage trunk for you—there's a key in the lock. It's not very big—but make sure you put anything of value in there and secure it. Sister Leah is a total klepto."

Leslie blinked at her.

"That was a joke," Gina told him. Apparently she was wrong about the sense of humor thing. "We don't even have a Sister Leah and . . . Never mind. Third tent on the left. It's the one with a tin of tea out on the table, along with the sign that says, 'Welcome, Ms. Pollard.' Please make yourself at home."

And with that, she squished off to find some water.

Leslie Pollard stood with all his gear just inside the door of the tent.

There, on the table was the tin of tea—Earl Grey—that what's-her-name—Gina—had mentioned. It was next to a kettle, a can of Sterno, and an obviously coveted Tupperware container of Fig Newtons. His stomach rumbled just at the sight of them. Of course, his stomach rumbled pretty damn constantly these days as he tried to keep his weight down.

The sign she'd described was there, too. "Welcome to our home, Ms. Pollard."

As far as homes went, from the outside this was one of the shabbiest tents he'd ever seen in his life. The canvas had been repaired so many times it was more patch than original fabric. And the frame reminded him of a swayback mule. Old and ugly, and probably unreliable in a storm, but able to get the job done on an average day.

As if there were any average days here in this camp—this holier-than-thou den of do-gooders on a mission to save this extra-crappy section of an all-but-irredeemable world.

No doubt about it, though, this part of Africa had more priests and nuns per square mile than just about anywhere he'd ever traveled. If someone needed saving, this was the place to come.

And yet Gina, of the dark brown hair and killer bod, actually thought no one would . . . what? Care? Or maybe not notice that the volunteers were suddenly having co-ed sleepovers?

According to the rules and regulations of AAI—he'd been given an entire booklet from the office in Nairobi—unmarried men and women were not allowed to "fraternize individually." This included any travel outside of the camp. Relief workers were encouraged to travel and socialize in groups, three being the magic number.

The booklet claimed these rules were created both to provide protection for the relief workers, and to be an obvious example of AAI's utmost respect of all of the varying customs and cultures in Kenya.

So . . . share a tent in an AAI camp with two very attractive women?

Not bloody likely.

He had gone, brimming with disbelief, to talk to the stern-faced Nazi nun. He figured he'd go straight to the source to find out where he really would bunk down tonight.

But apparently the camp had some kind of pamper-the-new-guy policy, and Sister Brunhilda also agreed that having him stay temporarily in this tent while the two women slept in the hospital—where, on the floor?—was the best solution to their overcrowding problem. She did let him know that it would all be under her watchful eyes. And he could tell just from looking that she was the type who slept with one eye open.

When she bothered to sleep at all.

So here he was.

He set his cane and his bag down on the bed nearest the door—the one with the empty trunk chained to its metal frame.

The two women had sewn brightly patterned fabric to the inside top panels of the tent, and it drooped down in places—somehow managing to make the space look exotic instead of pathetic. There were richly dyed spreads on their cots, a cozy homemade table and chairs, bookshelves crafted from old crates that were stuffed to overflowing.

Every available surface was covered with candles and carvings and all of the little knickknacks and photographs and drawings and collectibles, each with its own story, that made this faded tent in a godforsaken corner of the world into more of a home than any place he had stayed for more years than he could remember.

But there was another sign on the table, too: "Only drink bottled water," with about six exclamation points, underlined three times.

It reminded him of the puking priests. Going out there and offering to help would win him salvation points.

It would also remove him from the temptation of rifling through private papers, letters, diaries. He'd sworn to himself that he wouldn't do that.

Or at least that he wouldn't get caught.

And there'd be less of a chance of someone walking in on his unauthorized browsing after the camp was asleep.

Besides, it looked as if anything of interest was securely locked up in one of the larger trunks.

Trunks that had locks any beginner criminal could pop in a heartbeat.

He quickly unzipped his bag and put his clothing into the one empty trunk and locked it.

His real valuables would go elsewhere. Not that he had much. His cans of "Silver Fox" theatrical hairspray—irreplaceable out here in Nowhereland—went up between the top of the tent and the fabric faux-ceiling. He hung them from the tent pole, so that they wouldn't be seen, either from inside or out. His passport he kept with him, along with the remainder of his cash.

He went out the door and was already several steps toward the mess tent before he remembered and scrambled back inside. Jesus! It was a careless mistake, a stupid mistake. What the hell was wrong with him, after coming so far?

But no one had seen him. Thank God for that.

Heart still pounding, he picked up his cane and, leaning on it heavily, he limped out the door.

CHAPTER
THREE

Jules drove Max to the airport.

A surprisingly lively discussion on alternatives to fossil fuel was being broadcast on NPR and that plus the wipers, slapping in rhythm as they cleared the early evening rain from the windshield, had kept them from having to speak more than necessary.

But now Max cleared his throat. "Did you call the hotel in Hamburg?"

Jules turned down the radio's volume. "The one where Gina was—"

"Yes."

Staying. "Yes. They haven't touched her room," Jules reported. "As long as you're willing to pay for the extra nights—"

"I said I was."

"Yes, sir, I told them that. The hotel manager said he'd put a do-not-disturb sign on the door," Jules told him. "The room'll be exactly as she left it."

Max nodded grimly. "Good." He turned the radio back up.

Jules felt compelled to turn it back down. "Her room's

not a crime scene," he gently reminded his boss. "She wasn't—"

Max cut him off. "I know," he said, but Jules had to wonder.

"It was random," he reminded Max. "Gina's death. It had nothing to do with you. You can't blame yourself because she was in the wrong place at the wrong time."

Max reached over and turned up the volume on the radio again. "Just drive," he ordered.

So Jules drove as Teri Gross interviewed Willie Nelson—of all people—about fuel made from vegetable oil.

He glanced again at Max.

His carry-on bag wasn't much larger than an oversized briefcase. Jules took that as a good sign, that his boss truly was going to arrive in Hamburg, identify Gina, pack up her things from her hotel, and then return with her body—oh, God—on the next available flight home.

Gina's brother Victor was planning to meet them at the airport in New York. Jules was to call him with information about their return flight. Jules had spoken to Vic on the phone several times already today—to let the Vitagliano family know that Max was going to bring Gina home.

The usually abrasive and tough talking New Yawker's expression of gratitude had been heartbreakingly eloquent in its simplicity. Vic had told Jules that Max's generosity would allow him and his brothers to comfort their parents during this time of sorrow.

They deserved to have Gina's body returned to them as quickly as possible.

Jules glanced at Max again. Surely, if he were intending to do some serious terrorist hunting, he wouldn't've packed quite so lightly.

Still, Jules would never dare to hazard a guess about exactly what might be in Max's bag. It was too small for a bazooka or a sawed off shotgun. Although, a dismantled semiautomatic would fit, no problem. Along with a small arsenal of handguns.

It would be interesting to see if the mighty and powerful Max Bhagat would be required to run his bag through the X-ray machines at the entrance to the airport gate, or if he'd simply get waved through.

The rain got lighter but the traffic much heavier as they entered the airport loop. Jules followed the signs to the garage, and Max finally spoke.

"Just drop me at departures."

It was the moment of truth.

For most of the trip, Jules had purposely focused on learning about fuel made from soybeans to keep himself from obsessing over exactly how he was going to tell Max when the time came.

"Don't be mad," he started, then inwardly rolled his eyes. *Don't be mad?* Of course Max was going to be mad. The man was running on rage. Sure, he was keeping it locked inside, but Jules knew it was there. Because he was feeling it, too.

There was a reason for all those clichéd movies where the FBI agent went on a vengeful rampage after a loved one was murdered. The same qualities that made both Max and Jules good candidates for a long-term career in law enforcement naturally made it hard for them to sit back and let someone else's team find the terrorists responsible for Gina's death.

Jules cleared his throat and started over. "Sir, I know you're not going to like this—"

As they rolled past, Max gazed with undisguised longing at the ramp that led to the drop-off for people taking departing flights. "I don't need a babysitter."

"No, sir," Jules agreed. "You don't. You do, however, need a friend."

Max snorted his disgust. "We're not friends, Cassidy."

Jules pulled up to the garage's automated machine, and

he reached out through his window to punch the button and take a ticket as Max continued, "And if you really think I want your company—"

"I think you want Gina," Jules said quietly. "And I think everyone else in the world is going to fall way short."

Max wasn't done. He gave Jules his most terrifyingly disdainful stare. "You must really want that promotion."

Ouch.

"You know I do," Jules answered, as the gate opened and he pulled through, leaning forward to peer through the still wet windshield, searching for the sign to long-term parking. There it was. Dead ahead. He kept his eyes on it, because Max's scary face was known to make underlings crap their pants, and the overnight bag Jules kept in his car trunk contained only clean shirts and one neatly rolled pair of jeans.

He could feel Max's melt-solid-rock stare as he passed a sign saying "Lot Full," and went up a ramp to the next level.

"Although, you know, I think manhandling and shouting at Peggy Ryan already did the trick," Jules told his boss. "Impressed the shit out of her, don't you think? I'm in. Big time. This paying out of pocket for a last-minute airline ticket to Hamburg—this is just insurance. Because I figured, you know, that you probably wouldn't want sexual favors."

Max made that almost-laughter sound again, but Jules couldn't tell if that was a good or a bad sign. "I should fire you."

"You could go that way," Jules agreed. "But you know, Peggy would probably walk out, too. In solidarity, because she just likes me so much. And I'm still going to Hamburg with you, fired or not, so really what good does it do you?"

Jules found what might well have been the very last parking spot in the entire garage. It was about as far as possible from the walkway to the terminal. Still, as he pulled in he said a prayer of thanks to the patron saint of parking garages, along with his knighted brother—the hero who'd invented luggage with wheels.

Max had gone back to being silent. But now he gave it one last try as Jules took the key out of the ignition. "We're not friends."

Jules braced himself and met Max's extremely evil eye. "You may not think of *me* as a friend," he said, "but I think of you as one. You've always treated me with kindness and respect so I'm going to return the favor, whether you like it or not. I'm not going to pretend to know what you must be feeling right now, but Gina was my friend, too, and I *do* know how badly *I'm* hurting. So, go ahead, sweetie. Have at me. Be as rude to me as you need to be. Or you don't even have to talk to me—I won't take it personally. I'll just sit next to you on the flight. I'll handle all the arrangements. I'll take care of the details about where we need to go and what we need to do, so you won't have to. And whether you like it or not, I'm going with you to that morgue. Because no one should ever have to do something like that alone, especially when a friend who loves them is standing by."

Max didn't say a word for a very, very long time. He just sat there, trying to incinerate Jules with his eyes. "I should just kill you and stuff you into the trunk," he said, when he finally spoke.

Shit. Jules worked hard not to react. He just nodded, and even managed to shrug nonchalantly. "Well, I guess you could certainly *try* . . ."

Max just sat there, glaring. But then he shook his head. He got out of the car and started the trek toward the terminal, not bothering to wait for Jules.

Who grabbed his raincoat and his bag and followed.

SHEFFIELD PHYSICAL REHAB CENTER, MCLEAN, VIRGINIA
NOVEMBER 11, 2003
NINETEEN MONTHS AGO

"Don't," Max said, closing his eyes to keep Gina from taking another picture with her new digital camera, recording for posterity just how much of a wimp he was—dressed in his jammies and tucked in his bed here at the Sheffield Physical Rehab Center at four in the afternoon, ready for a nap.

"How'd it go?" she asked.

"It was fine," he lied. In truth, the session had hurt. Like hell. He'd been discouraged, too, by how weak he was, how quickly he'd tired. How exhausted it had made him.

Gina crossed to the desk that was built into the wall beside his bed, and carefully put down her camera. She'd gotten the damn thing for her trip to Kenya. Max hoped the fact that she'd taken it out of the box and was learning how to use it didn't mean she'd rescheduled her flight.

Kenya. God.

He'd been trying to talk her into embracing the excitement and adventure of law school. He had an in at NYU. Gina would be accepted there, based on Max's recommendation, in a heartbeat.

"Kevin said he thought you were in some serious pain but that you just wouldn't quit," she told him as she nudged his legs over and sat down on the bed. "He was very impressed."

Kevin was one of those touchy-feely physical therapists who had his cheerleading pompoms ready to wave for even the most insignificant events. Old Mrs. Klinger, recovering from a stroke, had lifted the index finger on her right hand a whole half an inch! Rah-rah-rah! Ajay Moseley held a pencil and wrote a note to his grandmother for the first time since the car accident! Whoo-hoo! Forget about the fact that the kid would never walk again. Forget about the fact that he'd suffered so much damage to his skinny little body that he needed a new kidney, that he was on dialysis just to stay alive.

Max gazed impassively at Gina. "If you already asked Kevin how it went, why bother asking me?"

"Because I love it when you do that stoic he-man thing," she said, leaning toward him, her mouth now dangerously close to his, her hand burning his thigh. "It makes me really hot."

She was kidding. It was supposed to be funny. A joke. He knew that, but his mouth went dry anyway.

He found himself gazing into her eyes at a very close proximity.

And wanting her. Badly. Yup, Doctor Yao was right. He was definitely starting to feel far more like his old self again.

He had to use every ounce of self-control that he owned to keep himself from reaching for her.

Every ounce.

The good news was that she was as rattled as he was by the sudden, nearly palpable sexual energy that surrounded them.

She turned away. Stood up, moving to look out of the window.

Rattled and vulnerable.

They hadn't so much as kissed since that night before he'd been shot, that night that he'd . . . that they'd . . .

Correction—Gina had kissed him frequently, back in the hospital, both in Florida and after he'd been moved up to D.C. But they were all "see you later" kisses. Nothing like the way they'd kissed that night.

Not that they'd had the opportunity to soul-kiss while he was hooked up to all those tubes and machines. Not with the high volume of traffic in and out of his hospital room, day and night.

Now, as he watched, she leaned her head against the windowpane. His room here—a single—was small, but the view of the surrounding countryside was nice. Nicer than that grungy back-alley dumpster that he could see from the bedroom window in his D.C. apartment.

"My brother called. Victor. Just out of the blue." Gina glanced over her shoulder at Max. "He's flying in this evening. He's never been to Washington—he missed his seventh-grade class trip. Strep throat."

"Make sure you take him to the World War Two Memorial," Max said, glad that she'd changed the subject. He'd half expected her to go the other way. Confront. Ask, *Were you thinking about kissing me just then, because I had the sense that you really wanted to.*

And then what was he supposed to say? *Honey, not a moment of the day goes by that I don't think about kissing you* . . . Yeah, that would help.

"It's on the list," Gina said, finally turning to face him, sitting on the windowsill, her skirt blowing in the breeze from the air conditioner's fan. She had to hold it down. "We've got a whole day of sightseeing lined up. Vietnam Wall, Holocaust Museum, Korean War, Lincoln Memorial . . ." She ticked them off on her fingers. "But I'm pretty sure the real reason he's coming is to check up on me. I think my entire family's a little freaked. You know, because I'm staying with Jules."

Imagine how freaked they would have been if Max had opted for outpatient therapy, if he'd moved back into his apartment instead of coming to live here. If he'd done that, Gina would have come along to make sure he had everything he needed, and ten minutes after they were alone together, they would have been back in bed. Ten minutes after that, she would've been unpacking her suitcase, hanging her clothes in his closet.

Because the truth was, Max had enough willpower to keep his distance from her for only a very short time. If she'd persisted and tried to turn her "stoic men make me hot" thing into more than just a joke, he would have been cooked. He had zero resistance to her. He prayed she'd never figure that out. If she did . . .

Although, okay. This place wasn't as public as the hospital, but he still had people knocking on his door at random times of the day. She wasn't going to jump him here. She just wasn't.

Which was the second reason he'd chosen inpatient physical rehab.

And so, instead of moving in with Max, Gina had gone to stay with Jules Cassidy. The younger agent's condo was relatively close to this facility. Besides, there was no way Max would've ever agreed to let Gina stay in his place by herself. His neighborhood wasn't safe. Not for a young woman living alone.

He'd been burgled twice in the past ten months.

Not that he had anything worth stealing.

"I don't think they really believe that Jules is gay," Gina continued now, coming back toward him. "Or maybe they're afraid I'm so irresistible, I'll turn him straight." She rolled her eyes and laughed. "Vic isn't exactly Mr. Politically Correct—I don't even think he knows anyone who's gay. Jules and I have a bet going—I give Vic twelve hours, tops, before he makes up some excuse and runs back home. Jules thinks he'll stay longer." She stopped at the end of his bed. "The nurse said you just had a massage, but you don't look very relaxed."

Man, she was beautiful. There was a Van Morrison song, "Brown Eyed Girl." It played in Max's head whenever Gina smiled at him the way she was smiling now.

"You know what you need?" she asked. He braced himself because he knew that the words about to come out of her mouth could be damn near anything.

"I need a lot of things," he said evenly. "World peace. A nonviolent society. The extinction of religious fanaticism—"

"A happy ending. You should have asked for one," Gina cut him off, mischief and laughter in her eyes.

For about a half a second he didn't get it. And then he did. And he laughed, too. "Yeah, I don't think that's on the massage menu here. Besides, the masseur—big guy, name of Pete?—not my type."

"I'm your type," she pointed out, and he stopped laughing.

Oh, hell.

And okay. Yeah. Max had had his share of healthy sexual fantasies, starting when he was around ten years old and saw Ann-Margret for the first time, when *Viva Las Vegas* played on channel eleven's Million Dollar Movie. Then, as now, his fantasy usually involved a well-endowed, unbelievably gorgeous young woman locking the door to the—fill in the blank. Office, classroom, bathroom, conference room, bedroom—and approaching him with a knowing smile, as she stripped down to her unbelievably sexy underwear.

"Hey," he said as Gina's skirt hit the floor, but he sounded decidedly less than enthusiastic in his attempt to make her stop. "This isn't—"

"Shhh," she admonished, finger to her lips. "Don't talk."

Gina, apparently, still shopped at Victoria's Secret. Today, as it turned out, she was wearing an extremely attractive sheer black bra and panties that were remarkably miniscule and . . . Thong. Yes. God. The late-afternoon sunlight streaming in through the window made her belly-button ring sparkle and her bare skin glow.

She had such beautiful skin. Max knew for a fact just how soft she would feel beneath his hands, his mouth . . .

"Gina," he said, but it came out sounding like a sigh.

She smiled as she joined him on the bed, on her knees this time, and she leaned toward him again. This time, however, she didn't stop.

This time, she kissed him.

First on the mouth, as she worked the bed controls, lowering him down into more of a prone position, as all that skin slid beneath his fingers.

"Gina," he tried again, but she silenced him with another deep, searingly sweet kiss.

As she kept on kissing him, she pulled back the blankets, unfastened his pajamas, and then . . . She kissed him yet again.

Hoh yeah.

This was where—since his mouth was now free—he was supposed to tell her to stop, to put her clothes back on. They were friends.

Remember how they'd had that discussion—all two sentences of it—while he was in the hospital? He'd said, "I don't want to mislead you. What happened between us that night—" and she'd cut him off, saying, "I'm here as a friend."

But his "friend" was now . . .

Oh, man.

"Gina," he managed again, but couldn't quite find the air needed to tell her that he loved her dearly, he truly did, but this wasn't the kind of relationship he wanted from her.

Liar. In truth he wanted her to live beneath his desk, so she could do exactly what she was doing, six, seven times a day and . . . Gohhhd . . .

Her underwear joined her other clothes on the floor. She'd covered him with a condom that she'd conjured out of nowhere and she straddled him now, the most beautiful, vibrant, magnificent, courageous, smart, funny, exciting woman he'd ever known—naked and gasping with pleasure because he was inside of her.

It was an unbelievable turn on.

She moved slowly on top of him, her eyes closed, face upturned, hair tumbled down around her shoulders, and Max felt himself start to sweat as he tried to hang on, as he watched her, memorized her, burning an indelible picture of this moment, this woman, into his brain. This woman that he lusted after with every cell in his body, with every single breath he took . . .

Her mouth, slightly open, lips soft and moist. Her throat, so elegantly, gracefully long. Her eyelashes dark against the smoothness of her cheeks. Her breasts so full, her body taut with desire, smooth and soft and welcoming. And his.

All his.

He came with a rush that caught him off-guard, ripping through him with an intensity and power that made him shout nonsense.

Yes.

Yes?

Yes, what? Yes, he was coming. Yes, it felt unbelievably great.

No fucking kidding.

He felt her release, too, and he opened his eyes and made himself focus as his heart tried to pound its way out of his chest. He wanted to watch her, wanted to take the most from this stupidly bad mistake that he possibly could.

It was a mistake he couldn't let happen again.

After she finished, she didn't collapse against him, still considerably careful of the new scars on his chest, of the tenderness from his barely healed collarbone. She just sat atop him, arms wrapped around herself, clasping him tightly with her thighs, eyes still closed, face still upturned, as she struggled to regain her breath.

With the sunlight streaming in behind her, she looked like some pagan celebrant at worship.

And then she opened her eyes and looked down at him, frowning slightly. "Is that Spy Museum exhibit still open? I bet Vic would really like to go there."

What?

"No, I think it closed," she answered herself. "It was only a limited run exhibition. Right?"

"I don't, um . . ." Max shook his head. "Remember."

One part of him was amazed that they were just continuing their conversation about her brother's visit, as if they hadn't just had sex, as if he wasn't still inside of her. Another part of him—the part that always waited with amused excitement to see just what she'd say or do next, was already starting to get turned on again.

Naked women did that to him, and Gina was one of those women who managed to be naked with a capital N.

She was unbelievably beautiful.

"You mind if I use your laptop to Google it?" she asked.

As long as you don't put on your clothes first. Max clenched his teeth over the words. Lighthearted banter would turn what they'd just done from a crazy mistake into the beginning of a real relationship.

Happy ending, his ass. Gina wasn't looking for an end to anything.

And he opened his mouth to tell her that he couldn't do this, that he wasn't ready yet—that he might never be ready for what she wanted, when someone knocked loudly on his door.

"Blood pressure check!" The doorknob rattled, as if the nurse were intending just to walk in, but the lock held, thank God. The nurse knocked again.

"Oh, shit," Gina breathed, laughing as she scrambled off of him. She reached to remove the condom they'd just used, encountered . . . him, and met his eyes. But then she scooped her clothes off the floor and ran into the bathroom.

"Mr. Bhagat?" The nurse knocked on the door again. Even louder this time. "Are you all right?"

Oh, shit, indeed. "Come in," Max called as he pulled up the blanket and leaned on the button that put his bed back up into a sitting position. The same control device had a "call nurse" button as well as the clearly marked one that would unlock the door.

"It's locked," the nurse called back, as well he knew.

"Oh, I'm sorry," he said, as he wiped off his face with the edge of the sheet. Sweat much in bed, all alone, Mr. Bhagat? "I must've . . . Here, let me figure out how to . . ." He took an extra second to smooth his hair, his pajama top, and then, praying that the nurse had a cold and couldn't smell the scent of sex that lingered in the air, he hit the release.

"Please don't lock your door during the day," the woman scolded him as she came into the room, around to the side of his bed. It was Debra Forsythe, a woman around his age, whom Max had met briefly at his check-in. She had been on her way home to deal with some crisis with her kids, and hadn't been happy then, either. "And not at night either," she added, "until you've been here a few days."

"Sorry." He gave her an apologetic smile, hanging on to it as the woman gazed at him through narrowed eyes.

She didn't say anything, she just wrapped the blood pressure cuff around his arm, and pumped it a little too full of air—ow—as Gina opened the bathroom door. "Did I hear someone at the door?" she asked brightly. "Oh, hi. Debbie, right?"

"Debra." She glanced at Gina, and then back, her disgust for Max apparent in the tightness of her lips. But then she focused on the gauge, stethoscope to his arm.

Gina came out into the room, crossing around behind the nurse, making a face at him that meant . . . ?

Max sent her a questioning look, and she flashed him. She just lifted her skirt and gave him a quick but total eyeful. Which meant . . . Ah, Christ.

The nurse turned to glare at Gina, who quickly straightened up from searching the floor.

What was it with him and missing underwear?

Gina smiled sweetly. "His blood pressure should be nice and low. He's very relaxed—he just had a massage."

"You know, I didn't peg you for a troublemaker when

you checked in yesterday," Debra said to Max, as she wrote his numbers on the chart.

Gina was back to scanning the floor, but again, she straightened up innocently when the nurse turned toward her.

"I think you're probably looking for this." Debra leaned over and . . .

Gina's panties dangled off the edge of her pen. They'd been on the floor, right at the woman's sensibly clad feet.

"Oops," Gina said. Max could tell that she was mortified, but only because he knew her so well. She forced an even sunnier smile, and attempted to explain. "It was just . . . he was in the hospital for so long and . . ."

"And men have needs," Debra droned, clearly unmoved. "Believe me, I've heard it all before."

"No, actually," Gina said, still trying to turn this into something they could all laugh about, "*I* have needs."

But it was obvious that this nurse hadn't laughed since 1985. "Then maybe you should find someone your own age to play with. A professional hockey player just arrived. He's in the east wing. Second floor." She lowered her voice conspiratorially. "Lots of money. Just your type, I'm sure."

"Ex*cuse* me?" Gina wasn't going to let that one go past. She may not have been wearing any panties, but her Long Island attitude now waved around her like a superhero's cape. She even assumed the battle position, hands on her hips.

Debra pointed her pursed lips in Max's direction. "Overnight guests are forbidden. No exceptions."

"Did you just have the audacity to judge me?" Gina blocked the nurse's route to the door. "Without knowing the least little thing about me?"

Debra lifted an eyebrow. "Well, I *have* seen your underwear, dear."

"Exactly," Gina said. "You've seen my underwear—not

my personality profile, or my resume, or my college transcript, or—"

"If you think for one second," the nurse countered, "that anything about this situation is even remotely unique—"

"That's enough," Max said.

Gina, of course, ignored him. "I don't just think it, I know it," she said. "It's unique because I'm unique, because Max is unique, because—"

Debra finally laughed. "Oh, honey, you are so . . . *young.* Here's a tip I don't usually bother to tell girls like you: If I find one pair of panties on the floor, it's only a matter of time before I find another. And I hate to break it to you, hon, but the girl who comes out of the bathroom next time, well . . . She isn't going to be you."

"First of all," Gina said grimly, "I'm a woman, not a girl. And second, *Grandma* . . . You want to bet it's not going to be me?"

"I said, *that's enough,*" Max repeated, and they both turned to look at him. About time. He was used to clearing his throat and having an entire room jump to full attention. "Ms. Forsythe, you took my blood pressure—you have the information you needed, good day to you, ma'am. Gina . . ." He wanted to tell her to untwist her panties and put them back on, but he didn't dare. "Sit," he ordered instead, motioning to the desk chair that could be pulled beside the bed. "Please," he added when Nurse Evil smirked on her way out the door.

"I can't stay. Vic's flight comes in just after seven. If I don't leave now, I'll be late." Gina swooped in to kiss him, full on the mouth. "Mmmm," she said, and kissed him again, longer this time, lingering, now that they were once again alone. She smoothed back his hair. "Thank you for a lovely afternoon."

Yeah. About that . . . "We need to—," Max started.

But she grabbed her camera and waved as she sailed out the door.

Leaving him holding . . .

Yes, she'd tucked them into his hand during that last kiss.

Her panties.

Of course.

Her intention was obvious. She wanted him to spend the next few hours thinking about her walking around the Baltimore-Washington Airport terminal without them.

Yeah.

So much for his nap.

CHAPTER
FOUR

Forty-eight grueling hours after poor Narari breathed her last breath, it finally became apparent to Molly that the three other girls were going to survive.

For now, anyway. Women who'd been cut like this often struggled with recurring infections. Serious ones. Childbirth would be difficult, if not flat-out dangerous. And if the men that they married—the men to whom their parents all but sold them—were HIV positive, they, too had a far greater risk of becoming infected.

Risk? For most of them, it was practically a guarantee.

Molly made sure she was in the shower when Narari's family came to claim her body, because Sister Double-M forbade her to speak to them. She stood there for much longer than she should have, letting the water pound on her head as she cried. Trying, with her tears, to release her anger at Narari's parents, at the nun, at herself.

For not taking the time to get to know those girls better. For not sensing that they were in danger and urging them to run away.

For not protecting them.

It was a long time before Molly finally turned off the water. Exhausted, she then just stood and let herself drip, not wanting to move, but knowing that eventually she must.

The truth was, there just wasn't anywhere that she wanted to go right now.

Gina was asleep in their tent. Having a roommate had its pros and cons.

But at least she didn't have *two* roommates. They'd reclaimed their quarters from their English guest just this morning, when the busload of priests had retreated to Nairobi.

Molly was sorry she'd missed meeting them. A conversation with someone new would have been nice. But some of the visitors were still quite ill and the hospital facility here couldn't continue to handle their care.

Gina had told her of the vomit-between-her-toes incident, which had made Molly think of Dave Jones, which was, of course, not the man's real name.

She'd learned to speak of him only as Jones, even though his real name was Grady Morant, because too many nasty people wanted Morant dead. And although Molly doubted that they would travel all the way from the jungles of South Asia to the gorgeous desolation of this part of Kenya, she'd learned the hard way that evil could have a very long reach.

Because of that, she was training herself to *think* of him only as Jones, too—during those rare times she actually let herself think about him, of course.

Such as right now.

And, considering that one of her very first interactions with Jones had included his barfing on her running shoes, there was a solid reason why she was thinking about him now.

Unlike Gina's episode with Father Dieter, the shoes hadn't been on Molly's feet at the time of the barfing, thank goodness. Both they and Jones had been in her tent, in a camp much like this one—except for the fact that it was on the other side of the world, on a small, lush, green island in Indonesia.

The American expat and entrepreneur—which was the polite word for black market smuggler—had been sick, and Molly had been a Good Samaritan and taken care of him. With the same exact amount of kindness that she would have shown him even if she hadn't found him unbelievably attractive.

The flu-related event was the start of what had eventually become a torrid love affair. And, as most torrid love affairs tended to do, it had ended badly.

Still, there had been a time when Molly had looked for Jones wherever she went. She'd expected to turn around one day and see him standing there.

She'd honestly thought he'd find her, that he wouldn't be able to stay away. He'd loved her. And wherever he was, he loved her still. She believed that with all of her heart.

But, after nearly three long years, she was no longer waiting and watching for him.

And she really only obsessed about him at those moments when a good romantic obsession could be used to blot out the day's real-life pain.

Such as when a thirteen-year-old child died as the result of misogynistic ignorance.

Molly finished brushing out her hair and stashed her shower supplies back in her locker. She hung her towel out on the line, contemplating which she needed most—food or sleep.

Food won, and she headed for the mess tent.

At this time of early afternoon, it was deserted. Even Sister Helen, the self-anointed queen of the kitchen—terribly sweet but extremely talkative—was nowhere to be found. The solitude was just what Molly needed, and she knew that, despite the fact that their vastly different personalities often clashed, Sister Double-M was responsible for Helen's disappearing act.

Molly took a tray from the stack and poured herself a glass of tea, then helped herself to bread and some of a divine-smelling vegetable dish that Helen had kept warm for the hospital staff.

It more than made up for the serious lack of chocolate.

She turned to carry her tray to a table and . . .

The Englishman, Leslie Whoosis, was leaning heavily on his cane just inside the door. Odd, she hadn't heard it open. It was almost as if he'd materialized there.

She'd only seen him from the distance since he'd arrived in camp. This was their first face-to-face.

And he was exactly as Gina had described him—almost painfully thin, with terrible posture. He was, indeed as Gina said, the poster-child for tragically bad haircuts, with enough sunblock on his face to protect him should he decide to take wing and do a tight orbit around the sun. Glasses with twenty-year-old frames combined with his slightly dazed silence completed the time-traveling anthropology professor look.

Molly wasn't close enough to tell if Gina's rather unkind guess was on target—that he had bad breath, too—but she wouldn't have been at all surprised if she were correct. At the very least, he looked as if he reeked of emotional neglect.

"It's Leslie, right?" she said, finding a smile for him, because it wasn't his fault that he'd wandered in here during her alone time, an Englishman in perpetual search of tea. "I'm Molly Anderson."

He didn't move an inch, and there was something about the way he was clutching his cane that made her notice his hands. They were big and not as pale as she'd expected them to be, not by a long shot. He had long, sturdy fingers that he used to grip that cane so tightly his knuckles were nearly white.

His hands were . . .

Dear Heavenly Father. She looked hard at his eyes, hidden behind those glasses and . . .

He lunged toward her, but he was too late. Her tray hit the wooden floor with a smash and a clatter of metal utensils, loud enough to wake the dead.

.He swore sharply, David Jones's still-so-familiar voice coming out of that stranger's body. "Do you have any idea how unbelievably hard it's been to get you alone?"

Had she finally started hallucinating?

But he took off his glasses, and she could see his eyes more clearly and . . . "It's you," she breathed, tears welling. "It's really you." She reached for him, but he stepped back.

Sisters Helen and Grace were hurrying across the compound, coming to see what the ruckus was, shading their eyes and peering so they could see in through the screens.

"You can't let on that you know me," Jones told Molly quickly, his voice low, rough. "You can't tell anyone—not even your friend the priest during confession, do you understand?"

"Are you in some kind of danger?" she asked him. Dear God, he was so thin. And was the cane necessary or just a prop? "Stand still, will you, so I can—"

"No. Don't. We can't . . ." He backed away again. "If you say anything, Mol, I swear, I'll vanish, and I will not come back. Unless . . . if you don't want me here—and I don't blame you if you don't—"

"No!" was all she managed to say before Sister Helen opened the door and looked from the mess on the floor to Molly's stricken expression.

"Oh, dear."

"I'm afraid it's my fault," Jones said in a British accent, in a voice that was completely different from his own, as Helen rushed to Molly's side. "My fault entirely. I brought Miss Anderson some bad news. I didn't realize just how devastating it would be."

Molly started crying. It was more than just a good way

to hide her laughter at that accent—those were real tears streaming down her face and she couldn't stop them. Helen led her to one of the tables, helped her sit down.

"Oh, my dear," the nun said, kneeling in front of her, concern on her round face, holding her hand. "What happened?"

"We have a mutual friend," Jones answered for her. "Bill Bolten. He found out I was heading to Kenya, and he thought if I happened to run into Miss Anderson that she would want to know that a friend of theirs recently . . . well, passed. Cat's out of the bag, right? Fellow name of Grady Morant, who went by the alias of Jones."

"Oh, dear," Helen said again, hand to her mouth in genuine sympathy.

Jones leaned closer to the nun, his voice low, but not low enough for Molly to miss hearing. "His plane went down—burned—gas tank exploded . . . Ghastly mess. Not a prayer that he survived."

Molly buried her face in her hands, hardly able to think.

"Bill was worried that she might've heard it first from someone else," he said. "But apparently she hadn't."

Molly shook her head, no. News *did* travel fast via the grapevine. Relief workers tended to know other relief workers and . . . She could well have heard about Jones's death *without* him standing right in front of her.

Wouldn't *that* have been awful?

"I'm very glad," Jones continued fervently, sounding like a card-carrying Colin Firth impersonator. "So very glad. You can't know how glad . . ." He cleared his throat. "I hate to be the bearer of more bad tidings, but your . . . friend was something of a criminal, the way I heard it. He had a price on his head—millions—from some druglord who wanted him dead. Chased him mercilessly, for years. I guess this Jones fellow used to work for him—it's all very sordid, I'm afraid. And dangerous. He had to be on the move constantly. It was risky just to have a drink with Jones—you might've gotten killed in the crossfire. Of course, the big irony here is that the druglord died two weeks before Jones. He never knew it, but he was finally free."

As he looked at her with those eyes that she'd dreamed about for so many months, Molly understood. Jones was here, now, only because the druglord known as Chai, a dangerous and sadistic bastard who'd spent years hunting him, was finally dead.

"It's entirely possible that whoever's taken over business for this druglord," he continued, "would've gone after this Jones, too. Of course, he probably wouldn't have searched to the ends of the earth for him . . . Although, when dealing with such dangerous types, it pays to be cautious, I suppose."

Message received.

"Not that that's anything Jones needs to worry about," he added. "Considering he's left his earthly cares behind. Still, I suspect it's rather hot where he's gone."

Yes, it certainly was hot in Kenya right now. Molly covered her mouth, pretending to sob instead of laugh.

"Shhh," Helen admonished him, thinking, of course, that he was referring to an unearthly heat. "Don't say such a thing. She loved him." She turned back to Molly. "This Jones *is* the man that you spoke of so many times?"

Molly could see from the expression on Jones's face that Helen had given her away. She might as well go big with the truth.

She wiped her eyes with a handkerchief that Helen had at the ready, then met his gaze.

"I loved him very much. I'll always love him," she told this man who'd traveled halfway around the world for her, who apparently had waited years for it to be safe enough for him to join her, who had actually thought that, once he arrived, she might send him away.

If you don't want me here—and I don't blame you if you don't—just say the word . . .

"He was a good man," Molly said, "with a good heart." Her voice shook, because, dear Lord, there were now tears in his eyes, too. "He deserved forgiveness—I'm positive he's in heaven."

"I don't think it's going to be that easy for him," he whispered. "It shouldn't be . . ." He cleared his throat, put his glasses back on. "I'm so sorry to have distressed you, Miss Anderson. And I haven't even properly introduced myself. Where are my manners?" He held out his hand to her. "Leslie Pollard."

Even with his glasses on, she could see quite clearly that he'd far rather be kissing her.

But that would have to wait for later, when he came to her tent . . . No, wait, Gina would be there. Molly would have to go to his.

Later, she told him with her eyes, as she reached out and, for the first time in years, touched the hand of the man that she loved.

She didn't have to work at all to make her tears appear convincing, and Helen helped her to her feet. "Come, dear, let's get you to your tent. I'll bring a tray with something for you to eat."

As Molly left the mess tent, she looked back at Leslie Pollard, who was already helping Sister Grace clean up the mess she'd made.

Gina was wrong. He didn't have bad breath at all.

SHEFFIELD PHYSICAL REHAB CENTER, MCLEAN, VIRGINIA
NOVEMBER 13, 2003
NINETEEN MONTHS AGO

Gina found Max in the recreation room.

Sitting at a table by the window, with a cup of coffee, engrossed in a book.

A steamy romance novel, perhaps?

She smiled at the ridiculous idea of Max reading anything that wasn't directly related to his job as she stopped just outside the door, in the shadows, where he'd have trouble seeing her if he glanced up. She was waiting for her brother to finish up in the men's room—she didn't want to disappear on him. And she also didn't want to walk in there alone, giving Max the opportunity to tell her that the sex they'd shared had been a huge mistake.

It had been the first time since . . . that other first time, back months ago, before Max had been shot. That it had happened again—here at the rehab facility, no less—had been almost as surprising to her as it obviously had been to him. She didn't want to debate the issue, although she was prepared to go into battle, if need be.

Because, God, the way he looked at her when he didn't think she was watching . . .

It didn't happen very often. Mostly when he was exhausted, or just waking up.

But Max wanted her, and Gina knew it. She was as sure of that as she was that the sky was blue, and the earth was round.

That knowledge had given her the courage to play out her little seduction scene, day before last. That, and the realization she'd come to during those endless days and nights in the hospital, as Max had hovered close to death.

She loved this man with all of her heart and soul.

And all of those reasons she'd been so ready to walk away from him, to go to Kenya and move on with her life—they so didn't matter anymore.

So he'd asked someone else—Alyssa Locke, a gorgeous, perfect woman who'd worked with him at the Bureau—to marry him. So what? Alyssa didn't want him. She'd foolishly turned him down. Her loss.

And Gina's gain.

Because so what if that meant Gina was getting him on

the rebound? She no longer cared that she was Max's second choice. She wouldn't care if she was his *fifth* choice.

Max's nearly dying had brought it all down to the bottom line for her. Which was that she just wanted to be with him.

And two days ago, she'd proven her theory that sex was the chink in his armor. She now knew that their mutual attraction was going to be her way in. And she was going to use it shamelessly to get what she wanted—a chance to be a part of this man's life.

And if rebound relationships tended to end because the reboundee bounced away—well, that wasn't going to happen here. Gina was going to hold on to Max with all of her might.

Across the room, he turned a page of his book.

It was nice to be able to look at him without him looking back at her.

Without him going to DEFCON 1.

He was wearing faded jeans and a subdued second cousin to a Hawaiian shirt, flip-flops on his feet. The shirt and sandals were fashion by necessity—his still healing collarbone made it impossible to pull a T-shirt over his head. And he'd actually admitted that tying his sneakers was painful for him.

He had on his reading glasses, and Gina knew if she approached, he'd quickly take them off. It might've been because he couldn't see her with them on. Or it might've been vanity.

A fear of appearing old, perhaps?

She had to figure out exactly why their age difference was such a big problem for him. Of course, talking about it with him would be nice.

Ha. As if he'd ever volunteer to do that.

What was that expression she'd recently heard? Not until snow falls on the hills of hell.

She used to think that Max was good at talking. God

knows they'd spent hours on the phone, back when she was struggling to put her life back together, after the hijacking. But it wasn't until recently that she realized—it wasn't talking he was good at. He was good at *listening*.

She'd opened herself up to him, told him her secrets, her dreams, her hopes—and he'd told her very little in return. He loved Jimi Hendrix. His parents had divorced while he was in college. He had a sister with mental health issues. He was too much of a nerd to have had a girlfriend in high school, but while at Princeton, he'd been hot and heavy for three years with a girl named Beverly. They'd split up when he graduated early. She'd married someone else a year later, and had two kids.

Gina was pretty sure he hadn't told her all of *that* story, although he *had* made a point to tell her those kids were both close to Gina's age.

She now leaned against the door frame, watching as Max used a highlighter to mark a passage in his book. So much for her theory about the romance novel, unless he was taking notes for the next time they were together and naked.

A clatter and raised voice over by the pool table made him look up and she shrank farther back.

"Yes! *Yes!*"

There was a young boy in a special, funky, extra-tall wheelchair, working with one of the female staff members, playing the game. He looked about twelve years old, but Gina suspected he was just small for his age.

He'd dropped his pool cue onto the tile floor and was taking victory laps around the table as he continued to whoop and chant. "Who won? I did! Who won? I did!"

His face was angelic—big brown eyes, rich, dark brown skin. But his arms and hands looked as if he'd done some serious time in hell. He'd been so badly burned, his hands weren't really hands anymore. What was left of his fingers were twisted and claw-like from thick scar tissue.

"Ajay, Ajay!" the staff member said, laughing. "Shhh! The gentleman is trying to read."

The boy sat in a position that looked as if he were unable to use his legs—knees over slightly to one side, feet together. But he motored swiftly and expertly over to Max, using a hand control on the right arm of the wheelchair. "I'm in training to be a pool hustler, you know, for when the insurance money runs out? You up for losing twenty bucks?"

Max smiled as he put his book down. "Not right now, thanks. I've got a friend coming to visit."

Gina was that friend to whom he'd referred. Friend. Not girlfriend. Not lover.

But okay. As depressing as that news was, it was good to know where she stood.

As Gina continued to watch, Ajay held out his hand to Max. "I'm Ajay Moseley. Car accident."

It was clearly a test, and Max passed with flying colors. He took the boy's misshapen hand without hesitation and shook. "Max Bhagat. Gunshot."

"Yeah, I know. You're the big hero everyone's buzzing about. Mr. FBI—who caught a terrorist bullet to the chest but still managed to take the scumbag down. Snaps." Ajay sat back in his chair. "So what's the word on me these days? 'Poor little Ajay, gon' die soon, he don't find hisself a new kidney?' " He pretended to sniff and wipe a tear from his eye.

Max shook his head. "Nah. You're like me. You've got yourself a solid Triple-T-K rating around here."

Ajay sat back in his chair, eyes narrowed for several seconds. "Aiight, dawg," he finally said. "I'll bite. What's a whatsis-K . . . ?"

"Too tough to kill," Max told him.

Ajay laughed, clearly pleased. "That's for damn sure."

The staff member approached. "Ajay, it's time to go see Kevin."

"Kevin the torturer," Ajay said. "Oh, happy day! You meet the Kevster yet, Mr. FBI?" He slipped effortlessly into a California surfer accent. "Dude! Way to go! Push it harder! We both know you'll be so much happier tomorrow if it hurts so much today that you bleed from your ears, dude!"

Max laughed. "Yeah," he told him. "I visit his torture chamber twice a day for physical therapy. And the name's Max."

"How about a friendly game of pool tomorrow morning?" Ajay said. "Around ten? No need to bring your wallet just yet. At least not until I find out if you're better'n me."

The nurse gently pulled his chair away. "I'm sure Mr. Bhagat has things he needs to—"

"Tomorrow morning sounds good," Max interrupted. "But I've got Kevin until ten, and I'll need a hosing down after. Want to make it ten-thirty? If I survive?"

"Ms. LeBlanc," Ajay said to the staff member, in an exaggerated English accent. "Please check my schedule—" he pronounced it the British way: shed-dule "—and pencil in my morning engagement with my good friend Max." He grinned. "Later, bro."

Gina pulled even farther back into the hallway as the boy and the nurse left the room.

But it was too late—Max had spotted her.

"Victor head back to New York?" he asked.

"No, he's here." Gina pointed over her shoulder, down the hall to where she'd last seen her brother. "I think he's flirting with the nurses." She came into the room. "How *are* you?"

His eyes were guarded, his expression neutral. "Still sleeping too much."

"Sleep is good," she said. "You'll heal faster."

And there they were, face to face. Both obviously thinking about the last time they were together, about the way she'd pushed him back in his bed and climbed on top of him and . . .

Oh, yes, he was definitely thinking about that. He was trying to hide it, but she could tell.

Maybe bringing her brother along to play chaperone had been a bad idea. Maybe if she'd come here by herself, they wouldn't have had the discussion she'd been dreading. Maybe all she had to do was let Max look into her eyes and see how badly she wanted to make love to him again and hold out her hand and . . .

"Excuse me."

Both Gina and Max turned to see that same staff member who'd been playing pool with Ajay standing just inside the door.

"I'm sorry to interrupt," the woman said. "I just . . . I'm Gail," she said, coming over to shake their hands. "We haven't been introduced yet. I work mostly with Ajay." She had a sweet face, a warm smile. "I just wanted to . . . Well, it's a favor and I hope you don't mind too much, but Ajay has a brother—Rick—who's always promising to come visit and he's only shown up maybe once in the past year and a half, and . . . I just wanted to ask you not to make any plans with Ajay that you can't keep. I'm sorry, that sounds so insulting. But the disappointment . . . He puts on such a positive face for the world and . . . I'm the one who hears him cry at night," she finished apologetically.

"How old is he?" Max asked.

"Fourteen," Gail told him. "I'm not sure if it was the accident or the treatments that stunted his growth. All I know is it's a miracle he's alive. His entire family was killed—except for Rick, who wasn't in the car. It's been three years—he's been in and out of here. Each time he has a new surgery, he's back and . . . He's had trouble with scarring, and now with his kidney . . ."

Max nodded. "You can tell him I'll see him tomorrow at ten-thirty."

Gail nodded, too, but she was obviously still worried.

"Max'll be there," Gina told her. "But I'm sure he won't mind if you want to call his room, to remind him."

"Absolutely," Max said. "If it makes you feel better . . ."

"Thank you," Gail said.

"Gee," Gina said after the nurse had left the room. "This place has some seriously devoted staff. Should I be jealous?"

Stupid question. It opened up all kinds of doors.

"We need to talk about what happened the other day," Max told her.

"Okay." She sat down across from him. "Which part do you want to talk about first, Wild Thing? The part where you gave me what's probably the best orgasm I've ever had in my entire life?"

He closed his eyes. "Gina—"

She leaned forward as she lowered her voice. "Or the part where I first pushed you all the way inside of me, *all* the way and God, it felt *so* amazingly—"

"Stop."

"—good." Not a chance. Gina reached for his hand. "Ever since I left here, I've been thinking about making love to you again. About how great it was. About how just sitting here like this makes me hot for you."

He didn't pull his hand away. And when he looked up to meet her gaze, there was heat in his eyes. "I know what you're trying to do," he said. "And it's . . ."

"Working?" she finished for him, laughing, because yes, her words were working. At least they were working for her. If they were in his room right now, she would lock his door.

And he would not argue. She knew it.

At least not very much.

So she pushed him harder. "You know, I thought maybe if we had sex again it would make me stop wanting you so much. But all it's done is make me want you more." She leaned closer. Spoke even more softly. "Day and night, Max. I've been thinking about you constantly. Sometimes I think even if we could make love every hour on the hour, it still wouldn't be enough. I want to spend, like, two weeks with you inside me, nonstop."

Ooh, yeah. Direct hit. Her point-blank approach was both making him uncomfortable and turning him on. Wasn't *this* going to be fun?

"But then what?" he asked. "After those two weeks . . . ?"

"I don't know," she told him honestly. "Why don't we try it and find out? What can it hurt—"

"You," he said, his voice rough. "It could hurt you, and I don't want to do that. Gina—"

"Hey, there you are."

Gina looked up to see her brother coming toward them, and Max took the opportunity to pull his hand away. Shoot, Victor had lousy timing. Or maybe it was good timing.

"Hey, Max," Vic said.

Max stayed in his seat as he shook Victor's hand. Of course, he still kept his cane nearby. He might have been feeling unsteady on his feet.

Or maybe he didn't stand for a different reason.

Gina could only hope.

Vic, of course, clasped Max's hand, obviously sizing him up, doing that macho squeeze thing that drove Gina nuts. "He's younger than I remember," he said to Gina. Perfect. Thank you *so* much, Victor. Then, back to Max, "We met— very briefly—a few years ago. Looks like being shot has agreed with you."

"That is *the* stupidest thing I've ever heard you say," Gina told the man who had just moved into first place as the most stupid of her three very stupid brothers.

"What?" Vic shrugged as he dragged over a chair. "I'm just saying—Max looks good. You know, for an older guy. What'd, ya lose weight while you were in the hospital?"

"Yes, Victor," Gina said. "They call it the Almost Dying Diet." She turned to Max. "My brother is an idiot."

"It's all right," he said, flexing his fingers—no doubt checking to make sure Victor hadn't broken his hand. "Still living in Manhattan, Vic?"

"Nah, the office moved to Jersey about a year after 9/11. The commute was killing me, so I finally loaded up the old U-Haul and crossed the river," Victor said. "I'm in frickin' Hackensack. I wake up most mornings and wonder how the hell did *this* happen?"

"I know the feeling," Max said. It was a comment that was so aimed at her, but Gina refused to accept it.

"You could look for a new job," she suggested to her brother.

"In this market? I don't think so." Vic shook his head. "With my luck, word would get out I was looking and I'd be given notice. We're not all lucky enough to have some big airline lawsuit settlement in our savings account, Geen."

"Lucky?" Max repeated, incredulity dripping from that single word.

Gina knew he was thinking that Victor actually believed it was lucky that terrorists had hijacked the airliner that her college jazz band had taken on their European tour. That the money she'd received as a settlement from the airline made the entire ordeal worthwhile.

She touched Max's arm. "He didn't mean it like that."

Victor was oblivious to the fact that he'd just jumped, with both feet, on one of Max's buttons. "Besides, I bought the condo when interest rates were low. I couldn't get those numbers anymore."

The muscles in the sides of Max's face were jumping as he clenched his teeth.

"It's all right," Gina said softly. "It doesn't bother me."

He didn't say the words—he wouldn't dare admit it—but she knew that everything about her experience on that hijacked plane still bothered him.

Very much.

Mr. Clueless was checking his watch. "We should probably take off," her brother announced as he pushed himself to his feet. "We're meeting a coupla college friends down in Fairfax." He held out his hand again. "Max. Nice seeing you again, even though it is a little creepy that you and my baby sister are—"

"Thank you, Victor," Gina interrupted.

He shrugged. "I'm just saying. Just being honest. You're always saying 'be honest'—"

"Go be honest out in the hall. I'll catch up to you in a sec," she ordered.

"Feel better, man," Vic called as he sauntered out.

"If he doesn't go home soon," Gina said, "I may be facing homicide charges. You should hear some of the things he's asked Jules." She rolled her eyes. "He's been trying to get him to admit he's not really gay. 'Catherine Zeta-Jones, man,' " she imitated her brother's voice. " 'You come home from work and she's naked on your bed—are you really saying you're going to walk away from that magic? And if you do say it, you expect me to believe you?' "

Max smiled, but it was still pretty grim. "You should've just let me kill him for you."

"It still really freaks you out," Gina asked. "Doesn't it? What happened to me on the plane." She didn't wait for him to answer. "You should've seen how tense you got when he made that stupid comment about the settlement. We really should talk about it sometime. Like, in two weeks . . . ?"

She'd hoped her reference to their earlier conversation would make him smile again, but he just ground his teeth even harder.

She leaned across the table to kiss him. He didn't exactly respond, but he didn't pull away either.

"His plane leaves at twelve-thirty tomorrow," Gina told him. "I'll be dropping him at the airport in the morning. I'll meet you in your room after your pool game. You won't have any trouble recognizing me—I'll be the soon-to-be-naked woman sitting on your bed holding a picnic lunch."

She kissed him again, and headed for the door before he could argue.

It was, of course, entirely possible that he wouldn't show up. That he would—how had Victor said it?—just walk away from that magic.

But Gina looked back and saw that heat in his eyes.

And she knew he'd be there.

CHAPTER
FIVE

Gina's body was being held at the airport.

Upper-echelon FBI team leader Walter Frisk himself met Max at the plane—which had to be Jules Cassidy's doing.

Frisk didn't do more than shake Max's hand, murmur something extremely brief about sorrow and loss, and then use his local clout to lead the way unchallenged through customs, through the terminal, and down into the airport morgue.

All of that was Jules's doing, too. The junior agent had balls, that was for sure. When they arrived at the door to the room where the body was being held, Jules thanked Frisk and then politely but firmly dismissed the man, telling—not asking—him to wait outside in the outer hall with the security guard.

Giving Max privacy to go in on his own.

Which he did. On legs that were suddenly leaden. As bad as the past twenty-odd hours had been, these next few minutes were going to be worse, and he steeled himself.

Gina wasn't alone in the holding area. There were dozens of the white space-age-looking body boxes tagged and stacked against the wall. They belonged, no doubt, to the other victims of the terrorist attack, along with tourists who'd had heart attacks and car accidents, as well as a few expats who were finally ready to return home.

Someone had moved Gina's open container—Max just couldn't bring himself to think of it as a *coffin*—to a table in the center of the room. They'd also pulled a white sheet up and over her face. He just stood there, staring at the profile of her face beneath that shroud.

Her prominent nose.

Gina had laughingly called it her beak. Her passport to an extra large piece of tiramisu when she had dinner in Little Italy.

He'd never told her that he thought it made her face even more exotically beautiful. He'd never said just how much he'd loved it.

How much he'd loved her.

Time passed. Minutes. Many, many of them.

And Max didn't lift that sheet. He could not make himself move.

He didn't want to see her dead.

Yet he knew he had to look. He couldn't put her on that flight home until he'd provided a positive identification.

But until he saw her, until he touched her cold, lifeless face, he could pretend that they were wrong. That Gina wasn't really dead.

That her eyes were still sparkling the way they sparkled whenever she laughed and leaned in close to kiss him.

I'll stay as long as you need me.

But she hadn't stayed. Probably because Max had convinced her that he didn't need her.

And now he would never be kissed by her again.

Because he'd been too goddamn afraid.

"Max, I'm coming in." Jules Cassidy closed the door behind him with a solid-sounding thunk.

Jesus. Max somehow found his voice. "Don't." The word was little more than a growl.

Cassidy didn't flinch or falter. "Sweetie, you've been

standing in here for nearly half an hour," he said gently. "I'm just going to pull this from her face so we can see her, okay?"

It was obviously not a question Jules wanted Max to answer, because he didn't give him time to respond. He just reached out and . . .

God God God! Gina was horribly, hideously burned. Max recoiled, taking a step back, but then . . .

He stopped. All air had left his body, as if he'd been slammed in the stomach, and he couldn't breathe, couldn't speak.

But Jules could. "It's not her," he whispered, wonder in his voice. "Holy shit, it's not Gina."

Whoever was in that coffin was young, female, with long, dark hair and a prominent nose. When she was alive, she had probably looked a lot like Gina, particularly from the distance. At dusk.

But whoever she was, she was *not* Gina Vitagliano.

It was entirely possible that Max was going to throw up.

But he knew that he couldn't, because throwing up would take far too much time.

Instead, he spun to look at the rows of other coffins lining the room, and Jules—good man—knew exactly what he was thinking. He quickly moved to help.

The latches weren't locked. They popped open and . . .

Old man.

"Sorry to disturb you, sir." Jules Cassidy gently closed the lid.

Max moved on to the next, barking, "He's dead, he doesn't care."

He flipped the latches, and opened the lid and his heart stopped because it was another young, dark-haired woman lying there, but thank God again because she, too, wasn't Gina.

Still, something inside of him finally snapped.

He must've made some sort of sound, because Jules was

right there, next to him. Jules—the only man Max knew who would apologize to a corpse.

Or dare to put comforting arms around his boss, a man whose hardassed intolerance for stupid mistakes—one strike and you were off his team—was legendary.

"We'll find her," Jules told Max, his voice in his ear. "We will. But I honestly don't think we're going to find her in here."

For several dizzying seconds, it was possible Jules was the only thing holding Max up.

"God, I want her to be alive," Max squeezed the words out, daring to put voice to his emotions. He wanted it so badly, he didn't trust himself to be unbiased about the odds. He pulled away from Jules, wiping the tears from his face. Fuck that, until he found Gina, he didn't have time to cry. "Do you really think she's still alive?"

The kindness and sympathy he saw in Jules's eyes pissed him off.

"And don't goddamn answer that as my friend. You're not my friend. Fuck friendship," Max said, even though he knew damn well he wouldn't be having this conversation with any random subordinate. "You work for me. Answer as if your job depended on your telling the truth as you see it—as an experienced field agent."

Jules nodded as he closed the second coffin, keeping his apology to its occupant silent this time. "It wouldn't be the first time it's happened." He glanced at Max as they moved on to the next box. "A misplaced body. You know that as well as I do, sir. It falls under the way too common *snafu* heading."

He opened the locks and Max braced himself as they lifted the lid and . . .

Young man. Very battered, very dead young man. Somewhere his mother was crying.

"But I think," Jules continued as they moved to the next,

"that at this point, it's okay if you allow yourself to feel at least a little bit of hope."

Max had to wipe his face again. He hadn't cried at all when he'd thought Gina was dead. He'd just turned his heart into solid stone. But now these freaking tears just would not stop.

Because his heart was beating again. He could feel it, thumping wildly in his chest.

Hope wasn't the only thing he was feeling. He was also feeling fear. If Gina was alive, then where the hell *was* she? If she wasn't dead, then she could be in danger.

"We're going to need some assistance in here," Jules continued, looking over to where the coffins were stacked, some six high. "I'll stay. Frisk can send some of his team to help." He paused. Made sure Max was listening. "We'll also need to double-check with the lab doing DNA identifications. You know that, right?"

"Yeah." Some of the people killed in the terrorist blast were little more than jumbled body parts. That grim knowledge made it easier to stop the motherfucking crying.

"Why don't you go over to the hotel," Jules suggested. "I'll check with Frisk's team, find out why they put this other girl on their list as Gina Vitagliano. You know, was she carrying Gina's passport, or was the passport found somewhere in the rubble and assumed to be this girl's? God, Max, if Gina's passport was lost or stolen . . ."

It could have happened. Gina might have taken a side trip to, say, Berlin. Somewhere in-country. It was possible she might not know her passport was gone. Hell, she might not even know she was believed to be dead.

If Gina's passport had been stolen, she could be back at her hotel, right now.

"I know it's a long shot," Jules was saying, "but it wouldn't be the first time that type of *snafu* has happened, either and . . . Whoa!"

That much hope had brought Max to his knees.

Apparently if he didn't let himself weep like a little girl to relieve this emotional pressure building inside of him, he was in danger of hitting the ground in a dead faint.

Jules crouched beside him, checking for his pulse. "Are you okay? You're not, like, having a heart attack or a stroke, are you?"

"Fuck you," Max managed, swatting his hand away. "I'm not that old."

"If you really think heart disease is about age, then you definitely need to make an appointment with a cardiologist, like, tomorrow—"

"I just . . . tripped," Max said, but when he tried to get up, he found he still hadn't regained his equilibrium. Shit.

"Or maybe you needed to get on your knees to pray," Jules said as Max put his head down and waited for the dizziness to pass. "That excuse sounds a little more believable, if you want to know the truth. 'Hello God? It's me, Max. I know I've been lax in my attention to You over the past forty-mmph years, but if You give me a second chance, I'll make absolutely certain that this time around I'll tell Gina just how much I love her. Because withholding that information sure as hell didn't do either of us one bit of good, now did it?' "

"I did what I—" Max stopped himself. To hell with that. "I don't have to explain myself to you."

"That's right, you don't." Jules ignored Max's attempt to push him away, and helped him to his feet. "But you might want to work up some kind of Forgive-Me-For-Being-a-Butthead speech for when you come face to face with Gina. Although, I've got to admit that the falling to the knees thing might make an impact. You'll definitely get big points for drama."

Max straightened his suit, brushed off his pants. He took a deep breath, blew it out hard. He had to remember to keep breathing.

Because Gina was *not* going to be waiting for him in her hotel room. Life just wasn't that simple or easy.

He still didn't know why she had left Kenya in the first place, or even who she was traveling with, for that matter.

"You want me to come with?" Jules asked him. "To the hotel? So you don't *trip* again and maybe break your nose this time and—"

Max shook his head. "I need you here." Jules was the only one besides Max who could identify Gina. There was still a chance she was in one of those boxes—her body merely misplaced.

There was an even bigger chance she was still going to need one of those boxes for her flight home.

He had to remember that.

Even if she was alive, she was missing.

But the odds were that she was not alive. Because even if she hadn't been killed in the bombing, her passport may have been taken by someone who wouldn't have wanted her to report it as stolen. One best-case scenario had her tied up and locked in some ancient cellar somewhere. Worst had her already under the cellar's dirt floor.

Still, the odds of Max finding Gina alive were greater than they had been when he'd first walked into this room. And for that he was grateful.

Jules had his hand on the doorknob, his body language clear—*ready?*

Max wiped his face one last time. He was as ready as he'd ever be, but first he cleared his throat. "Thank you."

For maybe the first time in his life, Jules Cassidy didn't try to make a joke. He didn't make a big deal out of it in any other way, either. He just nodded and pushed open the door, saying, "You're more than welcome, sir," as they both went out of the room.

Sir.

Not "sweetie." Not even Max.

Not out here where someone might overhear.

But as they walked down the hall toward both Frisk and the security guard, Jules just couldn't keep himself completely in line. "So about that promotion," he murmured in a voice so low that even Max had trouble hearing it. "It's in the bag, right, crybaby-man?"

And Max did the one thing he thought he'd never do again, a mere hour ago as he'd entered the Hamburg terminal to identify Gina's body for air passage home.

He actually laughed.

KENYA, AFRICA
FEBRUARY 23, 2005
FOUR MONTHS AGO

It was after midnight when Molly finally came to his tent.

Jones had been expecting it, expecting her, and he knew what he had to do.

He just hadn't realized how difficult it was going to be to do it.

"You can't come in," he told her, but she spoke right over him as she pushed her way inside.

"No one saw me," she said and then she kissed him.

What had he been thinking? That Molly would meekly wait outside, that she'd understand that although the threat was diminished, it wasn't gone, and that they couldn't know for sure that no one had seen her coming in here?

And Jesus, had he really—stupidly—believed that when he was with her again, like this, in private, that he'd be able to step back and tell her not to kiss him?

He'd waited an eternity to be with her—it had been so goddamn long . . .

She was kissing the shit out of him. And hero that he was, he didn't stop himself from kissing the shit out of her, right back.

He kissed her, even though he knew he shouldn't, couldn't.

Because fuck that. She was fire in his arms as she pressed herself against him, as his eyes damn near rolled back in his head from all those years of wanting her so badly.

She was touching him, running her hands down his back and across his shoulders, up his neck and through his hair, as if checking to make sure he was really all there. True gentleman, his focus and both hands were on her amazing ass, as she opened herself to him, wrapping one leg around him in an attempt to get even closer.

"You're so thin, Dave," she breathed. "And that cane— are you all right?"

"Yeah," he said. "I'm fine. The cane's a prop." He knew he had to tell her to call him Leslie now, or Les. But damn, he loved being Dave Jones. It was Jones who'd first met her. It was Jones with whom she'd fallen in love.

She kissed him again, and yeah, she definitely wanted to be closer—she unfastened his pants and lifted her skirt, shifted and . . .

Molly made a sound that Jones knew he was making, too, and it was only that sudden awareness that they were being too loud that kept him from coming right then and right there, with that first sweet push inside of her.

Oh, God, oh God . . . *Thank you thank you thank you* . . .

Except, this wasn't happening the way he'd imagined it.

In his ultimate fantasy version of their reunion, Molly had always kissed him hello so sweetly, the gentlest of homecomings. She was so soft and warm and her beautiful eyes were always filled with tears. One would escape, and he'd brush it away with his thumb as he cupped the soft curve of her beautiful face, as he whispered that he'd dreamed about this day.

Instead, he kissed her hungrily, trying to absorb the sounds she was making as she strained against him, balancing on one foot, on tip-toes, as he fucked her.

Or rather, made love to her, vigorously. Molly didn't particularly like the F-word.

Despite the fact that she sure liked F-word-ing. He'd never factored that into his little fantasy, but he should have. He wasn't the only one, apparently, who'd been on a no-sex diet for way too long.

She'd waited for him, too—only she'd been running on pure faith. She hadn't known about his plan to find her. She'd had no idea that he'd spent every single day since he'd last seen her, working for this very moment.

Emotion crashed through him, and he knew that the salt he was tasting as he kissed her wasn't only from her tears.

And as long as he was thanking God, he added the darkness in that tent to his Things to be Grateful For list. There were limits to what a man could endure.

He felt her release—thanks again, God—because he had maybe three seconds left before he—

Jesus!—he wasn't wearing a condom. He pulled out of her, fast, and she immediately knew why.

"I have one," she said, fumbling in her pocket.

She'd brought one with her—and Jones knew this wasn't an accident. She'd come here tonight, intending to jump right back into their relationship, hot and heavy, just the way they'd left off. No questions, no "so, what exactly have you been up to for the past three years?"

And standing there, breathing hard, struggling to see her face in the darkness, he fell in love with her, all over again.

His woman.

Well, okay, so he'd never actually call her that to her face.

But right now they were out of time. "Save it," he told her, but she reached for him.

"No, Molly, *stop*." He could see her incredulity even in the dimness. "We've already been in here too long," he said as he zipped his pants back up—not easy to do—leaving his shirt untucked. He wiped his eyes on his sleeve, smoothed down his hair, found Leslie's glasses, hooking the wire frames around his ears. "Fix your skirt."

She didn't understand, and she didn't move to straighten herself until he grabbed her with one hand and his cane with the other and pulled her out of the tent and into the moonlight.

"I'm afraid it's terribly inappropriate," he said in Leslie Pollard's Brit accent as he led the way, limping toward the still-lit mess tent, "for you to come to my tent, unchaparoned, at this late hour, Miss Anderson."

"I'm sorry," she said. She didn't necessarily look like a woman who'd just had sex. No, the flushed, tear-streaked face and crazy hair could've belonged to a woman who was grieving and distraught. If you had a G-rated imagination. "But I . . ."

"I know you have more questions about him. Your dead friend. Dave Jones." He fished in his pants pocket for his handkerchief, taking advantage of the opportunity to try to adjust himself so his balls would end up only half crushed. But nope, it was hopeless. He was doomed.

Before he handed the handkerchief to Molly, he used it to wipe his mouth—God forbid she'd started wearing lipstick and had left a telltale streak on his face. "I'm not sure, though, what more I can tell you," he added. "I only met him a few times."

It was hard to tell what bemused her more—his pretense of propriety, his painfully real limping, or the fact that he was carrying a handkerchief. She wiped her eyes, blew her nose. "I'd heard rumors that . . . Crazy stuff, like, he'd killed this man, and, I don't know, run off, I guess, with his wife," she said. "But then someone said that he killed her, too . . ."

No way. That old story had made it all the way to *Africa* . . . ? It apparently had been twisted and changed, like the message in a worldwide game of telephone, but still . . .

"I knew him well," Molly continued. "Dave Jones. He would never have hurt anyone."

Um . . . Jones made a mental note—file this under things to talk about at another time. Right now, though, he had other priorities. They'd finally moved out of hearing range of the other sleeping tents, so he leaned closer to her, lowering his voice, and changing the subject. "It's important that you don't do anything out of the ordinary, Mol. This might be crazy and paranoid, but damn it, if you managed to hear about . . . Look, I don't want word getting back to the wrong people that my do-gooder ex-girlfriend has suddenly gotten very cozy with some guy she supposedly just met. Unless you've added casual sleepovers with strangers to your repertoire—"

"You know I haven't," she told him.

Yeah. He nodded. "That means anyone with brains will put two and two together and know it's gotta be me."

She stopped him with a hand on his arm. But she didn't touch him for long—as aware as he was that Sister Maura was in the mess, making herself a cup of tea, taking a break from the hospital's night shift. The nun didn't seem to have seen them out here in the moonlight, but they couldn't know that for sure.

"So we'll need to be discreet," she said. Her eyes welled with tears again. "I can't believe that you're really here. Wow, that is one awful haircut."

"We were discreet in Indonesia," Jones told her. He took off his glasses, polishing them with the edge of his shirt. It was something to do with his hands. As opposed to reaching to push her hair back from her face. Or pulling her into his arms again, to kiss her, to finish what they'd started. "And how long was it before your entire camp knew? Two days or three?"

"Then we'll have to be even more—" she started.

He cut her off. "Discreet's not good enough." He put his glasses back on. "What happened in my tent tonight . . . Mol, it's not going to happen again."

"What happened in your tent," she pointed out, "only half happened."

Yeah. He was well aware of that. "Not for a while, anyway," he added.

"You're serious, aren't you?" she said, searching his eyes.

He tried hard to look resolute. This had been way easier in theory, as part of his grand plan. "We need to do this right," he told her, reminding himself as well.

"When?" she asked. "How long is *a while*?"

"Months," he said.

Molly laughed—a burst of disbelief. "You came all the way around the world to—"

"Have coffee." He nodded. "With you. To sit at the same table, across from you. Shit, Mol, to sit in the same mess tent with you is enough—I don't even need to be at the same table."

"For months," she clarified. "Units of time, usually consisting of a complete lunar cycle."

"Yeah," Jones said. "And we should start with you not talking to me again for, I don't know, maybe even a couple of weeks."

She was starting to get mad. She just didn't get it. "You can't be serious—"

"Jones is dead," he told her. "Think about it. I'm the one who brought you that news. What's that expression, you know, about shooting the messenger . . . ? So okay, church ladies usually don't shoot people, but they probably avoid 'em for a while."

"I'm certainly mature enough to be able to separate the bad news from the bearer of the bad news," she shot back. "Or haven't you noticed three additional years of wrinkles on my face—"

"We need to make this look real," he interrupted her again. "Don't you get the fact that just being here scares the shit out of me? I won't put you into danger. Again. God knows I'll burn in hell for what I did the last time—"

She interrupted him, waving away both his mortal sins and the years he'd spent trying desperately to redeem himself. "So you think my ignoring you for a week or two is going to convince all the people who are watching us—who might not even be watching, might I add—that you're not you. So then what?"

One of the people who might not even be watching—the battle-ax, Sister Maria-Margarit—had opened the squeaky screen door of the nuns' larger, wooden-framed tent. She tied the belt of her robe around her waist as she started toward them.

He had to talk fast. "Then we take it slowly. We have a conversation in the mess tent every now and then. Eventually you invite me over for tea. In the daylight. With your roommate there. We stretch it out—over as many months as it would take for a geek like Leslie Pollard to realize he's in love with you—and then to get up enough nerve to actually do something about it."

And the sister was upon them.

Leslie turned toward her. "I'm so sorry, did we wake you? Miss Anderson was having trouble sleeping, naturally, after receiving such bad news . . . She came to my tent with some questions, and of course, that's not the proper place for a conversation, so . . . I thought perhaps a glass of warm milk . . . ?" He lowered his voice conspiratorially. "She was so upset, I didn't want to leave her alone."

Sister Maria-Margarit didn't cluck, didn't hug Molly, didn't show a snippet of sympathy. In fact, the look she gave Jones was filled with suspicion.

But it was probably no different than the way she looked at every man who walked God's earth.

He turned back to Molly, sending her a silent apology as he nodded his farewell. "I'll leave you in good hands then, Miss Anderson."

"Thank you for being so kind," she said. "Mr. Pollard.

And I apologize again for disturbing you and . . . everything."

He knew exactly what she meant by everything, and, yeah, as he walked back to his tent, he knew that the next few months were going to be among the longest of his entire life.

CHAPTER SIX

"What were you like when you were a kid?" Gina interrupted the post-sex glow to ask.

There was a short time, right after they made love, when Max held her in his arms and seemed almost relaxed.

It had occurred to her that, instead of lying back and enjoying the moment, this might be the time to get him talking.

But Max now shook his head. "I was never a kid."

She laughed, turning to look up at him. "Yes, you were. Come on. What was your favorite . . . TV show growing up?"

He shook his head again. "I didn't watch much TV."

"*Charlie's Angels,*" she guessed, laughing when he rolled his eyes. "I bet you were one of those guys who had a picture of what's-her-name—Farrah—on your wall at college."

"No comment." But he smiled. "I was more into music than TV during college. I mean, we watched *Saturday Night Live,* sure, but . . . Give me Chrissie Hynde from the Pretenders any day. She was hot. And she could really sing."

Music. They talked music a lot. It was easy to talk about

music. "What was your favorite TV show when you were, like, ten?" she asked him.

"Jeez, I don't know," he said. "I watched what my brother and sister wanted to watch. They were so much older . . . Tim was a sports fan, so we saw a lot of baseball and basketball. And when they weren't around . . . My grandfather was really into Elvis. I watched a lot of Elvis movies with him."

Elvis movies. That was too funny. "How old were you," Gina asked, "when your grandfather had his stroke?"

"Nine."

"That must've sucked."

"Yeah."

She was silent for a moment, just watching him, half hoping he'd say more, but knowing that he wouldn't. He'd told her once—a long time ago—that he was nine when his sister first tried to kill herself. It must've been one hell of a year.

The first of many.

No wonder he felt as if he hadn't had a childhood.

She leaned forward to kiss him on the side of his face, but he turned and caught her mouth with his.

God, the man knew how to kiss. It would have been so easy to let this be the final punctuation mark at the end of the conversation. To let this kiss slide them into one of those two-condom nights.

But it was getting late and she couldn't stay forever.

As much as she would have liked to.

She gently pulled away.

"So what's your favorite Elvis movie?" she asked.

He laughed.

"Come on," she said. "This isn't heavy stuff—you're allowed to answer."

"I don't know," he said. "I really only watched because my grandfather wanted to."

"So . . . What?" Gina asked, propping herself up on one

elbow to look down at him. "You sat there with him in the living room and did quadratic equations in your head while staring into space?"

He rolled his eyes again. "Okay," he said. "Just . . . gimme a break—I was nine, okay? And my grandfather stopped being able to talk, but when he watched these movies, he, I don't know. He looked almost happy. Sometimes he even laughed out loud. Shit, I would've climbed into one of those movies to live there permanently if I could've. So yeah, I had a favorite. *Follow That Dream*. Which probably means nothing to you."

"Hey, I had some significant Elvis exposure," she said. "That's the one with all the kids and the station wagon, right?"

He laughed. "Wow. Secret Elvis fans unite."

God, she loved it when he smiled like that.

"I had a great-aunt who had two pictures hanging in her apartment in Bayside," Gina told him. "One was Jesus, the other was Elvis."

"Black velvet?"

"You know it. My idiot brother told me that he was one of the most important saints, and I . . . Well, I actually believed him. I'm embarrassed to say how old I was before I realized it was only a joke." It was her turn to roll her eyes now.

It earned her a soft laugh. "The patron saint of rock and roll," Max said. "I like it. I mean, he was a stepping stone to more sophisticated music, but for me, it pretty much all started with Elvis."

Back again to music. But okay.

"Did you ever play an instrument when you were a kid?" Gina asked him.

He looked at her, apparently decided the topic was still safe enough, and said, "When I was in middle school, I really wanted to play the guitar. I'd discovered Hendrix by then, you know?"

She nodded.

"So I went to the school music teacher, and . . . She got me this violin that she kept on hand—for kids who wanted to try it out before renting one for an entire year."

"A violin?"

"Yeah," Max said. "Apparently that was where you had to start in the string department in our school. I remember her telling me that I had to earn the right to play the guitar."

"Oh, man," Gina said. "Your middle school music teacher would've made *my* middle school music teacher have a heart attack. I mean, there would have been a knife fight in the teacher's lounge. Did you, like, totally never go back to the music room ever again?"

"Not quite," he admitted. "I was . . . Well, I figured, how hard could it be?" He made a disgusted noise. "What a disaster. I was always good at everything but . . ."

"Not the violin," she said. "That's one of *the* hardest instruments to play. That was so stupid of that teacher."

"Yeah," Max agreed. "I was listening to stuff like 'Crosstown Traffic' and 'All Along the Watchtower' and the teacher wanted me to master 'Three Blind Mice' on this piece of crap that I never managed to get in tune. It didn't help that the tolerance for noise in our house had dropped to negative five. I mean, I could listen to Hendrix with my headphones on. But practicing was . . ." He shrugged. "I quit after a week."

"Was that when your sister was—"

"Yeah," he said. "What was *your* favorite Elvis movie?"

Okay. Gina had gotten more than she'd expected with that story about the violin, so she backed down. "The one where he plays the priest," she told him. "Well, he's really a doctor, but I always thought he was a priest. He worked with nuns, so . . . And I thought he was a saint, right?"

"So how old were you when you found out he wasn't?" Max asked.

"Third grade," she said. "It was ugly. This stupid fifth-grade boy—Patrick O'Brien—wouldn't stop talking about how Elvis sucked and how he'd died of an overdose. So I gave him a bloody lip and a black eye—I really kicked the crap out of him, out on the playground. I got into *so* much trouble. The principal made me go to the library right then and there—my clothes were all muddy, it was *so* humiliating. But she made me research the details of Elvis's death." She sighed. "It was not a good day. I remember my mother was at work, so my Uncle Frank—he was living in our basement because he was having trouble finding work—he came to school to pick me up. Fighting was a serious deal. I was suspended for two days, and I had to apologize to Patrick and his parents before I could come back. Only, I knew that would make it all worse, right? Imagine if you were that kid, and this third-grade girl comes to your house and . . ."

Max was smiling. "Poor bastard."

"Yeah, you think it's funny, but I was despondent," she told him. "Heartbroken. All those prayers—going out to some phony antisaint? This hero of mine—a drug addict? You know, I come from a long line of firefighters and cops. Doing drugs was on par with murder and arson in our family." She spooned back against him, pulling his arm more tightly around her. "I can't believe I haven't told you this story before. I haven't, have I?"

"No." He reached up to brush her hair away from his face.

"Uncle Frank sat me down and told me that heroes sometimes make mistakes," Gina said. "He told me that despite the mistakes he'd made, Elvis maybe should've been made a saint anyway, because he brought so much light into so many people's lives. Like Great-Aunt Tilly, who didn't have a lot to be happy about after Great-Uncle Herman died.

"He also made me take a shower and change my clothes,"

she continued, "and he took me right over to the O'Briens' house, and he told me what to say so Patrick wouldn't terrorize me for the rest of the year." She snorted. "Frank told me that I had to restore his pride and that I had to say to him, 'I'm sorry, I was wrong. Thank you for not hitting me because I'm just a girl and I'm littler than you, too, and you obviously know that boys shouldn't hit girls.' And I was all like, 'But he *did* hit me—I won that fight, fair and square! What about *my* pride?' And so Frankie let me write a note, to give to Patrick without his parents seeing, and it said, 'If I ever hear you say that Elvis sucks again, I will make you sorry.' " Gina laughed. "And after we got back home, Frank let me play his drum kit for the first time. We kids weren't allowed to touch it, but that day he let me sit down—he actually gave me a lesson, and it was magical . . . Of course from then on, I would sneak downstairs when no one else was home and play. I think he must have known . . . Anyway, Patrick O'Brien always avoided me on the playground after that."

Max was smiling. "My grandfather would've adored you."

A long time ago, Max had told her the story of how his grandfather met his grandmother—an American—in India in the 1920s. They were both thirteen when his grandmother, Wendy, got separated from her school group. Raza Bhagat had walked her safely home. He'd then gone and learned English in some remarkably insane amount of time, like two weeks, so that he could talk to her more easily.

Apparently, the attraction went both ways. They were married in 1930—and back then their relationship was considered interracial and quite scandalous. It was made worse by the fact that Raza wasn't high caste.

After the second world war, Raza, Wendy, and their son Timothy—Max's dad—moved to America, where they were slightly less outcast, especially when Raza got a high-paying job in the aviation industry.

Raza embraced his wife's country with enthusiasm—a place where a rocket scientist born in a laborer's body didn't have to spend his entire life hauling manure.

"I would've loved to have met him," Gina said. "Your parents, too."

The look Max shot her was filled with disbelief.

"What?" Gina said.

"Nothing."

"How old were you when they got divorced?" Gina asked.

He sighed. "First year of college," he said. "Do we really have to go here?"

"That must've been hard for you," she said. *Come on, Max, talk about something that matters* . . .

"Nah," he said. "It was all over by then."

"If that's the case, why don't you want to talk about it?"

"Because there's nothing to say," Max told her. "I did what I always did. Got straight As. Graduated early. Look, Gina, it's getting late."

Oh, good. The conversation had moved into slightly less comfortable territory for him, so he did what he always did. Tried to get rid of her.

It wouldn't do any good to get pissed off. If she did that, Max would just shut down even tighter.

So she kept it light. "Big day tomorrow?" she teased. "Playing gin rummy with Ajay?"

"I meant for you. You've got to drive back to Jules's tonight."

"Yeah, and then pick up your mail tomorrow. Exhausting," she said.

He didn't smile. He was so on the verge of saying something about her going back to New York and applying to law school at NYU—she just knew it. And then she wouldn't be able to keep from getting pissed off at him and . . .

She'd end up walking out, upset. It had been too nice a

night for that—even though she'd been the one doing most of the talking.

"So what do you use as an outlet for your creativity?" Gina asked him before he could say something stupid.

"What?"

She'd confused him. Good. "Since you gave up the violin," she explained. "If I didn't have my drums, I'd go crazy."

"You don't have your drums," he pointed out. "They're in New York."

Grrrr.

"Yeah," she said, "no, I found this recording studio about two blocks from Jules's apartment. They've got a kit set up. The owner, Ernie, doesn't mind if I come in, off hours, and . . . Didn't I tell you about this?"

"No." Max frowned. "Ernie?"

"Ooh." She kissed him. "Jealous?" She didn't let him answer. "He's married with two kids. So stop dodging my question. What do you do? Write poetry? Or—I know—you scrapbook, right?"

He laughed, as she'd hoped he would. "Yeah. In all my copious free time."

"Seriously," she said. "Have you ever tried painting or sculpting or—"

"Some people are born to create art, others are born to sit in the audience."

Gina sat up, turning to face him. "You don't really believe that, do you?" She was outraged. "That's as stupid as telling a kid that in order to play the guitar he needs to master the violin first. They're two completely different instruments, by the way—"

"Shhhh," he said, but he was smiling. "People are sleeping."

"I love when you smile," she told him. "You don't do that enough."

And just like that, his smile was gone. "I know," he said. "I'm sorry."

And there they were, just gazing at each other.

Tired. And scared. Or at least *she* was scared. Uncertain. Emotionally exhausted from having to be so freaking careful around him all the time. Fearful he was finally going to tell her that enough was enough, that they couldn't go on.

She didn't know how *he* felt because he would never tell her.

Please, she prayed to Saint Elvis, *give me some sort of sign* . . . She didn't need Max to tell her that he loved her, but it sure as heck wouldn't hurt.

The fact that they were naked and in his bed probably played into it, but, as always, when they looked at each other that way, something sparked. It flashed and crackled and snapped around them.

What are we doing here, Max? Gina didn't ask him that. Instead, she said, "It's late."

"Yeah," he agreed. And then he surprised her. He actually sang to her. It was soft and a little off-key, but it was definitely meant to be an Elvis imitation. "Lord Almighty, I feel my temperature rising . . ."

Gina laughed.

Max reached for her, the heat in his eyes telling her she wasn't going anywhere.

Not for a while, at least.

HOTEL ELBE HOF, HAMBURG, GERMANY
JUNE 21, 2005
PRESENT DAY

Gina wasn't waiting for him in her room at the Elbe Hof hotel.

Max hadn't really expected her to be.

But, Christ, how he'd hoped.

There was an envelope on the floor just inside the room, no doubt a hotel bill that had been pushed through the crack under the door. Max scooped it up on his way in.

He didn't bother to turn on the light as he shut the door behind him—the curtains were open, bathing the two neatly made beds in late-afternoon sunlight. The room had a typical hotel setup—beds, dresser, desk with a telephone, TV. Overstuffed chair and a standing lamp. Breakfast table and chairs next to the window.

The decor was blandly generic—he could have been anywhere in the world that catered to American travelers.

Except it smelled like Gina in here. She didn't wear perfume, at least not the kind that came in a bottle, but her shampoo, soap, and lotions were sweetly scented.

The smell was stronger in the bathroom. As if she were in there. Just invisible.

Makeup was out on the counter as if she'd just used it. As if she'd left this room with every intention of coming right back.

In the bedroom, paperback books were stacked on the dresser, on the desk, even on the floor. Gina used to joke that her segment in a "Girls Gone Wild" video would take place in a bookstore. The only thing that could get her to lift her shirt in public would be the promise of an advance copy of the latest Dean Koontz or J.D. Robb.

There were no bookstores in the remote part of Kenya where she was working, and Max felt a stab of remorse. He should have thought of that and bought her the latest releases. He could have had Jules send them to her—it would have taken both of them so little time and effort.

Max tossed the envelope onto the bed nearest the bathroom to free up his hands so he could open all the drawers.

Gina was an unpacker. Instead of keeping her things in her bag when she traveled, the way normal people did, she actually used the hotel dresser.

Sure enough, she'd done the same here.

There were clothes hanging in the closet, too, and Max moved closer to look.

Gina's clothes and someone else's.

But there were no shirts or suits hanging, no man-sized sneakers on the closet floor. That someone else was female.

Max stood there looking at a dress that was neither Gina's style nor size, feeling . . . What? Relief?

Not really.

Although, yeah, okay. Maybe a little. The hotel registration had been for Gina Vitagliano and guest. Up to this moment, Max had been going on the assumption that the guest in question was a man.

Leslie Pollard, who'd arrived at Gina's camp in Kenya around four months ago. British. Mid-thirties. Scholarly.

Fascinating.

Or so Gina had described the son of a bitch in a brief letter to Jules. *I have met the most fascinating man!*

But unless part of what made Pollard so fascinating was his tendency to wear dresses in bold floral prints, he wasn't her current traveling companion.

Jules had showed Gina's note to Max only after he'd done some digging and found out that, according to AAI records, Pollard had signed on as a volunteer after his wife of more than ten years had passed away.

The man had worked for awhile for other volunteer organizations—in China, in Southeast Asia, and in India. He hailed from a little town in England, where he'd taught in a private school for wealthy girls. The school's scrutiny, done before they even considered hiring him, was more in-depth than most government security clearances.

Leslie Pollard was—the AAI office had informed Jules, who in turn relayed the information to Max—a quiet, spiritual man who mourned the loss of a wife whom he still loved quite deeply.

But Gina, with her love of life, her forthright attitude,

her sense of humor, and that movie-star body, had what it took to teach any man to embrace life—and to love again.

Christ, it was like something out of a novel. Gina flees to Kenya, running from a broken heart caused by a bad relationship with Max, who was happy to sleep with her whenever she asked, but who was too much of a coldhearted prick to be able to open up and share his true feelings.

Pollard, meanwhile, dedicates himself to serving his fellow man after his wife dies—probably from something painful and lingering, like cancer. He's gentle, sensitive, and wounded—yet unafraid to speak his heart. She's frank and funny and so goddamn beautiful and vibrant, she takes his breath away.

While helping to search for a missing goat—no, make it a lost child—they get stranded together in the wilderness, far from the camp. Forced to huddle together to stay warm, their passion ignites and . . .

Yeah. *This* was really helping. Imagining what it was like the first time Gina and that goddamn Englishman made love was really going to help Max find her.

He went through Gina's clothes more thoroughly, searching her pockets for a restaurant matchbook or some other clue that might help them retrace her steps. He tried to keep himself focused by thinking about how devastatingly difficult it would have been to do this if that body in the morgue really had been hers.

It kept him from thinking about her having sex with Mr. Fascinating, but he goddamn made himself tear up again in the process.

Yeah, that, too, wasn't helping. *Crybaby-man.* Shit. What was wrong with him?

Gina had mostly sturdy camping attire in her drawer. Cargo shorts. Jeans. T-shirts. Lightweight overshirts. Thick socks. Underwear—not quite of the sturdy variety. She had a generous supply of her usual lacy, frilly fare.

Ah, God.

But there were no business cards from Osama bin Laden or any of his associates tucked in among her clothes.

Out on the desk was a pile of papers. Brochures advertising local museums. A ragged map of the city. A short list of items to pick up from a drugstore, in Gina's familiar messy handwriting. "Soap, sunblock, Q-tips & cotton balls, bottled water, crackers . . ."

But there were no credit card receipts—no receipts of any kind.

Max scanned for her luggage, and found a pair of empty duffle bags tucked onto the shelf in the closet.

He reached to take them down and . . . What the hell was in here?

The bag on the bottom was much heavier than an empty bag should have been. It was also locked and attached to the wire shelf with one of those cheap bicycle locks, the kind that had its own little combination clasp. It was looped around the duffel's handle.

As if any of that would keep a burglar from absconding with the contents.

Max got out his penknife and cut the handle.

The bag was Gina's. Her last name was clearly on it, written in indelible marker. He took it over to the bed, pushing aside the envelope he'd tossed there . . .

Okay. Whoa. He was either exhausted or slipping, because that envelope wasn't from the hotel as he'd assumed. It had come through the mail—there was a cancelled stamp on it. It was addressed to Gina, care of the hotel, room 817. The sender was something called A.M.C., located here in Hamburg.

Since he already had his knife out and open, he took care of the bag first, slicing through the canvas alongside the zipper.

Inside was . . .

Gina's digital camera, and, yes, as he'd hoped—a pile of receipts.

Max sat down on the bed, leafing through the scraps of paper. She'd written directly on them, when it wasn't obvious what they were for. Dinner, dinner, dinner, lunch, breakfast, lunch. Books, books, books, books.

There were about two dozen receipts of various sizes and shapes, with varying legibility. He'd go through them in detail after he found out what A.M.C. was—

Hold on.

At the bottom of the pile was a larger piece of paper that had been folded into thirds to better fit with the others. It was that really thin kind of paper, almost translucent, and Max could read through it, backwards and upside down, the bold letters proclaiming American Medical Clinic.

A.M.C.

He unfolded it and . . .

It was a receipt for medical services.

Gina's full name was printed at the top, with her address care of this hotel, room 817. Apparently, she'd seen a doctor and . . .

Jesus.

She'd had a pregnancy test.

Max tore open the sealed envelope. It contained a letter. He pulled it out, shook it open and . . .

A.M.C. was indeed the American Medical Clinic.

Again, Gina's name and temporary address was in print at the top. "Dear Patient," it started.

There were several brief paragraphs in English. The first informed her that her test results were in, but didn't say what those results were.

Of course not.

The second chided her for missing a scheduled appointment and told her payment was due anyway since she hadn't cancelled twenty-four hours in advance.

And the third was the kicker. It reminded her of the importance of good prenatal care.

He read it again, and that word was still there. *Prenatal.*

Was Gina actually *pregnant*?

Except, okay. This was clearly a form letter. Her missed appointment date—yesterday—had been written in by hand.

This type of women's health clinic probably pushed the importance of prenatal care whenever possible.

This didn't mean anything.

And even if she was pregnant, so what? He'd take her alive and pregnant any day, over not pregnant but dead.

Still, how could he have been such a total, flipping fool? Max had to put his head between his knees—he was suddenly feeling so short of air, so damn dizzy. She would have stayed if he'd asked her to. She'd've been safe and . . .

If she'd stayed, her baby could've been his.

And wasn't *that* a terrifying thought? What the hell would *he* do with a baby?

The question was moot. She hadn't stayed.

And apparently, Max had done what he'd set out to do— pushed her from his life for good. Lost her to another man, who'd either been too stupid, selfish, or careless to properly protect her.

Unless she loved this son of a bitch and her pregnancy was intentional.

But if that was the case, why hadn't he come along on this trip with her? And who the hell was this woman she *was* traveling with?

Aside from her clothes, there was nothing in this room that would identify her.

Max had found Gina's receipts—where were hers?

He got off the bed to finish his search—starting with the wastebaskets.

KENYA, AFRICA
FEBRUARY 23, 2005
FOUR MONTHS AGO

David Jones was dead.

Gina helped Molly cope with the devastating news by taking over her shifts in the hospital.

She'd also suggested that they hold a wake tonight. Just the two of them, a bottle of wine that Sister Helen had donated to the cause, and all the stories that Molly could share—without blushing—about her too-short time with this man that she'd loved.

Molly had agreed—it was a good idea, but she'd surprised Gina. Twice.

First, with the news that she was a recovering alcoholic, so she'd just as soon skip the wine, but thanks anyway.

This information, had Gina stopped to consider, wasn't all that much of a surprise. Molly had told her she'd started her relief work career as a bona fide Type B volunteer. A teenage pregnancy with the baby given up for adoption, a dead boyfriend . . . Molly had struggled for years before finding her way.

The second surprise was that Molly planned to invite Leslie Pollard to their wake.

As weird as that seemed at first, Gina quickly realized that Molly didn't just want to *tell* stories about Jones. She wanted to *hear* stories, too. And the stammering and lank-haired Brit had known the man. Or at least he'd met him a few times.

It was going to make for one odd vibe in the tent tonight.

Assuming, of course, ol' Humor-Les accepted the invitation.

Gina finished sterilizing the hospital's bedpans and headed to the mess tent to get Winnie and the other girls their lunch.

The camp slowed down considerably in the midday heat.

And wasn't that an understatement.

This camp, which tended to groove along at an eat-the-dust-of-a-passing-tortoise pace, went into a coma every day, just around noon.

As a born-and-bred New Yorker, the lazy pace had frustrated Gina at first. She'd had to take deep breaths to keep herself from clapping her hands and shouting, "Faster! Walk faster!" And since she wasn't into napping, the midday breaks seemed a waste of time.

But now she liked it. The entire camp fell asleep, and she had the place to herself. It was like stepping into that episode of *Star Trek* where Captain Kirk found himself alone on the *Enterprise*. Turned out he'd been accelerated to a point where he was moving so fast, his crewmembers couldn't see him and . . . No, she was getting that episode confused with the one where the aliens created a mock-up of the starship and . . .

Crap. Eighteen months without sex, and she was turning into her cousin, Karol-with-a-K, who spent way too much time wondering if Mr. Spock would've fallen in love with Winifred, had he been able to warp into the Buffyverse.

Karol-with-a-K was a freak, and not just because it was so obvious that opposites attracted and that Spock would've been crushing on Buffy, big time.

"Miss! Pardon me, Miss!"

Gina turned to see a woman lurking in the shadows near the shower tent. She was young, a girl really, barely eighteen if that, and dressed in a vibrantly-colored robe that screamed money. Where on earth had she come from?

"I must speak with you." Her English was upper-class London, her face flawlessly beautiful, with its rich, dark brown skin, and her wide, expressive eyes. "But we must not be seen together. May we go inside?"

Into the shower tent?

The girl's anxiety was palpable, and Gina nodded. "Of course."

The sign outside the tent was flipped to "Men," but the camp would stay asleep for another solid hour. Besides, the generator was turned off at this time of day. Anyone showering now would get only tepid water at best.

The girl opened the wooden-framed door. "Hurry," she urged Gina, which was kind of a sick joke, considering she moved the way far too many local women moved—slowly, with careful, pain-ridden steps.

It was also obvious as she moved that she wasn't just pleasantly, healthily plump as Gina had assumed. She was pregnant.

"Do you need a doctor?" Gina asked her. "Or a nurse?"

Many women in this region of Kenya refused treatment from male doctors. Or rather, their husbands refused it for them.

Both Father Ben and AAI had been trying, for years now, to find a female doctor for this camp. The nuns had gone so far as to start raising money with a plan to send Sister Maria-Margarit to medical school. Although at this point, Gina was pretty sure that Sister Double-M could teach the OB/GYN instructors at Harvard Med a thing or two about providing pre- and neo-natal care to women in third world countries.

"We have a very good nurse practitioner here," Gina continued, trying to reassure her.

"Oh, yes, I know," the girl said. "We came here—my husband and I, to visit your nurse. But my husband, he's enlightened, you see. He's decided I should see the doctor, which unfortunately means he'll be with me during the examination and . . ." She opened the door a crack and peeked out. "I don't have much time. I'm supposed to be resting right now. They brought me to a tent and . . . You *are* the American woman I've heard so much about?"

"I'm an American," Gina told her. "Yeah. But—"

The woman took her hands. "I need your help," she said. "My sister, Lucy, will turn sixteen in a few weeks. And when she does, they'll claim she gave consent and they'll do to her what they did to me."

Oh, *crap.* "But that's illegal," Gina said, and immediately felt like an idiot. What a stupid thing to say. Of course it was illegal.

"Yes, isn't it?" the girl agreed. "Try prosecuting, though, in a town like Narok. That's the big city, out where my uncle has his farm, where Lucy still lives. She's visiting me now, but she and my aunt will be going back a week from Wednesday. So you see, we've got to do this very soon."

"Do this?" Gina echoed lamely.

"I'm going to create a diversion," the girl told her. "Some time in the next few days. I've already given Lucy what little money I have, some jewelry . . . We have a friend up north in Marsabit who'll help her get to London. We lived in Great Britain for a year, before my father died. We have friends there who'll care for her. She's ready to go, Miss. Please say that I can tell her to come here, to you, that you'll help her get to Marsabit."

"Of course," Gina said. Holy shit . . .

"Thank you." The girl started to cry. "Bless you. A woman who works in my mother-in-law's kitchen told me you helped all seven of her daughters flee—that you are an angel to have risked so much for her children. She said there are people angry enough to make you vanish forever if you dared step outside the boundaries of this camp, but that you still would help me."

And there it was.

The reason why Molly—the only other American woman in camp—repeatedly turned down opportunities to go on safaris and trips into the Kenyan countryside. Because she was targeted for running a twenty-first-century version of the underground railroad for Kenyan girls.

"Go back to your tent," Gina told her, leading her back to the door. "I'll find Molly, okay? She's the woman your friend told you about—I'm just her . . . assistant." At least she was from now on. She checked to make sure no one was outside the tent. "Tell Lucy to ask for Molly or Gina when she comes, all right? Tell her that we'll be ready for her. We'll get her safely to Marsabit."

With a nod, the girl—shoot, Gina hadn't asked her name—was gone.

Gina shook her head as she waited there in the tent. Just in case someone was watching, she didn't want to follow the girl right outside. Although, if someone was watching, counting to ten or even ten hundred before she left wasn't going to make a difference. It was obvious, since this tent didn't have a back door, that if two people came out within a few minutes of each other, they'd been in there together.

So why bother to wait at all?

She was only doing it because that's what spies did in the movies. Which was a pretty stupid reason.

Of course, she *was* the world's worst liar. Subterfuge was not one of her strengths.

Molly, on the other hand, apparently excelled at it.

All these months they'd been close friends, and Gina hadn't had a clue.

What other secrets had her tentmate been keeping from her?

Gina peeked out the door and—oh, crap! Leslie Pollard was heading straight for this tent, towel over his shoulder.

It seemed that he'd chosen today for his monthly bleaching.

Instinct made her back up. Instinct made her duck and hide in one of the partitioned changing areas.

Her instinct sucked. In retrospect—a very quickly occurring retrospect, which bloomed instantly to life behind that canvas curtain—she realized that instead of hiding, she should have pushed open that door and breezed out. She should have waved cheerily to Humor-Les Pollard and announced loudly—in case he cared—that that plumbing problem was definitely fixed.

Of course, that *was* still an option.

And then the sound of a zipper being pulled down seemed to echo in the tent.

Oh double crap.

Except that was a good thing—right? It meant he was safely ensconced in another of the changing areas, doing whatever meditations were required to enable him to allow soap and water to touch his body.

All she had to do was slip quietly past this curtain and tiptoe toward the door and . . .

Screeeee! If her life had a soundtrack, the noise of a needle scraping across an old-fashioned LP would have woken up the entire camp.

Because apparently Leslie Pollard didn't feel the need to step into the changing area when he thought himself alone in the shower tent.

He seemed as stunned to see her as she was to see so very much of him. That was good news, since he didn't find his voice to ask her what she was doing in the shower tent when it clearly said MEN on the sign on the door.

But one of them very definitely had to say *some*thing, so Gina said, "Hi," because, *shit,* Leslie Pollard in his tightie-whities was . . . Way not as skinny and raw-chicken-skin pale as she'd imagined.

Not that she'd spent a whole lot of time imagining, because she honestly hadn't.

But the man was a whole lot younger than she'd thought, too—far closer to thirty than fifty.

He was also ripped. Six-pack ripped, with a tan that was fading, but still quite dark. No doubt about it, there was not a bit of chicken skin in sight. Although his tan faded away completely to pale at the very tops of his thighs and . . .

And *shee-yit.*

He could've turned his back on her. Instead, he reached for his towel, wrapping it around his waist in one smooth motion. Which made the muscles in his arms and upper body flex and ripple like those of an action-hero in a movie.

Leslie Pollard Saves the Day.

Gina laughed at the idea of *that* movie poster, which was wrong, very wrong, to do. God forbid some strange man burst in on her in her underwear and break into giggles, so she turned it into a cough.

"Sorry. Dust in my . . . Ignore me—I was just checking the . . ." Plumbing, she was going to say, but she stopped herself, because, oh my God. It was a double entendre. Check the plumbing as in checking *your* plumbing. Which she really hadn't meant to do. At all. Except, pretowel, when she was noticing his tan, or lack thereof in certain areas, it was just so . . . there.

"Water pressure," she said instead. "Good news. There's water pressure. It's very . . . waterlike and pressure-ish . . ." Somehow she managed to stumble to the door. "Have a nice day."

Well, okay.

Most of the camp was still in coma-mode, and Gina managed to make it back to the tent she shared with Molly without seeing any other of her coworkers nearly naked. Sister Maria-Margarit, for instance. Yeeks.

As she burst through the door, Molly knocked over a bottle of nail-polish, clearly startled. "Shoot," she said crossly, trying to contain the mess.

She was wearing her silk turquoise robe, a towel wrapped around her head, some of Gina's mudpack on her face.

So, *this* afternoon was getting weirder and weirder. Instead of grieving, tears soaking her pillow, Molly was giving herself what Gina called a "spa day," complete with painting her toenails red.

Of course, everyone grieved in their own way.

"I'm so sorry to bother you," Gina told her friend, "but this can't wait . . ."

HOTEL ELBE HOF, HAMBURG, GERMANY
JUNE 21, 2005
PRESENT DAY

Max was wasting his time, trying to talk the administrative staff at the American Medical Clinic into violating the rules of their patient privacy policy.

He knew that they couldn't give out Gina's personal information, especially not over the phone, but he couldn't not try.

As he started to explain who he was, why he was in Hamburg, his discovery of both the receipt and the letter from A.M.C., the woman who'd answered the phone interrupted him.

"Hold please."

So he held. And held. He knew this was meant to discourage him, but he had so few leads to go on.

As he waited, he spread Gina's receipts out on the bed, arranging them according to date.

He discovered, upon closer perusal of those very receipts, that Gina had paid for her friend's lunches, breakfasts, and dinners.

Unless, of course, she was literally eating for two.

So great. Now he had a good sense of where and what Gina had eaten during her visit to Hamburg, as well as where she'd shopped for books—all within close proximity of this hotel—but little else.

His survey of her trash had told him nothing. And his careful search of the rest of the hotel room hadn't clued him in as to the identity of Gina's traveling companion.

It was freaking weird—as if she were traveling with Jane Anonymous. Or maybe Jane Bond. Whoever this woman was, she was better sanitized than some of the top No-Name Agency field operatives Max had come into contact with during his career.

What were the chances of such a lack of identifiers being unintentional?

While he waited, on hold, he checked her clothes a second time for laundry markings, and discovered that she'd once had what looked to be name tags sewn into just about every item. Two little bumps of extra fabric.

Name tags that had been cut out.

The woman with the crisp German accent came back on the line. "I'm sorry, sir. Without a release form signed by the patient—"

"I'd like to make an appointment to speak to the doctor who examined her," Max said. He squinted at the receipt. "Dr. Liesle Kramer."

She was silent for a moment, then said, "How's September? The seventh. It's a Wednesday—"

That was three months away. "I'm sorry, you don't understand. I'm with—"

"Yes," she cut him off. "I do. You're with the FBI—or so you say. Your story is not very original, I'm afraid."

"What?"

"We get quite a few calls each week from the FBI, the police, the CIA. As if they are magic words that will make us hand over private information."

His phone beeped—he another call coming in. He glanced at the number. It was Jules.

"Yeah," Max said to the A.M.C. administrator, "but I'm really—"

"I'm sorry, sir, I suggest you speak directly to your friend, if you wish to inquire about her health. We do *not* give out information without a release form signed by—"

"Look," he said. "She's missing. I'm trying to find her. I want to talk to Dr. Kramer to see if Gina was with someone or by herself when she came to her appointment."

"I'm sorry, sir—"

"Is Dr. Kramer in tonight?" He saw from the letterhead that A.M.C. had evening hours today.

"I'm sorry, sir, we do not reveal information about our staff."

To potential lunatics. She didn't say the words, but Max knew she was thinking it.

"Good-bye," she said, and hung up on him.

Damn it.

Jules had given up on him. Max called him back.

"What have you got on the woman Gina's traveling with?" he asked as Jules picked up.

The younger agent wasn't fazed by the lack of a more traditional greeting, such as *hello*.

"Nothing," he said. "Yet. Although I am expecting a call from George. He's contacted an operative in Nairobi who's actually going out to the camp so we can talk to the priest who runs the place. Communication is spotty at best out there and we haven't been able to reach him any other way. His name's Ben Soldano. The priest, that is. I'll let you know as soon as I hear anything from George."

"What else have you got?" Max asked.

"We've been in touch with Gina's credit card company. There've been no charges since the day of the bombing."

"Shit," Max said.

"Yeah, sorry," Jules said. "And you're going to hate this even more. On that same day that the bomb went off, there was a charge made for a one-way plane ticket to New York City from Hamburg—departing late that afternoon. In Gina's name. Even earlier that same day, there was a very large charge—twenty thousand dollars—to a company called NTS International, that oddly doesn't seem to exist anymore."

Jesus.

"We're trying to trace it," Jules said, "but no luck so far."

"So the credit card was stolen," Max said. He didn't want to think about what that might mean. If Gina's passport and wallet had both been stolen . . .

"That's what we're thinking," Jules said. "Although, wait, there's more. This is extra freaky. Gina had a second card with a different company. She took a major cash advance—ten thousand dollars—on *that* card ten days before the bombing, at a bank in Nairobi."

"What the hell?" Max said. Ten thousand dollars in *cash*?

"Ooh," Jules said. "I'm getting that call from George. Let me call you back. It might be a few minutes—"

He cut the connection, and Max shut his cell phone. Goddamn it—what was Gina involved with?

Some lowlife scum who not only got her pregnant but extorted large sums of money from her, then stole her credit card and passport and . . .

And killed her.

No.

Please God, no.

Gina's digital camera was lying there on the bed, and Max picked it up.

Come on, Cassidy. Call back.

And report that they'd reached the priest from the Kenyan camp only to discover that Gina had returned there, safe and sound—

Leaving all of her belongings behind?

If it was just her clothes and makeup, Max might've let himself hope.

But no way would she leave all those books.

His phone didn't ring, and it still didn't ring, so Max turned on the camera's power—as usual, Gina had dozens of photos saved—and . . .

The very first picture that came up on the camera's little view screen was of him.

What did that mean that she'd kept this picture of him?

Was it because she still cared?

Or had she saved it as a warning? Like, "Never forget

how completely screwed up your relationship was with *this* loser . . ."

It wasn't a particularly good picture. In fact, it was pretty embarrassing.

Sitting up in his bed, Max was in his room at Sheffield. It was the photo Gina had taken the day after he'd arrived there. He looked like crap warmed over after his very first physical therapy session, and he was glowering into the camera because he goddamn didn't want his picture taken.

He hadn't wanted her in his room, either.

As if that had stopped her from coming in . . .

You know what you need? A happy ending . . .

He toggled the switch and moved to the next picture.

It was another shot of Max. With Ajay this time.

Ah, God.

They were at a table in the rec room at the physical rehab center, playing cards—Ajay with a big smile on his face, despite the fact that he was sitting there in a wheelchair, despite the fact that the scar tissue on his badly burned hands had turned them into frightening-looking claws.

It was Christmas, and decorations adorned the room. Max was cracking up at something the boy had just said— no doubt some ridiculously silly fart joke. The kid had learned, right from their very first card game, that potty humor made Gina laugh. And that when Gina laughed, Max laughed.

The next photo was one that Ajay had taken of Max with Gina. She was sitting on his lap, at that same table in the rec center, arm looped around his neck, wearing the reindeer antler hat she'd brought for Ajay.

Max's smile was forced, and he looked like he was afraid to touch her.

Afraid to let her know how much he loved touching her. Afraid to have it recorded on film, afraid . . .

Goddamn it, but he wanted to step into that photograph.

He wanted to slap himself upside his head and tell himself . . . What?

Enjoy this moment. Take your time with it. Savor it. Treasure it.

Because it sure as shit wasn't going to last.

CHAPTER
SEVEN

It had become a game.

Max would try to keep Jules or Ajay around, Gina would gently try to get rid of them. To be alone with Max.

Although, truth be told, Max didn't try very hard at all. Every other day or so, he gave in.

It soon became his favorite part of the week. Gina. Atop him.

It was interesting, too, to see how quickly sex moved from its position as an occasional luxury to a deep-rooted necessity.

An addiction.

The truly dangerous thing was that Gina knew it.

"Good morning, Debra." Max heard her greet the nurse out in the hallway.

Just the sound of Gina's voice was enough to get his blood pressure rising. Jules wasn't with her today, which meant now was the time he should reach for the telephone and tell Ajay to drop over for a game of cards.

Except he didn't move. He didn't want to play cards today. He just sat, listening to the two women discuss the weather.

". . . few snowflakes and everyone starts driving like my Great Aunt Lucia."

Actually, Gina discussed. Debra gave noncommittal responses. "Yeah." "Mmmm." "Uh-huh."

"I have a cousin who's a fifth-grade teacher just outside of Boston. He told me they don't close school for anything less than a blizzard. Is Max in his room?"

"He's napping."

"Thanks, I'll be quiet."

"Hmph."

It was then that Gina did it. Apparently, she'd had enough. "What do you have against me?" she asked. Just point-blank. *Pow.*

Her voice was low. The only reason he could hear them was because they were standing right outside his partly open door.

Debra let out a nervous laugh. Yes, Debra. Be afraid. Be very afraid. Gina could be a pit bull. She was not likely to walk away without an answer that satisfied her.

And Debra didn't have the option of distracting her with sex.

"Don't be ridiculous, dear. I have nothing against you."

Not even close. Max could picture Gina crossing her arms. Sign number one that she had gone into battle.

Surrender was no longer an option—for either opponent.

"Oh, come on. We both know you're not being honest. I know exactly what you're thinking every time I come in here." Gina did a pitch perfect imitation of the older woman's voice. "Well hello, dear. Time for Mr. Bhagat's shagging, is it?"

Now Debra's voice was tight. "Do you deny—"

"No."

Ah, Christ.

"Sex is an important part of our relationship. I'm not going to deny that," Gina said. "I'm not ashamed of it—why should I be? I love him."

This wasn't news, still to hear her say it aloud . . .

She wasn't done: "Can't we start over? Or at least can't you be civil to me? You were wrong about the whole panties on the floor thing, right? He hasn't had a stream of women coming in here—"

"I'm afraid I can't comment. You'll have to ask him about that."

"You are *such* a bitch," Gina said, and the nurse gasped her outrage. "Why do you insist on insinuating—"

Debra's voice got louder, talking over her. "I don't need to tolerate—"

"And I don't need to tolerate your narrow-minded assumptions one second longer," Gina shot back. "You think younger woman, older man—that I broke up his happy home, don't you? Well, guess what? Max has never been married, you've got it entirely wrong. Nobody wants him but me! I'm the only one crazy enough to hope for a long-term relationship with him, and I'll tell you right now that it already sucks!"

Ouch.

Gina wasn't done. "Just because your husband left you for someone younger—"

"Where did you hear . . . My personal life is of no—" Debra sputtered.

But Gina steamrolled over her. "Deb. I'm sorry that your ex is a prick, that he hurt you that way, but Max is nothing like him. He's lived in this total hole of an apartment, all by himself for years. He's married to his job and if that makes me his mistress, well all right. That's what I'm willing to be. Hey, don't you walk away from me! I've endured your silent disapproval for too many weeks now! If you have something to say to me, say it!"

"You're *not* the only woman who comes to see him," Debra said tightly. "It's not my place to tell you who goes in there and closes the door, but if you had any brains, you'd know that every guest who visits signs in at the front desk."

"Peggy Ryan, Deb Erlanger, his assistant Laronda," Gina listed them. "Frannie Stuart . . . These are all women who work for him, period, the end, and you know it. You know what? Forget it, Debra, okay? You can just go back to ignoring me. I'm not interested in making friends with someone as incredibly toxic as you."

Max shut his eyes as he heard Gina open his door, then close it behind her. "Shit," she said. "*Shit*. Why do I even *bother*?"

She was silent for a moment then, just watching him, and he made his breathing slow and steady.

As if he were sleeping.

She'd told him she was bringing over lunch, and he finally heard her move and set at least two paper bags on his desk.

She sat down, not on his bed, but on the chair nearby. And she sighed. "I know you're not asleep. I know you heard every word of that."

Max opened his eyes and looked at her. The blinds were closed in such a way as to throw a pattern of light on the ceiling. It lit her face with the softest glow, making her sadness seem to shine. He found himself wishing for her camera.

"When I said that it sucks," she tried to explain, "what I meant was . . ." She faltered.

"That it sucks?" he finished for her.

She laughed, but there was still so much unhappiness in her eyes. His heart broke because he didn't want this for her.

She had to be crazy to want him. It was good that she knew that. Because the next step was for her to realize that she wasn't quite crazy enough.

As for what he wanted . . .

"I just . . ." Gina started. "I thought . . . I don't know

what I think anymore, Max. I just . . . I love you, but . . . God."

She gazed at him and for once he couldn't read her. She was usually filled to overflowing with hope and optimism. With confidence. But now all he could see was sadness.

Maybe this was it for them. Maybe she was going to stand up and walk out of his room.

Out of his life.

It was then that he watched himself do it. He knew he shouldn't, that he should just sit still and let it happen.

Instead, he held out his hand to her. His message was clear: Come here.

He'd never made the first move before. She was always the instigator, so to speak.

And if the sadness in her eyes changed to something else, if she got a little misty as she took his hand, he didn't see it. He closed his eyes and tugged her into his bed.

She was usually naked when she slipped in with him, but this time she had all of her clothes on. It was sexy in a backwards kind of way.

Of course, he thought Gina was sexy when she greeted the nurses in the hall. When she played gin rummy with Ajay. When she made a face at the pink snowball cupcakes that Ajay thought were the ultimate dessert food. When she laughed, when she spoke, when she breathed . . .

He'd intended just to hold her, to let her rest against him, in the circle of his arms, but when she drew her leg across him, she encountered his . . . enthusiastic response to her presence.

She laughed and reached up to lock his door with the remote. "Well, at least now I feel a little less unwanted."

She kissed him, but he pulled back to meet her eyes. "I've always wanted you, Gina. That's never been the issue."

"So what is the issue?" she asked. "And if you give me some crap about how you don't deserve me, I'm going to scream."

"What I deserve doesn't play into it," he told her. "I just don't think . . ." He corrected himself. "I know that I can't give you what you need."

"You want to bet?" She kissed him again and as always, he was lost.

He helped her remove just enough of her clothing, his fingers gliding against the smoothness of her skin as she reached for a condom and . . .

Yes.

"Max."

He opened his eyes to find her gazing down at him, hair tousled, shirt half unbuttoned, black sheen of her bra barely restraining the fullness of her perfect breasts.

Face serious. Eyes filled with a question.

"Is this really just sex for you?" she whispered. "Is it all just . . . some game that we're playing?"

He hesitated, and in the silence he could hear the earth come screeching to a halt in its orbit, as the entire universe waited on his reply.

The two obvious options were A, no and B, yes. Max chose C. He closed his eyes and kissed her, praying that she both would and wouldn't understand something that he himself couldn't begin to comprehend.

And apparently, even if it wasn't the absolute right answer, it was close enough for jazz.

KENYA, AFRICA
FEBRUARY 23, 2005
FOUR MONTHS AGO

"Everyone," Gina said as Molly finished preparing the tent for Dave Jones's visit, "okay, *almost* everybody in our line of work has had some kind of tragedy in their past."

Molly straightened her bedspread, then checked to see if

the water had started to boil. It had. She poured it into her teapot.

"Sister Helen," Gina said. "She told me she gave her life to God after her sister was murdered right in her living room."

Gina was still upset with Molly. It had been something of a shock for her this afternoon—finding out about Molly's . . . extracurricular activities helping runaway girls.

"And Sister Double-M carries some pretty heavy baggage," Gina continued. She was still trying to talk Molly into letting her help.

"I know," Molly told her. "And I wouldn't ask either of them to help me get Lucy to Marsabit, either." She made sure nothing ugly had crawled into any of the tea mugs, holding them up to the flickering light from the lantern.

In Molly's opinion, Gina would not benefit from putting herself at risk. It had only been a few short years since she'd survived the hellish experience of being aboard a hijacked airplane.

"Besides," Molly added, "I'm not going to make the trip north myself. I have a contact who's reliable." She held up her hand to stop the questions she knew would come. "You don't need to know who, you just need to know that Lucy will be taken care of."

"So . . . What?" Gina said. "I'm just supposed to forget that I know anything about this? How about when the next girl shows up?"

"You do what you did today and you tell me. And I'll take care of her, too," Molly said. "Gina, look, I'm sorry. I should have told you about this a long time ago."

"Yeah," Gina said. "You should have." Molly knew Gina wasn't just angry because Molly wouldn't let her participate. She was angry because Molly had kept a very major secret from her for the entire length of their friendship.

But now Molly had another secret. An even bigger one.

But if she had anything to say about it, she'd be sharing it with Gina in just a few minutes.

After Jones arrived.

It was such an obvious solution—to tell Gina that Leslie Pollard and Dave Jones were one and the same. Then there'd be no awkward curiosity as to why Molly was painting her toenails rather than overcome with grief. And Molly wouldn't have to bear the guilt of keeping yet another secret from her best friend.

Best of all, Jones could visit their tent for tea and it would all seem very proper to the outside world—except he and Molly would have the chance to speak openly.

In front of Gina, of course. Camp rules required a chaperone.

But it would be far better than the occasional whisper as they passed in the mess tent.

Surely Jones would agree.

"Come on," Molly told Gina now. "Help me."

Gina halfheartedly finished cleaning up her side of the tent. She took a pair of socks off their clothesline—socks she'd washed out and hung to dry days ago.

"You don't really think Leslie's going to show up tonight, do you?" she asked, tossing the socks into her trunk.

Molly didn't just think it, she knew it. "Why wouldn't he?" she asked.

Gina shook her head.

And Jones knocked on the frame of the tent.

Molly's heart leapt. Except this was supposed to be a wake. She made herself look properly subdued as she opened the door. "Mr. Pollard. Please come in."

"Thank you." He met her eyes only briefly, but it was enough to make her want to grin foolishly. *Don't smile.*

He was wearing one of his awful plaid shirts, buttoned at his neck as well as both wrists. His sun hat adorned his head, even though it was dark outside. He didn't smile at her, either. But he did manage to brush against her as he came into the tent.

Dear Lord. "Tea?" she asked, her voice coming out unnaturally high.

"Please," he said, giving Gina a nod hello as he lowered himself into one of their two chairs.

Molly could feel him watching her as she poured. Suddenly it was quite warm in here.

Gina cleared her throat. "So, uh, Leslie," she said, awkwardly—which was odd. When was Gina ever awkward with anyone? "How well did you, um, know David Jones?"

He cleared his throat, too. "Not very well, I'm afraid," he said.

Molly gave him his tea mug and an imploring look. "I really think we should tell Gina the truth about—"

The look he gave her in return was pure warning. "The truth is that Jones incurred the wrath of some very dangerous men back in Indonesia," he said in that Merchant-Ivory accent. "If he hadn't died when he did, some very bad men would have caught up with him eventually—because he wasn't cautious enough."

And, in case she hadn't received his message loud and clear, he leapt immediately into a long-winded story about his journey here from Nairobi with that busload of priests.

Her back to Gina, Molly made a face at him.

He didn't so much as break stride, describing the bus in painfully precise detail, and then starting in on his fellow passengers.

"Father Dieter—well, you met him, of course. He has really quite a lovely singing voice . . ."

Molly would've been happy just to sit, sipping tea, and listen to him recite the phonebook. Watching his hands as he held that mug, just basking in the memory of his touch . . .

How long did they have to play this game?

He surely knew what she was thinking, because he purposely avoided her gaze.

He just kept on with his story. "Father Tom told us he lived in Manila as a child. He was seven years old when the Japanese attacked."

Across the room, Gina was unnaturally quiet. She was sitting on her bed, as far from Jones as humanly possible, her body language completely closed. She was turned slightly away from him, her arms tightly crossed.

"Tom's mother was killed," Jones continued. "Rather brutally, I imagine. His older brother, Alvin, escaped with him into the jungle."

As Molly watched, Gina examined a worn spot on the sleeve of her shirt. It was as if she'd rather look at anything else other than Jones.

Who was still talking. "They were quite the pair of guerrillas, responsible for a serious bit of sabotage during the war."

Was it possible Gina was uncomfortable with him being in here? It wasn't as if they had men in their tent every day. And, when they did, those men were usually priests. Or kindly Triple Fs as Gina called them: fifty, friendly, and faithfully married.

"They blended with the locals and were never captured." Jones kept going. "No one expected children to be responsible for such major disruptions in the supply line. Remarkable men. Alvin is still alive and living in San Francisco. He was only eleven at the time."

He moved on to a detailed description of Father Jurgen.

Maybe Jones had the same height and build as one of the men who'd taken Gina hostage and held her at gunpoint. Or maybe it was his ridiculous fake accent that was similar to that of one of her captors.

Gina seemed to have come to terms with her ordeal rather easily, despite the fact that it had happened just a few short years ago. She seemed mentally healthy and well adjusted.

Of course, the keyword there was *seemed*. Molly couldn't get inside of Gina's head.

It was entirely possible it was all just a big, fat act.

Bottom line, Molly and Gina had to talk.

"I don't quite remember," Jones was saying, "whether it was Father Dieter or Father Jurgen who sang Balthazar's verse of 'We Three Kings' as we pulled into Nakuru, although I believe it *was* Father Jurgen."

He took a breath, and Molly interrupted him. "More tea, Mr. Pollard?"

He glanced at his watch. "No. Thank you. It's late. I should go."

Was he kidding? He'd barely arrived fifteen minutes ago. Molly couldn't help herself—she made a sound of dismay.

Which made Gina lean forward. "We're supposed to be sharing our memories of Dave Jones. I never met him, so I'm not much help, but you did. What was he like?"

Jones glanced at Molly. "Well. He was . . . tall."

"Tall," Gina shot Molly a look, too. Except hers was loaded with *Can you believe this idiot?*

"Very tall," Jones told her. "Taller than me." He stood up. "I really must go."

He handed Molly his mug, making sure their fingers touched, albeit too briefly, then thank-you-ed and good-evening-ed his way out of the tent.

Molly didn't wait for his footsteps to fade away before turning to Gina. "Are you all right?"

"Are *you* all right?" Gina countered, sotto voce. "Brother, could this guy be any more clueless? You wanted to talk about Jones and . . . Best he can manage is that he's *tall*? And did he really think I was interested in whether the fourth seat or the fifth seat behind the bus driver had more of its original padding?"

Molly covered her smile with her hand. That *had* been

excessive. "Some people talk when they're nervous," she suggested. And some people talked when they wanted to make sure other people *wouldn't* talk.

Gina flopped back on her cot, arm up over her eyes. "Oh, my God, Molly, what am I going to do? The fact that he came here tonight at all is . . . He's so clearly interested, but that's probably just because he thinks I'm a total perv."

"Whoa," Molly said. "Wait. You lost me there."

Gina sat up, a mix of earnestness, horror, and amusement on her pretty face. "I didn't tell you this, but after I first spoke to Lucy's sister—we were in the shower tent so no one would see us—I let her leave first and then I waited, like, a minute, thinking we shouldn't be seen leaving the tent together. And before I could go, *he* came in."

He. "Leslie Pollard?" Molly clarified.

Gina nodded. "I freaked when I saw him coming, and it's stupid, I know, but I hid. And I should have just waited until I heard the shower go on, but God, maybe he wouldn't have pulled the curtain, because he obviously thought he was in there alone . . ."

Molly started to laugh. "Oh my."

"Yeah," Gina said. "Oh my. So I decide to run for it, only he's not in one of the changing booths, he's over by the bench, you know?"

Molly nodded. The bench in the main part of the room.

"In only his underwear," Gina finished, with a roll of her eyes. "Oh, my God."

"Really?" Molly asked. Apparently Jones was taking his change of identity very seriously. He hated wearing underwear of any kind, but obviously he thought it wouldn't be in character for Leslie Pollard to go commando. "Boxers or briefs?"

Gina gave her a look, but she was starting to laugh now, too, thank goodness. "Briefs. Very brief briefs." She covered her mouth with her hands. "Oh, my God, Molly, he was . . . I think he showers at noon because he knows no one else will be in there, so he can, you know, have an intimate visit with Mr. Hand."

Oh, dear.

"And now I know, and he *knows* I know, and he also probably thinks I lurk in the men's shower," Gina continued. "And the fact that he actually came to tea tonight, instead of hiding from me, in his tent, forever, means . . . something awful, don't you think? Did I mention he has, like, an incredible body?"

Molly shook her head. *Oh* dear. "No."

"Yes," Gina said just a little too grimly, considering the topic. "Who would've guessed that underneath those awful shirts he's a total god? And maybe that's what's freaking me out the most."

"You mean because . . . you're attracted to him?" Molly asked.

"No!" Gina said. "God! Because I'm *not*. I felt nothing. I'm standing there and he's . . . You know how I said he reminds me of Hugh Grant?"

Molly nodded, too relieved to speak.

"Well, I got the wrong Hugh. This guy is built like Hugh Jackman. And beneath the hats and sunblock and glasses, he's actually got cheekbones and a jaw line, too. I'm talking total hottie. And, yes, I can definitely appreciate that on one level, but . . ." She glanced over at the desk, at her digital camera. She'd gotten it out of her trunk earlier today.

Which, Molly had learned, meant that she'd spent some time this afternoon looking at her saved pictures.

Which included at least a few of Max.

Molly's relief over not having to deal with the complications of Gina having a crush on Leslie felt a whole lot less good. She wished someone would just go ahead and steal Gina's camera already. Maybe that would help her move on. "Honey, you don't have to have a reason for not being attracted to Leslie Pollard," she said, reaching for Gina's hands. "Sooner or later, you'll meet someone and it'll feel right and . . ."

Gina sighed. "I know. I just . . ." She rolled her eyes again. "Aside from the fact that Leslie's only interested in me because he thinks I'm a pervert, I think he's . . . Well, he's here, right? With AAI. So he's got to be nice. Dull, but nice. And I don't want to hurt his feelings. So just . . . Don't invite him for tea again, please? Keep him out of our tent. I think if I avoid him for a while, he'll get the message that I'm not interested."

Don't invite him for tea? Not a chance.

"You know, it's funny," Gina mused, "seeing someone like Leslie in a completely different, unexpected light. Like, you don't look at him and think, 'Wow, he must look great naked.' I mean, what else don't we know about him? Do you think he's one of those guys who's got a name for his penis? Or maybe he's got a pierced tongue, or—"

"What if you're mistaken?" Molly asked. "What if it's not you he's interested in?"

"What?" And wasn't *that* an expression of total incomprehension on Gina's face.

Apparently the thought that Leslie Pollard might've come to tea because of Molly, not Gina, hadn't thrown the palest of shadows across the younger woman's mind.

That stung, and Molly's temper sparked. "Do you think I'm too old for him?" she asked, her voice just a little too sharp.

"You? And . . . Leslie?" Gina's surprise slipped out, but she quickly realized how insulting she sounded and immediately began to backpedal. "Of course you're not too old. I mean, you're not old. I mean, yeah, you're probably older than he is. And he's probably younger than you think—I thought he was older, too, but now after, you know . . . I'm guessing he's in his early thirties at most."

She was just digging herself in deeper, and she knew it. "Which isn't too young for you," she continued. "I just . . .

I didn't think you were . . . I mean . . . You're in mourning," she added, but—smart woman—she thought about what she'd just said. And then, as she looked down at Molly's red-polished toenails and then back up into her eyes, it was suddenly quite apparent to her that Molly *wasn't* in mourning. Not really. "Oh, my God." Full realization dawned. "Leslie is—"

"Shhh—don't say it," Molly stopped her.

Gina stared at her, eyes enormous in her face. "Oh, shit. I'm right?"

Oh, *damn*.

"I am," Gina breathed. "God. Another secret that you were, what? Just never going to tell me?" Her anger morphed almost instantly into joy. "Oh, Mol, you suck and I'm going to be so mad at you later, I promise, but this is wonderful! I'm *so* happy for you—I think I'm going to hyperventilate!" Gina hugged her. "Did you know he was coming? Did he write or—"

Molly shook her head.

"He just showed up?" Gina was working to keep her voice low. "Oh my God! Did you totally shit monkeys?"

Molly nodded, tears in her eyes. "Gorillas. Gina, you can't tell anyone."

"I won't. I swear."

"I wanted to tell you, but he's the one who . . . He had such a high price on his head, he's afraid people are still going to be looking for him."

"People?" Gina asked.

"People connected to the man who put the price on his head," Molly explained. "Maybe even bounty hunters, I don't know. All I know is he's determined to take this really slowly. He's afraid if word gets out that I'm suddenly all hot and heavy with some new man in camp, that'll raise a red flag. And he's right. People gossip and . . ." She shook her head. "As much as I want to, I'm not going to be sneaking over to his tent in the near future. He's says there's no such thing as discreet—that we need to wait months before we can even, I don't know, hold hands . . ."

"My God."

"He says he won't even come to tea that often, because it could draw attention to me."

"Not necessarily," Gina said. "People see what they expect to see—especially if we give them a little help. *I'll* invite him to tea. I'll sit next to him at dinner—then you can join us, right? I'll write some letters—to Pammy in the Nairobi office. And didn't you tell me Electra was going to Sri Lanka? I'll write to her, too. *I have met the most fascinating man . . .* Then, in a coupla months, I'll dump him, and you can catch him on the rebound. You slut."

Molly started to laugh, hope dawning. "Could this really work?"

"You bet your ass, it could," Gina said. "Now. The million-dollar question. Does Jones—"

"Leslie. That's his name now."

"Right. Does he know that you can't leave this camp without some kind of armed guard, because if you did, you might be hunted down and killed? And that's a direct quote, thank you, Lucy's sister."

"Oh, come on," Molly said. "That's an exaggeration, and you know it." And she'd actually thought the million-dollar question would have to do with penis names. It figured Gina would come up with a question that made her even more uncomfortable.

Gina persisted. "Does he know?"

"You know he doesn't," Molly countered. "And no, I'm not going to tell him. Not right away. He's going to be unhappy enough when he finds out you know who he is. Gina, he said he'd leave if I didn't play by his rules."

"Well, okay then," Gina said, sitting cross-legged on her bed. "I won't tell him either. *If* you let me help Lucy, too."

CHAPTER EIGHT

Gina's brother Victor called Jules back after he stopped crying. Vic had made up some ridiculous excuse for why he'd had to hang up—his call waiting was beeping—but Jules didn't buy it for one second. *What's that you say? My sister, whom we'd been told died in a horrible terrorist bombing may not be dead after all? Whoops, I have to take this call, it's the library. That book I wanted has finally come in . . .*

All-righty then.

"It's definitely not Gina?" Victor asked him now.

"It's definitely not." Jules told him what he'd just told Max. "It's not a case of her body being misplaced, either. She's not in the morgue. And so far all the DNA testing has come back negative." He took a deep breath. "Which doesn't mean she's not dead."

He'd been saying that a lot lately, Little Johnny Doom, spreading gloom and despair as he oozed—well, was driven, actually—through the streets of Hamburg.

His driver was tall and blond with a cute accent, but alas, he was about as gay as a November day in Schenectady. He wove his way through the crowded city with ease, taking Jules over to the blast site at Max's request.

Jules would have preferred joining his boss over at Gina's hotel. He wasn't sure what good surveying the damage was going to do. But it was not his to ask why. It was his to do or die, stick a needle in his eye. Or however that went.

But, unless Max thought he might find something of Gina's in the rubble—her shoe or that ring she used to wear—his going there seemed pointless.

Almost as if Max were finding him busywork to do, to keep him away from the hotel.

And there—aha!—was the point, Jules realized. Max wanted privacy as he went through Gina's things, as he faced the fact that letting her leave in the first place had been one mondo stupidass freakadelic mistake.

"This is awesome," Victor was saying, completely ignoring Jules's gloomy words of warning.

"It doesn't mean," he started again, but Vic cut him off.

"Yeah, yeah," he said. "That she's *not* dead. I got that. But we don't need any glass-half-empty bullshit right now. Can you stick to the facts that you do know for sure?"

But Victor didn't want all the facts—he only wanted the ones that were positive and hopeful.

Hope, Jules knew, could be a wonderful thing—in manageable doses. But if it grew too large, if it overshadowed reality, if all bad news was ignored in order to support the theory that Gina was still alive, well, it could prove to be very messy when the truth finally did rear its ugly head.

"Gina's passport was in the possession of a young woman we now believe to be a terrorist," Jules repeated the news he'd just shared with Max. In his opinion, it wasn't particularly good news. In fact, it was very ungood. It meant that although Gina probably hadn't died in the blast, it was likely that she'd died several days earlier. But if he said it cheerfully enough, maybe Victor wouldn't catch on. "This woman had it in a security pocket that she wore underneath her blouse," he continued.

Eyewitnesses put the woman he and Max had found in

Gina's coffin leaving a Volkswagen Jetta and running into a pastry shop moments before the car exploded.

This was a detail Jules had told Max, but couldn't yet share with Gina's family. He also couldn't share the fact that there had been a ticket bought in Gina's name for a flight to New York—one way—scheduled for the same day that the bomb had gone off.

In FBI-speak, that was called a Big Freaking Clue. As in, hello, if someone had just paid a bazillion euros for a plane ticket to New York, it seemed crazy to then go and blow oneself up in an out-of-the-way Hamburg cafe.

Still, they didn't know for absolute sure that Gina herself hadn't bought that ticket. Which was one of the reasons why Jules needed to talk to her brother.

"Last time Gina spoke to you she didn't mention anything about coming home, did she?" Jules asked Victor now. "You know, for a quick visit?"

"No."

"She wouldn't, like, want to surprise you," he persisted. "You don't have a grandmother or someone with a birthday, or maybe a family reunion? Wedding? Funeral? You know, something that everyone thought she was going to have to miss, but then . . . ?"

"No. We didn't even know she was in fucking Germany," Vic answered flatly. "Last we heard, she was staying in Kenya an extra nine months." He paused. "Is it possible she's still in Africa? That her passport was stolen or copied or something?"

"No. We finally spoke to Ben Soldano, the head of Gina's AAI camp." Jules had already thought of that. "She and a friend—a woman named Molly Anderson—left Kenya last Thursday."

"You sure this guy's telling the truth?"

"Considering they were on the passenger manifest for a Lufthansa flight into Hamburg—not to mention the fact that Soldano is a priest and God really doesn't like it when priests lie—Holy shit!" Jules stared out the car window as a bus roared past with both Adam and Robin's face on the side—part of a giant advertisement for the movie *American Hero. Der Amerikanische Held. Ab Donnerstag. Manche Kriege führst Du in Dir*—which had to be a translation of the movie's tag line, The War is Within. "Jesus!"

"What?"

"Nothing," Jules said. "Sorry." He'd thought he'd be safe here, that Hollywood movies about World War II wouldn't be particularly well received in Germany.

Color him one very deep shade of wrong.

"What?" Vic persisted. "You can't just go *holy shit* and *Jesus* and then *nothing*."

"It's not about Gina." Jules laughed. "Really, Victor, you don't want to know."

"Fuck you, douchebag—tell me what just happened."

Okay. "An ex-lover and his . . . new boyfriend are both actors in a movie that's apparently getting worldwide distribution," Jules told him, even though it wasn't quite true. Robin had only slept with Adam that once—he'd been experimenting, or so the allegedly straight actor had claimed. But no way was Jules going to attempt to explain *that* to Victor. "I see their picture—movie ads—wherever I go. Here I am, in fucking Germany—" he used Victor's adjective "—and I still can't get away from them."

Silence.

"You still there?" Jules asked. "Or did my use of the words *ex-lover* and *his* cause a massive heart attack?"

"No," Victor said. "I just . . . it must suck, is all. Is it . . . Tom Cruise?"

Jules laughed. Why did the entire straight and vaguely homophobic male population of America think that Tom Cruise was gay? Was it because they found him attractive and that frightened them? "No, sweetie. His name is Adam. You wouldn't know him—this is his first real movie." But apparently, from the amount of buzz *American Hero* was getting, it wasn't going to be his last.

"I'd hate it if one of my exes were, like, on some billboard." Victor actually sounded sympathetic. "I'm sorry you have to deal with that. I mean, on top of . . . I just . . . I know how much you care about Gina."

It was weird hearing those sensitive words from the mouth of the man who'd once asked him if the gay thing was just a scam to meet chicks. Vic had actually used that word—*chicks*. Who talked like that? Although this was also the gentleman who'd asked if didn't Jules think it was creepy, a guy as old as Max dipping his wick in someone as young as Gina?

Well, *yeah*, it was *really* creepy when Vic put it like that. Especially since it was his sister he was talking about.

Ew.

"Thanks, but an ex on a billboard is nothing compared to what your family is going through," Jules said as the driver took a corner onto a street that was actually cobblestone. The buildings in this part of town looked like something out of a fairytale. "Hey, did Gina ever mention anyone named Leslie Pollard? From England? He showed up at the AAI camp in Kenya about four months ago . . . ?"

"Doesn't ring a bell," Vic said, "but I'll ask Leo and Bobby. And Ma. She and Geenie aren't as close as they used to be. You know. Before the, uh, hijacking. Lester, you said his name was . . . ?"

"Leslie," Jules corrected.

"Dude, that's a girl's name."

"Actually," Jules said, "it's not. Well, it's both."

"Yeah, but what kind of parents name their son Leslie?" Vic asked. "Jesus, just fuckin' tattoo *I am a fag* on the poor asshole's forehead and send him off to school to be killed."

Jules cleared his throat. So much for sensitivity.

"I'm just saying," Victor said. "No offense."

"Yeah, that wasn't offensive at all."

"You know it's true. I mean, come on."

"That actually makes it more offensive," Jules pointed out as his driver pulled up to the curb. He was going to have to walk the rest of the way to the blast site. "Wait for me, please," he ordered the driver as he got out of the car. He didn't expect to be here long.

Victor tactfully, if not exactly eloquently, changed the subject as Jules flashed his badge to the armed guard standing next to big concrete barriers that would . . . what? Prevent another suicide bomber from driving his car into the wreckage?

Too little, too late.

But perhaps the idea was to create an illusion of security in a world that simply was no longer safe.

"So what is this we've been hearing on the news," Vic asked. "That the explosion in Hamburg was some big-ass mistake—some terrorist screwup that wasn't supposed to happen . . . ? What's up with that?"

The going theory was that the Hamburg blast was indeed an error. "We think it's likely that the explosives went off accidentally," Jules told him, using his handkerchief to cover his nose as he picked his way down the debris filled street. Jesus, the smell.

"What the fuck does that mean?" Vic asked.

It meant that instead of one mega explosion in a not-very-strategic part of the city, the analysts suspected that terrorists had intended for there to be four separate blasts.

Taking out four different commercial airliners, heading for not just New York, but also London, Paris, and Madrid.

It made sense. It explained the passport, the airline ticket in Gina's name, the inanity of four suicide bombers in the car when a single martyr would have done the job just fine.

That is, if blowing up the regulars at Schneider's bakery and cafe had really been their plan.

"Sorry, Vic, I can't go into any details about this," Jules said. "Not right now."

But Victor wasn't as stupid as he sometimes sounded. "That girl in Gina's coffin," he said. "The one who had her passport. If she was a terrorist . . . She was going to come to New York and either take out the plane and a chunk of the airport—or hit some target in Manhattan, am I right?" He laughed. "Yeah, don't answer that. I don't want you to get in trouble. It's just . . . people like that—people who'd plan something as fucked up as that . . . They wouldn't've said *please* when they took Gina's passport from her, would they?"

"No," Jules said quietly.

Victor was silent for a moment, reality making his hope shine a whole lot less brightly. "Are you going to be able to find her?" he finally asked, subdued. "If she's, you know . . ."

Dead.

"We'll do our best," Jules promised him.

As he hung up his cell phone, he rounded the corner and stopped.

Whoa.

The crater from the blast was huge and deep, and now he really knew why Max had sent him here. It was so that he'd see this. With his own two eyes. Which were the only two eyes on the European continent that Max trusted as much as the two that were in his own head. Which was one hell of a compliment. Jules would have to take some time to think about that—later.

Right now . . .

God-a-mighty, this had to have been an accident.

And one hell of a miracle. The fact that the bomb had gone off in such an ineffective location truly was miraculous. If the car had been another half a block north, the death toll could have been in the thousands, rather than mere dozens. This was definitely the result of a bomb-maker's equivalent of premature ejaculation.

Also, just looking at the depth of that crater, Jules knew that if the terrorists had intended for this to be a true car bomb, they would have reinforced the car's trunk in such a way as to send the explosion up and out instead of down into the ground. If they'd done that, far more people would have died, as well.

As it was, judging from that hole, anyone close to the car—say, a body belonging to someone who might have been killed for her passport and tossed in the trunk—would have been vaporized.

It was likely there'd be no DNA evidence left at all.

Of course, looking at that crater, and having a vague idea of the cubic footage of a Jetta's trunk—which was large for a small car, but not enormous . . . With the amount of explosives needed to make this hole, Jules couldn't believe there was room in that trunk for a body, too.

All this wasn't particularly useful information in terms of finding Gina. But it did help them cross one more location off the list titled "Possible Places in Hamburg Where Gina Vitagliano May Have Died."

Problem was, infinity minus one was still a huge number.

Still holding his handkerchief over his nose, Jules turned and headed back to his waiting car and driver.

KENYA, AFRICA
FEBRUARY 25, 2005
FOUR MONTHS AGO

"I can't believe you told him!" Gina whispered.

"And I can't believe you would think I *wouldn't* tell him," Molly said just as quietly, but no less intense. "Since when do friends resort to blackmail?"

"Hey," Jones tried to interrupt, but they both flat-out ignored him. He sat down on Molly's bed.

"Probably," Gina said, "right after one friend finds out that the other has been lying to her."

"Oh, no you don't." Molly got in her face. "I never lied to you."

" 'Where are you going?' " Gina imitated herself and then Molly's response: " 'Just out for some air.' Left out a little, didn't you? Like, 'And to help some local girls escape from their parents to a place where they won't be harmed.' "

Their argument—done in whispers so that no one would overhear—was all the more strange due to the fact that Gina was shivering in her bed, sick from what was looking more and more like an early version of the stomach virus that had taken down that busload of visiting priests.

Jones hadn't caught it. Probably because there was nothing about him that was even remotely holy.

Molly alternately scolded Gina and pressed a cool cloth to her head. "Don't be melodramatic," she told her now. "I'm just the intermediary."

"These days," Gina corrected her. "Because you're a potential target." She looked over at Jones. "She'd probably be attacked if she left the camp. Did she tell you that?"

Attacked? "Jesus, Molly!" Frustration rang in Jones's voice.

They finally both turned to look at him. "Shhhh!"

It would have been funny if this wasn't so serious. The thought of Molly putting herself in danger made his stomach churn.

"My turn to talk," he said, working hard to keep his voice low.

"Okay," Molly admitted, "at one time, I may have put myself into danger, but over the past year, Paul Jimmo has smuggled the girls up to his farm and then—"

"*My*," he said, "turn to talk."

Or not talk, as he tried to make sense of all the information that had come flying at him over the past few minutes.

Starting with the fact that Gina had "figured out"—according to Molly—that he was really Dave Jones.

Which, in itself was a mind-bender, considering that he wasn't "really" Jones. His real name was Grady Morant. Jones was just another AKA in a string of AKAs. But at least Gina didn't know that.

Some of the facts were far more clear.

Paul Jimmo, a friendly young Kenyan man who frequently visited this camp, had just been badly injured in a tribal dispute over water rights. He'd been airlifted to the hospital in Nairobi. It wasn't yet known whether he would survive.

A fifteen-year-old Kenyan girl named Lucy was currently hiding here—in Jones's very own tent, as a matter of fact. Apparently, yesterday Molly had made an arrangement with Paul Jimmo to take the girl north to Marsabit.

Which Jimmo obviously now couldn't do.

"What's the girl running from?" Jones asked. "An arranged marriage?"

Molly and Gina exchanged a look, and his heart sank. Whatever they were about to tell him couldn't be good.

"Do you know what FGM is?" Molly asked him.

He shook his head. "No." But he knew he was about to find out.

"Female genital mutilation," Gina said. "Also known less descriptively as female circumcision . . . ?"

Oh, *shit.* "Okay, yeah," Jones said. "I know what that is." It was a rite of passage ritual done to women, and it was as awful as it sounded. The medical term was clitoridectomy. But it was usually performed by people with no medical training, using knives or even chunks of glass that were nowhere near sterile. The idea of it made him shudder.

"I used to think I knew what it was," Gina said. "And then I came here."

"It's a purification ritual," Molly explained. "Certain cultures believe that female genitals are unclean—that contact with an uncut woman can be dangerous to a man."

Jones laughed his disbelief. "So, like: 'Look out, I'm going to touch you with my unclean parts!' And all the men run away screaming?"

He came from a very different culture.

"The cutting is just one part of the process," Molly told him. "Some tribes perform something called infibulation, too."

"That's where they sew what's left together, so that when it heals, the girl is essentially scarred shut, with an opening that's maybe a little bigger than a pinhole," Gina said. "It's the equivalent of a physical chastity belt—what a terrific way to keep all the girls and women in line, huh? If the fact that their clitoris is completely gone doesn't put a damper on their hankerin' to step out, they're stopped because penetration is impossible."

"And it gets worse," Molly said, sympathetic to the fact that he was turning pale. "When they marry, on their wedding night, their bridegroom has to cut or tear open the scar tissue in order to—"

"Yeah," Jones said. "I get it." Okay, that would make *him* run away, screaming.

"That's if they survive the initial ritual," Gina said. "Narari didn't."

Narari was . . . Oh, damn, those little girls who were still in the hospital . . . ?

They couldn't have been more than thirteen years old. He looked at Molly, who nodded.

"There's a new law in Kenya," Molly told him, "that allegedly prohibits the cutting of any girl younger than sixteen. At which time, she supposedly has to give her consent to have the procedure done."

"But there's not a lot of Grrl Power in this part of the world," Gina added. "An unscarred girl can't prove her purity, so men don't want to marry her. Which means a family will lose her bride price. A girl may say no, but when the family who feeds and houses her says yes . . ."

"This girl—Lucy," Molly told him, "has said no."

Jones nodded. "Okay," he said. "With Paul Jimmo in the ICU, how're we going to get her to Marsabit?"

SHEFFIELD REHAB HOSPITAL, MCLEAN, VIRGINIA
JANUARY 9, 2004
SEVENTEEN MONTHS AGO

Ajay's older brother finally came to visit.

After being noticeably absent during both Christmas and New Year's, he just appeared, without advance notice, walking into the rec room where Ajay and Max were playing a hand of their ongoing game of gin rummy, while waiting for Gina to show up.

"Yo, Jay-man . . ."

Ajay looked up. Blinked. "Hey, wow, Ricky." The kid was remarkably unenthusiastic, considering he always spoke of his brother with such reverence. "Finally found the place, huh?"

Tall and skinny, Rick Moseley was much older than Max had imagined—in his mid-twenties. He was also much whiter—as in Scandinavian—with hair that might've been blond if he'd bothered to wash it. He hadn't. He also wore clothes that looked as if he slept in them.

Even though a lot of younger people worked hard to achieve that rumpled, messy-haired look, this was obviously not a fashion statement. The kid was ripe, like he'd done his sleeping in his clothes behind a dumpster.

He also moved like he couldn't stand still for too long.

"Dude!" Rick took a wide berth around the table, heading for the big picture windows that looked out over the countryside. "You got some kind of view here, huh?"

"Yeah," Ajay said. "It's great."

Rick hadn't given Ajay a hug, hadn't so much as touched the boy's shoulder. It was possible he didn't want to get too close, so as not to offend with his stench, but Max doubted it. Rick didn't even look at Ajay. He just gazed out at the view during their whole conversation. If you could call this wimpy exchange of words a conversation. How about asking, *How are you?*

Ajay tried a variation on that theme, since it was obvious that Rick wasn't doing too well himself. "Hey, how's Cindy?"

"Ashley," Rick corrected him. "Cindy is so over. Ashley's much cooler. She's uh, you know, out in the car . . . Yeah, this is some view . . ."

Max cleared his throat.

"Oh, hey, this is Max," Ajay said, taking the cue. "Max, Ricky. We're stepbrothers, in case you were wondering," he explained. "My dad did the Brady Bunch thing with his mom. We shared a half-sister, but she didn't . . . you know."

Max did know. She hadn't survived the crash.

Over by the window, Rick ran his hands down his face.

Granted, it had to have been difficult for him to deal with the loss of his entire family. No doubt it was hard, too, to see his little brother in a wheelchair, unable to walk, with those terribly scarred hands. Max could only imagine.

Still, Rick's refusal to look at the boy came across as revulsion—at least that was the way Ajay appeared to interpret it. He'd tucked his hands out of sight, beneath the tails of his too-big shirt, as if they were something he had to hide.

"Max," Rick said, finally turning. "You work here, Max? 'Cause I'm wondering if you can't push Jay's chair to his room, so we can—"

"Max is a patient," Ajay said, his voice a little higher

pitched than usual. "Believe it or not, he plays cards with me because he wants to."

"Lucky Max," Rick said, approaching the back of Ajay's chair. "Some of us have bills to pay." He tugged on the chair, which didn't budge. "How the fuck do you work this thing?"

"There's a brake," Max said, pointing. "You have to release . . . You know, Ajay can use the controls—"

"No, I can—" Rick tried to release the brake a little too forcefully, which made Ajay grab for the armrests. But he quickly hid his hands again.

Max pushed himself to his feet, but Rick finally got it, and rolled his brother away.

"How're the nurses treating you? Good?" Max heard him ask Ajay as they went out into the hall.

He didn't hear Ajay's response.

Max found himself following them—not right on their heels. He still wasn't up to that kind of speed.

By the time he reached the reception desk, the hallway that led down to Ajay's room was empty. He and his brother had disappeared.

Max stood there, tempted to stroll past Ajay's door, see if they'd shut it, see if he couldn't hear them talking.

But that was just crazy. He'd definitely been in law enforcement for too many years. Not everyone was a criminal.

Rick wasn't dangerous, he wasn't a threat—at least not to his own brother. He was merely a twenty-something slacker who'd had a rough Saturday night, who was struggling to get his life back together after a terrible tragedy. He hadn't been in that car with Ajay, but it was obvious that, in some ways, he was as badly scarred.

Max made himself take a right turn, going through the front doors toward the garden with its pretty sitting area, sheltered from the wind. On an unseasonably warm day like today, it was a good place to wait for Gina.

Nice and public.

He'd just sat down when the front door opened with too much force, hitting the side of the building with a crash.

It was Ajay's stepbrother, coming back out.

Some visit. It hadn't even been five whole minutes since he'd pushed Ajay out of the rec room.

The kid was moving fast and, cursing loudly, he nearly knocked over an elderly man—nice guy named Ted, served on a sub in World War II—who was on his way inside to visit his sister.

Max stood up. "Hey!"

Rick didn't stop, he didn't even slow down.

As Max shuffled for the rehab center door, Rick ran for his vehicle—a beat-up pickup truck with West Virginia plates—climbed in the driver's side, and left the lot, tires squealing.

Old Mrs. Lane had left her wheelchair outside the ladies room, and Max appropriated it, throwing himself onto the seat. He zoomed down the hall.

Ajay's door was ajar.

He nearly killed himself braking, steering into the wall to come to a complete stop, instinctively reaching too far to stop himself and zinging his broken collarbone. *Christ.* He pulled himself up, shoved the chair back down the hall, then went in, knocking on the door as he opened it wider.

Ajay was sitting by the window.

"Are you okay?" Max asked. "Rick left in such a hurry . . ."

"Ashley was waiting for him in the car," Ajay said, but he was close to tears.

There were pills on the floor. Lots of them, crunching underfoot.

"What just happened here?" Max asked.

"Nothing."

"Did you spill a bottle of Tylenol?" he asked, knowing

that wasn't the case, bending down to pick one up, take a closer look.

"Yeah," Ajay said. "That's what happened. I have a headache. A bad one. I think I'm going to lie down—"

"These aren't Tylenol," Max said.

"That's funny," Ajay said. "Because the bottle said—"

"What'dya do?" Max asked him. "Steal these from the medicine lockup for your brother, only you took the wrong bottle by mistake?"

"No! Screw you! You don't know *shit*—"

"I know Ricky was tweaked. What's he using, Ajay? Crystal Meth?"

"Get out!"

"He must need money, right? That kind of habit is expensive—"

"You don't have the right to come in here—"

"I also know," Max said, speaking over him, "what happens when stolen prescription drugs are sold on the street for recreational use. Someone takes them for shits and giggles, doesn't realize how much their judgment is impaired, gets behind the wheel and drives their car into another car and kills an entire family. Just wipes them off the face of the earth."

"I didn't steal them!" Ajay was crying now. "I didn't! He wanted me to, but I didn't. He said they kept something called Oxy-something in the closet, that there were bottles of it here, that I could just help myself and no one would even notice. Only, they keep the drugs locked up and inventoried, and even if they didn't, I'm not a thief—he might be but I'm not! These were *my* pills, only he didn't want these . . ."

Max realized that there was more than one type of medication on the floor—dozens of doses of medicine that Ajay apparently had fooled the nurses into thinking he was taking, but had actually never even put in his mouth.

Because he was saving it for his tweaked-out, wicked stepbrother.

God*damn* it.

"Hey, guys." Gina knocked as she pushed open the door. "What's . . ."

"Get the nurse," Max ordered. "This idiot hasn't been taking any of his meds for—" He looked at Ajay. "How long?"

"Since Christmas," he admitted through his tears. "I'm so sorry. I just wanted him to come see me, so I told him I had the stuff he wanted, only it wasn't, so he threw it at me . . ."

Gina was back almost instantly, followed by not just Gail, but Debra and the facility's doctor, too.

"You messed up," Max told him.

"I know," Ajay wept. "I know."

Gina was tugging on his arm, pulling him toward the door. "They need to examine him."

"I'm sorry," Ajay told him. "I don't want you to be mad at me, Max."

"Too bad—I am mad at you," Max said. "You knew your brother had a problem and you didn't ask for help. You know what I would do if I found out my brother had a problem with drugs? I would ask for help, because even though I know a lot, I don't know anything about helping an addict. You're a kid. In a wheelchair. With serious medical issues. How are you supposed to help Ricky? By bribing him to come see you?"

"I think he probably feels badly enough," the nurse named Gail said as she tried to herd him the rest of the way into the hall.

But Max wasn't done. "That wasn't you helping him," he told Ajay. "That was you being selfish."

"I know," Ajay sobbed. "I know."

"You want to help your brother?" Max asked the kid. "I'll help you figure out who we need to talk to, what we need to do, although, I've got to warn you, some people just can't be saved. He's got to want to help himself—"

"Mr. Bhagat, this really isn't helping right now." Gail looked ready to deck him.

Max stood his ground. "After the doctor checks you out—if stupidly not taking your meds for more than three weeks hasn't won you a trip to the hospital," he said to Ajay, "come into the rec room. I'll be there with Gina. Maybe Gail can join us, too. She might have some suggestions for how to help your brother. Then after we talk, we can finish our card game, because I've got a hand I'm not just going to throw away."

Gina's pulling and the nurse's pushing finally got him into the hall, where the door closed, practically in his face.

He stood there, shaking his head, breathing hard, pissed as all hell. Three *weeks*. What was Ajay thinking?

And what was *he* thinking, to let his anger loose like that?

Gina slipped her arms around his waist, hugging him from behind, her body soft against him. "She was wrong, you know. About it not helping."

"Yeah," Max scoffed. "It's always good to call a crippled kid stupid and selfish."

"You were being honest," Gina said. "That's why he likes you so much, you know. You don't BS him. You don't talk down to him, either. You just . . . talk to him." She hugged him harder, then let him go. "My brother's a social worker." She took out her cell phone as she led him back toward the rec room, searching through her list of saved phone numbers. "He's in New York, but he might know of some programs down here in D.C. You know, for Rick."

Which of her three older brothers was a . . . ? "Stockbroker, teacher, firefighter . . ."

Gina put the phone to her ear. "The firefighter—Rob—is also a teacher at Hofstra. Vic's the broker, but Leo worked on Wall Street, too. He made enough money to retire at, like, twenty-eight, but got bored and went back to school and—" She turned away, speaking into her phone. "Yeah, Tammy, this is Gina. Is my brother around?" She laughed. "Yeah, thanks." Back to Max. "You might be able to keep my brothers straight if we spent more time talking instead of—Yeah, Lee, it's me. Hi." She wiggled her eyebrows meaningfully at Max, a silent end to her unfinished sentence. "No, I'm still here in D.C.," she told her brother, "Well, really it's the burbs, in Virginia . . ."

The rec room was empty, and Max wandered to the window as Gina spoke on the phone, her laughter winding around him.

The irony was that they'd reached a place in their relationship—if you could call it that—where he was the one who didn't want to talk. He'd gotten really good at feigning sleep.

Gina, in return, had gotten really good at steering clear of volatile subjects.

"He's going to call back with some phone numbers," Gina told Max as she put her phone into her shoulder bag. She sat on the window sill, facing him, her back to the view. "You know, I really wish you could be as honest with me as you are with Ajay."

Damn. Max sighed.

"Look, I know you don't need this now," Gina told him quietly. "I know you're worried about Ajay, and . . . Well, Jules told me he dropped off a couple more files—that you're doing even more work—which is *not* what the doctor ordered, I might add, but . . . I found this woman, a therapist, who does some couples counseling."

Ah, God. "Gina—"

"I spoke to her on the phone," Gina said. "For about two hours. I told her everything. About the rape and . . . everything."

If there was anything she could have said to shut him up, it was that. He closed his eyes against the sudden image of

Gina thrown to the deck of that airliner's cockpit, struggling to get away, crying out in panic and pain . . .

"I like her," Gina admitted. "Most therapists piss me off, but she's . . . I think she really cares. So. I made an appointment to go see her on Wednesday." She smiled ruefully as Max met her gaze. He'd been urging her to get back into therapy for as long as they both could remember. "Big step, huh? Will you, you know, come with me?"

"Absolutely," Max said. "But . . ." She wanted honesty. "Are we really a couple?" Okay, that came out sounding far more harsh than it had seemed as a mere thought running through his head. "I mean, it's just so . . . I don't know, isolated here, I guess. Like it's not real." He tried to explain. "I know it's January, but it feels like we're having a summer fling."

And he couldn't begin to figure out what was going to happen when he left here, and returned to his real life.

"Doctor says I'm gonna live."

They both turned to see Ajay wheeling his way into the room.

"Give us a sec," Max called to the boy, but Gina was already on her feet.

"Don't bother, I understand what you meant," Gina said, but it was clear that he'd hurt her.

Goddamn it.

It wasn't the first time he'd hurt her, and it wasn't going to be the last.

And so it began.

The beginning of the end.

CHAPTER
NINE

Max had to put his cell phone down because his hands were shaking.

Molly Anderson.

That was the name of Gina's traveling companion, confirmed by yet another phone call from Jules Cassidy. The aid worker hadn't changed much since Max had met her a few years back. She still wore her long, curly, reddish-brown hair San Francisco earthmother style. Her smile was still as warm and sincere.

As he'd looked through the photos stored in that digital camera, Max knew why Gina was missing, why her passport had turned up in another woman's possession. He knew what this was about.

It had to do with a man named Grady Morant, aka David Jones, and probably a dozen other aliases as well.

Had to be.

Grady Morant was a dangerous man—an expatriated American and former Army NCO who was wanted by the U.S. for a long list of crimes, including desertion and drug trafficking.

For a short time, Morant had fancied himself in love

with Molly Anderson. But that had ended when he'd sold her out for a suitcase filled with cash.

Max sat on one of the hotel room's beds.

And blamed himself.

If Gina was dead, it was because of him.

Christ.

He picked up the camera and toggled through the pictures again, unable to keep from looking at them. Gina with Molly and a group of women, some smiling, some stern-faced. Gina, her hair cut short, laughing as she held the hands of two Kenyan children. Molly, wearing a Hawaiian shirt, dancing against the backdrop of a tent's interior. A man, with graying hair and glasses that reflected the camera's flash, sitting properly—back straight, tea cup in his hands. Gina behind his chair, laughing into the camera, her arms wrapped affectionately around his neck. Another shot of the same man, all alone this time, in a pose that looked as if it were meant to be a passport photo.

Max didn't need to see the name tag sewn into the back of his undershirt to know that this was the ever-so-fascinating Leslie Pollard.

They'd gotten his description from the priest who ran the AAI camp. Along with the breaking news that Pollard had disappeared right after Molly and Gina left for Germany.

Yes, that's right. Pollard had pulled a complete *adios* two days before that bomb went off outside the Hamburg cafe and killed a young woman who had Gina's passport in her possession.

As a rule, Max didn't believe in coincidences. Pollard had to be involved in this . . . whatever this was. Abduction. Kidnapping.

Please God, not homicide.

According to U.S. Intel—Jules had the information available even before Max asked for it—there was no record of a Leslie Pollard flying out of any airport in Kenya to any destination in Europe. Nor had a man by that name flown into any airport in Germany. Max had his team widening their search, checking passenger lists for trains and steamships. But he already knew what they'd find.

Nothing.

He stared again at the picture in Gina's camera, trying to turn the Englishman's face into that of Grady Morant, but he couldn't do it. He'd only seen Morant once—and it was after the man had received a rather savage beating.

Max now opened his phone, dialed the D.C. office and told Peggy Ryan to find a photo from Morant's service in the army and e-mail it to him.

As he shut off the camera's power, he realized that the sun was setting. It had slipped behind the building across the street, which cast a long shadow. Without the light from the camera, the hotel room was dark and . . .

Over on the desk, the telephone's red message light was on—a feeble flicker in the dimness.

Max stood up.

How the hell had he missed seeing that?

Was he completely losing it? Except, he'd made a point to look at the phone when he first came in. He remembered noting quite specifically that the message light was not on.

Max flipped on the desk light—and even that low wattage bulb generated enough glare to make the message light appear to be unlit.

Sonuvabitch.

He picked up the phone, pushing the buttons that would play the message.

It was probably only a greeting from hotel housekeeping, making sure Gina and Molly were comfortable and—

"You have one new message," the automated voice mail computer told him in a crisp female voice. It spoke perfect English, with a pleasant German accent. "First message, dated 19 June. 6:57 A.M."

"Shit, where are you?" Now the voice was male, and ragged with stress. "You've got to get out of Hamburg."

The connection was terrible and the line crackled. It was hard to tell if the voice was British or American. Max had to strain just to discern the words. "Get out of the hotel right now—don't pack, leave your things. Just go. Jesus, to the American Embassy if you have to. Go and stay there, don't leave for anything, do you hear me? You're in danger—"

There was a crackle of static, then silence.

"End of message," the computer told him. "To delete this message, press seven. To replay this message press two. To save this message—"

Max hit two. One *new* message, the computer had said. Which meant that Gina and Molly had never received it. Still, as he listened to the message again, he opened his cell phone, dialing Jules Cassidy.

"Where are you?" Max asked when Jules picked up.

"Just leaving the blast site," the younger agent reported. "Traffic sucks. It was definitely an accident, by the way— the bombing. What's up, boss? What do you need me to do?"

"I need you here," Max told him. "Now. I need a digital copy of a message left on Gina's hotel voice mail from an unidentified male." As the message played yet again, he held his phone so Jules could hear it.

"You think it's Pollard?" Jules asked.

"I don't know," Max told him grimly, making sure he saved the voice mail before hanging up the hotel phone. "Look, I'm going to need your laptop ASAP to download a photo from Gina's camera."

He could then send the electronic file to his own lab, his own team, back in D.C. It would be faster than sending the entire camera to the FBI's facility here in Hamburg. Besides, Frisk's team had enough on their plate.

"The driver says we're still forty minutes away," Jules reported, "and that's best case scenario—if the traffic lets up. What's in the photo?"

"Not what," Max told him. "Who. Leslie Pollard. Gina's got a snapshot that's got to be him. Meanwhile, Peggy's locating a photo of Grady Morant. I'm going to have the analysts run a computer comparison of the two men's faces."

"Okay," Jules said. "Whoa. Grady *Morant*. The same Grady Morant you asked me to do low-pro on . . . when was that? It was after the von Hopf kidnapping case, right?"

A few years back, Max had included Jules in the team he'd used to help track down a kidnapped VIP—the son of a retired CIA agent. The VIP had been snatched by one of the many groups of rebels, drug smugglers, terrorists, and thieves who set up camp on a remote island in Indonesia.

It was the same remote island where Molly Anderson had been working at the time as a Peace Corps–type volunteer.

The VIP had been returned to his family alive, but before the dust had settled, Molly Anderson had gotten herself into the thick of the danger, due to her relationship with—ding, ding, ding, correct for two points—Grady Morant.

After they'd returned to D.C., Max had given Jules an assignment. An extremely low-profile off-the-record gathering of information. "Find out what you can about a former Army Special Forces NCO named Grady Morant, but keep it under the radar." At Jules's puzzled look Max had added, "I don't want to get a what-the-fuck call from either the Pentagon or the CIA, is that clear?"

"He was the alleged deserter, right?" Jules said now. "And you're . . . thinking Morant is Pollard?"

"I'm thinking we need to eliminate that possibility," Max told Jules. "Which we can do by comparing the two photos."

Morant had to be involved in this.

God*damn* it.

Back when Gina had signed up with AIDS Awareness International, Max had been alarmed that she'd volunteered to go to Kenya to work with this very same Molly Anderson. A mutual friend—Navy SEAL Chief Ken Karmody, damn him to hell—had introduced the two women, and they'd instantly hit it off via e-mail.

But after a thorough investigation, Max had been convinced that Molly had severed all ties with Morant. She'd moved to Africa while, until just recently, Morant was still regularly spotted in his beat-up little airplane in the skies over Indonesia. Molly had had no further contact with the man—at least none that Max had known about.

And didn't *that* sting. Max made a point to know everything, to stay in control, to ward off disaster, avert tragedy.

"Wait a minute," Jules said now, breaking the silence that was becoming more and more grim by the second. "Didn't we get some kind of intra-agency report—a 'case closed' doc that had Morant's name on it as reported dead? I showed that to you, didn't I, sir? It was about, what? Four or five months ago?"

"Yeah," Max said. And he'd actually been foolish enough to feel a twinge of remorse at the news. "I need that information checked. I want to know if anyone saw the body, if dental records were matched."

"I'm on it," Jules said.

Max suspected the answer he'd find was a resounding no. And that Morant was still very much alive.

Jules was trying to keep up. "So you think . . . Morant faked his death in order to come after Molly Anderson because . . . he can't live without her?"

Cassidy was a hopeless romantic. "I think he heard about the reward Molly got for helping to rescue what's-his-name von Hopf," Max said grimly.

"Alex," Jules supplied the man's name. As if it mattered.

"I think Morant went to Kenya, to claim his share." And if Molly objected, Morant would disappear her and take it all. Gina would have been just an innocent bystander, but it also fit Morant's profile for him to turn a profit by selling her passport to the highest bidder.

Christ.

Max should never have let Gina anywhere near Molly Anderson—a concept that worked well in theory. But in reality, Max knew he hadn't had the power to let or not let Gina do anything.

He could have, though. He could have said, "Stay, because I love you, because my crappy life will be even crappier without you." Maybe then she would've hung around.

For a while, anyway.

"I just don't buy it," Jules said. "It doesn't fit with Morant's record back when he was in the service. He was exemplary—"

"He was also exemplary," Max pointed out, "when he taught security teams how to guard shipments of heroin for Nang-Klao Chai."

"He didn't give them any information that wasn't readily available over the Internet," Jules countered. "And most of his time with Chai was spent as a medic." He could, no doubt, make a case for Satan. *His fall from heaven was not his fault* . . . "Remember, Chai got him out of prison. Do you know what kind of torture went on, daily, in that place?"

"The kind that would twist a man, permanently?" Max answered, his voice tight.

"Hey," Jules said. "Sweetie, I know what you're thinking, but come on. It's unlikely this is some kind of revenge. And even if it is, it's certainly not against you. You all but let the guy go."

Yes. Yes, Max had.

He'd let.

The fucker.

Go.

He'd had Morant in custody—and he'd let him go in a moment of softhearted insanity.

Because the bastard had pulled a Han Solo, because he'd ended up sacrificing both himself and that suitcase of cash, and ultimately saved a crapload of lives—including that kidnapped VIP. Morant had been beaten to a pulp for his trouble, too, hovering in a haze of pain, ready to be shipped back to Chai for more torture, until a team of SEALs had gone in after him and pulled him out.

So Max had made it easy for Morant to escape from the hospital.

True, he didn't make it too easy. The son of a bitch had had to walk out on a broken leg.

But he'd walked. And he'd vanished.

And now Gina was missing, and probably dead.

Jules, perceptive little bastard, correctly read Max's silence. He sighed. "You cannot blame yourself for this."

"Call Frisk," Max ordered tightly. "See if any of his agents are near this hotel. They're going to need to take a look at this room anyway—just have them bump it up in priority. Make sure they bring the equipment they'll need to copy this voice mail. And call the American Embassy. Verify that Gina and Molly aren't sitting in some safe room somewhere."

As he said the words, his gut twisted. Goddamn it, there was nothing he wouldn't give for that to be so.

But Jules dashed his hopes. "They're not," he said. "I'm sorry, sir, I already thought of that and—shit on a *stick*! We're stopping. Aw, crap, it's a total parking lot—someone's actually getting out of their car up ahead. Sir, let me call the hotel. They must have a business center, or I don't know, a laptop you can rent or borrow to download that photo."

Of course. Thank God one of them was thinking clearly. "I'll call the front desk," Max said. "Just . . . get here as soon as you can."

KENYA, AFRICA
FEBRUARY 25, 2005
FOUR MONTHS AGO

Molly was ready to scream.

According to the rules of AAI, they needed a flipping chaperone. In order to respect the various customs of the indigenous people, an unmarried man and woman could not go on a four-day journey to the north.

Heck, they couldn't take a ten-minute trip to the grocery store—were there a grocery store to go to.

She and Jones, aka Leslie Pollard, needed a third person to go with them as they delivered little Lucy northward.

But Gina had just spent the past half hour getting violently ill.

"I'll go with you anyway," Gina said now. She was pale and shaking with the chills and sweats of a fever, but she dragged her mouth up into a smile. "I can go. I can do it. It was just something I ate. I feel much better now."

Her message lost some of its believability as she once again leaned over the side of her bed, grabbing for her bucket.

And it was more than obvious that she hadn't eaten something bad. She'd caught the same bug that the visiting priests had suffered from. They'd brought it with them, special delivery.

Please God, Molly prayed as she used a wet cloth to wipe Gina's face, *don't let me get this until Lucy is in Marsabit.* "I think it's safe to say that you're not going anywhere," she told her friend.

"You could put me in the back of the truck," Gina gasped.

"What, tie you down, so you don't bounce out when the road is rough? Gee, why didn't I think of that?"

"I'm serious." Gina grabbed her hand. "Mol, any minute

Lucy's uncles are going to realize she's gone, and they are going to do the math and come straight here."

Molly was well aware of that. They needed to leave the area.

Now.

Jones was ready to take Lucy and head north, on his own. But a Western male, traveling alone with an underage girl . . . They would be noticed. And stopped for questioning. Child trafficking was a problem here, as it was in most underdeveloped countries around the world. It was too dangerous an endeavor.

And there were obvious reasons why Molly couldn't go off with the girl on *her* own. One of them being that Jones would—what was that expression Gina used? Shit monkeys.

Which was why she'd sent him out to fetch Sister Helen. Except, when he knocked on the door, he came back inside the tent with Sister Maria-Margarit, the dreaded Double-M.

What was he thinking? Molly made giant "no" eyes at him.

He shook his head. "We got a problem," he said. "Everyone in camp's got what Gina's got. Sister Helen, Sister Grace . . . All down for the count. I give you the last nun standing."

"Where's the girl?" Sister Double-M grimly asked.

Oh, dear Lord, he'd *told* her . . . ? But Jones was shaking his head. "Hey, I didn't say a word."

"Don't look so surprised," the nun chided. "I'm not stupid. I saw her arrive. And when we received the message from Mr. Jimmo's wife, about his being in hospital, it included the curious line, 'Thus, he cannot help the girl.'" She gazed at Molly. "I knew you'd be part of this. I just didn't expect you to get Mr. Pollard involved. At least not quite so soon."

Molly had two choices. Tell the truth, or lie. "I'm taking the girl to safety." She hated liars. "Mr. Pollard has agreed to come along. We were hoping Helen would come, too, as our third."

The nun was shaking her head. "She's ill. And even if she weren't, this is not what we do."

Molly's heart sank. "You know that the AAI rule about chaperones is outdated—"

"If you're asking for permission to break it," Double-M said sternly, "my answer is unequivocally no."

"We could put on rings," Jones suggested. "Pretend we're married."

"And if someone sees you along the way?" the sister asked. "Which they surely will." She shook her head. "AAI's rule was created to win and maintain the trust of all of the many cultures in this region—some deeply religious. Yes, you save one child by breaking this rule. But how many do we lose later? We've worked hard for acceptance, for a chance to suggest alternative, less harmful initiation ceremonies for these girls, for a chance to educate, to teach . . ."

"Lucy will be our chaperone," Molly said. "At least for the trip north. And we can hire someone in Marsabit to travel south with us." This was the solution—it had to be.

But Sister Double-M wasn't impressed.

"And when Lucy's uncles and cousins arrive?" the nun asked. "Searching for her? Angry? Certain that we have spirited away the girl? What do I tell them when they ask where you have gone?"

"To Paul Jimmo's farm," Molly said. "To help his family while he's in the hospital. It won't be a lie—we'll stop there on our way north."

"And when they find out it wasn't your final destination?" The sister shook her head. "They will see through your story. And AAI will be known not as the organization that helps and educates, but rather the organization that steals their girls." She kept on shaking her head. "No. If you leave this camp tonight, I will not allow you to return."

Molly sat down on her bunk. It had been a gamble, going to the nuns for help—and she'd lost.

"Then I'll pack my things," she said quietly. The people here were her friends, her family, and leaving was going to break her heart, but a girl's life was at stake. What, was she just supposed to stand by and let Lucy's uncles take her home? Kicking and screaming—crying out for help?

Molly reached under her bed for her backpack, swinging it up next to her, unzipping its many compartments. "Gina, will you box up whatever I can't—"

"What if you can tell them—Lucy's uncles—that we're on a legitimate trip?" Jones interrupted. "What if you tell them we've gone on our honeymoon?"

What?

"Molly and I," he clarified.

She wasn't the only one staring at him, frozen.

"It solves both problems, doesn't it?" he said. "The chaperone thing as well as the other? We'll borrow the camp truck and head out, on a camping trip—a chance to spend some time alone. God knows I've always dreamed of seeing Marsabit. And if we happen to pick up a hitchhiker on our way, well, that's our business, and our business alone. It will have nothing to do with AAI."

"Is anyone going to believe you got married during an epidemic?" Gina spoke up.

"White lie," Jones said. "We left just before the fireworks started." He directed his words to the nun. "You'd tell a white lie to save a girl, wouldn't you?" He didn't wait for her answer before turning to Molly. "Are you up for getting married?"

He was actually serious. What about his fear that someone would notice—that if she suddenly started sharing a tent with him, a red flag would go up . . . ? Speaking of that, his accent was slipping. "Leslie," she said, to remind him. "That's crazy."

"Not if we do it to save Lucy," he added, his accent back

in place. "Yes, we hardly know each other, although I *do* like you. Very much. Yes, it'll seem hasty to some, but to the people—your friends—who are familiar with your generosity . . . They'll understand that it was to save Lucy."

And with that, Molly understood, too. Via the relief worker grapevine, word would get out that she'd married a near stranger—in order to save a girl's life. The locals could and would believe that theirs was love at first sight—since it wasn't the locals Jones was worried about.

"Do you really think it would work?" she breathed.

"Yes," he whispered, his eyes never leaving hers. "I do."

Sister Double-M was trying her best to be a wet blanket. "A white lie is one thing. But marriage is a sacrament, not to be taken lightly—"

"No one's taking this lightly, sister." Gina cut her off. She was sick as a dog, but she had something to say. "If you're going to do this, Leslie, you need to get down on one knee, and do it right."

Jones was ignoring both of them. "Do you want to?" he asked Molly, his accent seriously slipping again. "I mean, really do this? Because we could get it annulled, later, if . . . you didn't want to really be . . . you know, married. To me."

Molly stood there, looking into the eyes of this man that she loved with all her heart. The doubt she saw there was real. He actually thought . . .

"Are you really asking me?" she said. "Because you haven't asked the question that, if you were to actually ask, I'd definitely answer with . . . a yes."

He didn't kiss her. Not with Attila the Nun watching. But Molly knew that he wanted to.

Instead, he got down on one knee in front of her, glancing at Gina. "This right?"

"Works for me," Gina said.

He took Molly's hand, gazed up at her. "Marry me."

"That's not a question, it's an order," Gina complained. "Try again."

Molly started to laugh—it was either that or cry.

"Molly, will you marry me?"

"Yes," Molly told him, adding, "To save Lucy," for Sister Double-M's sake.

The nun cleared her throat, and Molly turned toward her, prepared to do battle.

But the old woman had tears in her eyes. "I'll get Father Ben," she said. "God certainly works to help his children in mysterious ways."

Five minutes later, as they took their vows right there in the tent, with Gina, still in bed, as their witness, they both added, "To save Lucy," after saying "I do."

Although they both knew that it wasn't true.

Lucy, as it turned out, had saved them.

McLean, Virginia
January 28, 2004
Seventeen Months Ago

Gina couldn't believe it. "You said no?"

Jules glanced into the rearview mirror before signaling and moving into the passing lane. "It's a big step."

"It's just a date," she told him from the passenger seat as he drove her out to Sheffield, to see Max. They'd just dropped her car at the shop—the electrical system was going haywire again. "And it's only a little date. Meeting for drinks after work? It's not even dinner."

Even though Jules was working from home today—a definite challenge since Gina had become the houseguest who wouldn't leave—he was dressed in his FBI clothes. He'd taken off his suit jacket before getting into the car but he still looked amazing. With his white shirt, sleeves rolled up, tie loosened, sunglasses on, perfect hair, perfect nose, perfect jawline, perfect cheekbones, and of course, that perfect, white-toothed killer smile, he was, quite possibly, the most beautiful man she'd ever seen in her life.

It was odd that he didn't get hit on by handsome strangers more often.

Or maybe it wasn't. Gina had had a roommate, freshman year of college, who, like Jules, was drop-dead gorgeous. She'd spent a lot of nights alone—guys were too scared to ask her out.

"It's not like you're not attracted to Stephen," Gina pointed out.

Jules had started announcing twinkie sightings right from the moment the van pulled up and his newest neighbor began moving his furniture into the apartment down the street. Over the past few weeks, both he and Gina had spent an awful lot of time peering out the windows and giggling—or running out to get something they "forgot" in one of their cars—just to catch a glimpse of Mr. Wonderful.

Tall, dark, and truly fabulous, Stephen-the-new-neighbor had *the* prettiest hazel eyes and longest eyelashes Gina had ever seen on a man. Besides Jules. The eyelashes, that is. Jules's eyes were a rich, chocolate brown.

"Yeah, well, attraction from afar is one thing." Jules sighed. "It's just . . . I know I'll be disappointed. My fantasy Stephen is so much more . . . perfect than the real life version."

"But what if he's not? What if the real guy is even better than your wildest imaginings?" Gina asked.

Jules laughed his scorn. "I doubt that. Besides, he walks around like he's got cruise control—his trolling is on auto-drive."

"Correct me if I'm wrong," Gina said. "But a guy who's cruising, who only wants sex, doesn't he tend to skip the invite for drinks?"

"Well, yeah," Jules admitted. "But . . . maybe he was thirsty."

"Maybe," Gina countered, "you're a coward."

Jules made an insulted sound. "I am *not*."

"Yeah, you are. And you never answered my question," Gina pointed out. "What if you go have drinks and find out that Stephen is great?"

Jules signaled for the exit that would take them to the rehab center. "I just . . . I don't think I'm ready for this. Great or not . . ."

And Gina understood. "You're, like, a double coward, because you're afraid this guy *is* going to be great. You're afraid you're going to get involved with him—at which point, you think Adam will dump Branford and finally come crawling back, and *then* what'll you do?"

Jules sighed. "Go ahead. I know you're not done. You might as well finish."

"How long are you going to sit around, waiting for this . . . this . . ."

"Total asshole?" Jules supplied.

"Right! To come back and tell you he made a mistake—again?" Gina asked. "And what kind of pretentious L.A. plastic name is Branford anyway? Yuck. Adam has no taste. Get over him, already. I'm serious. Stephen could be perfect—"

"You know I love you," he cut her off, "but as long as we're flinging our weaknesses and failings about, I'd like to point out to you that I'm not the one who's not in Kenya right now. 'Hello, AAI?' " he did a mock imitation of Gina's voice, higher-pitched and breathy, " 'I just want to let you know that I'm going to be putting my entire life on hold, indefinitely, for a man who can't or won't admit that he loves me, and who just compared our entire relationship, excuse me, *friend*ship—we do the musicless mambo every chance we get but we're really only friends. Anyway, he just compared our friendship to a high-school summer fling.' "

Gina forced a laugh. "Wow, I really must've hit a nerve

bringing up Adam," she said, unable to keep her voice from shaking, "because that was really, *really* bitchy."

Jules sighed. "I'm sorry," he said, and so obviously meant it, distress on his face.

He reached for her hand, and she met him halfway, lacing their fingers together and giving him a squeeze. "It's okay," she said. "Because, you know, you're right."

"And you're right, too," he told her. "Stephen scares me because, yes, I think he might be perfect. He's so . . . nice—and smart and funny. It's almost a joke. I didn't tell you, but he was out walking his dog when I got home a few days ago, and we talked a little bit and . . . Merciful God. But you're so right. I don't want to have to admit to myself that I'm not over What's-his-name. Because what kind of . . . of . . ."

"Fool?" Gina suggested.

"Yeah," he said. "What kind of fool would still be jonesing for a crud like Adam—when Mr. Potentially Perfect is standing right in front of him?"

Gina's heart was breaking for him. "So okay," she said. "Maybe you're right. Maybe you're not ready to date."

"How about you, Kimosabe?" Jules asked, pulling into the rehab lot. He headed for a spot near the door. "You about ready to pack it in with Mr. Grumpy?"

"I don't know," Gina said. "I just . . ." She shook her head as he parked the car. "I promised I'd stay as long as he needs me. Maybe it's wishful thinking, but I can't shake this feeling that he does. Need me."

"Oh, sweetie . . ." Jules hugged her. "I'm sorry I was so mean."

Interesting that he didn't say whether or not he thought that Max truly did need her. Gina changed the subject, too. "So what's this important thing Max has been working on?"

The past couple days, he'd been glued to his phone. Yesterday, she hadn't seen him at all.

She was supposed to meet him for dinner, but traffic was terrible, it was raining like crazy, the car's airbag light was on, and she'd had bad cramps. When she'd called to say she was going to be late and he was barely monosyllabic, she'd cancelled instead.

Hoping he'd be disappointed.

He hadn't said a thing. Except, "I've got to take this call . . ."

"You know I can't tell you anything," Jules said now as he got out of the car.

"It's got something to do with that assassination attempt in Afghanistan," Gina said, climbing out, too. "Doesn't it? There's some terrorist who's—"

"There's always some terrorist, somewhere," Jules said. "Gina, you know that's what we do. Do yourself a favor, and don't ask Max about it."

He put his jacket on, and his overcoat, too. It was chilly out today.

"Great," Gina grumbled as she wrapped her scarf around her neck. "More topics to avoid." She gathered up the latest armload of comic books she'd gotten for Ajay. And Max. She suspected he liked reading them, too. She juggled them with the flowers she'd brought for elderly Mrs. Klinger. "Grab that, will you?"

Jules lifted the guitar case out of the backseat by its handle. "You're really going to just . . . give this to Max?"

Gina knew Max would never buy one for himself. "He's always wanted a guitar," she said.

"Max?" Jules looked skeptical.

"I thought I could give him a lesson or two."

"You play?"

"A little," she said. "You know, enough to fake my way through a few choruses of 'All Shook Up.' "

"Can I watch him learn to play that?" Jules said. "Pretty please? Max playing an Elvis song." He laughed. "Then again, I may never recover from the sight."

"Max is an Elvis fan," Gina told him as she led the way across the parking lot.

"No. Way."

"He is."

"He told you that?" Jules didn't believe her.

"Yeah," Gina said. "You know, he does talk to me occasionally. With complete sentences and everything."

"He said those words," Jules said. "He said, 'I, Max Bhagat, am an Elvis fan.' "

"Please don't even think about teasing him," Gina said. "I swear, this assassination thing that I'm not supposed to know anything about is making him really grim. Extra grim. I can't even remember the last time I saw him smile."

"Max smiles?" Jules said, incredulity in his voice. "He's an Elvis fan, and you've actually seen him *smile* . . . ?"

"Stop," Gina said, laughing. "Or I'm going to invite Stephen-the-new-neighbor over for dinner. With my brother Victor. 'Dude, no, no, dude—three words. Sarah Michelle Gellar. Tell me to my face, right to my face, dude, that you wouldn't do it with Sarah Michelle Gellar.' "

"All right, all right," Jules said, as he opened the door for her. "You win."

CHAPTER
TEN

As Max downloaded the photos from Gina's camera onto the computer he'd appropriated from the hotel's business center, he cursed himself for the fortieth time in the past half hour for not bringing along his own familiar laptop.

The knock at the door came just at the perfect moment—right before he popped a vein, ground his teeth into shards, and flung the fucking hard drive through the window.

"You made good time," he told Jules curtly as he opened the door and—

"Hey, Max."

The world went into super-slow-mo.

For about half a lifetime, Max stood stone still and stared into the eyes of Grady Morant, aka Dave Jones, aka the motherfucker who, along with Max, was responsible for Gina's disappearance.

The part of him that had been an FBI agent for two decades went into autopilot, rapidly taking note of important information.

Hands—up and empty, intentionally placed where Max could see them.

Bulge, under jacket's left arm—possible large wallet, probable sidearm.

"Hey, Max"—Morant expected him to open this door, knew he'd be here.

Taller, bigger—he had at least twenty-five pounds on Max.

Special Forces—he'd been trained in some serious hand-to-hand.

Back in 1990-something. Lotta years since Morant had been in the Army. Lotta years to lose his edge, get out of shape, go soft.

Motherfucker didn't look soft.

His doctor's gentle voice—"Looking good, Max. Collarbone's healed nicely. Just . . . try to take it easy for awhile."

The part of Max that was a fucking madman lunatic didn't wait to sort through the rapid-fire information and come to the conclusion that reaching beneath his own jacket to pull out his weapon and usher Morant into the hotel room at gunpoint to question him on Gina's whereabouts was the smart move.

The part of him that was a fucking madman lunatic was swallowed up by the chaos, by the fury and the fear and the bitter frustration.

That heartstopping memory of Gina's name—in harsh black and white on an official list of the dead.

That body, beneath a shroud—with a face that wasn't hers.

A freefall of shock, as rage and grief still swirled and danced, parrying now with hope, the tiniest speck of which had already begun to unravel him.

Max must've grabbed Morant and pulled him into the room. The door must've swung shut behind them, but Max didn't hear it close.

He just knew that Morant crashed over the chair and smashed into the wall next to the window.

Max was right behind him, a pistol in his hand—an unfamiliar Astra that he must've somehow taken from Morant.

He threw it across the room, then heaved the chair out of the way.

Morant pushed himself to his feet, saying something that Max couldn't hear over the thunderous storm inside his head.

"Where's Gina?" Max roared over it. "You fucking better tell me where Gina is or I'll fucking kill you. I'll rip you to pieces, right fucking now, you son of a bitch!"

Morant tried to escape around the breakfast table, but Max grabbed him, tripped him, and together they went down, taking out a lamp that broke with a crash.

His head hit the frame of the bed, hard, but the dancing lights that temporarily blinded him didn't even start to slow him down. He was going for Morant's throat whether he could see it or not, grabbing handfuls of his belt, his shirt, his hair.

"I said, I don't know where she—Ow, *Jesus*!"

A fist to Max's face didn't do the fucker a bit of good—no velocity. But then he tasted blood. Maybe he'd just gone past pain as Morant again tried to scramble free.

An elbow caught Max in the side, taking his air with a sharp stab, but he still didn't back off.

Morant thought he'd bought himself a second or two of time—his mistake. He moved onto his hands and knees to get away and put himself right where Max wanted him—into a chokehold, Max's arm around his throat, his knee pressing into his back, grinding into his spine.

"Are you out of your mind?" Morant spat out before Max tightened his grip, keeping him from getting the air he needed to speak.

The air he needed to breathe.

Morant, of course, was too well trained to just lie there and die. He rolled, onto his back, onto Max, trying to break the smaller man's grip. He shoved himself, hard, against the wall, repeatedly trying to crush Max with his body weight, trying at least to loosen his death grip.

And it was a death grip.

Max wanted to kill Morant.

Max *was* killing Morant.

The man clawed at Max's arm, trying desperately to reach Max's face, his eyes, all to no avail. He struggled then, squirming like a beached fish—until Max realized he was reaching into his pocket, reaching for something.

Not a knife, not a gun—a pen. Cheap plastic, with a point that clicked out.

A well-trained man could kill with a pen—or at least wound, and Max tucked his face into Morant's broad back and braced himself for another attack.

Max Bhagat had clearly snapped. Jones had seen it before— in training for Special Forces as well as in Chai's employ— with men who'd been pushed too hard, too far.

He'd even experienced it himself, in prison.

Torture—a tongue-loosening tactic that was apparently now in America's arsenal—could do that to a man.

Sanity vanished and instinct ruled. Decisions were made, choices taken that had little to do with personal beliefs, with long-held perceptions of right or wrong.

It was pretty damn obvious that Max either was unable to listen or had retreated to some dark place where he couldn't hear Jones's gasped explanations: "I don't know where Gina is, but I know she's with Molly, and they're both still alive."

Or "Hey, shit-for-brains! We're on the same side!"

And then, as Max's grip tightened on his throat, Jones could no longer speak. He could no longer breathe.

What the fuck . . . ?

The possibility that he was going to die in the very near future was highly likely.

It just seemed unbelievable that it would happen right here. Right now.

Like this.

He wasn't ready.

He thought of Molly, and he fought harder, but light sparked and black patches popped, messing up his vision, and he knew he was going down.

Without telling Max what he needed to know.

God*damn* it. He dug for the pen he was carrying in his pants, cursing himself for taking care to follow the rules—to never write anything down. Never leave a paper trail. When Max went through his pockets, he'd find nothing.

He clicked the pen—his husband pen—thanking God that he had it with him. He'd started carrying it to keep from having to run back to their tent or the hospital office whenever Molly turned to him and asked, "Do you have a pen?"

Jesus—the wall was too far away to write on.

His hand spasmed and he dropped it. Groped for it, got it.

And then he pushed back his sleeve and he wrote, for the last few seconds of his life, directly on his other arm, right until the world faded for the very last time, and went permanently black.

SHEFFIELD PHYSICAL REHAB CENTER, MCLEAN, VIRGINIA
JANUARY 28, 2004
SEVENTEEN MONTHS AGO

Jules followed Gina into the building, carrying Max's guitar.

Well, okay. It wasn't Max's yet, but Jules liked calling it that. It was just so totally un-Max-ish. Kind of similar to the outlandishly out-of-character plaid PJ pants and Snoopy T-shirt Jules had seen his boss wearing late one night, some months ago.

Gina had been involved in *that* surprise-fest, too.

Today, Nurse Horrible was over at the reception desk,

and Saint Gina greeted her cheerfully despite their ongoing feud, waving those comic books she'd brought. "Hi, Debra. Where's Ajay hiding? I found the latest *X-Men*."

Jules didn't hear Deb's reply as he held the door for a pair of what had to be professional hockey players, visiting their recuperating teammate.

And, whoa, the cute blond one actually held Jules's gaze as he thanked him. Wasn't *that* interesting. Of course, the boy was barely twenty, so maybe he was just some naïve Canadian and . . . Nope. Jules got a bona fide over-the-shoulder second glance and a pretty obvious once-over from the sports twinkie—with more eye contact that ended in an actual wink.

So okay. Wow. He was going to have to start watching hockey.

The sound of breaking glass made Jules turn away from the scenery in the parking lot. Oops. Gina had dropped the flowers she'd brought for old Mrs. Klinger. The mayonnaise jar she was using to transport them had shattered on the tile floor.

The comic books had gone flying, too, and at first Jules thought she'd dropped to her knees to pick them up, but as he hurried toward her, Debra came out from behind the counter and . . .

The two women clung to each other . . . ?

Oh, dear Jesus . . . Jules broke into a run as he saw that Gina was in tears, and he heard her ask, "Does Max know?"

Which was good, because it meant that it wasn't Max who had dropped dead. Instead, it was someone else, only now Deb was crying, too, and with heartsickening certainty, Jules knew that could mean only one thing. These two women who so totally disliked each other had something in common . . .

"Max found him," Deb told Gina.

"Oh, God, no," Gina wept.

"Found who?" Jules asked, crouching down next to them, even though he already knew.

Ajay. They'd both adored Ajay.

"But he was doing so well," Gina said, as if a good, solid argument as to why he shouldn't have died could bring the boy back to life.

"Was it kidney failure?" Jules asked.

Deb shook her head as she wiped her eyes. "Infection. It ripped through his immune system. He complained of a sore throat at dinner, so I took his temperature. It wasn't more than a little bit higher than normal. None of us thought . . . But by the time Max found him, just a few hours later, he was burning up. We rushed him to the hospital, where he died in the ER around midnight. His poor little heart just gave up the fight."

Now they were all crying.

"Poor Max," Gina said. "He must be devastated." She began pushing herself up. "I better find him. I can't believe he didn't call me."

Jules could believe it. Max may have been devastated, but he'd never let anyone know. Not even Gina. Maybe especially not Gina. He helped Deb to her feet, too.

"This must've happened right after I called last night," Gina realized.

"No, no, hon," Debra said. "This wasn't last night. It was the night before."

Oh, crap.

Gina didn't believe it at first. Jules could see her struggling to make sense of this information. "Are you sure? I spoke to Max yesterday and . . ."

Jules knew what she was thinking: *And he hadn't said a word about it.*

Ajay had *died* and Max hadn't even bothered to tell her.

Gina abruptly turned and headed toward Max's room.

"Oh, dear." Deb gestured toward the broken glass on the

floor. "I'll take care of this mess," she told Jules. "You go try to handle that one."

Good verb choice—try. Jules grabbed Max's guitar and ran after Gina. "Sweetie, maybe you should slow down, count to ten—"

"Why? So I don't say something I'm going to regret? Don't worry, I've got it down to three perfect, regret-proof words: *Go fuck yourself.* Maybe I'll add a fourth: *Max.*"

"Gina—"

"I actually thought he needed me," she said. "Wow, did I ever get *that* wrong!"

Max's door was closed, but Gina just went on in without even knocking.

He was on the phone, standing and looking out of the window, but he turned. Maybe it was the fire shooting out of Gina's ears, but he knew that telling her to hold on a sec wasn't going to cut it. "I'm going to have to call you back," he said into his phone and snapped it shut.

Max was a master negotiator, but it was going to take a miracle to talk his way out of this one.

Jules stood in the hall. He knew he should turn around, walk away, but he couldn't. It was like watching a train wreck happening in slow motion.

"Didn't you think," Gina said, "that Ajay's dying just might be something that I'd want to know?"

Max got very still. "I thought . . ." He shook his head. "You weren't feeling well," he said.

"I wasn't feeling well at 5:25 P.M.," she lit into him. "A solid, what, sixteen hours after Ajay died?" She started to cry. "Jesus, Max! You couldn't pick up the phone before that?"

He didn't say anything. What could he say?

"What, were you too busy?" she asked him. "Like, oh, well. Shit happens. Little boys die every day, what's the big deal about one more?"

It was so obvious to Jules that Max felt awful. That he

was devastated. That he hadn't known how to tell her, that he didn't know what to say right now, that he was unable to find any words at all to express his pain.

Or maybe that was just what Jules wanted to see. Instead of this silent, expressionless, emotional void of a man.

"What is *wrong* with you?" Gina whispered.

Her words seemed to hang, like the dust in the sunlight streaming in through the window, as they all stood in silence.

Until Max's phone started ringing.

He cleared his throat. "I'm sorry," he said, his voice tight. "I told you often enough—I can't give you what you want."

"I guess not," Gina said. "But thanks so much for trying—oh. Wait. You *didn't* try." She turned to Jules, still standing there like an idiot in the hall. "I'm going to get a cab back to your place."

"Jules can drive you," Max said, as his phone just kept ringing and ringing.

"I know you have business to discuss," Gina said stiffly.

"It can wait," Max said.

"Whatever," Gina said, and left the room.

Jules was holding that guitar. "You want me to—"

"Leave it," she said as she walked away.

Jules went into the room as his boss answered the phone. "Bhagat," Max said. "Yeah." He closed his eyes. "Yeah." He had to know that Gina wasn't coming back.

Didn't he care that she hadn't even bothered to say goodbye?

Jules's stomach hurt for both of them as he set the guitar down in the corner. What a waste.

Max opened his eyes, saw Jules was still standing there, and waved him away, mouthing, *Go*, from between clenched teeth.

"I'm sorry for your loss, sir," Jules said, but he wasn't even sure that Max heard him.

HOTEL ELBE HOF, HAMBURG, GERMANY
JUNE 21, 2005
PRESENT DAY

There was no doubt about it, good FBI agent/crazy FBI agent didn't work so well when there wasn't a good FBI agent in the room.

Not to mention the fact that the insanity was supposed to be part of an act.

As Grady Morant went limp, reality slapped Max in the face with two hard facts: One, the son of a bitch hadn't tried to jab him with that pen, and two, if he was dead, he couldn't help Max find Gina.

Correction. If Morant *stayed* dead, he couldn't help find Gina.

Carefully, in case the limpness was feigned, Max let go of the bastard and . . .

The good news was that Max didn't have to fight off an attempt by Morant to put that pen in his eye.

The bad news was that he had absolutely no idea how much time had passed since he'd grabbed Morant in that chokehold—or how long it had been since oxygen had last reached the man's brain.

Max rolled the body onto its back, lifted the chin, checked for obstructions in the airway—yeah, right, whoops, that was unnecessary. *He'd* been the cause of the obstruction in the bastard's airway.

He breathed into Morant's mouth—come on, come on—quickly tossing the pen out of reach, searching for any other weapons he might've missed during their fight, checking for a pulse on a wrist that had blue ink on it. What the . . . ? Instead of stabbing Max with that pen, Morant had started to write a novel. On his freaking arm.

The words *Gina* and *alive* stood out—ah, Christ!—but there was no pulse there, goddamn it. He tried the pulse point in Morant's throat as he breathed for the son of a bitch. If it was back there, it was flipping faint, and whatever he felt may have been just his own wishful thinking.

Fuck, fuck, fuck.

Max leaned on Morant's chest, training kicking in as he automatically pressed, breathed, pressed, getting into the rhythm.

Come on, come on, please God, come on . . .

He was on the verge of sticking his fingers down the bastard's throat, to try to see if he'd damaged something in their struggle. If Morant's throat had swollen, if air couldn't get through . . .

But then he got a pulse—yes!—right as Morant coughed up a spray of spit and blood and God knows what directly into Max's face.

At least it wasn't vomit.

With shaking hands—that had been too damn close—Max wiped his face as he nudged Morant onto his side, letting him gasp and wheeze and cough up the rest of the smoke and embers and poisonous slime of hell that had slipped down into his lungs during those long moments that he'd been dead.

Max leaned back against the wall, and tried to steady his own breathing. His nose was bleeding—not too badly. Just enough to be annoying.

"Do you need a hospital?" he finally asked. Sometimes the throat tissue got so badly bruised that medical attention was necessary. Sometimes it wasn't enough merely to stop strangling someone and then bring them back to life.

Not that he was in the habit of throttling people. He had, however, studied anatomy. He was very familiar with all of the various kill points—and the throat was particularly vulnerable.

But Morant shook his head. "No." It was little more than a whisper, but he left no room for doubt. As Max watched, he rolled onto his back, eyes closed, as he just breathed.

His clothes weren't as badly torn as Max's.

One sleeve of Max's suit jacket was completely down around his wrist. And he'd ripped out the back seam. He could feel cool air against the sweat that drenched his shirt.

Morant, however, looked pretty damn good for a man who'd just returned from the dead, for a man who'd allegedly died months ago, for a man wanted by too many different governments on too many different charges to count.

His clothes weren't expensive—typical relief worker gear—and thus were harder to destroy in a brawl. Cargo pants, boots, denim shirt, denim jacket.

The man himself looked like Africa agreed with him. Healthy. Trim.

Max nudged Morant's hand with his foot, so he could read what was written on his arm.

It looked like an e-mail address—*RoyallyEffed@freemail. com.* Then the letters P and W, and what looked like . . . *chair?*

Gina + Molly alive then *SAVE THEM*—underlined three times. Then something that looked like *trace . . . the . . . form*-squiggle. It was impossible to read.

The rest, too, was illegible, but Max didn't need to see more to know that he'd come goddamn close to killing an innocent man.

A man who'd used what he thought were his last moments of life to try to get Max the information he would need to save Gina and Molly.

It was humbling.

"I'm really sorry," Max said. It seemed like such an inadequate thing to say. *Sorry I tried to kill you?* It wasn't even honest. He hadn't merely tried, he'd succeeded.

Morant turned his head to look at Max. "Smells like her in here," he whispered. "My wife."

His . . . ? Max took a deep breath. Remembering to breathe was good.

"Bet you never thought I'd use those two words one after the other like that," Morant continued. He coughed again. Tried to clear his throat. "Never thought I would either."

"Molly?" Max asked.

"Yeah, Molly," Morant said with a look of incredulity. He was hoarse—he would be for a while. "Who'd you think I meant? Gina?"

Max blotted his nose on his ruined sleeve. "I've been having a particularly bad day." Gina finally finding happiness with a dangerous, wanted criminal would've fit the running pattern. Although *day* wasn't quite accurate. Bad year was more appropriate.

"She always said how brilliant you were," Morant said. "A total prick, but brilliant. Don't prove her wrong."

Was *prick* her word or Morant's? And wasn't *that* the last question he should be asking. "Where are they?" Max asked instead. "Who has them—Leslie Pollard? Did you ask for proof of life?"

"Indonesia," Morant said. "All I have for the man who grabbed them is an initial—E.—and a description. Don't get excited. It's just this side of useless. He's medium height, medium build, medium complexion, dark hair, mustache, speaks the Queen's English with an accent, possibly French. Unless maybe he's a friend of yours . . . ?"

Max shook his head. Although with that description, this could have been anyone. It could've been Max, with fake facial hair, doing his Inspector Clouseau impression.

"Didn't think so," Morant continued. "What I *do* know is he's not Leslie Pollard because I buried him—what was left of him—in Thailand. And thanks to the indigenous fauna, there wasn't that much left by the time I found him." His smile was grim. "I figured he didn't need his name anymore. His passport, sadly, was chewed into unsalvageable bits."

So Grady Morant, aka Dave Jones, was also Leslie

Pollard—who was married to Molly Anderson. Or so he claimed.

The pieces of the puzzle that were still missing had to do with Gina. Her letter to Jules—*I have met the most fascinating man*!

"Did you know Gina's pregnant?" Max asked Morant.

He got a flash of total surprise in response. Surprise and something else. Max wasn't exactly sure what else, but the surprise was real. No one was that good an actor. "Gina?"

"So the baby's not yours," Max said.

"Hell, no." Morant laughed, but then stopped. "Jesus, was that why you tried to kill me?"

"Was she seeing anyone?" Max asked. "This E., maybe?"

"No." Morant was certain. "He showed up at the camp—at least I'm assuming he's the same man who e-mailed me—but it wasn't until after Molly and Gina left for Germany. He flew in, in a rented helicopter, spoke to Sister Helen—who told me she'd never seen him before. She was the one who gave me the description—I only saw him from a distance. He walks like an operator, by the way."

Terrific. "Did Gina leave the camp?" Max asked. "On weekends or . . . I don't know, her days off?" It was possible she'd met this E., whoever he was, in Nairobi.

"Nah," Morant said. "I mean, she and Molly went into Nairobi only once the entire time I was at the camp. As far as days off . . . She never stopped working. She also never talked about anyone else—a boyfriend or lover or . . . But I was only at the camp for about four months, so . . ."

So it was possible the relationship had already ended.

Did she ever talk about Max? Besides, of course, calling him a brilliant prick.

The question was not relevant to this investigation. But she must have—how else would Morant have known he'd be here, in Hamburg, searching for her?

"What about Molly?" Max asked instead. "Did she ever

leave the camp without you? Was it possible she might've hooked up with—"

"No." Morant bristled. "And fuck you for suggesting it."

It was standard in an investigation to raise questions about whether the abductees were familiar with the abductor. It was easier, from a kidnapping standpoint, to befriend the victims and have them willingly get into the car. If this guy had been hanging around—not at the camp, because it was clear he was a stranger there, but in Nairobi . . .

If Max was going to find Gina, he was going to follow every lead possible. He'd already made a mental note to have Peggy check out helicopter rentals in Kenya.

"Just because you don't want to believe that Gina's not this perfect little angel," Morant was saying, "instead of what she really is—a flesh-and-blood woman who—" He cut himself off. "You know, maybe I'm wrong about the no boyfriend thing. There was this one Kenyan man . . . Paul Jimmo. He was killed shortly after I arrived. The entire camp took it pretty hard, Gina in particular."

Paul Jimmo.

His intense hatred of a dead man named Paul Jimmo wasn't helping him find Gina. Still Max couldn't let that one word slide past without asking, "Killed?"

"Part of some ongoing battle over water rights," Morant told him. "I don't think he was involved. I think it was a wrong place, wrong time, innocent bystander thing."

And wasn't *that* just swell. Max didn't want to think about the fact that, if it turned out to be true that Gina was romantically entangled with this Jimmo, it was just luck that she hadn't been with him at the time.

But right now he had to focus on finding her. "Did you leave that message, on the hotel phone?" Max asked. "Telling Gina and Molly to go to the Embassy?"

"Yeah. That was me."

"They didn't get it," Max told him. "It was new on the voice mail when I got here."

"I figured. Considering they didn't go to the Embassy. E. did send proof of life, by the way—a photo in a j-peg file—via e-mail. It was a picture of them both, sitting next to a TV showing Sunday's soccer game. Yeah, it could have been digitally altered, but I doubt it. It looked like they were in some kind of warehouse. The TV was one of those little cheap ones."

Gina was alive. Or at least she was as of Sunday night. Now Max's hands were really shaking.

"You all right?" As Morant sat up, he grabbed his head. "Ow, Jesus!"

Along with the hoarse thing, he was going to experience a headache and dizziness for a while, too.

He wasn't the only one. Max was actually seeing stars. "I want to see the picture," he said.

"They're okay," Morant told him, back on the floor. "They look okay—not too happy, but they haven't been hurt. Whoever has them knows the abduction business. They're being taken care of."

"I want to see the picture," Max said again. "And then we need to e-mail this son of a bitch and tell him that nothing happens—nothing—until I talk to Gina on the phone."

And tell her . . . what? *I'm so sorry . . .*

"What we need to do is get out of here," Morant said, sitting up again, more slowly and carefully this time. "I've already been here too long." He tilted his head from side to side, hand up on the back of his neck.

Whoever has them knows the abduction business. Considering the company Grady Morant had kept back in Indonesia, it could be said that *he* knew the abduction business. And it *was* a business in that part of the world.

"If we take the time now to sign online," Morant was saying.

Max cut him off. "You had Internet access at the camp in Kenya?" He knew for a fact that wasn't true. Yet this E. had allegedly e-mailed Morant?

"No," Morant said. "We were lucky if we had warm water when we showered."

"But you have an e-mail address . . . ?"

Morant had a nifty explanation all ready to go. "When I worked for Chai—"

"That would be the notorious drug lord and murderer Nang-Klao Chai?" Max clarified.

Morant was silent then, just looking at Max. "Okay," he finally said. "Yes, I'm talking about the same Chai. And point taken. You have plenty of reasons not to trust me. Are you going to hear me out or do you want to beat the shit out of me again? I'm ready, either way."

"I'm listening," Max said.

"What I'm not ready to do, is to sit here, fucking around, until enough reinforcements arrive so you can drag my ass to jail," Morant told him. "If that's your plan—"

"When you worked for Chai," Max prompted.

Morant started over. He knew damn well he had no choice. "When I worked for Chai, we sometimes used an Internet message board to communicate. When I arrived here in Hamburg, sure enough, there was a message waiting for me there. Same code we used to use, directing me to an e-mail account already set up. Whoever the kidnappers are, they're good."

"How much money do they want?" Max asked, as Morant began to pull himself to his feet. He drew his own weapon, aimed it at the other man. "I didn't say you could stand."

Morant looked at him, looked at the gun. He didn't seem impressed. "If we don't leave here, some time in the very near future, very close to *now,* your friends from the Hamburg office are going to come in here, see me, and do their best to ship me back to the States. At which point, we're fucked. You, me, Molly, and Gina."

Of course Morant might not feel so threatened by a gun

held in the hand of the man who'd already killed him once today. Killed him, but then brought him back to life.

"I *will* shoot you," Max said. "I know you don't think I'll do it—"

"Actually, I do," Morant said. "In fact, I'm counting on it—if it comes down to that. A word of warning though. If you do it here, it's going to make transporting my body all the way to Indonesia one giant, sucking pain in the balls."

And suddenly, it all made sense. The nearly illegible words on Morant's arm. It wasn't *trace the form,* it was *trade them for me.*

They didn't want money—the people who took Molly and Gina. They wanted Grady Morant.

And, if they couldn't get them out any other way, Morant was ready to deliver.

"I don't know for sure who wants me," Morant said quietly, "but whoever they are, they're connected to Chai. And that means they're not going to play by the rules—their goal is going to be to hurt me as badly as they possibly can. If they get me alive, they're not going to release Molly and Gina. Instead they'll make me watch them die."

Christ.

"I will not let that happen," Morant continued. "But I'm going to need your help." He smiled grimly. "Yours and those Navy SEALs' you had working with you last time we met. Here's how it's going to work—and by the way, this deal is nonnegotiable. You use your resources to help me find Molly and Gina. You and your supermen help me get them out alive. If everything goes well and I'm still standing when it's over, I'm all yours. You can write the confession yourself—I'll sign whatever you want. But you and your fucked-up government don't get to touch me until Molly is safe and secure. And guaranteed to stay that way."

Max gazed at Morant. Correct procedure had him stepping back from this. He was involved—he couldn't be called upon to make the right decisions when Gina's life was on the line. But was he really going to put Gina's life into someone else's hands?

Who could he trust with something like that?

Morant was right—first thing they needed to do was to get out of here. Once Frisk's team showed up, he'd have far fewer choices.

Max put the safety back on his gun. Reholstered it. Took off what was left of his jacket. "Get your weapon," he ordered Morant. "Let's go."

And, of course, because it had been exactly that sort of crazy, bad-luck, fucked-up year, it was too late.

Someone knocked on the hotel room door.

CHAPTER ELEVEN

They were alive.

So far, at least, they were still alive.

Gina had always heard that the survival rate of abductees dropped significantly the moment they got into a car with their abductor.

She wondered what the odds were for abductees who were put into a metal shipping container.

Although, for the first time in days they weren't being held at gunpoint by a WWE–sized woman who spoke just enough English to be able to order them not to talk.

"Are you all right?" Molly whispered now from the darkness.

Gina had a splinter in her butt from an unfortunate encounter with a wooden pallet. And she had been certain not just once, but many times over the past blur of days that her life was about to end violently. Oh, yeah, and she was currently sitting in a box without any source of light.

All right didn't quite cut it.

Still at least this was a fairly large box. It wasn't large enough for them to stand up, but they could both sit comfortably, and even lie down.

"Yeah, I'm okay. Are *you* all right?" she asked, because a

butt-splinter was nothing compared to what Molly must've been feeling. This was *so* not what the doctor had had in mind when he'd given Molly instructions to take it easy for a few days.

"I'm a little sore," Molly admitted. "And queasy. What else is new? Gina, I am *so* sorry—"

"Me, too," Gina said.

As the darkness pressed in on her, she moved her face closer to the short length of hose that provided them with outside air. Wherever they were, it smelled like diesel. It was dank and polluted.

And very, very dark.

God, she wanted Max. She wanted him to come and rescue her. She wanted to hear his voice, to have him tell her to stay calm, that he was on his way.

That he was sorry for being such a jerk, and that he loved her and wanted to spend the entire rest of his life as her personal slave, to try to make up for it.

Hey, as long as she was fantasizing about the impossible, she might as well dream big.

"I can't believe you didn't run away when you had the chance." Gina's voice shook. "His gun was on me."

"And leave you?" Molly countered. Gina heard her moving around. "Never. Besides, I'm the one they want. There's something in here with us. Bottles. Plastic ones."

"That name the Italian man kept mentioning," Gina asked Molly, as she, too, gingerly reached out in the darkness to see what she could feel. "Grady Morant?"

"That's Jones's real name."

That was what Gina had thought. Molly had told her that Dave Jones was as much of an alias as Leslie Pollard, but had never told her exactly what her husband's name truly was.

Grady. Huh. He didn't look like a Grady.

"And those people with the guns in Gretta's studio?"

Gina asked as her hand closed around a blanket. Not one but two. "Are they looking for Grady Morant, too?"

The angry people with the guns who'd all started shooting in the forger's studio . . . It was a miracle Gina and Molly hadn't been killed.

That woman, Gretta—the one who had made Jones his new and very expensive fake passport—*had* been killed. Bullets had hit her and her blood had sprayed, and for quite a few horrific moments Gina had been back on that hijacked airliner, back when the terrorists killed the pilot, as he fell onto the deck beside her, half of his head gone, as Alojzije Nabulsi battered and beat her, slamming himself inside of her in that act of violence and hatred that so wasn't her fault.

Oh God, oh God, oh God, she was going to be sick.

"I don't know who they were," Molly was saying as Gina put her head down, praying that the waves of dizziness would subside. "He saved us, you know—the Italian man?"

Saved them? Was she nuts?

Saved them by taking them, at gunpoint, to a dingy, dank warehouse and making them sit on wooden pallets in silence for hours and hours while he went off to finalize arrangements for their luxury accommodations here in this metal box . . . ?

The biggest question, of course, was, *saved them for what*?

"He seemed apologetic," Molly pointed out. "When he shut us in here. He said he doesn't want to hurt us."

"He's lying," Gina said, and her voice was like something out of *The Exorcist*, a raspy squawk, only Molly didn't hear her.

She was counting aloud.

"Nineteen, twenty . . . Twenty-one," Molly announced. "I've got twenty-one bottles of water, and a pack of adult diapers—thank God for small favors."

Thank God? Thank *God* that their armed and dangerous Italian kidnapper had thrown a package of freaking adult diapers into this shipping crate, so that while he sent them God knows where, they'd be able to pee not *quite* in their pants?

Molly had been hit by disaster after disaster over the past few weeks, and yet her optimistic attitude continuously put Gina to shame. And Gina was usually no slouch herself in the positive thinking department.

"Water is good," Molly continued. "Water implies that he wants us to arrive alive."

Yeah, but what was going to happen to them when they were unpacked at their destination—wherever that was?

The fact that they were bait was a no-brainer. And bait only had to be kept fresh to a certain point.

Gina had been sure Italian Gun Man was going to kill them after taking that photograph of them next to the TV set, when they'd first arrived at the warehouse. Proof of life, it was called. Usually it was done with hostages holding a newspaper, but a live broadcast soccer game on cable TV apparently worked, too.

Sometimes it wasn't proof of life. Sometimes it was proof of possession. And after that was established, hostages could become unnecessary.

There was a loud noise now—the sound of an engine being started. And then a lurch, and they were moving.

Heading God knows where.

Hurtling toward their fate.

Gina couldn't help herself. She started to cry.

Molly shuffled toward her in the darkness, finding her and wrapping her arms around her. "Lord, Gina, I'm scared to death—and I can only imagine what this is like for you."

"It's like," Gina said, wiping her face with her grubby hands, no doubt creating some real mud, "I've been sealed in a box." Like she was already dead, but she just didn't know it yet. Her voice wobbled. "I really miss Max."

"I know, honey," Molly said, hugging her. "Right now, even *I* miss Max, and I hold a grudge against him for hurting you."

Gina laughed. It was shaky but it was laughter. "You've never held a grudge in your life." Along with being ridiculously optimistic, Molly was quick to forgive. Jones—Grady—had once teased her by saying she'd give Hannibal Lecter a second chance. Which brought Gina back to a far less humorless subject.

"Don't let Gun Man—the Italian guy—fool you," she told her friend. "He doesn't see us as people. We're worms on his hook. If it suits his purpose to keep us alive, we'll stay alive. If not . . . You know that saying, 'When you expect the best of people, you'll get the best . . . ?' This is not one of those times."

Molly was silent. She wasn't usually silent when she disagreed, but this time she restrained herself. Gina knew if there had been light in there, the expression on her face would have given her away. Her rebuttal would start with "But . . ." *But he seems so soft-spoken. But he seems like a gentleman. But . . .*

"I'm serious, Mol," Gina said. "Don't make friends with this guy."

Because when he savagely beat and raped them before he finally killed them, it would be just that much worse.

"You're not alone this time, Gina," Molly told her. "We're going to get through this. Together. Jones is going to come and—"

"Get himself killed," Gina pointed out.

"Not if I have anything to say about that." Conviction rang in Molly's voice. "And not if you do, either."

HOTEL ELBE HOF, HAMBURG, GERMANY
JUNE 21, 2005
PRESENT DAY

Jules stood back as Agent Jim Ulster knocked on the hotel room door again.

"You sure we got the right room?" Ulster asked his partner, a stocky, friendly faced woman that he called Goldie.

"This is the one," Jules told them. "Eight-seventeen."

Goldie—her real name was Vera Goldstein—double-checked her notepad. "Yes," she verified. "It's the room. Maybe Mr. Bhagat stepped out."

"Unlikely," Jules said.

"It *is* dinner time," she said. "Even legends need to eat."

"Trust me," he said. "Max doesn't stop for dinner even when the case he's working on *isn't* personal. He's in there. But he may not want to be disturbed."

"I heard he's a little strange that way," Goldie said. "That you need an engraved invitation to go into his office."

Short, whip-thin, and radiating impatience, Ulster was the Ren to Goldie's gentle Stimpy. The man didn't want to stand around shooting the breeze. He knocked on the door again. Louder.

"No," Jules said, "that's not true. I mean, yes, when you talk to him, you better know exactly what you're going to say. If you waste his time, he'll let you know, but . . ."

"I really don't think he's here," Ulster said, managing to check his watch, his cell phone, and surreptitiously adjust his balls in one swift movement.

And the door opened.

"Sorry to keep you waiting," Max said. "I had a little accident, and I was getting cleaned up."

Hello! Lying liar at twelve o'clock.

Goldie and Ulster were definitely fooled, blinded as they were by the shining glory of he-who-was-Max Bhagat. Although calling him *shining* in his current condition was a real stretch.

It was clear to Jules that someone had—quite recently—kicked the crap out of his legendary boss.

Recently enough so that his nose was still bleeding. Max had changed his shirt, sure, but his jacket and tie were noticeably absent. He held a washcloth up to his nose as the two agents introduced themselves like a pair of star-struck schoolgirls. Even Ulster was stammering now.

"I caught my foot in the electric cord for the lamp," he told them, a charming, chatty Max Bhagat—lying his ass off. "Broke the damn thing. The lamp, not my nose. Thank God for that at least."

It was definitely weird. With Max looking the way Max looked, there should have been a body or at least a very sore and aching loser, handcuffed to the pipe under the bathroom sink. And, as was appropriate in the law enforcement biz, when gathering for a meeting, post–body-accumulating, nose-bleed-inducing encounter, Max should have pointed to said loser and said, "Book 'em, Dano."

Or, in this case, "Book 'em, Goldie." Not blah, blah, lamp, blah, blah, nose.

As Jules stood there in the hall, he had a sudden vision of Max, as the completely insane but utterly delicious Edward Norton character in *Fight Club*, beating the hell out of himself in quite a few rounds of down and dirty, no rules, ultraviolent brawling.

Weird was putting it mildly.

And then . . . it got even weirder.

"Have you met Bill Jones, from the D.C. office?" Max asked Ulster and Goldstein as he stood back and let them into the room.

What the *who*?

But there was, indeed, a man in the room, sitting at the desk, using the hotel phone, as if he were taking a Very Important Call, hence his inability to answer the door.

Sure.

Most people sucked at faking a phone call, and Bill Jones was no exception.

He was tall, dark, and ruggedly handsome, and Jules had met him once before, only it wasn't anywhere near the D.C. office. And the name he'd been using at the time sure as shit wasn't Bill.

He hung up the phone, but as Max introduced him to Frisk's agents, he didn't get to his feet.

Possibly because Max had broken both his knees.

What was going on here?

"You've worked with Bill before, right, Cassidy?" Max had structured it as a question, but in truth, it was a direct order.

So Jules answered it the same way he answered all orders from his boss. "Yes, sir." He held out his hand for Jones to shake. "Bill. How are you, buddy? Nice to see you again."

And with that, Max was no longer the only liar in the room.

Yup, Billski had battered knuckles. And the shadow of a bruise was forming on the man's jaw. And what *was* he holding onto with his left hand, hidden there in the pocket of his jacket?

Odds were it wasn't his favorite Beanie Baby.

And, lookee over there, stuffed in yonder wastebasket. That wad of dark fabric had to be the tattered remains of Max's suit jacket.

Torn and bloodied, no doubt, while tripping over a lamp cord.

Glad they got *that* all straightened out.

"You came all this way for nothing, I'm afraid," Max—that gracious, charismatic, friendly Max—said as he smiled ruefully at Ulster and Goldstein.

It was kind of like stepping into an alternate universe. One where Mr. Spock had a beard, and Max was jovial.

"I managed to download the picture from the camera,"

Happy-Max continued. "I already sent it in a J-peg file to my team back in the States. The good news is that's one less thing for your team to do. I know Frisk's pushing you hard—everyone's tired."

Jules headed toward the window, pretending to check out the early evening view of the city's twinkly lights. He stepped over the broken lamp, leaning toward the glass to look down at the bustling street below.

His good friend Billy Jones didn't like that he was over there at all. It meant he had to divide his attention between watching Jules and watching Max, who was still over on the other side of the room. It meant if he were going to discharge that Beanie Baby, he'd have to choose who to shoot first.

Dude made his choice, and watched Jules.

Possibly because he'd already disarmed Max. Although, wait. Wasn't that Max's shoulder holster and sidearm over there on the bed? As if he'd placed it there while he'd changed his bloody shirt?

Curiouser and curiouser.

Max was deep in discussion with Ulster and Goldie—talking about the information that had turned up after the analysts had poured over thousands of satellite images.

They'd traced the vehicle that had exploded near the cafe, backwards chronologically on the day of the explosion, all the way to the rundown apartment where this particular terrorist cell had been squatting. They also noted that the tangos had made a pit stop while en route to the airport that very same morning.

"They stopped at the home and workshop of . . ." Goldie consulted her little notepad but apparently couldn't read her handwriting. She frowned at Ulstie. "Is it Gretl or Gretta?"

God forbid she make a mistake while talking to Max Bhagat.

Jules could relate.

He, too, was not eager to make a mistake in front of Max. Such as allowing a dangerous criminal who might know Gina's whereabouts to sit with a loaded weapon in his hidden left hand.

"Gretta Kraus," Ulster said with confidence that quickly wavered. "I think."

Over at the desk, Bill Jones finally gave Jules an opening as he turned back toward Max. "Gretta Kraus?" he repeated. "The counterfeit artist?"

Jules took advantage, moving swiftly behind Jones. Bending down, he pretended to pick something up off the floor as he removed his sidearm from his shoulder holster. Keeping it concealed, he straightened up. And, behind the chair's padded back, where Goldie and Ulster couldn't see it, he aimed the barrel of his weapon at the man's spine.

Jules put his other hand on Jones's very broad, very muscular shoulder as he spoke quietly, right into the man's attractive ear. He smiled, as if they were sharing a friendly secret or a workplace complaint. *Can you believe this dickweed boss of ours won't let us have even ten minutes to grab a slice of pizza?* "Left hand up and on the table, friend."

"Gretta Kraus, the forger," Goldie was telling Max. "She had a lucrative business creating passports, driver's licenses, birth certificates—you name it, she'd make it. And, yeah, I'm sure in certain circles she was thought of as an artist."

"Back off," Jones muttered to Jules. Louder, he said, "Was?"

His hand stayed in his pocket.

Which pissed Jules off. He leaned close again to whisper to Jones that until he put his hand on that desk, he better not so much as pass gas or he'd end up extremely dead, but the man actually shushed him.

And Max, as usual, aware of everything going on around him, met Jules's eyes and shook his head. It was the slightest movement, done while he smiled—yes, and smiled patiently, boys and girls—at Vera Goldstein.

That head-shake was an obvious warning, a silent echo of Jones's own words, *back off*. But now Jules had to wonder if Max, who was probably being coerced, was capable of making the right choices.

So he stayed exactly where he was.

"We went over there, to ask some questions," Goldie was reporting, "and everyone was dead—Gretta, her husband, their sons, her assistant."

"Oh shit," Jones breathed.

"Forensics estimates they died on the same day as the bombing," Goldie continued, starting to dig for something in her shoulder bag. "But they lived in a part of town where gunshots go unreported, so . . ."

Max was nodding to show he was listening, but he'd moved to the bed, where he picked up his shoulder holster and put it on. A message to Jules?

Definitely. But Jones could well have taken all of the bullets out of that handgun that Max slid home and locked down with velcro.

Goldie was still talking as she searched through her massive shoulder bag. "The security cameras in Gretta's workshop were all destroyed, so we were working on the theory that the terrorist cell came in, killed them, and then took what they wanted—forged passports and visas and ID cards. But then we did an electronics sweep . . ." She triumphantly came up with a DVD in a plastic jewel case. "And we found backup security—one of those hidden nanny-cams. There's no sound, but the picture's very clear. We made you a copy of the digital recording, sir, so you don't have to go all the way downtown to see it." She presented it to Max with a flourish.

"Thank you," Max said, reaching out to shake her hand, even as he moved back toward the door. He was very good at signaling the end of a conversation, although he usually did it with a flat *Shut the door behind you.* "I'll definitely review it later—"

Ulster, however, didn't budge. "No, sir, I'm sorry—we didn't make it clear." He ruined the generous, blame-embracing effect of the word *we* by shooting a look at his partner that broadcast *You Stupid Eeee-diot* quite loudly. "We're not certain, but we think your, uh, friend, Gina, and her traveling companion had an, um . . ."

"Less-than-kosher connection to Gretta Kraus," Goldie finished for him. "This is probably the last thing you want to hear, sir, but according to this footage—" she tapped the DVD "—they were there, in the studio, when the terrorists arrived. They barely made it out alive."

"Oh, shit," seemed to be Jones's new mantra.

Happy-Max had vanished. His replacement brought the DVD over to the desk, as Jones woke up the computer.

"Why, for the love of God, would they go to Gretta Kraus's workshop?" Max asked it as a rhetorical question.

Jones kept his mouth shut, although it was clear to Jules that he knew the answer.

"We were hoping you'd be able to tell us," Ulster said to Max.

The DVD began to play, and both Max and Jones leaned in to watch. Jules had a clear view over Jones's broad shoulder.

Max—the real Max who could turn coal to diamonds with certain tightly clenched muscles—used the opportunity to tell Jones, sotto voce and through gritted teeth, "I'm going to kill you. More slowly and painfully this time so that—"

But then Goldie was upon them, leaving the rest of Max's threat hanging. *This time?* Jules could only guess what that meant.

The female agent used her pen to point to the screen, which revealed a stagnant shot of what could have been an architect's studio. Slanted work surfaces, stools, clean lines, bright colors, cut flowers in ceramic vases—it looked like a page from the upscale section of an Ikea catalogue. She tapped. "This is Gretta."

Gretta was neither typical Hollywood thriller forger-nerd, with pocket protector, thick glasses and streaks of ink on her face and hands, nor James Bondian catsuit-wearing babe-of-evil. She was, instead, 100 percent German haus-frau. Fifty and frumpy. Good for her, for not conforming to expectations.

Except wait. Not so good for her—considering they were watching the last few minutes of her life. She was about to become the newest poster girl for the Crime Doesn't Pay campaign.

"Gretta's husband and her sons," Goldie pointed again with her pen to three men leaning over a computer, much the way Max, Jones, and Jules were doing now. Except Max, Jones, and Jules had all of their teeth. As they watched, the oldest of the three men took his out, putting it—them?—on a plate alongside of what looked like a donut.

Yikes.

A youngish woman entered the frame, "Gretta's assis-tant," Goldie narrated. "And watch Mr. Kraus as she brings the women in. He makes a phone call."

On the screen, the assistant was followed by . . . Yes, that was definitely Gina, but with an adorable haircut, along with another woman. And sure enough, over by the com-puter Mr. Kraus looked at them, then slipped in his teeth and picked up the phone.

As Jules watched, both Max and Jones tensed, and Jones oh shitted.

"That's her," Max told Goldie and Ulster, trying hard to resurrect Happy-Max, but not quite able, considering. "Gina. And her friend, Molly Anderson." He looked at Jules. "Also known as Mrs. Leslie Pollard. She was married recently. When was it exactly . . . ? Do you remember what Father Soldano told us, Bill?"

"About four months ago," Jones said, his voice tight as he stared at the screen.

And Jules finally backed off, because he now understood. Jones was apparently as invested in finding Molly and Gina as Max was. And, for various reasons—the most obvious being that the man would be wrestled to the floor, handcuffed, and immediately extradited to the United States—Max wasn't ready to disclose Jones's true identity to Ulster and Goldstein.

Jules, however, was trusted with the truth. He reholstered his weapon, pretending he had an itch under his arm.

On the screen, Molly seemed *pissed*. A statuesque redhead whose entire attire and attitude screamed crunchy-granola Unicef Mama, she was talking and talking, but Gretta just kept shaking her sullen head. "I'm sorry," it looked as if she were saying. And, No. *"Nein."*

Gina stood there, hugging her nifty ergonomic backpack, as if she'd rather be anywhere else in the world.

Jules couldn't wait to find out what they were doing there. Although he suspected if he asked, "Who here needs a professionally forged passport and ID?" only one of them would raise his battered-knuckled hand.

But what kind of lowlife scum willingly sent two women into a literal den of thieves?

Jules predicted that after Max got rid of Ulster and Goldie someone and someone else might just trip over the ol' lamp cord again.

On screen, Molly didn't give up. She just kept talking. Jules wished this recording had a soundtrack. He could only imagine how frustrated Max must be.

Gretta now looked pissed. She pulled out a file from a cabinet, tossed it on her desk, gesturing to Molly.

Maybe it was just Jules's vivid imagination, but Gretta had to be saying, *auf Deutsch*, of course: "So who's going to pay for this? Huh? Huh? Huh?"

This being the masterpiece of forgery that was surely in that file. Whatever it was, the camera angle didn't pick it up. Jules guessed passport. And he'd bet big *dinero* that the photo used in the official document would show a remarkable likeness to the man sitting directly in front of him.

The name on the passport, of course, could have been anything. Anything except for Grady Morant, David Jones, or Leslie Pollard.

"Bill" had already used those names—he would surely have chosen something fresh and new. Something, oh, say, *not* on anyone's Most Wanted List.

On the computer screen, Gina was now digging in her bag. Opening her wallet. As she and Molly now argued, she handed Gretta a . . . credit card?

Even more absurd was the fact that Gretta took it. She vanished out of range of the camera as Molly and Gina stepped closer to each other to continue their disagreement.

"NTS International," Max murmured.

Of course. That mysterious twenty-thousand-dollar charge to Gina's credit card. NTS International was a temporary front for Gretta Kraus's lucrative illegal business. No wonder they were having trouble tracking them.

"Now, here's where the husband gets a phone call, probably from the front office," Goldie pointed to the screen. Sure enough, in the background, Mr. Kraus again picked up the phone. What were the chances that the old guy's first name was Klaus? "And now he goes out front and . . ."

Mr. Kraus came back into the workshop with another man.

Jules had never seen him before, but Gina and Molly sure as hell seemed to recognize him. They backed away. As if they were afraid of him.

"Motherfucker," Jones expleted, apparently having used up his *oh shit* reserve. "He's clearly our guy and those assholes just walked him in."

"Do you know him?" Max asked Jones, who was probably still alive thanks only to Goldie and Ulster's continued presence.

"No. You?"

"No."

As everyone on that screen did more of that silent talking, the man—dark hair, medium height and build, mustache, maybe mid-fifties—casually took out a handgun. His demeanor wasn't threatening, but that weapon really ramped up the mood from frightened to scared shitless.

Gretta Kraus got into the discussion then, as Gina stepped slightly in front of Molly.

And it was Max's turn to cuss. He glared at Goldie. "Do we have an ID on him?"

"Not yet, sir," she said. "It was lower priority, since he doesn't seem to be connected to the terrorists and . . . See, here's where Gina's got her passport behind her—it's in her wallet. See, she's backed up against Gretta's desk and . . ."

As they watched, courtesy of the camera positioned back behind that desk, Gina slipped her wallet—large, made of brown leather—beneath some of the papers scattered there.

Maybe she was trying to hide her identity. Or maybe she thought that without her passport, she wouldn't be able to leave the country.

"Molly's passport was in there, too," Jones said. He glanced up at Goldie, adding, "Probably. I mean, she's not carrying a purse or anything, so I'm guessing . . ."

"And now the shooting starts," Jim Ulster took over the narration.

On the screen, everyone jumped, as if there was a sudden loud noise from out in the other room.

Gretta, who'd been standing close to Gina, went down, hard, with a spray of blood.

"Ah, God," Max breathed, no doubt noticing the look of

pure horror on Gina's face. She didn't quite know what had happened. She was still just standing there.

The room exploded around her as bullets hit the plaster walls, the lamps, those vases with cut flowers. And the mustached gunman, who'd already tackled Molly, dragged Gina down with him to the floor.

On the far side of the room, the two younger Kraus men grabbed for weapons—serious-ass military-type machine guns—ready to fight back. But their as-of-yet unidentified gunman didn't waste a single second returning fire. He shouted something to Gina—he had her by the wrist—and she grabbed Molly. And he pulled them both with him out of camera range.

"Back door's back behind the camera, to the left on your screen," Ulster told them, as they watched the last two Krauses get riddled with bullets and fall.

"Whoever he was," Goldie said, "he definitely saved Gina and her friend's lives."

Maybe so. But it was obvious to Jules that Max wasn't on the verge of giving Mr. Mustache-Man a medal.

Goldie reached over and paused the DVD. "The rest of the footage is the terrorists trashing the place as they look for passports. They find Gina's wallet on Gretta's desk—it's clear this is how they got hold of it. It also explains why the same-day, one-way airline ticket that was made in her name was paid for with her own credit card. We're no longer looking at her as a possible connection to the cell."

They'd actually thought Gina was . . . ? Jules made a noise of indignation, even though he knew they'd had to consider all possibilities.

"I want an ID for that gunman," Max ordered. "Bump it higher in priority." His phone rang. "Excuse me."

He turned away to answer it, and Jules's phone rang, too.

As he reached for it, Goldie and Ulster also started ringing.

That was never a good sign. Four agents, all getting called at once?

Something big had happened—an attempt on the President's life, a nuclear meltdown, or . . .

"Goddamn it!" The real Max came roaring back to life, full force this time. He hit the mute button on his phone. "Don't answer that, Cassidy!"

Or a terrorist attack.

Jules had his phone in his hand. He recognized the caller's number. "It's Yashi." From the D.C. headquarters.

Max had already turned back to his call. "Please repeat— I'm having trouble hearing you."

"Oh, my God," Goldie was saying into her phone. "Right away. Yes, ma'am. *Yes*, ma'am!"

"They did *what*?" Ulster was equally distressed, one finger in his non-phone ear. "Oh, crap. Okay. Yeah, okay. We'll be right in."

Jesus, this couldn't be good.

"What's going on?" Jones asked Ulster as he hung up.

"We've got to go," Ulster said. "We've got at least three commercial passenger planes in the air sending out an SOS. Air marshals have prevented hijackings, but they believe there are bombs on board that'll go off if the planes try to land."

"We've also uncovered a plot to set off a series of dirty bombs in U.S. and European cities," Goldie gathered up her shoulder bag and headed for the door. "We've located three of the bombs, but at least two are still at large."

"The connection's bad," Max said into his phone. "I can't hear you. Call me back." He hung up as Ulster and Goldstein paused at the door, waiting for him to dismiss them. "Go," he said, and they went. "Jules."

"Yes, sir."

"You heard what's going down?"

"Yes, sir." Apparently, they were on the verge of a global terrorist attack. The one they always said was coming—

and this time they'd been ready. They'd apparently already stopped much of it from happening, now they were going to stop the rest.

"That call you didn't take," Max told him grimly, "It's someone telling you to get your ass back to D.C. When you call them back, they're going to say you'll have to catch a military transport, because all commercial airports in the U.S. have been shut down."

Sweet baby Jesus. "*All* of them?"

"Yeah. I'm not going in," Max told him. "For obvious reasons. But Peggy Ryan will take over—I have total faith in her. In the entire team. In you, too. But I know you and Peggy have knocked heads, so . . . Just tell me where you want to be assigned, and you'll go there. As a team leader. She'll eventually get used to you."

What? "Excuse me, sir, you're talking like you're never coming back."

Max nodded. "Yeah."

Shit.

Double shit.

Jules hadn't expected Max to ask him to stay and help find Gina and Molly. Not in so many words, anyway. But he really hadn't expected this *tell me where you want to be assigned,* "have a nice life" bullshit.

Which didn't mean that Jules couldn't volunteer to stay right here. Especially considering the manpower needed for a hostage rescue. If Max had been thinking he was going to be able to utilize any type of Special Ops group like SEAL Team Sixteen to assist in Molly and Gina's rescue . . . Honey, he was going to have to think again.

Those guys were going to be a little busy over the next few days, saving the world and whatnot.

Which meant . . . what? Max and No-name Jones over there, kicking down the kidnapper's door all by their little lonesome?

"God, you know, I really hate Peggy Ryan," Jules told

Max now. "She is such a pain in my ass. If it's all the same to you, sir, I'll just keep on keeping on, assisting you with this case. Just because the rest of the world's on fire doesn't mean two kidnapped women don't matter. They need saving, so let's go save 'em."

Max was shaking his head. "Careers are going to be made, based on what happens over the next few days," he pointed out.

Jules just looked at him for several long seconds. "That might be truly *the* most offensive thing you've ever said to me."

Max didn't look even slightly ashamed. His nose, however, was a little swollen. "That doesn't make it any less true."

Jones, aka Grady Morant, was watching them from his seat at the desk. Now that the comedy team of Ulster and Goldstein had left the building, his left hand, Jules noted, was no longer in his pocket.

"Why is it," Jules asked Jones, "that Max can't simply look me in the eye and tell me he wants me to stay, that he needs my help?"

Jones shook his head. Shrugged. "I'm not," he said, "you know. Gay."

Jules laughed his surprise. "What does that have to do with . . . ?" Did Jones think . . . ? Okay. Apparently no help would be coming from that quarter.

Jones stood up. "Can we get out of here? We need to figure out how the hell we're getting to Jakarta. If commercial airports are shutting down . . ."

Jules's phone started ringing again. He turned to Max. "You said tell me where I want to be assigned, I told you. What more do you need me to say?"

Max seemed to make up his mind. He nodded. "Answer that," he ordered Jules. "And tell Yashi that I made you a team leader—that you're in charge of this kidnapping investigation, and that you need three seats on the next flight to Indonesia—civilian or military, it doesn't matter which, as long as you can board unchallenged with two passengers."

"*I'm* in charge? As in, what? You're assisting me?" Jules laughed. But Max didn't join in. "Whoa. Wait, sir. I—"

"Tell him," Max spoke over him, "as team leader, I tendered my resignation to you, and you accepted."

What?

The ringing was driving him nuts. Jules answered his phone. "Yash, I've got to call you right back." He hung up. "I beg your pardon, sir, but what the *hell*?"

"I can't be in charge of this case," Max said. "I can't participate in any official capacity. Gina's my . . . girlfriend."

It was entirely possible, that was the first time he'd ever called her that. As it was, he practically choked on the word.

But before Jules could scoff at him—what a baby, and what a stupid word to choke on, for crying out loud, because Gina was not a girl and hello, he hadn't even seen her in a year and a half—Max spoke again.

"She means everything to me," he whispered. "She's my life. Without her . . ." He shook his head.

And Jules realized with a jolt of shock that Max had tears in his eyes. It was one thing to see the man cry upon discovery that Gina wasn't dead, but this . . .

"I'd sacrifice anything for her," Max admitted now. "Including your career. So, yes, I *will* say it. I want you to stay and help me get her back."

Jules didn't hesitate. "I accept the position," he told his friend. "And I accept your . . . you know." Resignation. He accepted it, but couldn't quite bring himself to utter the word.

Max nodded. "Call Yashi," he ordered. "I'll pack the laptop so we can communicate with the kidnapper—he calls himself E. We need to e-mail him—he's already contacted Morant here through a special account. I'm going to demand additional proof of life. He sent a photo, but I want phone contact. Oh, and you should probably be aware, before I quit, I cut a deal with Mr. Morant. We don't touch him until Molly and Gina are safely in our custody. After that, he's all ours." He caught himself. "Yours."

"Only in my dreams," Jules said, as he dialed his cell phone. "Because, you know, dude says he's not gay."

Jones ignored him. "I know it's a long shot, but we should get whatever information we can about both e-mail accounts—his and the one he set up for me. Maybe we can trace his location."

"Roger that," Jules said. He'd also see if the D.C. office could spare any personnel, although it was extremely unlikely. Peggy Ryan wouldn't miss him—he had no doubts about that. He also knew that she wouldn't willingly assign away any other members of her team during a situation that involved a possible dirty bomb in the nation's capital.

Still, maybe there was someone else on the team whom she suspected of being gay.

As he got bumped to Yashi's voice mail, his phone beeped. He had an incoming call—from Peggy Ryan. Terrific. He was going to have to talk directly to the Wicked Witch of the West.

He anticipated the subtext of her message: "Good, you go to Indonesia and be gay there, thousands of miles away from me and the important press conferences I'm going to be holding."

He could even imagine her barely concealed amused condescension that he was finally a team leader—without a real team.

"Hey, Peg," Jules said as he answered his phone, as he watched Jones wind up the laptop's power cord and hand it to Max, who was securing the computer in its carrying case.

Who said he didn't have a real team to lead? And this wasn't just a real team—it was a dream team.

Except wait—that was the hotel's computer. Max realized it at the same moment that Jules did. Only Jones seemed to want to take it anyway, as backup.

And then, whoops, as he watched, Max grabbed Jones by the shirt and shoved him up against the wall.

"Hold please," Jules said over Peggy's terse list of orders. He muted his phone. "Back off," he told Max.

Max didn't move. "This son of a bitch sent his wife and Gina to pick up a new passport from—"

"I did not," Jones said hotly. "She wasn't supposed to go there."

"Oh, so she and Gina just flew to Hamburg to, what? Shop?" Max said.

Jules's entire team was on the verge of tripping over that dang lamp cord again.

"Back," he ordered through gritted teeth, "Off. Let me talk to Peggy, and then we'll sort this out." Max still didn't move. "That was not a request. *Max*."

Wonder of wonders, the man actually obeyed. He released Jones with only a minimum of alpha-male jostling.

The two of them stood there then, eyeing each other with obvious distaste.

Jules unmuted his phone. "Sorry, Peg. Go ahead."

It was possible that calling them a "dream team" was a teensy exaggeration.

CHAPTER TWELVE

PULAU MEDA, INDONESIA
EXACT DATE: UNKNOWN
PRESENT DAY

Molly squinted at the sudden bright light as the container she and Gina had traveled in for the past fifteen hours was finally opened.

The fresh air was a godsend, and both women gulped it in.

Their captor made an apologetic face as he held his handkerchief to his nose. "The Depends didn't work as well as I'd hoped."

"No," Gina told him, "they didn't." Particularly not when she'd gotten seasick on the last leg of their journey.

"Ah, well, it was worth a try."

Trim and elegant, with gray at his temples, the Italian man who'd ordered them at gunpoint into this container spoke perfect English, with only the faintest trace of an accent. He was still as apologetically polite as he'd been back in Hamburg.

"My friend is ill, too," Gina said. "She needs ginger ale or cola—something to settle her stomach."

Molly was beyond queasy, and so hungry she was light-headed. It wasn't a good combination. It was a miracle that she hadn't thrown up as well.

Of course, she still might.

"By all means," the man said. "We'll just dial up room service."

She was so fuzzy-headed, she couldn't tell if he was mocking Gina or if he meant what he'd said. Of course, it was hard to completely trust a man who'd pack two grown women in a container and ship them . . .

Molly didn't know where they'd been shipped, only that it was much warmer here than it had been in Germany. And it was sunnier, too, although the light that had made her squint came from a bare bulb hanging down from the ceiling.

As another man—younger, darker, shorter, but wider— peered in at them, still brandishing the crowbar he'd used to pry the container open, Molly helped Gina to her feet. Or maybe Gina helped Molly. It was difficult to tell which of them was steadier on her feet.

The older man spoke sharply to the younger one in what sounded like Italian—no doubt a warning to be careful of the car that was parked beside them. A navy blue Impala, it dated back to the days when bigger was better. It was in very good shape for its age—similar to its owner.

"We'll need a shower and a change of clothes," Molly told him with as much dignity as she could muster, considering the circumstances.

They were in a garage with shuttered windows and a concrete floor. Concrete with bits of shells mixed in—similar to the way they made it back on Parwati Island.

"Are you all right?" Gina whispered to Molly.

"I'll live." Besides her churning stomach, Molly's heels were bruised from their attempts to get attention by kicking the metal sides of their prison. She was hoarse, too, from screaming for help.

No one had heard them. No one, at least, who had cared.

The older man led them into the house, down a hallway into a room that was nicely furnished. A king-sized bed. A sofa with bamboo legs and sides. A TV even, though what were the odds that it worked?

An open doorway revealed an attached modern bathroom—all gleaming white tile and chrome fixtures.

It was air conditioned and cool, thank you, Lord Jesus. It was nicer than many of the hotel rooms she'd ever stayed in—except for the decided lack of view.

Due to the fact that there were no windows whatsoever.

"If you put your clothes outside the door," their captor said, "my daughter-in-law will wash them for you."

With a stately bow, he closed the door behind him.

Was he just leaving it unlocked?

Gina was thinking the same thing, and went over to it. Opened it.

The younger man they'd seen in the garage was standing guard out in the hall. He still held the crowbar.

Gina closed the door, fast. "Okay," she said. "Okay." She moved away from the door, lowered her voice. She was clearly feeling better.

Molly wished she could say the same.

"There are three of them," Gina continued. "We've only seen two, but he mentioned a third—his daughter-in-law. So far I've only seen one gun, and I haven't seen it lately. What we need to do is be ready for them to come back in here. Maybe we can ask Crowbar for help, like the toilet won't flush, and when he comes in, we'll hit him over the head." She crossed toward the bed, pulling up the cover to look at the metal frame. "We need to make a run for it. Now—before any reinforcements arrive."

Gina's voice was getting more and more faint, as if she were talking from a great distance, instead of just a few feet away. That couldn't be good.

"Help me with this, will you?" Gina said, trying to move the mattress.

Molly tried to go toward her, and ended up sitting right on the bed. Her legs weren't working right.

"Oh, *that's* really helping." Gina's voice was sharp, until she looked up. "Molly? Are you okay?"

Molly's cheek was against the crispness of the sheets. How'd she get there?

"Just gotta . . . close my eyes," she said. "Just for a sec . . . Can we . . . make a run for it . . . a little later?"

RAMSTEIN AIR BASE, GERMANY
JUNE 22, 2005
PRESENT DAY

Jules Cassidy had called a time-out as they drove to Ramstein Air Base.

It was not unlike the time-outs Max's father had called during long family road trips.

Max had sat in the backseat of the car, in between his sister and brother, not just because he was the youngest, but because he usually got along with them both.

When they'd started to fight, they'd had to fight over him.

Although there *had* been quite a few frustrating times when they joined forces and ganged up on him.

At which point, his father usually called for total silence.

Just like Jules had as they'd left the hotel.

They'd stopped only twice on their way to the airbase—to pick up a rental car to make the journey, and then at a shopping mall.

A good leader, Jules had made sure his team was properly—and literally—outfitted. He grabbed a pair of jeans from the shelf, without even asking Max's size. Apparently, he already knew what Max wore, down to the style and brand.

A pair of sneakers—again he knew which rack to approach—and a lightweight jacket later, they were back in the car and on their way.

It wasn't until after midnight, when they hit the airbase, that Jules let Max and Morant speak to each other, let alone get into it.

But first he checked in to make sure they still had an hour to kill before boarding the transport heading for Indonesia. He also led them to a patch of tarmac from which they would not be overheard.

"Who goes first?" Jules asked, light on the balls of his feet, like a boxing referee.

Grady Morant, aka Leslie Pollard, aka Dave Jones, raised his hand, but then didn't speak right away. He scanned the area, taking in the activity on the airfield. He did it automatically, out of habit.

Same way Max did. He knew if they went inside the terminal, they'd both head directly for the same seat. Back against the wall, easier to see anyone coming or going.

He and Morant were a lot alike.

Except Max hadn't turned to a life of crime.

Morant finally cleared his throat, then got the party started with a totally unexpected acceptance of blame.

"Look, I know it's on me—completely—that Molly and Gina were grabbed." He took a deep breath. "But—"

Okay, here it came. The part where it really wasn't his fault.

"I swear," he continued, "I didn't send them to Kraus's workshop. I didn't even tell Molly where it was. I have no idea how she found the place, and . . . As for why they went there, the only reason I can come up with is that Molly realized she was being followed. Maybe she wanted to try to warn me." He shook his head, misery on his face. "Goddamn it. I should have known not to trust Kraus."

It was pretty obvious that was how the kidnapper had found him, found Molly and Gina, too. They'd all watched it play out on the DVD. Molly and Gina had walked in, Mr. Kraus made that phone call, and five minutes later, the man who'd ID'd himself as E. showed up.

Coincidence? Not likely.

Morant wasn't done. "I just . . . I had to risk it. There were reasons for haste."

Reasons. For. Haste. Max resisted the urge to rip out the bastard's throat. Reasons like a chance to make a million dollars in some business deal that was mostly legal—oh, except for the parts that were felonies? Or maybe Morant was going to try to tug on their heartstrings with *reasons* that were sentimental. His dear old mother was ill, for example. Or his cousin needed a kidney transplant.

Max couldn't wait to hear this.

But Jules stepped in and took the discussion in a different direction. "If you weren't intending to send Molly to Kraus's workshop, how exactly were you going to get that passport?"

"The plan was to meet in a bar," Morant explained. "In Hamburg. Me," he added. "For me to meet one of Kraus's sons. And pay for it, in cash. Believe me, I had no intention of Molly getting anywhere near any of that."

"Gina was a different story, though, right?" Max asked, his anger making little lights flash at the edges of his peripheral vision. "You didn't give a damn about her, so using her credit card for the down payment was a no brainer."

That was surely what that ten-thousand-dollar cash advance in Nairobi had been about.

"Or maybe you stole her card," Max added, "Without her even knowing."

Morant looked like he was seconds from swinging at Max. "Fuck you."

"Fuck you!" Max just hoped he'd try it.

Jules stepped between them. "This is not useful."

"I didn't steal Gina's credit card," Morant said heatedly. "She knew what I was doing—she *insisted*. And we didn't *use* her card. She got the cash from one bank, I took it to another and wired it to Kraus."

"Were both banks in Nairobi?"

"No," Morant said. "We flew to Paris—of course they were both in Nairobi. Look, I know you're angry . . ."

Max was beyond angry. Anyone with a little computer hacking know-how could have traced that money back to Gina's credit card. It was just one of the many, many ways E-the-kidnapper could have used Morant's business transaction with Kraus to locate him. "How many banks are there in Nairobi, Morant?"

"Shit, I don't know," Morant said. "Yes, I trusted Kraus and . . . It was obviously a mistake. I gambled, all right? I didn't know what else to do. I had to get Molly back to Iowa, and she wouldn't go without me!"

"You took the photo for your new passport with Gina's camera, right?" Max asked him. "Sent it electronically to Kraus? A copy was still in there, saved in a file."

"If you know that," Morant's defiance was edged with despair, "why ask? Yes. I mean, what? Are you hoping I'm going to lie about it—"

"It would have taken my team approximately ten minutes to identify you as Grady Morant from that photo," Max raised his voice and spoke over him. "The same photo you sent to Kraus. It probably took her a little bit longer—maybe an hour—to figure out who the hell she was doing business with—" he was full-out shouting now "—and that her new customer still had a price on his goddamn head. So much for honor among thieves, huh, *Grady*?"

"I said it's my fault," Morant shouted back. "It's my fault. *It's my fault!* What more do you want me to say? You know, Gina *wanted* to help. She *asked* if she could help—"

"And you goddamn didn't keep her safe," Max snarled at him. "What the hell were you thinking?"

"I was thinking, *fuck*," Morant roared, "if I don't do something, my wife is going to die of fucking cancer!"

It was then, shaking with anger, that Grady Morant

nearly started to cry. "You stupid self-absorbed asshole," he whispered through clenched teeth, "you may have been willing just to throw Gina away, but I have no intention of losing Molly without a fight!"

NAIROBI, KENYA
JUNE 8, 2005
THIRTEEN DAYS AGO

"They want me to go to Hamburg for a biopsy," Molly said, as she came out into the doctor's waiting room, her face pale.

"What?" Jones stood up.

"They want me to go to Hamburg," she said again. "In Germany."

"I know where Hamburg is," he said. Jesus, this couldn't be happening.

This was supposed to be a minibreak—Molly was reading about one of her other favorite Joneses again. They were supposed to drive into Nairobi, visit a doctor who'd actually gotten a medical degree, find out that the lump she'd discovered was either normal or imaginary, have dinner, spend the night in a fancy hotel screaming lustily the entire time, and then drive back to camp in the morning.

He hadn't planned at all for "They want me to go to Hamburg."

Yes, she was almost exactly the same age as her mother had been, when her mother was diagnosed with breast cancer. Yes, the lump she'd found was similar to her mother's in size and consistency. It was even in the same breast.

"What do they think it is?" he asked, even though he knew. Biopsy. They didn't do biopsies for swollen glands or viruses.

Molly slipped her arms around his waist, holding him tight. "It's probably nothing."

"Mol, it's not *probably nothing* if they fucking want you to go to Germany." She winced, and he turned to the people—mostly women—who were filling most of those waiting room seats. "Excuse me. This doctor thinks my wife, whom I love more than life, has breast cancer, so I'm going to say fuck probably about ten more times. Is that okay with all of you?"

She took his hand, pulling him toward the door. "Let's take a walk."

"I don't think you should go to Hamburg," Jones said, as she led him into the stairwell and down toward the street level. "I think you should go home. To Iowa. I think you should see your mother's oncologist. Because your mother's fine, right? It's been, like, twenty years and she's fine."

The lobby was mostly empty, and much cooler than the sun-drenched street. There was a bench, off to the side, beneath a brightly colored wall mural.

"Let's sit down," Molly said.

She tried to tug him down with her, but he resisted.

If he was scared before, he was now petrified.

"Let's take a walk," he said. "Let's sit. Molly, whatever you have to tell me, just please tell me."

"I sort of don't know how to." She had tears in her eyes.

So Jones sat beside her. He laced his fingers with hers. "You know I love you, right?"

She nodded.

"Well, I don't love you for your breasts," he told her. "If one—or both of them's got to go, then they've got to go. It's not going to change the way I feel about you. It's not going to change anything."

Molly started to cry.

"Hey," he said, "that was supposed to make you, well, not exactly happy, but at least—"

She kissed him. *Happier.*

She pulled back to look at him. "I love you, too," she said, and somehow that unleashed a new flood of tears.

"Molly, you're really scaring me," Jones said. "Did the doctor give you a death sentence or something?"

"It's just . . ." She shook her head, looking down at their hands, clasped together. She exhaled before she spoke. "Remember the night that you came into the mess tent, and I realized it was you and I dropped my tray?"

It was Jones's turn to nod. He had no idea where she was going with this.

"And then, later, I came to your tent, and we kind of had . . . half-assed sex?"

He nodded again. Half-assed sex . . . He looked at her, realization dawning. Was she saying . . . ? They'd had half-assed sex without a condom. "But I didn't come. I mean, I remember that part really well."

"Apparently," she said, "you didn't have to."

Jones sat in silence for several long moments before he found the air to ask, "Are you serious? You're . . ."

"Pregnant," she said. "Not quite four months pregnant." Which meant in five months . . . Oh, shit.

"I thought you were, you know, in whatchamacallit," he said. "Perimenopause."

"Yes," Molly said. "I am. But apparently the last few months I missed my periods because of . . . this." She gazed at him, searchingly. "Are you completely horrified?"

"Shit yeah," he said, "but not for the reason you think. Can you be treated for cancer while you're pregnant?"

And there it was. She looked away from him. "It's not so much can I as *will* I. The doctor said that after the first trimester, some chemotherapy drugs pose no known danger to the baby."

But. Jones knew that look Molly was wearing on her face way too well. He said it for her. "But . . . ?"

"They haven't done enough long-term tests. I'm not going to poison this child."

And there it was. The doctor hadn't given Molly a death sentence. But she was potentially giving one to herself.

"This should be happy news," she said. "That I'm pregnant. It shouldn't be an add-on to, 'the doctor wants me to go to Hamburg for a biopsy.' "

Jones shook his head. "Surely it can't be good for the baby to just—"

She knew where he was going. "My having breast cancer won't harm the baby."

"Are you sure?" he said heatedly. "Have they done enough long fucking term tests on that?"

"Shhh," she said, glancing over at the security guard standing by the front door. "Come on—"

"No," Jones said. He stood up. "No, Molly. You can't honestly tell me that you want to have a baby that you won't be around to watch grow up."

"We don't know that. If the biopsy comes back and it's only stage one or two, then waiting a few months—"

"Five months," he said. "While the cancer is growing at an increased pace, feeding on all the estrogen and growth hormones that your body is making. It's insane to—"

She stood, too. "We don't have a choice anymore."

"Yes, we do!"

Now she was mad, too. "Okay," she said. "Yes. We have a choice. It's *my* choice. And I choose to do more research, talk to more doctors, and go to Hamburg for a biopsy. Is that okay with you?"

What the fuck was he doing? Arguing bitterly with a woman—his woman—who had just been told she could well have cancer. How could that be helping? Yes, he was scared, but she had to be, too.

Jones reached for her. Held her tightly. "Yeah," he said. "It's okay. Molly, God, I'm so sorry."

She clung to him. "I am, too."

He was not going to let her die. He was not going to lose her.

But Jones knew, as he held her, that there was really very little he could do.

Yeah, he'd already done far more than his share.

PULAU MEDA, INDONESIA
EXACT DATE: UNKNOWN
PRESENT DAY

Molly had been asleep for quite a few hours when Gina heard a soft knock on the door.

She'd been dozing herself, but she sat up now, her heart pounding.

At first, she'd been too busy to be scared. Helping Molly take off her soiled clothes and washing her face. Peeling back the edge of the bandage covering her biopsy stitches, making sure it was healing nicely and not infected. Tucking her under the cool cotton sheets on one side of that big bed.

She'd been sleeping on a camping cot for so long, an actual king-sized bed seemed ridiculously large. Did anyone on this planet really need a bed that big?

Gina had showered and rinsed out their clothes in the sink. No way was she putting them out in the hall for the invisible daughter-in-law to launder. If she did that, they might never get them back, making it that much harder for them to make a break for it.

Of course, in Molly's current condition, she was unable to run. If there only were a way to get her out of here . . .

If Gina were alone, she would've risked it already. She was taller than Crowbar Guy.

The door now opened. Just a crack at first, then wider, and Gina wrapped her robe more tightly around her.

As far as robes went, it was very nice, like something from an expensive hotel. But gleaming white, it practically glowed in the dark. Making a run while wearing it would be about as effective as having a neon hat that flashed "Here I am!"

Gina hadn't wanted to put it on—this *wasn't* a hotel, it was a prison—but the air conditioning had been set to a temperature that was a little too cool. She tightened the belt as she got to her feet.

It was dark in the hall, and she couldn't tell who was standing out there until he spoke.

"Anton said you refused the tray of food he brought." It was Gun Man. The Anton to whom he referred must be Tiny Crowbar Guy.

There were only two men holding them prisoner, with one gun between them. Gun Man had spoken of a third— that daughter-in-law—but Gina hadn't so much as heard the whisper of a female voice. It was possible he'd mentioned her to make them feel more relaxed. Like, they were going to think everything would be okay because one of their guards was a woman.

As if that made a bit of difference.

Gina wished, for the four thousandth time, that Molly was awake and alert, and ready to run like hell.

"We're not hungry," she lied as Gun Man came farther into the room. She was actually starving. But if *she* were holding two prisoners captive with only one helper and a single gun between then, she'd lace their food with tranquilizers.

"Ah," he said. "But when you do get hungry . . ." He was carrying a bag, the netting strained from the weight of its contents. He began unloading it on the dresser top. It was food—about a dozen cans of varying sizes. He stacked them neatly, and put a small, handcrank can-opener on top with a flourish. "If you should like any of this heated, we of course stand ready—"

"No," Gina said. She stood up, moving so that she blocked his view of Molly. She looked too vulnerable lying there like that, asleep, one smooth shoulder exposed.

"As you wish."

"We wish," Gina said sharply, "to go back to our hotel in Hamburg."

"I'm afraid that's not possible." He actually looked apologetic, but Gina knew better.

Her legs were shaking, but she locked her knees and lifted her chin. "Who are you working for?" she asked. "Whatever they're paying you, we'll pay you more."

He sighed heavily. "I'm afraid it's not that simple."

"It can be," she said, even though she knew in her heart that this man wasn't holding them for the money. This room was too nice, and his clothes—his entire appearance— screamed of wealth.

"You should expect to be here for a while," he said. "Please let me know if you need anything." He started for the door.

What Gina needed was Max.

God only knew where he was, what he was doing—if he even knew she was in danger.

Why would he? The only person who knew that she and Molly were missing was Leslie Pollard, aka David Jones, aka Grady Morant.

All things considered, Leslie-David-Grady was unlikely to turn to the FBI for help.

He would come for them, for Molly. Gina didn't doubt that for a heartbeat. But it wasn't going to be easy for him to get here—wherever here was.

It could take him weeks to find them.

Months.

For now at least, Gina was on her own.

Gun Man was going out the door, but Gina stopped him. "What's your name?"

"Emilio," he told her.

"I'm Molly," she lied. "Look, my friend is really sick. As a show of good faith—"

"I'm afraid that's impossible," he cut her off, already knowing she was going to ask him to let Molly go.

"Why?" Gina persisted. It didn't have anything to do with being selfless and courageous, although if Max were listening in, she knew he'd think otherwise. He'd be wrong. It was all about how fast Molly could run in her current condition. Which was not fast at all. Gina's chances of escaping were slim to none if she had to drag Molly with her.

"She says she's Molly, too," he said. "Which one of you do I believe?"

"Me," Gina said. "She's a liar. I mean, come on. Look at her. She's almost old enough to be my mother. Do you really think that she and Jones—" She corrected herself. "Grady—"

Again, he interrupted. "I think she is a beautiful woman, and that true love laughs in the face of convention," he told her. "I also think that she far more fits the description of this woman of Grady Morant's than you do. I believe, therefore, that you are the liar."

Figures she'd get a combination of Sherlock Holmes and Yoda for a captor.

"Why are you doing this?" Gina asked. "You seem like a decent man—"

"They have my wife," he said, and with a nod, went back out the door, closing it gently behind him.

CHAPTER THIRTEEN

It had been years since Jones had been a passenger on a U.S. military transport plane.

He'd never expected to board one again—at least not without handcuffs and leg shackles.

And never, not in his wildest dreams, had he imagined being asked, after achieving cruising altitude, by a gay FBI agent, no less—what was the world coming to?—whether he wanted cream and sugar in his coffee.

"Black's fine," he said.

As Jules Cassidy vanished toward the galley, Jones watched Max, who was talking on his cell phone on the other side of the cabin. One of the calls he was making was to some civilian security team called Troubleshooters Incorporated. He was hoping to hire some backup.

From the look on his face, the news he was getting wasn't good.

"You okay?" the little gay agent asked as he came back with the coffee in a styrofoam cup, genuine concern in his eyes.

"Yeah," Jones said. "Thanks." If being worried shitless about Molly could be called okay.

Jules sat down in the seat next to him. They had the entire space to themselves—not a lot of troops being moved today. At least not to Indonesia. The fact that they were in the air at all was entirely due to Max's clout. It was possible that one of the phone calls the former FBI bigwig had taken—out on the tarmac, after Jones had managed to completely embarrass himself—had been the U.S. vice president.

"We're going to find her," Jules said. For someone who was not only severely height challenged, but prettier than two-thirds of the women on the planet, Jules Cassidy exuded a christload of confidence. "Wherever she is, we'll get her out. Safely. Gina, too."

"With just the three of us?" Jones wasn't convinced. While he had to admit that there probably never was a good day for a terrorist attack, the timing of this one really sucked. Jules's request for support from SEAL Team Sixteen had already been denied.

"If we have to," Jules said, and he wasn't just bullshitting. He really believed it.

Over across the cabin, Max was still talking on the phone. Lines of weariness etched his face.

"I'm not sure what to call you," Jules continued, pulling Jones's attention back. "You know, what name to use. You have so many."

"You can call me whatever the hell you want." He took the lid off his coffee.

"You just . . . seemed uncomfortable before, when Max called you Morant."

Jones took a sip of coffee. It burned all the way down. "And my discomfort level is of concern to you because . . . ?"

Jules smiled. "It's been a long time since you've been a team player, Grady, hasn't it?"

"You know," he said, "I think I *would* prefer it if you called me Jones."

"Not feeling so much like Grady anymore, huh? That must be weird." Jules's eyes were sympathetic over the top of his coffee cup as he took a sip. "Plus, you were using the name Dave Jones when you first met Molly. I can see how that might make you attached to it. What does *she* call you?"

"None of your fucking business."

Jules sighed. "I know that you're worried—"

"You have no idea," Jones said.

"You're right," Jules told him mildly. "I don't. Except there are people that I love and worry about, too, so I can imagine how hard this is for you. If it's any help, my Aunt Sue is a breast cancer survivor. And about a dozen of the women in my mother's PFLAG chapter. People survive this."

Jones was plenty familiar with different leadership techniques—everything from the fear-of-pain method used by someone like Chai, to Max's holier-than-thou, double-dare method of leadership that Gina had so often talked about. Apparently working for Max Bhagat was a coveted assignment in the Bureau, but an agent had to earn it— even after they were on the man's team. *Let's just see if you're good enough to keep up, and if you are, maybe I'll let you kiss my ring.*

And then there was the touchy-feely leadership techniques that Jules employed. As a medic in the army, Jones had played the "we're all buddies" card many times himself. *How you doing, soldier? You're going to be just fine. Where you from? Looks like you're going to have a visit home if you just hang on a little bit longer . . .*

"Spare me the pep talk," Jones said. "Stop trying to handle me." He realized what he'd said. "I mean that figuratively," he quickly added. "I'm not accusing you of . . ."

Jules just sat back, smiling, and let him flounder.

"If you want, we could go through a list of things not to say," he said after Jones had sputtered to a stop. "*You don't know dick,* for example. If you ever feel the urge to say that, substitute *shit. Shit*'ll work."

Jones laughed despite himself.

Jules's smile was relaxed. Easygoing. He was completely comfortable with himself. It was hard not to like him, or at least be impressed by him.

"Just . . . stop trying to get inside my head, all right?" Jones said.

"FYI, I'm on your side," Jules told him. He glanced at Max, still talking on his phone across the cabin. The "bad cop" to Jules's "good cop"?

Jones put what they were both thinking into words. "As opposed to Max, who seriously wants to damage me. Thanks for, you know, keeping him in line."

Jules laughed again. But his smile faded as he looked at Jones's collection of bruises. "You two really got into it, back in the hotel, huh?" It wasn't really a question, and he didn't wait for Jones to answer it. "He didn't hurt you too badly, did he?"

Jones shook his head. It was actually embarrassing, considering he was so much bigger than Max. Taller, heavier. "I'm fine."

"I can just imagine him, like, throttling you to the point of . . ." He looked more closely at the bruises on Jones's throat. "Did he actually . . . ?"

"I'm fine."

But Jules seemed a little shaken as he gazed over at Max again.

They sat quietly for several minutes, then Jules cleared his throat.

"A few years ago," he said, "Max had me do a low-profile on you."

"I know what you're going to ask next," Jones said, "and the answer is yes, I really did work for Chai."

"Oh," Jules said. "No. There's no question about that. We have plenty of proof tying you to illegal activities—not just through Chai, but a whole parade of Indonesian drug lords, gun runners, and garden-variety thieves."

"Great," Jones said. "That's . . . just great." His ten to twenty years in prison just increased a decade. Or three.

"Any idea which one of them might be behind this kidnapping?" Jules finished the last of his coffee. "Any grudges or vendettas or even just hard feelings—"

"It might be quicker to make a list of the ones who *don't* have hard feelings."

"We've got a long flight. Go crazy." The FBI agent took a notepad from his pocket and handed it to Jones. Somewhere along their route, Jules had changed into jeans and a T-shirt, with a lightweight jacket to conceal his sidearm. He now fished for a pen. "I want to run a cross-check of records—see if anyone on your list comes up in connection with our kidnapper. Who, by the way, we've identified as Emilio Testa. Ring any bells?"

"None." Jones still had Molly's pen. He found it first. Waved it at Jules.

Who said, "I think Max must've stolen mine. Bastard. Anyway. Testa, Emilio Guiseppe. Born in Northern Italy, moved to Sri Lanka when he was in his late twenties. This was back during the Age of Aquarius—he's currently sixty-two. I estimated fifty, so he must be eating right. CIA in Jakarta had a pretty thick file on him. Lots of low-level stuff—fencing stolen goods, conning tourists, black marketeering. He did some informing, too. He'd drop our spooky cousins some breaking news, they'd provide occasional Get Out of Jail Free cards. Oh, here's something you'll like: About a dozen years ago, the authorities suspected Testa was involved in a kidnapping ring, but they didn't want to touch it, because the victims were always returned. That's good news, right? Although maybe not, considering that what he wants in exchange for the women is you. And we don't want to give him that."

Yeah, because they wanted to make sure Jones spent the next fifty years locked up. Terrific.

"Testa's allegedly been out of the game," Jules continued, "living clean—according to my contact—for about ten years now. Which is maybe why you never ran into him. Rumor is he got married, settled down, had kids. Retired from his life of petty crime."

"Not anymore," Jones said, adding the self-appointed "General" Badaruddin to the list he was scribbling, along with Chai's former dungeon master, Ram Subandrio. Last he knew, both were still alive and kicking. Although things changed fast in that part of the world.

"True," Jules agreed. "And what are the big three motivators, you know—to make a person forsake his retirement?" He didn't wait for Jones to respond. "Fear, pleasure, and/or greed."

Across the cabin, Max had ended his phone call. He came over to them now, looking grim. "It's a no-go. Everyone's stretched thin. Trouble-shooters' *receptionist* is gearing up, going out to assist on an op."

Jules nodded as Max sat down across the aisle. "The Jakarta office is overwhelmed, too. So okay. We're on our own. But it could be worse. There's a lot of good news here. Starting with the fact that Gina's smart. She's unlikely to have told the kidnapper that she's intimate friends with an FBI agent. That's going to come as a surprise. We'll locate him, we'll set up surveillance—"

Was this guy for real? Jones interrupted. "Have you been to Indonesia? It's huge—there are hundreds of islands. We're going to need a boat to get from one to another and . . ." He laughed his exasperation. "If this Testa guy doesn't want to be found, we're not going to just . . . locate him."

Jules gazed at him in surprise. "Didn't I tell you? I'm sorry. Apparently 'this Testa guy' wants to be found. My contact has him living on Pulau Meda. It's a small island near Pulau Romang, north of East Timor. Apparently he went on a trip about a week ago, but now he's back. He was spotted at the local market just this morning."

Jesus Christ. Jones was glad he was sitting down.

"We'll need a helo or waterplane to get to Meda from Jakarta, yeah," Jules continued, "but I don't think that's going to be a problem in this economy."

"Testa won't expect you to get from Hamburg to Jakarta quite so quickly," Max told Jones. "Particularly now that it's difficult for civilians to travel. We'll have the element of surprise in our favor."

Jules's phone rang. He stood up. "Excuse me."

Could this really be that simple?

Land in Jakarta, get a island-hopper to this Pulau Meda, make sure Testa didn't have an army guarding Molly and Gina, kick down the door . . .

And escort them safely home.

Jesus, how could it be that easy?

Probably because it couldn't be, wasn't going to be. The proximity to East Timor, where a deadly civil war had been raging for decades, wasn't a particularly good sign.

Jones glanced over at Max, but the man's eyes were closed. Probably not a good time to grill him on the current political situation in East Timor and Indonesia.

He closed his eyes as well, remembering his naiveté on his wedding night, back when he'd believed that the entire rest of his life was going to be blissfully easy.

Back before that visit to the doctor in Nairobi. Back before the cancer hit the fan.

The kicker was that he'd been fully prepared for it to be difficult. Being with Molly again, yet not able to *be* with her.

Not that he cared. He would have crawled, naked on his belly across hot coals, just to be with her. The other kind of being with her. The G-rated one.

And yet, there they suddenly were. Married. By a Catholic priest, no less. His mother would've cried tears of joy.

Mr. Pollard, you may kiss your bride.

Molly had dressed for the occasion in a brightly patterned dress that Sister Double-M clearly disapproved of, despite its long sleeves. It accentuated her curves, brought out the vivid color of her hair.

He'd loved it. Loved her.

But he'd kissed her as Leslie Pollard. Just the lightest, sweetest brushing of his lips across hers, there in a tent filled with flu-ridden nuns.

It wasn't until later that night, after driving with Lucy all the way out to the Jimmo's farm, that he'd truly kissed his bride the way he wanted to kiss her, during that ceremony.

Paul Jimmo was in the hospital in Nairobi—little did they realize then that he would die from his injuries early the next morning—but his mother and sisters welcomed them into their home.

It had been late, and Lucy had been assigned a bed in with the younger of the girls and quickly ushered off to sleep. He and Molly were given what was obviously the main bedroom.

Molly, of course, had wanted to use their unexpected privacy to talk. He'd barely closed the door behind them when she started.

"I want you to swear," she said, "on the Bible, that your marrying me like this doesn't put you into jeopardy."

He laughed at that. "You know, *my* swearing on the Bible is very different from you swearing on it. It just doesn't mean the same thing to me, Mol."

"Then swear on whatever does mean something to you," she countered.

"Whoever," he told her quietly. "And I already have—all those promises I made you tonight? I meant them. I'd never do anything that would put you in danger."

That was when he kissed her.

They had a whole night to share together and a real bed to spend it in. He shouldn't have been in such a hurry, but *damn*, she was fire in his arms.

He fumbled with the zipper that stretched down the back

of her dress. It took him too long to find the pull—he had to stop kissing her and turn her around.

But she moved away from him. Molly had never been shy before, but she went for the lantern, clearly intending to douse the light.

He caught her hand. "You're kidding, right?"

"I've gained weight," she said.

"I haven't noticed. And even if you have . . . so what? I love it. Gain more."

She laughed at that, as he'd hoped she would. "You're crazy."

"No," he said, kissing her again. "Molly, you're even more beautiful than I remembered. And believe me, I spent a lot of time these past few years with my memories. Fantasizing about . . . this. About making love to you. Like this. With the light blazing."

She gazed up at him, tears in her eyes. But she teased him. "Did you have to practice saying that? *Making love . . .* instead of . . . ?"

"No!" he said, as if he really were indignant, but she knew him too well. Amusement was now dancing in her eyes.

"Well . . . yeah, maybe a little," he admitted. He pushed her hair back from her face, winding one long curl around his finger. "I just . . . I don't know. Practiced saying a lot of things. *I came to find you as soon as I could.* And, *Not a day passed that I didn't think of you and long to be with you.*"

The tears were back. "That was a very nice one," she told him.

"I figured I'd have to grovel on my knees so you'd even talk to me, let alone . . ."

"Let you fuck my brains out?" She uttered the words he'd once used to describe that particular act.

Jones laughed. It always cracked him up to hear that

word coming from that mouth. "I'm your husband now. I don't think I'm allowed to do that anymore."

She laughed now, too. "You want to bet?"

This time she kissed him, pulling him back with her until they fell, in a tangle, on the bed.

But again, when he tried to take off her dress, she stopped him.

"I have a confession to make," she said. Her hair was spread out on the white linen of the pillow, her skirt riding up, revealing her long, long legs. "I lied. I really haven't gained that much weight."

Distracted, he kissed the smooth paleness of the inside of her thigh, pushing his way up under her skirt. Goddamn, she smelled good. Her panties were white lace—very pretty. Very fragile and bridelike. But they needed to be gone. He ripped them.

"Hey!" She was laughing. "Are you listening? I'm confessing here."

"No," he said, and kissed her.

It was possible she kept talking to him, but probably not. Even if she did, he didn't hear a word. Except when she started reaching for him, pulling him up and on top of her, begging him, "Please . . ."

She had a condom ready, but it occurred to him that they didn't have to use it. They were married—and what, was he crazy? No way were they having children. Had he completely lost his mind?

She helped him put it on, then reached to guide him inside of her with that goddamn dress and his shirt between them, his pants down around his ankles. Only it didn't matter, because she was clinging to him and he was home, and he was home, and he was home . . .

It wasn't until much, much later, when he was still sprawled partially atop her, as she ran her fingers through his hair and along the fabric stretched across his back, that he realized it was probably a good thing he still had his shirt on.

If he'd taken it off, she would've discovered the jagged scar near his right shoulder blade.

Jones had more than his share of scars on his back— souvenirs from his years in a prison where torture came in all forms and options. But this one was new. Seeing it was going to upset her and . . .

He pushed himself up and looked down at her, because he suddenly realized what her modesty was about.

She had been shot. Because of him. Back in Indonesia.

They'd found a suitcase filled with money. Everyone wanted it. Every two-bit thug, every terrorist wannabe. Together, he and Molly had done the right thing and returned it to its hiding place.

Only he'd gotten scared. He'd pretended to himself that it was greed. All that money—was he really going to leave it lying there? So he took it and ran. But he wasn't running from the thugs who wanted that cash. He was running from Molly. From how good it felt to be with her. From his knowledge that he couldn't protect her, couldn't keep her safe—not as long as Chai was alive.

Of course, the bad guys came looking for the money. And when they didn't find it, they'd shot her.

"Let me see it," he told her now, shifting off of her, helping her sit up in that bed.

Being Molly, she knew exactly what he was talking about. "It's not that bad."

"Then why keep the dress on?" he asked.

She answered honestly. "It's my wedding night, bucko. I'm supposed to have all kinds of wonderful memories of our first time together as man and wife. Forgive me for being shallow, but in my eyes, remembering that I made my bridegroom's manly splendor shrink to the size of a peanut when I took off my wedding dress doesn't qualify as wonderful."

Molly slipped her arms out of her sleeves and . . .

Oh, Jesus.

She tried to distract him by taking off her bra, too. He loved her breasts, so soft and full, and she knew it, but . . .

Jesus Christ.

In some ways, she was right. It wasn't that bad. It looked like what it was—a healed bullet wound in the soft part of her upper arm. Small, slightly puckered entry and exit scars.

But because it looked like what it was—the scars from a bullet wound—it was possible he was going to be sick.

"I'm so sorry," he whispered.

"I am, too," she said. "But it could have been so much worse."

No kidding. The bullet that had torn into the flesh of her arm could have hit her in the chest. Or the throat. Or the head.

If it had, she'd be three years in her grave. And he'd be dead, too. Maybe not physically, but certainly emotionally.

Panic hit him. What if he was wrong about this being easy?

He'd told her with confidence that he believed they were safe, and he still stood by that. The story of Molly Anderson marrying some AAI geek to save the life of a Kenyan girl would make the international rounds. If anything, it would work in his favor—to confirm the rumors of Grady Morant's—aka David Jones's—untimely death.

As long as they didn't draw any extra attention to themselves, they'd be fine. It was true, he'd have to be Leslie Pollard for the rest of his days, but there were certainly worse things.

No, it was the realization that Molly had people who wanted to shoot at her for reasons that had nothing to do with him that was making him crazy now.

Although, maybe, if he stayed very close to her, and never let her out of his sight . . .

She kissed him so sweetly. "Are you okay?"

He pulled back to look her in the eyes. "This is the last time we're doing something like this," he told her. "We get Lucy to Marsabit, we get back to camp, and we spend every free moment figuring out how to have sex silently." Canvas walls being so thin and all . . .

"I think I'm going to need lots of practice," she said, kissing him again.

"I guess the alternative is my learning how to say *who's your daddy?* in Leslie's accent." He tried it. "Who's your daddy?"

Molly laughed. He loved that sound. But she stopped laughing a little too soon. "I can't make you any promises," she said. "About . . . you know. If another girl comes to the camp, asking for help . . ."

"Yeah." Jones was afraid of that. "How about this—you don't leave the camp without me. Never. No exceptions. And if you *do* put yourself in danger, you have to do it knowing that when someone takes a shot at you, Mol, I will do my goddamn best to take that bullet for you."

He'd obviously shaken her with that revelation. Good. Maybe she'd think twice about putting herself in danger.

But she tried to lighten the mood. "Are you going to be one of those really bossy, demanding husbands?"

"The kind who gets upset when his wife gets shot?" he countered. "Yes." He kissed the scar on her arm, kissed her shoulder, her throat, her breasts as she tugged at his shirt, trying to get him to take it off. He helped her, letting her push him back against the bed, letting her straddle him. "The selfish kind who's going to keep her from going back to the States to live—have you really thought about that?" he asked. "Your family's there." In freakin' Iowa. What was she doing in Kenya?

"I have family here now," she told him.

She kissed him then, as if she knew how much those

words meant to him, as if she knew that she'd gone and made him get all choked up.

Big, tough, dangerous guy that he was, he wasn't supposed to get misty eyed and think, "Shit, those are the nicest words I've ever heard." He also wasn't supposed to get all giddy whenever he looked at this woman and thought, "Hey, she's my wife now."

He'd always pretended that his favorite three-word sentence was "Fuck me harder," not "I love you."

Of course, Molly being Molly, she whispered them both into his ear that night.

And Jones knew that the only reason she didn't shout it to the sky was that she was practicing being quiet.

They both were going to need a lot of work with that. A lot of work.

Of course, not all of this could be easy.

PULAU MEDA, INDONESIA
JUNE 24, 2005
PRESENT DAY

Gina ate monkey stew with her fingers, right out of the can, as she watched CNN on Emilio's hostage-ready TV set.

Okay, yeah, it probably wasn't monkey meat, but the label wasn't in English, and she couldn't begin to guess what it said. There was a small cartoon picture on the can—a monkey's head, wearing a jaunty red cap, winking. It was probably only the company's logo, though, not an identifier of what was inside.

Like that mermaid on those cans of tuna.

When she was little, she'd refused to eat tuna salad, afraid she might be chowing on one of Ariel's less-popular sisters.

Her three older brothers had mocked her mercilessly. It was still a joke in the Vitagliano household.

Here, way on the other side of the world from East Meadow, Long Island, Gina would have traded just about anything to be teased by her brothers again.

She wondered what they were thinking, what they were doing. If they'd stayed home from work, due to the terrorist threat.

When Gina had tried turning on the TV, she'd never expected it would actually work. Emilio must've had a satellite dish, because he got HBO and Showtime as well as the various cable news channels.

It had been over a year since she'd seen *Sex and the City,* and one of the channels was having a marathon, but she was glued to the news, volume turned low so as not to disturb Molly, who was still fast asleep.

She flipped back and forth among the news stations, watching all the different anchors make the most of this attempted terrorist attack. The color code had been raised to a shrill orange as al Qaeda's plots to explode dirty bombs in key cities around the world were exposed.

There was still one bomb at large, believed to be somewhere in the San Francisco area. Or maybe it was in D.C.

Coming up: How to survive a dirty bomb attack. Stay tuned for details . . .

Sheesh.

If a terrorist's goal was to terrify, they'd succeeded even without detonating a bomb, thanks to some of these news stations.

In other headlines, there had been three unsuccessful attempts to hijack commercial airliners. All of those flights had landed safely in Nova Scotia after lengthy and quite daring midair rescues—which had involved defusing deadly bombs that had been missed by the luggage screeners.

Gina could imagine what it must've been like to be on one of those planes. Yeah, she could imagine it a little too well.

The entire series of events had started with the explosion

of a bomb in a suburb of Hamburg—all on the very same day she and Molly had been kidnapped and stuffed into a shipping container.

So, wow. She'd been way wrong about that metal container. There *were* worse places on earth that she could have been.

Such as ground zero of that explosion.

Or in seat 24B, say, on any one of those hijacked planes.

And thank God she hadn't taken the time to call her parents, to tell them she was taking that side trip to Germany. If she had, they'd be crazy with worry right now.

The TV was showing footage of downtown Washington, D.C. Men and women wearing jackets clearly labeled FBI in big white letters on the back were part of some sort of perimeter of guards set up around the White House.

Gina leaned closer to the screen, searching for a glimpse of Jules. She didn't expect to see Max—he'd be inside the Situation Room, with the President. Or maybe he'd be in the Pentagon. Safe in some radioactiveproof chamber.

Which meant that he wasn't coming to rescue her.

At least not any time soon.

Sure, she'd been telling herself that right from the start, but from the waves of disappointment that had been rolling over her since she'd first turned on the TV, it was clear that she hadn't truly believed her own pessimistic spin.

She did now.

She was undeniably on her own.

She turned off the TV, and took the monkey stew can into the bathroom to rinse it out before putting it into the trash.

Her shirt, hanging over the shower bar, was mostly dry, but her pants were still damp.

What she wouldn't give for a chance to talk to Max. To hear his voice.

To say to him, *Hey, in case I die, I just want to make sure you know that I never stopped loving you. Right up to the very end.*

Yeah, he'd never let her get past the *in case I die* part. "Stop with the negative thinking. You're not going to die."

But you're not here to save me.

"I didn't save you last time either, did I?" She didn't have to work hard to imagine the strain that came into his voice whenever they talked about the hijacking she'd lived through all those years ago. "I didn't make the scene until the terrorists were dead. Until it was too late."

You were with me. The entire time. Gina truly hadn't felt alone on that airplane. She'd felt Max's presence, right from the moment he'd first made contact over the cockpit radio.

"Yeah, I was about as much use to you as an imaginary friend."

Gina smiled, remembering how mad she used to get when he'd said things like that to her.

Okay, my imaginary friend. What do I do now? She'd already checked the entire room, making sure there were no hidden doors behind the furniture or beneath the wall-to-wall carpeting. The air conditioning vents were too small to use to escape. The walls were solid—painted concrete.

The ceiling looked like plasterboard. She'd tried digging at it with the can opener, but didn't succeed at doing more than getting plaster dust in her hair. She'd need a saw to cut through it, and even then, it would take some serious time. Emilio or Crowbar Guy would notice the hole, and they'd be back to square one.

Or worse. Tied up.

She really didn't want to spend the rest of her life tied up.

Gina sat down on the edge of the tub, closed her eyes, and tried to conjure up Max. What would he tell her, if she had him on the phone or—better yet—in the room with her?

"Find out what they really want. The key to any negotiation is knowing not what the opposition says they want, but what they *really* want." If he were here, he'd be leaning against the counter, a picture of relaxed casualness.

What a joke. Of all the people she'd met in the world, Max was the most tightly wound. He was the most private, too, playing all of his cards close to his vest.

"Sometimes," he'd told her once, when they were talking— but not about the things that truly mattered, like where they were going in their relationship, or how they truly felt, deep in their hearts, "it's an even bigger challenge, because some people don't know what they really want."

He'd told her that he'd negotiated hostage situations where the hostage taker gave him a whole list of demands. Money, a helicopter to escape, a letter explaining his position printed in the newspaper, a pardon from the governor, and on and on. In truth, he'd just wanted someone to listen to him—really listen.

Max had also negotiated some situations where the hostage-taker was intent upon committing suicide by SWAT team. Not that the fool ever would have admitted it.

What Emilio wanted, however, seemed pretty cut and dried.

They have my wife.

Gina needed to find out who *they* were. *Who* had his wife, and why did they want Leslie/Dave/Grady in exchange for her?

Maybe she should sit down with Emilio and tell him about Max. Explain that he was a little tied up right now, but in a week or two he'd come here, and he and his FBI team would find and rescue Emilio's wife and—

And they'd all live happily ever after. Get a clue, her reflection seemed to mock her from the mirror over the sink. As Gina gazed at herself, she had a sudden clear image of her face, swollen and bruised.

The way she'd looked for weeks after being raped and beaten. She'd tried to talk to her captors while she'd been held hostage on that airplane. She'd thought she'd established a rapport with at least one of them. Brother, had she been wrong about that.

She hadn't understood what they'd truly wanted—that death was their prize. That *her* death was a given, even while they talked and joked and laughed with her. That she was already dead in their eyes.

It was a miracle that she'd made it out of there alive. A miracle orchestrated by Max and his entire task force. A miracle he saw as a failure. *His* failure.

They have my wife, Emilio's voice echoed.

Don't believe him, her swollen, bruised image scoffed. *Haven't you learned anything?*

But what if Emilio was telling the truth?

Open your eyes. Look around you. A windowless room. Locks on the outside of the door. This is not something that Emilio threw together for this particular occasion. What does he really want?

"What does he really want?" Max's voice echoed. "Sometimes *he* doesn't even know."

There was only one gun. Two men, one gun. If there ever was a time to fight their way out, it was now.

Don't forget the crowbar, her battered image reminded her. *You've been hit with the butt of a rifle. Can you imagine being hit with a crowbar? Besides, they've treated you decently up to now. If you attack them, you open the door to violence. God knows what they'll do to you. Although Crowbar Guy looked like he had a few ideas.*

No, he did not. It was her fear that had imagined whatever salaciousness she was remembering now. Crowbar Guy's face had been blank.

Yeah, you just keep telling yourself that, her own face mocked her, with its nearly swollen-shut eye. *So what are you going to do? Hit Emilio with the back cover to the toilet tank, smash his head in? Grab his gun, shoot Crowbar Guy . . . You've seen dead bodies, one of them quite re-*

cently, as a matter of fact. Are you really prepared to kill? Look at you. Your hands are shaking just thinking about it. Or maybe you won't get the gun. Maybe you'll miss his head, and he'll have the gun, and he'll shoot you instead. Maybe that's what you really want, because then it'll just be over. Maybe what you want is suicide-by-Emilio—

"No." Gina stood up, turned on the faucet, rinsed her face with cold water.

She was a survivor, not a victim, and certainly not a quitter. She was going to survive this, too. She just had to figure out how.

"What does Emilio really want?" Max's voice said again. "Sometimes he doesn't even know. Sometimes he can't admit it, even to himself . . ."

Gina grabbed a towel, drying her face. *What did you really want?* she would've asked him, if only he were truly standing in front of her. *From me, I mean.*

"What did *you* really want from me?" In a move that was typical Max, he would turn the question around on her.

Honesty, she'd tell him.

"Really."

What's that supposed to mean? Yes, really. I wanted you to talk to me. Really talk. You know, Max, all the years we've known each other, I can count on my fingers the times you told me about yourself—your childhood, for example. And even then? I had to drag it out of you.

Her imaginary Max smiled at her—the way he'd sometimes smile at her. As if he knew the punchline to some cosmic joke, and he was just waiting for her to catch up, catch on. "I am who I am—but apparently I'm not who you want me to be, am I?"

"Oh, blame me," Gina said crossly now. "It's all my fault, isn't it?"

"Isn't it?" He gazed at her with that calm lack of expression. Amazing. Even when he was imaginary, he could infuriate her. But then he dropped the bomb. "You're the one who left me."

"What?" Gina said. "Oh, perfect. Go away. Of course you're going to say that, because you're not really you, you're me." She was just imagining him, so of course her overinflated sense of guilt would play into it.

Yes, she'd left him. Because he shut her out. She'd left him because there was only so long a rational person could continue battering her head against an unmoving wall. She'd left him because she'd wanted more.

Except now all she could think about were the conversations they'd had where she'd asked about Max's family. His sister—plagued with depression, attempted suicide so often the sight of an ambulance in his driveway became almost commonplace. God, how awful must *that* have been to live with? His parents—always angry, always frightened, always fighting. His brilliant grandfather, a mentor and good friend—no longer able to communicate thanks to a devastating stroke. His best friend's brother—dead in Vietnam. His own brother, his one remaining ally, closest to him in age, but never a good student—escaped into the army the minute he turned eighteen, leaving him in a house that was dark with despair.

As for Max? How had he coped? Certainly not merely by watching Elvis movies.

"I got straight As."

She'd always thought it was a dodge, when he'd told her that. A comment that kept him from discussing his real feelings.

And yet . . . "You got straight As because your grades were one of the few things you were able to control, right?" she said to him now.

Imaginary Max gazed back at her impassively. "If that's what you want to think . . ."

"You tried to be perfect," she accused him. "But no one's perfect. And even if you're perfect, there are still things that you can't control. So you fail, and when you do, it drives you nuts, and you beat yourself up and blame yourself—even though it's not your fault."

She was his biggest failure. His words. He'd helped save an entire planeful of people, but he'd failed to keep her safe from that vicious attack. He wouldn't forgive himself for that.

It didn't matter that he'd failed for reasons not under his control. It didn't matter that, according to most people's definitions, he *hadn't* failed. Gina was alive—how could that be a failure?

It didn't make sense.

But it didn't have to. Because his reaction wasn't logical.

It was pure, raw emotion.

Here she'd thought he was hiding his true feelings from her, but all this time, he had been waving them, right in her face.

And no wonder he'd fought his attraction to her for all those years.

Whether or not he was right was moot. It really only mattered what he thought, what he felt. And, according to him, every time he was in the same room as Gina, he had to face the emotional pain of that devastating failure. He had to face that horrible self-blame.

"I can't give you what you want." How many times had Max said those words to her?

What if he'd been right?

What if he couldn't give her what she wanted, because she couldn't give him what *he'd* wanted—a chance to let the pain of his perceived failings fade into the past.

"*You* left *me*," he said now, again—her imaginary friend Max, still so accusatory.

"Yeah, but you didn't come after me," she told him. Told herself. Trying not to cry.

He hadn't come then, and he wasn't going to come now.

A soft knock made her jump. "Are you all right in there?" Molly's voice. She was finally awake.

Gina wiped her eyes then reached right through the place where Imaginary Max had been leaning and opened the bathroom door.

Molly was still pale, but she looked much better. At the very least, she was standing.

"Are *you* all right?" Gina asked her.

"Still a little shaky," Molly admitted. "Do you mind if I take a shower?"

She was too polite to ask who Gina had been talking to. Not when it was obvious with a quick glance around the tiny bathroom that she was quite alone.

"Of course not." Gina pulled their nearly dried clothes down from the bar that held the shower curtain. "Emilio— Gun Guy—brought canned food. After you shower, you need to eat something, and then we need to talk about getting out of here."

CHAPTER
FOURTEEN

PULAU MEDA, INDONESIA
JUNE 24, 2005
PRESENT DAY

Jules could tell that the waiting was driving Max crazy.

Crazier, that is, than usual.

Truth was, his former boss was seriously hurting. Jules had been around long enough to recognize burnout when he saw it. Of course, true to form, Max Bhagat didn't burn out quietly.

No, he was going down with full fireworks.

The fact that he'd gone twelve rounds with Grady Morant was one of those wildly waving red flags.

Even Max himself had noticed it. *I almost lost it,* he'd admitted to Jules.

Dude. Ya think?

And that *almost* was seriously in dispute.

That, plus the refusal to sleep, the hundred-mile stare, the complete transformation from a well-dressed FBI team leader to this ripe-smelling terrorist look-alike . . . True, the jeans and sneaks were Jules's contribution. But the GQ almost-beard and seriously grungy hat hair were all Max.

And yes, over the past few days their access to soap and water had been nonexistent, while their exposure to stifling heat had been unavoidable. But yikes.

Getting from Jakarta to the eastern part of Indonesia had

been a hellish series of hops from island to island via plane. And all legs of the journey had taken far longer than any of them had hoped. The very last segment, a boat ride in the darkness from Kupang to this remote island in the middle of nowhere, had been particularly unbelievable.

Then, of course, there'd been the hike up the mountain through the jungle—also in the pitch blackness of night—to this CIA surveillance post which just so happened to be right in Emilio Testa's neighborhood.

It was a modest corner apartment with windows looking out onto a central open square—which had, from the looks of it, been a marketplace during more prosperous times.

Apparently, back in the 1970s, Meda Island had been quite the tourist spot. It had had plenty of tony resorts as well as vacation houses—luxurious second homes to wealthy Europeans who had lots of frequent-flyer miles to kill. But Meda's proximity to East Timor's civil unrest—going on for decades now—brought new meaning to the travel bureau's promise of a unique, unforgettable vacation, and the richie rich peoples had stopped coming.

The less well-to-do folks who moved in to all those deserted elegant homes didn't have a problem with East Timor's violence going on virtually in their backyard. They were the types whose businesses weren't quite kosher—who not only thrived in the area's new lawlessness, but ramped it up to a whole new level.

This CIA apartment that they were currently occupying had been set up about a year ago to perform surveillance on a local baddie believed to have al Qaeda ties.

He was just one of the happy, friendly people in Mr. Testa's neighborhood, living two houses down from Mr. T himself.

Coincidence, much? God only knew. Although if Testa *did* have terrorist ties, it would make it that much easier for Jules to say yes after they captured him, when Max asked if he could throttle him.

Right now, however, all throttling was on hold. Max may have been seething with impatience, but Jules was glad for this necessary down time. And grateful that they had a home base that included a roof.

"Why don't you take a break, too?" Jules asked Max, sitting next to him, in front of the window. They'd confirmed that Testa's house, where Gina and Molly were being held, had no backdoor or even rear or side windows. Nestled up against the mountainside at the other end of that open square, there was only one way in or out—through the front.

If this was the right apartment. *If* Jules's CIA contact, a man with the sole moniker of Benny, had gotten his info about Emilio Testa right.

Benny had missed their rendezvous at the dock in Jakarta, which was a giant pain in Jules's ass because the agent was supposed to provide them with a CIA smorgasbord of techno-toys. Listening devices. Infrared goggles. A variety of microphones and minicams.

And Benny hadn't answered his cell phone, so they'd boarded the seaplane sans equipment.

Which had sparked another argument between the members of his illustrious, nonofficial, 50 percent criminal, 50 percent psycho dream team.

Max now glanced back into the dimness of the CIA apartment, to where Jones was stretched out on the couch.

Mr. Most Wanted had already spent several hours wandering the neighborhood, getting to know the lay of the land.

"I don't think I could sleep," Max admitted to Jules. "I took a nap on the flight to Kupang . . ."

"For about forty minutes," Jules pointed out. "And FYI, that was hours ago."

Max just shook his head. "I just can't . . ."

He looked out the window at the walls of that building across the dusty open market square, and Jules knew that

Max would have sold his soul to the devil for X-ray vision, for just a glimpse of Gina, alive and unharmed.

The windows were all mirrored, otherwise Max would have been over there, climbing the side of the building like Spiderman, trying to look inside.

Please God, let Gina and Molly still be alive.

"Maybe you should just lie down and at least *try* to—" Rest, he was going to say, again, but Max cut him off.

"No."

Instead of getting him to relax, Jules had incited that jumping muscle in the jaw thing. Damn it. "Sweetie, you're killing me."

He didn't know how to help. If Max were anyone else, Jules would sit with him for a while, looking out at the night, and then start to talk. About nothing too heavy at first. Warming up to get into the hard stuff.

Although, maybe, if he tried that now, the man would either open up—Ha, ha, ha! Riotous laughter. Like *that* would ever happen—or he'd stand up and move outside of talking range, which would put him away from the window with nothing to look at, at which point he might close his eyes for a while.

It was certainly worth a try.

Of course there were other possibilities. Max *could* put Jules into a chokehold until he passed out.

So okay. Start talking. Although why bother with inconsequential chitchat, designed to make Max relax? And weren't those words—*Max* and *relax*—two that had never before been used together in a sentence?

It wasn't going to happen, so it made sense to just jump right in.

Although, what was the best way to tell a friend that the choices he'd made were among the stupidest of all time, and that he was, in short, a complete dumbfuck?

Max was not oblivious to Jules's internal hemming and hawing. "If you have something you need to say, for the ove of God, just say it. Don't sit there making all those weird noises."

What? "What noises? I'm not making weird noises."

"Yeah," Max said. "You are."

"Like what? Like . . . ?" He held out his hands, inviting Max to demonstrate.

"Like . . ." Max sighed heavily. "Like . . ." He made a *sking* sound with his tongue.

Jules laughed. "Those aren't *weird* noises. Weird noises are like, *whup-whup-whup-whup*"—he imitated sounds from a Three Stooges movie—"or *Vrrrrr*."

"Sometimes I really have to work to remind myself that you're one of the Bureau's best agents," Max said. "You have something to say to me, Cassidy, say it. Or shut the fuck up."

"All right," Jules said. "I will." He took a deep breath. Exhaled. "Okay, see, I, well, I love you. Very, very much, and . . ." Where to go from here . . . ?

Except, his plain-spoken words earned him not just a glance but Max's sudden full and complete attention. Which was a little alarming.

But it was the genuine concern in Max's eyes that truly caught Jules off-guard.

Max actually thought . . . Jules laughed his surprise. "Oh! No, not like *that*. I meant it, you know, in a totally platonic, non-gay way."

Jules saw comprehension and relief on Max's face. The man *was* tired if he was letting such basic emotions show.

"Sorry." Max even smiled. "I just . . ." He let out a burst of air. "I mean, talk about making things even more complicated . . ."

It was amazing. Max hadn't recoiled in horror at the idea. His concern had been for Jules, about potentially hurting his tender feelings. And even now, he wasn't trying to turn it all into a bad joke.

And he claimed they weren't friends.

Jules felt his throat tighten. "You can't know," he told his friend quietly, "how much I appreciate your acceptance and respect."

"My father was born in India," Max told him, "in 1930. His mother was white—American. His father was not just Indian, but lower caste. The intolerance he experienced both there and later, even in America, made him a . . . very bitter, very hard, very, very unhappy man." He glanced at Jules again. "I know personality plays into it, and maybe you're just stronger than he was, but . . . People get knocked down all the time. They can either stay there, wallow in it, or . . . do what you've done—what you do. So yeah. I respect you more than *you* know."

Holy shit.

Weeping was probably a bad idea, so Jules grabbed onto the alternative. He made a joke. "I wasn't aware that you even had a father. I mean, rumors going around the office have you arriving via flying saucer—"

"I would prefer not to listen to aimless chatter all night long," Max interrupted him. "So if you've made your point . . . ?"

Ouch.

"Okay," Jules said. "I'm so not going to wallow in that. Because I *do* have a point. See, I said what I said because I thought I'd take the talk-to-an-eight-year-old approach with you. You know, tell you how much I love you and how great you are in part one of the speech—"

"Speech." Max echoed.

"Because part two is heavily loaded with the silent-but-implied 'you are such a freaking idiot.' "

"Ah, Christ," Max muttered.

"So, I love you," Jules said again, "in a totally buddy-movie way, and I just want to say that I also really love working for you, and I hope to God you'll come back so I can work for you again. See, I love the fact that you're my leader not because you were appointed by some suit, but because you earned every square inch of that gorgeous corner office. I love you because you're not just smart, you're open-minded—you're willing to talk to people who have a different point of view, and when they speak, you're willing to listen. Like right now, for instance. You're listening, right?"

"No."

"Liar." Jules kept going. "You know, the fact that so many people would sell their grandmother to become a part of your team is not an accident. Sir, you're beyond special—and your little speech to me before just clinched it. You scare us to death because we're afraid we won't be able to live up to your high standards. But your back is so strong, you always somehow manage to carry us with you even when we falter.

"Some people don't see that; they don't really get you—all they know is they would charge into hell without hesitation if you gave the order to go. But see, what *I* know is that you'd be right there, out in front—they'd have to run to keep up with you. You never flinch. You never hesitate. You never rest."

Max's unflinching gaze never left that house.

"What do you think's going to happen?" Jules asked him quietly, "if you let yourself peel that giant *S* off your shirt and take a nap? If you let yourself spend an hour, an evening, screw it, a whole weekend doing nothing more than breathing and taking enjoyment from living in the moment? What's going to happen, Max, if—after this is over—you give yourself permission to actually enjoy Gina's company? To sit with her arms around you and let yourself be happy. You don't have to be happy forever—just for that short amount of time."

Max didn't say anything.

So Jules went on. "And then maybe you could let yourself be happy again the next weekend. Not too happy," he added quickly. "We wouldn't want that. But just happy in a small way, because this amazing woman is part of your life, because she makes you smile and probably fucks like a dream and yeah—see? You *are* listening. Don't kill me, I was just making sure you hadn't checked out."

Max was giving him that look. "Are you done?"

"Oh, sweetie, we have nowhere to go and hours til dawn. I'm just getting started."

Shit, Max said with his body language. But he didn't stand up and walk away. He just sat there.

Across the street, nothing moved. And then it still didn't move. But once again, Max was back to watching it not move.

Jules let the silence go for an entire minute and a half. "Just in case I didn't make myself clear," he said, "I believe with all my heart that you deserve—completely—whatever happiness you can grab. I don't know what damage your father did to you but—"

"I don't know if I can do that," Max interrupted. "You know, what you said. Just go home from work and . . ."

Holy shit, Max was actually talking. About this. Or at least he had been talking. Jules waited for more, but Max just shook his head.

"You know what happens when you work your ass off?" Jules finally asked, and then answered the question for him. "There's no ass there the next time. So then you have to work off some other vital body part. You have to give yourself time to regrow, recharge. When was the last time you took a vacation? Was it nineteen ninety-one or ninety-two?"

"You know damn well that I took a really long vacation just—"

"No, sir, you did not. Hospitalization and recovery from a near-fatal gunshot wound is *not* a vacation," Jules blasted him. "Didn't you spend any of that time in ICU considering exactly *why* you made that stupid mistake that resulted in a bullet in your chest? Might it have been severe fatigue caused by asslessness, caused by working said ass off too many 24/7's in a row?"

Max sighed. Then nodded. "I know I fucked up. No doubt about that." He was silent for a moment. "I've been doing that a lot lately." He glanced over to where Jones was pretending to sleep, arm up and over his eyes. "I've been playing God too often, too. I don't know, maybe I'm starting to believe my own spin, and it's coming back to bite me."

"Not in the ass," Jules said.

Max smiled but it quickly faded. "Yeah, I think it's got me by the throat." He rubbed his forehead as Jules sat and watched him.

"It's always in my head," Max continued quietly. Almost too quietly for Jules to hear. "All the things I need to do. Everything I'm not doing. I can't leave it behind, like files on my desk, and just go home without it." He glanced at Jules and there was serious pain in his eyes. "How could I ever expect someone like Gina to put up with that?"

Whoa.

Okay. They weren't just talking now, they were *talking*.

"How did you expect Alyssa to put up with it?" Jules countered. "You asked *her* to marry you."

Silence. It stretched on, and Jules was just about to bitch-slap himself for bringing up Alyssa Locke—his friend and former FBI partner and obvious sore spot—when Max spoke.

"She used to put in even longer hours at work than I did," he said. "There were times she made me feel like a slacker."

Jules could relate. Whenever he'd gone in to work, no matter how early, Alyssa was already there. "For a while, I thought she was saving rent by living in her office." He laughed. Then stopped. "All kidding aside, you know that she was using work as a distraction, right? I mean, now that she works in the civilian sector—which she loves doing, by the way—she actually takes vacation days. Weekends. She and Sam just bought a new house—a total fixer-upper. They're going to do all the work themselves."

"That's . . ." Max laughed. "How would Sam put it? Un-fucking-believable."

"She's really happy," Jules said.

Max nodded. "I'm glad. She made the right choice—by not marrying me."

"Because . . . you didn't really love her?"

"Christ, I don't know," Max said. "Does love make you feel like you might need serious medication? Like you're going to explode because you both want this girl and you want to protect her—and it's got to be one or the other and you can't do either and it twists your gut into a knot and makes you act like a freaking crazy man and then everyone loses? *Shit*."

Jules pretended to think about that, his finger on his cheek. "Hmmm. I'm going to take that as a no," he said. "That you didn't really love Alyssa, because when you say *girl*, you're usually talking about Gina, and sweetie, hello, the Gina I know is one hundred percent woman. You need to start your metamorphosis into a real human boy by making yourself a little less nuts, okay? Please stop calling her something she's not."

Max gave him a look that was frosty. "So all I have to do is stop calling Gina a girl, and everything will be fine. Just like that, we live happily ever after."

"You're not going to be happy until you give yourself permission to be happy," Jules argued, "until you accept the fact that you cannot save the lives of everyone in the entire world. People die, Max. Every single day. You can't save them all, but you *can* save some of them. Unless you kill yourself working too hard. Then you end up saving . . . let's see, do the math, carry the no one . . . The number I come up with is zero."

"What if one of the people I want to save is Gina? What

if I want something . . . I don't know, better for her—damn it, that's not the right word—"

But Jules had already jumped on it. "Better than what?" He made a thoroughly disgusted noise. "Better than sharing her life with a man who's, in his own words, 'freaking crazy' about her? A man who's earned the respect and admiration of every single person he's ever worked with—including three different U.S. presidents? A man who manages to be sexy even when he smells bad? Max, come on, how much better do you need to be? IMO, you need some serious, *serious* therapy."

"No," Max said. "Not . . . I meant *different*. Less . . . I don't know, hard. Less . . ." He closed his eyes. Exhaled. "I imagine the future and I see myself hurting her. And . . . God, I see her hurting me. It's unavoidable. But I can't stay away from her. I'm going to go in there—" he gestured to the still-silent house across the square "—and I'm going to get her out, and I'm going to bring her home and I'm never going to let her go. Until I have to. Until the inevitable heartbreak."

Okay. Jules sat in silence for a good long time. "Well," he finally said. "Way to go, Mr. Romantic. And they lived pathetically and disgruntledly not-so-forever after."

The muscle was jumping again in Max's jaw. "Let's just stop talking about this, all right? It's not helping."

Jules let the quiet of the night weave its way around them for three whole minutes this time.

"You know, I spent years," he finally broke the silence, because damn it, maybe it would help if Max heard this, "in this really . . . toxic relationship with a man named Adam who just . . . He kept ripping my heart out of my chest and . . . No. I kept *letting* him rip my heart out. I just kept taking him back.

"Thing is, I got to the point where I knew he was going to hurt me again. I mean, I did learn, you know. I just didn't *learn*. And I made the same mistake over and over, because there was this undaunted part of me, this voice in my head that just didn't accept the reality—like, 'This time, it'll be different. This time, he'll really love me the way I want to be loved.'

"Eventually I reached this point where I had to silence that eternally optimistic, six-year-old, there-is-a-Santa part of me. I had to lock it away, and I did. And once I did, I could walk away from Adam. Screw it, I found out I could walk away from . . . anyone, if I needed to. Which didn't mean I didn't grieve the loss of that relationship, because shit, it sucked, and I did."

Jules was silent for a moment, thinking about those movie billboards, those pictures on the sides of all those buses, everywhere he went. But then he said, "Except, one day, when I woke up, I realized I was grieving more for the loss of my inner child. I didn't like the person I was becoming without that happy little voice—too grim, you know?" Too much like Max. He didn't say it, but he knew Max got the message.

"So I spent some serious time thinking about what my six-year-old self really wanted," Jules continued quietly. "And I discovered that it wasn't Adam in particular. It wasn't Robin, either—this other . . . Never mind. That's not . . ." He shook his head. "What I'm saying is that I realized I didn't want Adam—I wanted my *ideal* of Adam. What I wanted was someone *like* the Adam that I'd imagined. I wanted someone to love who would love me in return, according to *my* definition of love and respect."

Max sighed. "Do you ever just sit? Quietly? Without talking?"

"You want me to shut up before I even get to the actual point of the story?" Jules asked.

"Oh, there's a point? In that case—"

"Screw you. Sir."

"—carry on."

"The point is," Jules said, "that I was able to take that

clamoring, make some adjustments, and set my inner six-year-old free again."

Max obviously didn't get it.

"Instead of turning myself into some dark, grim, unhappy person," Jules explained, "with no sense of hope—oh, say, like your father—I changed the message. It's still a bona fide six-year-old war cry: Some day my prince will come. Which has certain problems, I know. I mean, hello. Looking for perfection much?

"Anyway. I'm a work in progress. But I'm telling you this because I know that somewhere inside of you, in some long-forgotten spider hole, is your inner hopeful child. You need to find him, sweetie. And you need to let him come back out to play. You don't need to spend a lot of time psycho-analyzing what it was—your father?—that made you lock up that Santa-believing part of you, if you don't want to. Although, it couldn't hurt. I'm a big fan of self-reflection and self-knowledge. But even if you don't, you can still give that part of you a new message: 'I'm allowed to be happy. I'm allowed to let Gina love me.' And maybe then, after we kick down those doors tomorrow, you *can* take her home without all that inevitable doom bullshit."

Max nodded. "Yeah," he said. "Except . . . I think Gina's pregnant."

What?

"No, she couldn't be," Jules said. "She wasn't seeing anyone. I mean, aside from the crush it sounded like she had on Leslie—Jones—when she first met him, and you *so* don't want to hear about that . . . Seriously though, I got a letter from her, just a month ago. She would've told me. And you know I would've told you."

"Yeah, apparently she was," Max told him. "A Kenyan. Paul Jimmo. He was killed a few months ago, in a fight over water rights."

"No," Jules said, relieved. "You're wrong. She mentioned him in one of her letters. He owned a farm about a hundred miles north of the camp. Where he lived with his wife and kids. Sweetie, he was married."

Max stared at him.

"Apparently, he asked Gina to be his second wife," Jules told him. "For a while it was kind of a running joke between them, because, well, *Gina*. Not exactly the co-wife type. And even if she liked him . . . Which she did at first, but then he started to get a little too persistent, which freaked her out . . . But even if, God, even if she *loved* him, which she didn't, she wouldn't have messed with a married man. Not Gina. You know that as well as I do."

The look on Max's face, as he took in that news, was terrible.

And Jules knew what he was thinking. If Gina hadn't been seeing someone . . .

"How do you know she's pregnant?" Jules asked.

Max took a piece of paper from his pocket, unfolded it. Handed it to him.

It was actually two pieces of paper. Some kind of letter and what looked like a receipt. Jules quickly read them both. "Did you call—"

"Yeah," Max said. "They wouldn't talk to me. I didn't have time to go through the right channels. I don't even know Germany's privacy laws—if there are even channels to go through."

"This is just a form letter," Jules pointed out. "And as for the test, maybe she went in for a checkup. Women are supposed to do that once a year, right? She'd been in Kenya, and suddenly here she was going to this health clinic with Molly, so she figured, what the heck. Maybe this place gives pregnancy tests as part of their regular annual exam."

"Yeah," Max said. "Maybe."

He didn't sound convinced.

"Okay. Let's run with the worst-case scenario. She *is* pregnant. I know it's not like her to have a one-night stand, but . . ." Jules said, but then stopped. His words were meant to help, but, *Hey, good news—the woman you love may have gotten knocked up from a night of casual sex with a stranger* were not going to provide a whole hell of a lot of comfort.

It didn't matter that the idea was less awful than the terrible alternative—that Paul Jimmo had continued to pressure Gina. And he hadn't taken no for an answer.

Which was obviously what Max was thinking, considering the way he was working to grind down his few remaining back teeth.

"So," Jules said. "Looks like our little talk didn't exactly succeed at putting you in a better place."

It was clear, when Max didn't respond, that he was concentrating on not leaping through the window and flying—using his rage as a form of propulsion—across the street and blasting a body-shaped hole in the wall of that building where Gina and Molly were being held prisoner—please, heavenly father, let them be in there.

And Jules knew that if it turned out that Paul Jimmo had so much as touched Gina without her consent, Max would find his grave, dig up his body, bring him back to life, and then kill the son of a bitch all over again.

When Molly came out of the bathroom, Gina was taking apart the metal bed-frame, unfastening the nuts and bolts with her bare fingers.

"We'll only have one chance for this," she said, handing Molly an ungainly length of metal, complete with bed leg and little wheel on the end. It was L-shaped the long way, designed to hold the bed's box spring, which made it hard to grip comfortably. "We have to be ready for 'em. You should definitely put your clothes on. They're still damp, but we have to be prepared to run."

"These people have guns," Molly pointed out. She tried to hold the piece of metal up like a baseball bat, over her shoulder, ready to swing. It was heavy, but was it really heavy enough to knock a grown man unconscious?

"Gun, singular," Gina said.

"We don't know that." The mattress was leaning up against the wall, so Molly pulled out one of the pair of chairs that were tucked under a small table, over in the corner.

"Last time Emilio came in here, his gun was nowhere in sight. You know, he may not have ammunition," Gina, who had never had the not-very-fun experience of being shot by a gun, informed her. "He never fired his weapon, even when we were being shot at."

"Or he might have lots and lots of ammunition." Molly sank down into the chair, still wobbly-legged. Truth was, he'd only need two bullets to end three lives.

"But maybe not." Gina was determined. "If he doesn't, it's only our fear holding us here."

"That and the angry little man in the hall with the crowbar," Molly reminded her.

Gina hesitated. "You thought he was angry?"

"Either that or badly constipated." While she was showering—carefully, and only small portions of herself at a time, thanks to that biopsy—Gina had filled her in on both the world events and the more local newsflash that the mysterious "they" who wanted Grady Morant had kidnapped Emilio's wife, creating a full-fledged chain of pain.

"Get dressed," Gina ordered her again, definitely one-track. "Seriously, Mol, get your sneakers on, too. As soon as you're ready, I'm going to open that door. For all we know, Crowbar Guy isn't even out there anymore. If he is . . ." She hefted her own length of metal, complete with castor.

"I'm not sure how much help I'm going to be," Molly told her as she pulled on her damp pants. "I'm still really dizzy. And queasy. And bashing people over the head isn't really my thing."

"You should have something to eat." Gina started for the cans of food.

Oh, urp. "No, actually, please, I shouldn't," Molly said.

"We better take it with us," Gina decided. She took one of the pillowcases off the bed, loaded the canned goods inside. "I know you don't like the idea of hurting anyone, but the alternatives—"

"I know what the alternatives are," Molly told her friend as she tied the laces to her sneakers. Jones—dead. Or worse. The two of them, including her baby—dead. Or worse. "And I'll bash if I have to. You better believe it. What I meant was I'm probably not very good at it." She sat down again. "You still haven't convinced me, though, that we stand a prayer of a chance against that gun."

"Shhh!" Gina said, holding up her hand.

There were voices in the hallway. Oh, Lord.

"We should run for the garage—it was straight down the hall, to the left," Gina instructed her, moving closer to the door, metal bed frame segment held up over her head, in prime bashing position.

Oh, Lord.

"Honey, please can't we try something else first?" Molly said as quickly as possible, moving to back her up, but not quite sure where to stand. The idea was to bash the person coming through that door, not Gina. And, likewise, not get bashed by Gina in return. "Like, pretending to be really sick? Pretending one of us needs to go to the hospital? Maybe Emilio'll—"

"He's not just going to let us go," Gina said. "You're crazy if you think—"

"We should talk to him at least," Molly said.

"Shhh," Gina said again.

What was that noise out in the hall? It sounded like some kind of animal or . . .

A very young child?

The door opened and a little boy—he couldn't have been more than two years old—stood teetering on the threshold.

"Don't!" Molly shouted at Gina.

But Gina was not about to hit a toddler. In fact, she stepped in front of Molly, ready to block her blow.

Emilio appeared then. He took one look at them—Molly still had that piece of metal raised over her head—and scooped the child into his arms.

Although it was hard to tell if his goal was to protect the boy or use him as a shield.

"I see you've been busy," he said to them in his charming accent. "May I introduce to you my grandson, Danjuma? I thank you both most humbly for not hurting him."

CHAPTER
FIFTEEN

With the dawn came movement out on the street.

Max sat back from the window and watched as people hurried to work or the market. Children came out to play in the dusty square.

When Jules's cell phone rang, Grady Morant—who wanted to be called Jones—got to his feet.

Like most operators Max had known through the years, Jones could go from asleep to completely alert in a heartbeat.

Of course, Max never had to worry about that. His solution was simply never to sleep.

At least he hadn't slept since Gina had left.

"We got another e-mail," Jules announced, phone to his ear. "It's Yashi," he told Max. "Joe Hirabayashi," he told Jones. "Teammate back in D.C." Back to Max. "I've had him watching that e-mail account, trying to trace . . . Yeah, Yash, go ahead. Wait, wait—you're breaking up . . ." He turned, walking closer to the window. "That's better. Go."

Max and Jones were left standing there, staring at each other.

"You really should get some rest," Jones said. "I heard you go out last night. After I got back. Did you sleep at all?"

Max just gazed at him. "It's probably better if you limit what you say over the next few days to *yes, sir* and *no, sir.*"

"Fuck off." Jones's laughter was closer to bared teeth

than true amusement. "You think you know me, asshole?" He stepped closer, lowered his voice, obviously aware that Jules was constantly monitoring the pair of them. "You think you have any idea who I am, and what I'm capable of?"

Max didn't move. "You're capable of putting two innocent women in danger, simply by association. What's your next stupid human trick going to be?"

"I'm ready to go," Jones said. "Right now. I'm rested—I'm ready to go in there and get them out. I came to you for help, but since you obviously can't deliver, I'm just going to—"

"That's a brilliant plan." Max blocked his path. "Walk across the street, kick down the door and . . . What? How do you get off this island?"

"There's an airstrip, about three miles up the road," Jones told him. "I guess you didn't make it that far. Lot of money on this island, in case you haven't noticed that either."

"So you help yourself to a plane and go . . . where?" Max asked.

"Does it really matter?"

"Considering your wife needs treatment for her cancer . . . You might want to work that little detail in somewhere."

Jones bristled. "You think I've forgotten that for one second?"

"I think you've forgotten," Max told him, "that whoever wants to find you had enough money to transport Gina and Molly here—without their passports—all the way from Germany. You really think they're not going to invest, heavily, in tracking you down? Dream on."

"There are ways to keep her safe," Jones said. "There's always a way."

"Like, what? Like taking her to the American Embassy? There's one in Dili," Max told him. "She'll be safe there—

except you won't. So what'll you do? Drop her off? Great, she'll be safe while she's within their walls. But the second she steps out of that building—like, to get into a car to be driven to the airport for a flight home?—she's a target again. How are you going to keep her safe then? You going to trust her life to some embassy guards? Maybe a few extra nineteen-year-old Marines?"

"So I won't take her to the embassy," Jones said.

"Ah. You'd rather have her be at risk—"

"You goddamn know I didn't want any of this to happen, you know I don't want her to be at risk. But guess what? She is. She would have been, sitting at home in Iowa with her mother. I did everything right," Jones told him. "I made goddamn sure she was safe before I went to Kenya. I waited *years* so she'd be safe. But shit, my mistake—I didn't factor in the possibility of her getting sick. And then she fucking wouldn't go to Iowa without me. She refused to leave—and believe me, I tried everything. I told her I was going to disappear, because then she'd be free to go, but she said she'd wait there for me—at the camp. That if I wanted to ensure that she *didn't* get state-of-the-art medical treatment, that was the way to do it and . . ."

Jones's anger temporarily spent, the emotion in his eyes made him look desperate and vulnerable. "I love her," he told Max quietly. "I took a gamble, trusting Kraus. If I could, I'd go back and do it over, differently. The story of my life, you know?"

Max did know.

Years ago, back when Jones was Grady Morant, his unit had gotten ambushed in an ongoing silent war that the United States was waging against a powerful Southeast Asian druglord.

His entire team had been wiped out. At least that was what the official reports Max had seen all said.

Apparently Morant's body had been found. Or—more

accurately—some body parts had been recovered along with his dog tags. But there wasn't enough of him left to verify his identity via fingerprints or dental records.

Rumors started, as rumors tended to do with the lack of identifiable physical remains for a soldier listed as KIA, but they were all written off as wishful thinking.

When the rumors persisted, rumors of an American being moved from prison to prison, there'd been a half-hearted investigation. It had cost too much time and too much money though, and eventually had been dropped. Results: inconclusive.

It wasn't until recently, until DNA testing was established, that proof came to light that the body buried in Grady Morant's grave was not, in fact, Grady Morant.

It was about that same time that stories of Chai's new first lieutenant, allegedly an American and former Special Forces soldier, started circulating.

Grady Morant hadn't died in that ambush. Instead, he'd spent years in a hellhole of a prison in Southeast Asia, tortured by his captors. Praying that someone would find him, that someone would come for him and bring him back home.

A few years ago, Max had felt sorry for Morant. It was clear, after meeting him, that those years in prison had been very real. He hadn't sold out his unit, as everyone had assumed after hearing he was working for Chai. He wasn't a deserter—on the contrary, his country had deserted him.

Life sucked.

But in Max's eyes, all the bad shit in the world didn't excuse what Morant did when the very drug lord he'd been fighting had finally come to his rescue and set him free.

Max would've rather died. He would've rather rotted in that prison than go to work for the enemy.

And here this piece of shit loser—at the very least a liar, smuggler, and thief—had found happiness. He'd found love. Molly Anderson had actually married the son of a bitch.

Okay, yeah, sure—life had thrown another suckbomb at them. But Max had absolutely no doubt whatsoever—once they got Gina and Molly safely home—that Molly would win her battle with cancer and live a long happy life.

As Mrs. Loser Morant or Pollard or Jones or Smith or whatever new alias he picked out for himself.

Shit, with his luck, Jones would probably go to trial for his various crimes, and get off on some technicality.

While Max lived on in misery.

While somewhere, hundreds of miles away from his personal hell, Gina raised a dead man's baby.

"Life doesn't give do-overs," Max told Jones now.

"No," the man agreed. "Just second chances."

"Okay," Jules said, coming back to join them, snapping his phone shut. "Here's the deal. Our guy sent another e-mail. He wants a phone number so he can contact us and give us further instructions. Yashi's setting up a number that Emilio won't be able to trace back to us. The call will get forwarded to my cell." He looked at Max. "I know you want to speak to Gina, but there's no way to ask for that. We want the kidnapper thinking Jones is alone. And we don't want to make too many demands—not at this point. After we get Testa on the phone—"

"I know," Max said.

"I *did* ask Yash to make sure the last four digits of the fictional number is the same as your personal cell phone. I wanted Gina to know—if she somehow sees it—that we're out here. It's a long shot, but . . ." Jules shrugged.

"Thank you," Max said.

"Yashi's also calling the Jakarta CIA office," Jules reported. "See if we can't track down ol' Benny. Either way, I'm trying to get that surveillance equipment."

"How about military assistance?" Jones asked.

Jules shook his head. "Everyone in this area's on standby.

Terrorist threat level's still high, and our case continues to be mega-low priority. I know this is driving you nuts, sweetie, but we've just got to sit and wait."

Molly pretended to faint.

Gina wanted to applaud, it was done with such perfect timing, but Emilio didn't leap to assist her. Instead, his squirming grandson still in his arms, he stepped back, well out of whacking range, barking out a command in what sounded like Italian.

Tiny Angry Crowbar Guy came into the room. He stopped short at the sight of the Molly doing her Swan Lake finale imitation. But then he quickly hopped to it, helping Gina put the mattress back down on the floor. The entire time, however, he eyed her makeshift weapon, now leaning against the wall.

As Gina rearranged the sheets and blankets, the vertically challenged man showed his stuff by effortlessly lifting Molly into his arms and carrying her to the bed.

Molly secured her spot in the race for the Best Actress Oscar by making the journey without shrieking or even opening her eyes.

In fact, it wasn't until she was on the bed, Gina leaning over her, that her eyelids even started to flutter.

Bravo.

Emilio was again shouting down the hall, and a dark-haired woman appeared, head down and shy, handing him several bottles of water before she again vanished.

"She needs to go to the hospital," Gina told Emilio, because they might as well try Molly's idea now that fighting their way out was no longer an option.

He gave the bottles of water to Crowbar Guy, who angrily held them out to Gina. She took them, mostly so that he wouldn't end up throwing them at her.

God, he scared her.

"As you can see," Emilio told her, "these, like the food, are sealed."

Gina opened one bottle, helped Molly sit up, helped her take a sip.

"She's burning up," she lied to Emilio, although, damn, Molly's skin did feel warm. As a matter of fact, she was showing signs of dehydration. "Are you okay?" she asked Molly, suddenly realizing that her entire Meryl Streep-worthy performance hadn't been a performance at all.

Molly was pulling away from the water with a grimace, pushing away Gina's hand. "Bathroom," she said, and Gina helped her up and into the tiny tiled room as quickly as humanly possible.

Urp. She closed the door on Molly's intimate conversation with the toilet, letting her very real concern for her friend color her voice. "She's been doing this for hours." Another lie, but why not? "She's severely dehydrated, with a high fever. Last time she was this sick, she started having seizures."

Emilio looked shaken at that news, although his dismay was probably also an act.

"She needs to go to the hospital," Gina said again.

Emilio shook his head. "That's impossible."

"Are you really prepared for her to die?"

From the bathroom came the sound of running water. Gina opened the door a crack, peeked in. Molly was at the sink, splashing water onto her face. Now was not the time for her to emerge, saying what she usually said after her rare bouts of morning sickness, "Wow, I feel *so* much better now."

Gina took the now-open bottle of water with her as she slipped into the bathroom. No point leaving it out there for them to monkey with.

"I'm going to help you get back out there, and into bed," she whispered to Molly. "I told them you need a hospital, so act like it, okay?"

Molly dried her face with a towel. "I don't want them to know that I'm pregnant," she whispered back.

"I know," Gina said. "I told him you were running a fever. Make it look good." She opened the door as Molly leaned on her.

Emilio was still out there, his grandson now on the floor, playing with their extra cans of food. The man moved, so that he was standing between them and the child as Gina helped Molly back into bed.

Like what? Gina was going to grab the little boy and threaten to break his neck?

God, what an awful idea. Would she do it—if it meant getting her freedom? What a twist—the hostage taking a hostage. She could demand Emilio surrender his gun. And once they had that gun . . .

Except what if he called her bluff? There was no way she would ever actually hurt a helpless little child, and surely Emilio would know that just by looking into her eyes.

People who take hostages, Max had told her once, had to be prepared to kill them. They had to be willing to end at least one human life. If they weren't, the negotiators would sense it, and they'd send in the takedown teams. They'd just kick in the doors and end the standoff without any bloodshed.

At least, without any innocent bloodshed.

"Your grandson is beautiful," Molly told Emilio as Gina handed her the bottle of water and opened a second one. "His name is . . . Danjuma?"

The boy looked up at his name, then laughed as one of the cans rolled away. He crawled after it.

"The resilience of children amazes me," Emilio murmured as he, too, watched the little boy. "Just last month, his father—my son—was executed, right in front of him."

Oh, God.

"I'm so sorry," Molly said.

"His mother," Emilio continued. "My daughter-in-law— you met her a few moments ago—was certain they would kill him, too. They do that, sometimes. Kill children, particularly our boys, so they don't grow up and become soldiers for the opposition. Instead, he was spared. Instead, he was thrown into prison. All three of them were—my wife was with them, you see. She watched her only son die."

Molly was buying this story, completely. She had tears in her eyes. Gina wasn't sure why he was telling them this. Was it to win their sympathy? To make them understand why they were here, as his hostages?

"Who are *they*?" she asked.

"Bad men," was his reply. "Greedy men, who stand to lose a great deal, should order and law come to East Timor."

"Do they have names?" she persisted.

"Their names would mean nothing to you," he said. "To me, and to my neighbors, they are cause to tremble in fear." He turned back to Molly—obviously he'd identified her as a better audience for his dramatic tale. "In prison, my grandson was separated from his mother for quite a few days. Imelda—Danjuma's mother—was frantic. When at last they put the boy back into her arms, she was ready to do their bidding." He glanced back at the door, moving closer and lowering his voice so that his daughter-in-law wouldn't overhear.

Assuming she could even speak English.

Molly was clutching Gina's hand, quite obviously believing every awful word of this story.

All Gina could think was, where was Emilio's gun right now, and how could she gain possession of it?

Was his story true? Maybe it was.

If there was one thing Gina had learned in life, it was that people were capable of doing terrible, atrocious things to each other.

She thought of Narari, back in Kenya, dead at age thirteen. And Lucy, who she'd helped to save, whose older sister was still back there, nearing her baby's delivery date—knowing that when her child was born, she'd have to be cut again.

She thought about the terrorist she'd nicknamed Bob, who had told her *his* story while he held her hostage on that airplane. She'd been sympathetic—his life had been one struggle after another. She'd seen him as a person, instead of a hijacker with a gun.

He'd seen her only as a means to a bloody end.

"I don't know all that they did to Imelda," Emilio continued, his voice quieter but much harder now. "She did tell me that, before she left, with Danjuma in her arms, they made her thank them for killing her husband. My son." His voice broke. "Forgive me."

"For turning around and kidnapping us?" Gina said. "No problem—we'll forgive you—just let us go."

But Molly was murmuring, "That's terrible."

"They told her," Emilio said, tears in his eyes, "to find me, and tell me that they had Sumaiya. My wife. If I wanted to see her again, I had to . . ." He gestured to the room around them. "I haven't used this room in over ten years, well, not for what it was intended. Yes, at one time, I made quite a fortune dealing in . . . others' misfortune, it's true. But that was years ago. My . . . skills have dulled. I knew it would be easier to lead Grady Morant here—have him come to me—"

Molly interrupted him. "There has to be another way to get your wife out of that prison." She turned to Gina. "You could call—"

Gina squeezed her fingers, hard, also warning her with her eyes not to say Max's name, or to mention his affiliation with the FBI. She spoke loudly over Molly, just in case she didn't get it. "My brother? He's a police officer in New Jersey," she lied to Emilio. "Maybe he knows somebody in,

I don't know, the FBI or CIA or something—someone who could help."

Molly got it. Ix-nay on entioning-may Ax-may.

Emilio, meanwhile, was sadly shaking his head. "It's too late."

Gina knew that that was her optimistic friend's least favorite sentence. Molly sat up again. "It's never too late."

"Sumaiya is dead," Emilio told them. "The message came this morning, from a contact within the prison. Her body was buried in a mass grave last week. I suspected as much—my repeated requests demanding proof of life—you know, as we did with the television in the warehouse? They have all been ignored."

He turned to Gina, who was trying to make sense of this latest twist in his tale. "I can see you are not impressed. Why should you believe anything I tell you? My fortune came from ransom money. I held you at gunpoint and packed you into a shipping crate, took you halfway around the world against your will. I can assure you until I drop dead from exertion that I have nothing against you, that I didn't wish to harm you, that my singleminded goal was to save the woman I love."

If he had started to cry, Gina would have remained skeptical, but he didn't. Instead, both his voice and eyes got hard. Bitter. Angry.

"Since she's dead, my goal has changed. The last thing I wish to do is give them what they want. I'm not sure how to protect you, since my enemy is here, all around us—everywhere on this island, on neighboring islands, too. I'd take you to the hospital in Dili, but I fear you'll be less safe there. I *do* have a friend who is a doctor, though. My new plan, if you'll agree, is to take you to his home where you'll receive the care you need. You'll be safe there."

"Why not take us to the American Embassy?" Gina was on her feet. Could this really be happening? Was he really going to just . . . let them go?

"There is none on this small island. And even if there were . . ." He laughed. "By helping you, I don't want to harm myself. Imelda, Danjuma, and I will have to leave our home forever, but we won't find sanctuary in your America, I can guarantee you that." He shook his head. "After I drop you at my doctor friend's, you may be able to convince him to fly you to the nearest embassy. He has a plane, although his pilot could be too easily bought. You see, it won't take long for my enemies to realize I'm gone. At which point there'll be an extensive search for the two of you."

He was fumbling in his pocket for something. His gun? Gina took a step back as he pulled out . . . a cell phone? "Here," he said, holding it out to her.

She opened it, hardly daring to believe . . . But the icons implied that both its battery and reception were strong.

He was getting something else of out his pocket now, too. A piece of paper. "My contacts in Jakarta have spotted Morant. He's here in Indonesia. Call him." He handed that to her, too.

It was . . . a printed e-mail? With a phone number on it. *I await your further communication. G.M.*

Although, hang on!

This was a phone number that Gina knew—at least in part—by heart.

The last four digits were the same as Max's number. She had to sit down.

Holy crap, Max was here, too.

The entire rest of the world was falling apart, and Max was here, trying to find her.

"Call him," Emilio said again. "Tell him I'll be taking you to the residence of Dr. Olhan Katip, on the north side of this island, Pulau Meda. We are near Pulau Wetar. Katip has a gated estate—"

He may have kept talking.

But Gina had stopped listening. She stood up and moved out of range as Molly tried to snatch both the phone and the paper from her.

Heart pounding, Gina dialed the phone, praying that life couldn't be so cruel as to make that number a mere coincidence.

At about ten A.M., Jules's cell phone rang again.

Jones was rummaging in the kitchen, searching among the well-stocked shelves for something to eat that was loaded with carbs.

He settled on one of the three cans of Beef-a-Roni that were front and center.

Which was quite a luxury—his not having to take a can from the long-forgotten back of the shelf in order to keep the apartment's owners from realizing they'd had unauthorized guests.

Jules had told him that this place was used by the CIA as part of an ongoing investigation into terrorist activity.

The terrorist in question lived two houses down from their kidnapping suspect.

What a lucky coincidence. Or it would be if Jones believed in either luck or coincidences.

He knew how things worked out here on these isolated little islands. Chances were if a suspected terrorist had moved in practically next door to Emilio Testa, there was a good reason for it.

Whatever the connection, this place was a godsend. It had kept them dry during the predawn rain showers. Without this apartment, they'd have been out on that roof last night, all night.

Of course, that was still an option for tonight—should they have to wait that long to kick down Emilio Testa's door.

Because today's fucking had started with news from

Jakarta that Benny, Jules's CIA contact, had turned up extremely dead.

Jules and Max were in the middle of a discussion about whether they should stay here or leave. Whether Benny's death had anything to do with them. And whether Jules should go all the way back to Jakarta to get that surveillance equipment they wanted.

But now Jules looked at his ringing phone. "Okay," he said, loudly enough to include Jones in the conversation. "This isn't Yashi—it's a number I don't recognize. It could be our man."

Jones came out of the kitchen. "I should answer it, then."

"I'm putting it on speaker," Jules agreed. "Remember, he might have his phone on speaker, too."

Jones felt adrenaline surge through him, and he forced himself to have faith in Jules's promise that Testa wouldn't be able to locate them via satellite, thanks to Yashi back in D.C. He forced himself to focus. It was easy to stop listening while amped up. It was easy to hear only what you wanted to hear, or misunderstand even the simplest of communications.

But Jones's mental prep didn't prepare him for what he heard after Jules answered the call, after he himself grunted an identifier. "Morant." He couldn't remember the last time he'd introduced himself that way.

"Hey. It's me." Holy Jesus. It was Gina.

Across the room, Max was still keeping an eye on Testa's house—where no one had entered or exited since they'd started watching. But now, he turned—signaling for Jules to mute the phone—so that Gina, or anyone else listening, wouldn't be able to hear him speak.

The relief Max must've been feeling had to be staggering—to actually hear Gina's voice and know she was still alive, at least for now. But as Jules hit the mute, it was clear to

Jones that Max's focus was on making sure Molly was alive, too—without jeopardizing the women's safety.

"She didn't say 'It's Gina.' " Max's words were rapid-fire. "She said, 'It's me.' Don't call her by name, don't talk about Molly by name, either. Testa may not know who's who, and we want to keep it that way. Ask her: Are you okay, are you *both* okay?"

At Max's nod, Jules unmuted the phone, and Jones said exactly that.

"Yes," Gina said, and Jones started breathing again. *Thank you, God.* He had to sit down, the relief was so intense. How did Max manage to stay standing?

"We're both fine," she continued. "Except Molly's, well, she's a little dehydrated."

So much for Max's theory about not naming names.

"We both are," Gina kept going. "And it's never fun to be a hostage—even if it's only one man running around with a little handgun."

Jules muted the phone, shaking his head in admiration. "She just told us—"

"Yeah," Max cut him off, because Gina was still talking.

"I mean, Imelda's pretty shy, and her son, Danjuma's only a two-year-old, but . . . Crowbar Guy's pretty scary. Of course, there could be more people in the house that we haven't seen . . ."

Jones stood up, realizing why Jules was grinning. Gina had just told them that her captors consisted of four people, who, between them, probably had only one small firearm. "Let's go kick in that fucking door," he said.

But Gina was speaking again. There had been a pause, a rumble of a voice in the background, and she then said, "Emilio says I'm wasting time. I'm sorry. But . . . Is Max with you? Because . . ." She laughed in something that sounded like disbelief. "Emilio is going to let us go."

"What?"

"They had his wife," she continued, "but he found out she's dead, that the people who took her killed her, so he doesn't want to . . . Look, it's complicated, but I just thought it would be easier to do this if maybe Max were with you. Is he there? Can I . . . Please, I need to talk to him."

Max took the phone from Jules. Unmuted it. "Gina," he said. "I'm here."

"Oh, Max," Gina's voice was thick with emotion. "Thank God—" But then she was gone.

Replaced by a male voice—it had to be Emilio. "This reunion is touching, but time is short. I'm going to bring the women to a friend on the northside of Pulau Meda, an island north of East Timor. They'll be quite safe there until you arrive."

A few minutes after Emilio took the phone from Gina, the excrement quite suddenly hit the fan.

One minute Emilio was calmly talking to Max on the phone, giving him directions to his doctor's house. But then he stopped talking, as if listening to something Max was telling him. And then he was shouting.

Molly's Italian was mostly limited to items she could order off a dessert cart, but she knew the word for *hurry*.

She was hearing it now, in abundance, from Emilio.

Imelda ran in, snatched her young son, ran out.

Crowbar Guy popped in, rattled off a stream of Italian, took what looked like a key ring from Emilio, then vanished.

And that nasty little gun that they hadn't seen since climbing into the shipping container appeared, in Emilio's very steady hand.

He aimed the barrel directly at Gina, who still looked stunned that Max had come looking for her, and that she'd actually spoken to him on the phone.

She fumbled as Emilio tossed her the cell phone, but managed to catch it.

"*What* is going on?" Molly asked.

"Tell your friend," Emilio ordered Gina, "that if anyone so much as sets foot inside this house, you'll be the first to die."

CHAPTER
SIXTEEN

Max's mistake had been in letting the kidnapper know that they were on Pulau Meda.

It was more than obvious that Emilio hadn't expected them to arrive in Indonesia quite so soon.

And it was pretty clear that Emilio had expected Jones to be alone, that Max's presence had rattled him.

Max had been in the middle of discussing Emilio's plan to take Molly and Gina to some doctor's estate. Where there was—oh-so conveniently—a plane that Jones could use to fly them out of there.

That was when Max had made the mistake of suggesting Emilio simply surrender his hostages right there, in his home. Max would see them safely off the island. While he didn't tip off Emilio to the fact that he was right across the street, he did let the kidnapper know he was close by.

There was a lot of shouting at that point—until Emilio took advantage of *his* phone's mute button.

Max should have said yes to everything, then intercepted them en route. Of course, then he had to factor in the inherent danger of surprising a man who was in possession of at least one deadly weapon. Guns and surprises were a bad mix.

"Damn it," he said now.

"Yeah," Jules agreed, watching the street. "I'm picking up a real mixed signal, too. It reads like a total trap. But if he sincerely wants to let them go—"

"Fuck what he wants or doesn't want." Jones was locked and loaded. "I'm going in, before he takes them and runs."

"Heads up," Jules announced. "I've got a garage door opening."

Just like that, Jones kicked out the screen and went out the side window.

Damn it. He should've been the last one out, not the first. He was the freaking target, for the love of God.

But then Max heard Gina's voice, over the phone: "Max, Emilio's got a gun, he says he doesn't want you to . . . come in . . . ? Where *are* you? Oh, my God, are you really that close? Yeah, yeah—I know," she sounded annoyed, obviously speaking to Emilio. "Max, he says to tell you if you come in here, he'll shoot me." Back to Emilio. "I told him, all right?"

"White van, leaving garage," Jules announced over the sound of tires squealing.

Goddamn it.

"Are you and Molly still inside the house?" Max asked Gina as he followed Jones. There was about a ten-foot drop to the alley alongside the building, but he landed on his feet. Jules was right behind him.

"Yes," Gina told him.

"You're not in a moving vehicle." He had to make sure.

There was a battered Ford Escort parked on the street—Jones had already opened the rusted door and started hot-wiring the damn thing.

"No." She was definite.

"And Molly's with you?" Max asked.

"She's right here," Gina said. "Max, what's going on?"

Jules was already inside the garage, weapon drawn. Whoever had driven away in that van had been in such a hurry, they'd not only left the garage bay open wide, but the door to the house was also ajar.

And it was some door, too. Like something you'd see on a bunker, built to withstand a major assault.

Max called to Jules in a low voice. "Hold up."

Jules jammed something between the door and the frame, making sure it wouldn't swing shut as he nodded, signaling that he copied—that he wasn't going any farther inside. "Jones," he hissed, to catch the man's eye as he came back out to the open bay door. He silently motioned for Jones to get out of the street. He also pointed into the garage and mimed holding a steering wheel. His meaning was quite clear. There was a car in there.

Jones nodded as he closed the Escort's door and jogged toward them.

Max was focusing on Gina, who was on the other end of that phone. "Tell Emilio I'm right outside, that I want to come in—just to talk. No weapons, completely unarmed— hands up and open. Tell him I'll strip naked if he wants me to. God knows I've done it before."

Gina actually laughed. "Really?"

"Yeah, tell him."

She sounded . . . exactly the way she'd always sounded. Max didn't know what he'd expected—maybe a subdued, frightened, defeated Gina, overcome with the terror of knowing just how slim her chances were of making it out of this situation unharmed.

"Oh, Max," she said, "you don't know how glad I am to hear your voice."

"Just tell him, Gina," he said, but he couldn't stop himself from adding, "And ditto." He muted the phone as she passed along his message, because he could see that Jules had something to add.

But Jones spoke first. "We don't have much time before reinforcements arrive."

"Are we sure he's not telling the truth?" Jules asked. "If I kidnapped someone, and decided to let her go, except suddenly her very angry husband showed up on my doorstep, I'd go into cornered animal mode, too. If Emilio's wife *is* dead—"

"If he even has a wife," Jones pointed out.

"Work your magic on this car," Jules ordered Jones. "Testa might not be willing to hand over his keys. Let's be ready to move. I'm going to call the embassy in Dili, give them a heads up as to the situation." He turned to Max. "I need your phone—you've got mine."

Max fished in his pocket and handed his over.

"Max?" Gina came back onto Jules's phone.

"I'm here," he told her.

"You can come in," she said. "But he wants you in a T-shirt, no jacket, nothing on your head, hands up and out, like you said. He says, while you're in here, if he hears a noise in the hall, he'll shoot me."

"Understood." Max was already stripping down, jacket, holster, weapons, all in a pile on the concrete floor. "I'm going in," he told Jules.

Jones pulled himself out of the car. "Don't let him hurt them."

"I won't," Max promised.

It couldn't have been easy—having to stay out here when Molly was in there, but Jones nodded.

"I'm not getting through to the embassy," Jules reported.

"Keep trying. Gina," Max said into the phone, "tell Emilio I'm opening the door from the garage to the house. Keep the phone line open if you can, okay? I'm giving this phone to Jules. I want him to be able to listen in." He handed it over, muted, his voice also lowered as he looked from Jules to Jones. "If I say *fire,* you come in fast and shoot to kill. Do you understand?"

Jones nodded.

"Max." Jules stopped him with a hand on his arm. "Don't do anything too stupid."

"Where were you with that advice a year and a half ago?" Max went into the house. "I'm coming down the hall," he called out loudly, his hands open and out.

* * *

Jules Cassidy was here, too?

Gina didn't have time to wonder how many other members of his team Max had brought with him, or how Jones had managed to get in touch with any of them, because Emilio moved his gun from her side to directly under her chin.

The barrel was cold and heavy. And capable of blowing her head completely off her shoulders if he pulled that trigger.

She stood very still, phone still open in her hands.

But then Max appeared in the doorway to the room.

He glanced quickly around, taking it all in—Molly still sitting on the bed, that gun in Emilio's hands—before meeting her gaze.

"Hi," he said, as if they'd run into each other in the cereal aisle of the supermarket.

Except, what *was* the correct greeting for this type of situation? On top of the etiquette confusion, Gina found herself distracted by how different Max looked.

She found herself thinking the most inane thoughts—that his broken collarbone must've been completely healed in order for him to hold his hands up in the air like that.

And maybe it was the way that black T-shirt hugged his upper body and shoulders, or the way he was holding his arms that made his muscles stretch the fabric of his sleeves, but he looked as if he'd gotten completely back into shape during the months she'd been gone.

Back in shape and then some.

But it wasn't just his super-buffness that made him look like a stranger. It had obviously been a while since he'd last shaved, and thick stubble covered his chin. His dark hair was uncombed and matted, too, as if he'd worn a hat for days on end.

Jeans and sneakers instead of a well-tailored suit—although she'd gotten used to seeing him dressed in casual clothes in the rehab center.

No, it was his eyes that made him look most like a stranger—as well as least like one.

Gina had always loved Max's eyes. They were bottomless and so exotically dark brown as to seem almost black.

He was looking at her now the way she'd always wanted him to look at her. With nothing hidden. With everything he was feeling right there for her to see.

Fear. Anger. Vulnerability. Frustration. It was all apparent, along with incredible relief.

And a boatload of hope.

"Hey, Max," she whispered back.

But he'd already focused his attention on Emilio. And that gun. "Step back from her, Mr. Testa. There's no need for that. Just let her go, take two steps back and point that thing at me."

"How many are here with you?" Emilio asked. His breathing was ragged, his muscles tense. Gina could feel his heart beating, hard, against her back. Or maybe that was her heart.

"Step away from the girl. Woman," Max corrected himself with a shake of his head and an apologetic grimace in her direction. "Then we'll talk."

"I'll make the rules," Emilio's voice was tight. "I've got the gun."

"I know you don't want to hurt her," Max's tone was soothing, calm, "so just aim your weapon at me and—"

"Is Grady Morant here, too?" Emilio asked. "He's out in the garage, isn't he? I don't want him coming in here."

"He won't. And if you step away from Gina," Max repeated, "we'll discuss the best way for all of us to get to safety."

Gina found herself praying that Emilio's finger didn't tighten on that trigger, that he didn't shoot her—either intentionally or accidentally. It wasn't just because she didn't want her brains sprayed onto the wall. It was because she knew that if Emilio killed her here, like this, Max would never recover.

And she'd already brought way too much pain into his life.

"Right about now," she told him, "that NYU law school thing is looking like a real missed opportunity."

He smiled, a brief and rueful twist of his lips. "Yeah." But he didn't even glance at her—he was busy staring down Emilio.

Who finally let her go.

Gina stumbled from suddenly having to hold herself up. She went down to her hands and knees, dropping the phone as she scrambled to get some distance between her head and that gun.

Except Emilio now aimed the damn thing at Max.

"Good," Max said, no doubt for Jules's benefit. "Keep it right here, right on me."

"Please don't shoot him," Gina begged. "I'd rather be shot myself, than have to—"

"That's not helping," Max told her.

"—live through that again," she finished. "Can't you just aim your gun at the floor? Please?"

"Max can keep his hands up," Molly chimed in. "We all want the same thing—to get out of here alive. So let's just bring this down a notch."

Emilio lowered his gun.

Relief made Gina's knees wobble, and she sat on the edge of the bed. "Thank you." Molly scrunched forward, put her arms around her.

And Max went to work. "Let's do this. Let me take Gina and Molly down to the dock. We'll hire a seaplane to take us to the American Embassy in Dili. We'll just walk out of here. We'll just walk away. We can all leave at the same time—you can go in one direction, we'll go in the other. We're not looking to jam you up, Testa. We just want Gina and Molly to be safe. I can see that you took good care of them. We all appreciate that very much—"

"How did you find me so quickly?" Emilio asked.

"That doesn't matter," Max said. "We need to focus—"

"Yes, it does," Emilio said. "Because I've had some time to think. I don't want the bastards who killed my wife to go unpunished. If you have . . . connections. To your government. To the CIA—I know they've been here, on Pulau Meda . . . If that was how you found me, and if you can guarantee . . . What is it called? Amnesty? And perhaps a financial incentive that will allow me to relocate . . . ? I have information I could share."

Emilio Testa had no doubt figured that if they were willing to cut a deal with Grady Morant, they'd be open to doing the same with just about anybody.

Jones himself didn't trust the scumbag, but Max and Jules were the ones talking to him—Jules via one cell phone, even as he used the other to keep trying the embassy—as if they were his new best friends. Of course, it was hard to tell with either of them if they really believed Emilio, or if they were just trying to make him *think* they believed him.

Whatever the case, it was radically different from the negotiating technique Max had used when he'd opened that Hamburg hotel room door to find Jones in the hall.

Still, whatever they were doing, they were doing it right.

"Jones," Jules called, and he looked up from trying to pick the lock on the trunk of that Impala.

Molly was standing just inside in the doorway that led to the house.

She looked tired and pale, her hair pulled back from her face in a braid. She was dressed for a summer day in Northern Germany—in long pants. She'd rolled up the bottoms to compensate for the Indonesian heat, and she'd tied the sleeves of her sweatshirt around her expanding waistline.

"Ma'am, do you need medical attention?" Jules asked her.

But she spotted Jones.

And ran to him.

And then, oh Jesus, he had his arms around her. "Please tell me—"

"Are you . . . ?" She pulled back, looking him over as thoroughly as he was looking at her.

"I'm all right." "I'm okay." They both said it at once, followed by "Are you sure?"

Jones didn't know whether to laugh or cry. Molly did both as he kissed her. But then she winced and he quickly loosened his grip. "You *are* hurt. I'm going to kill him—"

"No, no—it's the biopsy."

Oh, Jesus. He'd actually forgotten. Jones pulled back to look at her. "Is it . . . ?" He couldn't say it.

"I don't know." Molly shook her head. "It takes days to get the results." She wiped her tears from her face as she tried to smile at him. "I felt the baby move. Gina and I were at dinner, in Hamburg, and I felt him."

The baby. Jones knew he was supposed to say something, but he couldn't lie.

"It was so exciting," she continued. "The waiter gave us free dessert, to celebrate."

And God knows he couldn't tell her the truth. He pulled her close—gently—so that she wouldn't see his face, know what he was thinking.

"I'm so sorry," he whispered instead. "About all of this."

"I am, too." When she pulled back from him, she had on her school teacher face. "You shouldn't be here," she scolded.

"Yeah, well, neither should you."

"Although, I don't even know where *here* is," Molly admitted.

"Eastern Indonesia," he told her. "We're pretty close to East Timor."

"Of course we are," she said. "Of all the lawless islands out there, we're near the one that's the most lawless."

Across the garage, Jules was still working both his and Max's phones, and keeping an eye on the street. What were they doing inside the house?

Molly answered his unspoken question. "They're coming—they just have to figure out a way to do it so that Emilio doesn't feel threatened. I think he's afraid of you."

"Smart guy."

"I'm supposed to remind you that you're the target and tell you that you should keep your head down. I'm supposed to sit with you in the backseat of the car," she said, "and, I don't know, distract you, I guess, with my wifely skills. So that you don't shoot Emilio. Or something."

Molly had on her "But Face," that certain expression that she wore when she was on the verge of disagreeing.

Gina could do a pretty mean "But Face" but Molly was the undisputed queen. It involved eyebrows that were slightly raised, eyes opened wide, breath drawn in—the better to pronounce that slightly percussive B-sound. Her mouth would curl slightly up at the edges, either in appreciation of the argument that was on the verge of starting—for her, arguing was so much fun—or in bemused exasperation.

Right now it was all exasperation.

He pulled her into his arms again and kissed the *but* out of her. "I love you," he said. "Let's get in the car and speed this along. I want to get out of here."

She lowered her voice, glancing across the garage, over at Jules. "You *should* get out of here. Right now."

Jones shook his head. "I'm not leaving without you, babe."

"You have to." She was dead serious. "We're going to the embassy in Dili. If you come along—"

"Yeah, sorry, I'm not leaving until I know you're safe. It's a long way to Dili from here." He pulled her into the car with him.

"But they'll lock you up if—" she said.

"Probably," Jones told her. "But only after we're on our way back to the States." He kissed her again. "I gambled, Mol, and we lost."

"Gambled?" She didn't understand.

"By trying to get a passport that would let me go home. It was Kraus," he told her. "I still don't know who's behind all this, or what they want, but I do know that Gretta Kraus sold me out."

Molly nodded. "Emilio found us there, at her workshop."

"I know," he said grimly. "I saw the footage from a security camera. That was a terrorist cell that came in shooting and nearly killed you, by the way. Goddamn it."

"Lord," she said. "That was unbelievable. I didn't know what was happening at first and . . ."

"Unbelievable," Jones corrected her, "is when someone opens fire in a church or a shopping mall. When it's in the studio of a professional forger, where criminals go to reinvent themselves, it's a little less unbelievable. You shouldn't have been there."

But it was just as he'd suspected. She'd been worried about him.

"I wanted to warn you," Molly said. "I knew we were being followed. We spotted Emilio in the hallway outside our hotel room when we came back from church. I was afraid that—"

"I would have taken care of myself." He wanted to shake her. "You should have gone straight to the embassy."

"But that was the one place I was absolutely certain you *wouldn't* be," she retorted.

"How did you even find the studio?" He'd purposely not given her Kraus's address.

"We went to a . . . less than upscale establishment—it

was part pawn shop, part brothel, I think. We just pretended we needed passports to get to New York."

Jesus. He could only imagine the kind of dive it was. Just the thought of it made him want to . . . What was it Gina always said? Shit monkeys. Although, if it had been Jones trying to make contact with Gretta Kraus, it would've taken a week and a half, and way more than one visit to one crappy whorehouse.

"We walked in," Molly told him, "using fake accents, *Excuse please to help* . . . big puppy-dog eyes . . ." She demonstrated. "Plus a hacking cough to make sure no one got too close. I didn't even need to show any cleavage."

Jesus. He, too, had a facial expression that he found himself wearing occasionally. It was called "What-the-Fuck Face."

But the story wasn't over. "Gina stuck her jacket under her shirt," Molly was telling him, "and pretended she was pregnant, too. That was our character motivation—our reason for wanting to go to America. So our babies could be born there, right?"

She was so damned pleased with herself for having *character motivation* when she went into a brothel that was no doubt filled with the worst examples of humankind that the world had to offer. Thieves. Pimps and slavers. Drug users, pushers, killers, rapists . . .

"She just said *No speak English* and *Sprech' kein Deutsch* and pretended to start to cry whenever anyone looked in her direction," Molly finished her story. "She was brilliant." It was her turn to kiss him. "Please go," she said. "Let's plan to meet somewhere after this is all over. After I go home and do the hospital thing."

Do the hospital thing. Like ridding her body of cancer was going to be a walk in the park. And like it had a guaranteed happy ending.

But Molly was determined. "Somewhere like Perth or

Taiwan or maybe Kuala Lampur—we could help with the tsunami cleanup. They still need volunteers."

"I can't," Jones told her.

"Of course you can—"

"No," he said. "Even if you could convince me that you were safe from here on in, I wouldn't leave. I sold my soul to the devil to find you, Mol."

She didn't understand.

"I made a deal with Max," he explained. "Me for you and Gina. Unlike some people, at least he doesn't want me dead."

It was a bad attempt at a joke, and of course she didn't laugh.

But she stopped asking him to run away, as if she truly believed that he was a man of honor, a man who kept his word.

Over on the other side of the garage, Jules was arguing with Max over the phone.

"No," he was saying. "*I* will." Pause. "No. I'm doing it. Someone's got to stay with Gina and Molly and—"

They were having a testosterone-off. Apparently there was a dangerous job that needed to be done by a hero.

Man of honor that he was, Jones stayed right there in the car, his arms around his wife.

Jules made an exasperated noise. "No. *I'm* in charge, so zip it so I can tell you how this is going to go down."

The gay guy had balls.

"We'll get a lawyer," Molly told Jones, bringing him back to the yawning black hole of uncertainty that was their future.

"Yeah," he said, forcing a smile as he gazed into her eyes, praying that she wouldn't see the terror that gripped him every time he thought of losing her.

But even if they walked, right now, through a portal that led directly to her mother's home in Iowa, there was still a chance he'd have to bury Molly in the next few years.

Jones raised his voice, calling to Jules. "We need to get moving. What's taking so long?"

Jules got another busy signal, and finally gave up trying to call the embassy, pocketing his cell phone.

It was time to go.

He checked his weapons, wishing for the eight hundredth time that he had more ammo.

His consolation prize was a hat. A battered fedora that looked as if it had blown off of Humphrey Bogart during the filming of *Key Largo*. Sucked up into the atmosphere during the movie's hurricane, it had ended up here, on the other side of the world, sixty years later.

On his head.

Even though it had been enshrined in a closet inside the house, it kind of smelled as if it had spent about three of those decades at the bottom of a birdcage.

Yesirree. It was almost as fun to wear as the brown leather flight jacket.

Which really wasn't fair to the flight jacket. It was a gorgeously cared-for antique that didn't smell at all. And it definitely worked for him, in terms of some of his flyboy fantasies. But the day had turned into a scorcher. It was just shy of a bazillion degrees in the shade.

He needed mittens or perhaps a wool scarf to properly accessorize his impending heat stroke.

"Today, playing the role of Indiana Jones, aka Grady Morant, is Jules Cassidy," he said, as he slipped his arms into the sleeves.

Was anyone really going to be fooled by this? Jones was so much taller than he was.

But really, the big money question was, was anyone out there watching so that they *could* be fooled?

Emilio Testa was convinced there was.

He believed that if he were seen driving away from his house, holding another man at gunpoint, then whoever was watching would assume he had Grady Morant in his custody.

Theory number two—the first being that there were indeed people watching—was that said watchers would immediately leap into their own vehicles and follow Emilio. And if they were intercepted? Whoopsie, no Grady Morant in *this* car—only Jules.

Meanwhile, Jones and the others could leave in the Impala, unnoticed.

Theory number three was that a car the size of a battle-cruiser could actually go unnoticed, but okay.

The agreed-upon plan had them taking two cars, with the same final destination—the dock down at the harbor.

Jules and Emilio, heading out first, would meet a soon-to-be-arriving seaplane, owned by a man Emilio swore could be trusted. He'd fly them over to the American Embassy in Dili, East Timor.

The plan had the others hanging back, waiting for Jules to call with the all-clear.

Provided, of course, that all was clear.

There was still a significant amount of mistrust on both ends. For example, despite Emilio's insistence that they were all on the same side now, he'd refused to surrender his weapon.

And Jules didn't like being a downer, but there were some rather squishy, unexplained spots in E's drama-laden story of kidnapping and murder.

Such as, what about the fact that Jules, Max, and Morant had all entered the house via the open garage door a solid fifteen minutes ago? After that white van had vanished with a watcher-awakening squeal of tires on the potholed road?

Emilio's response had been to leap upon this point and use it as an argument for their immediate departure.

Okay. But hey, what *about* that white van? Who were the people driving it, and where did they go in such a rush?

Emilio told them that his assistant, Anton, was taking Emilio's daughter-in-law and grandson to safety.

Okay, except the CIA report had Emilio getting married only ten years ago. That was some precocious son—married, with a child, at age nine?

Pointing out the holes in Emilio's story wasn't going to speed things along, so Jules kept that comment to himself.

Negotiating with an armed gunman was more about the end than the means, and separating Molly and Gina from Emilio and his deadly weapon was their priority here.

Jules was still a little foggy on exactly who the "they" were—both they-the-watchers and they-to-whom-the-watchers-were-reporting, but it didn't matter at this point.

Emilio had referred to a contact he had with a man named Ram, but it wasn't quite clear whether this Ram had taken over for Chai, the recently deceased drug lord who'd had it in for Grady Morant, or whether Ram was working for the Indonesian government.

Of course, on this particular island, it was entirely possible he was doing both.

It would, no doubt, all get sorted out if and when they reached the sanctuary of the American Embassy.

Although yes, just to spice things up, Jules still hadn't made contact with the East Timor embassy in Dili. He'd called the diplo-folks in Jakarta, too, as well as the CIA office there, but all he got were relentless busy signals. Yashi, too, added to the festive international goatfuck atmosphere by failing to pick up from his desk back in D.C.

Whoo-hoo.

But finally, Gina emerged from the house. Emilio was holding tightly to her arm, his weapon pressed against her back. Max was several steps behind them, looking as if he were about to give birth to a pricker bush.

The E-meister looked much as he had in the video footage. Trim. Well-groomed. Even up close, he didn't look a day over fifty-five. Well, okay, his neck looked sixty. His cologne was nice, but it was applied a tad too heavily.

The man knew exactly how to ensure cooperation—by maintaining the least possible distance between the barrel of his handgun and his hostage—currently Gina.

If Emilio's finger tightened on that trigger, there was no chance at all that he would miss.

"Thank you for doing this," Gina said to Jules.

Yeah, like he would even consider letting Max go with Emilio.

And it wasn't just because Emilio was armed and dangerous and Max was no longer an agent of the U.S. Government.

Jules had listened in on nearly every word exchanged while they'd been back there together, and it was more than obvious that Max had yet to pull Gina into his arms and do his imitation of the Han Solo and Princess Leia big-moment kiss from *The Empire Strikes Back*.

Maybe when Jules and the E-man walked out of the garage and climbed into that ancient Escort—which turned out to be part of the Testa fleet—Max would take the opportunity to plant a big, wet one on this woman that he still so obviously adored.

Or maybe not.

"Sweetie, I love the haircut," Jules told Gina as he gave Max back his cell phone. "You look fabulous for a woman who's been dead for five days."

"What?" she said, but it was time to go.

"Max'll fill you in," he said. There. There was no way Max was going to be able to tell Gina about receiving that report of her death without getting a little misty-eyed. At which point Gina would, at the very least, throw her arms around him. If Max couldn't manage to turn *that* into a truth-revealing kiss, he didn't deserve the woman. "Ow," he added as Emilio pressed his weapon into Jules's kidney.

"Sorry." Emilio managed to put the right amount of

apology into his voice, but he was obviously so stressed that he didn't quite get the right facial expression to match. It was pretty odd. Particularly when he jabbed Jules again. "Let's go."

Wow, wasn't *this* going to be fun?

Max, meanwhile, had stepped protectively in front of Gina. He caught and held Jules's gaze. "We'll wait for your call." Silently, he sent another message entirely. If Emilio gave Jules any trouble, he should shoot him.

Never mind the fact that Emilio was the one with the drawn weapon. Never mind that Jules's hands were out and empty, and that he'd have a major bullet hole in his body if he so much as put said hands near his pockets.

Despite the seeming disadvantage, Max had unshakable faith in Jules's ability to gain the upper hand.

It was quite possibly the most glorious moment of Jules's entire career—here in this musty sweatbox of a garage with some dickhead jamming a pistol into his back.

"See you soon," Jules promised Max.

He pulled his hat down over his face, held his hands out slightly in front of him.

And away they went.

CHAPTER
SEVENTEEN

Max watched as Testa's Escort sputtered and coughed and finally pulled off down the street, Jules behind the steering wheel.

He turned. Gina was standing there, holding on to herself, looking at him as if he'd just killed her puppy.

"He'll be all right," he said.

"What did Jules mean back in the other room when he said you're not his boss anymore?" she asked.

"He meant I'm not his boss anymore," Max said. "Look, we've got to move fast, so—"

"Sorry. You're right. It's just . . . It's nice to see you, too. It's been a while." She was clearly pissed at him, which was just grand, as she turned toward the car.

Where Jones was pulling Molly out of the backseat.

"We're leaving on foot," Max explained before Gina could even ask. "And it is nice to see you." More than she could possibly imagine.

"On foot? But . . ."

He knew she'd heard him tell Emilio that they'd leave in the Impala.

"We're not taking the car," he clarified, "because he wanted us to take the car. We don't trust him." He turned to Jones. "Can you get us to that airfield that you found last night?"

"Absolutely."

Gina wasn't happy. "But you let Jules go with him."

"I didn't *let* Jules do anything. Besides, he can take care of himself. Do we have something Molly and Gina can use to put over their heads?" Max asked Jones.

"What, like paper bags?" Molly quipped. "I know we must look bad, but—"

"Scarves," Max said. "To hide your hair." How could she take the time to make a joke? But the two American women were going to stand out anyway, in their western clothes, even with their hair covered. Maybe it didn't matter. Except Molly's reddish hair was so noticeable.

"Maybe there's something in here." Jones had found a crowbar, and was using it to try to pop the Impala's trunk.

"We could look in the house," Gina suggested.

"No," Max decided. "I don't want to take the time. Let's just—"

"Whoa." Jones had gotten the trunk open.

Molly went to look. "Dear Lord."

Gina was slightly less reverent. "Holy shit."

Max was silent as he stared down at the collection of weaponry that filled the car's trunk. There was an abundance of everything from handguns to an array of your basic assault rifles to M3 and HK-MP5 submachine guns to Remington sniper rifles complete with scopes, to some extremely deadly-looking shotguns.

There was enough there to outfit a small army.

Or a dozen terrorist cells.

His gut had told him not to trust Emilio Testa. He just hadn't realized how much not to trust him.

"So I guess that 'Poor me, they kidnapped and killed my wife' thing was just a story," Jones said.

A well-executed story. Emilio had had his choice of weapons, yet he'd let them believe that he—and whoever had gone tearing out of here in that white van—had only one small handgun between them. Max almost admired the man. Almost.

Gina said, "Jules is with this guy." As if he'd forgotten.

"Yeah." Max took out his phone to try to call Jules even as, like Jones, he reached in and helped himself to one of those HKs and a generous amount of ammunition.

But, damn it, this wasn't his phone, it was Jules's. Somehow they'd gotten switched. Which meant Max had to call his own number, which he never did . . . He found himself on Jules's contact list under B. Not for Bhagat, but for *Boss, Max.* He dialed.

"Let's move." Phone to his ear, taking up the rear, he hit the street running.

Emilio opened his cell phone as Jules took the road down the mountain, toward the harbor.

The E-man had lowered his gun after they'd left the plaza, as they'd taken the turn onto this narrow, winding road that was surrounded by jungle.

It was then Jules gave some consideration to the fact that Emilio might be telling the truth. It became possible that the next few minutes were going to play out exactly as they'd planned, with a relatively uneventful drive to the dock.

"Excuse me," Jules said now. "I'd prefer it if you didn't make any calls until we arrive—"

"Yes," Emilio said into his phone. He wasn't just pointedly ignoring Jules. He'd also raised his weapon again.

Wasn't that just great.

Emilio spoke, rapid-fire, in a language that Jules couldn't understand. But he didn't need a graduate degree in Portunesian, or whatever this odd mix of Portuguese and Indonesian was called, to guess what Emilio was saying. *Change of plans. Morant's at my house, waiting for an all-clear call, at which time he'll be heading for the dock in my blue Chevy Impala. Get him, now.*

But then he did switch to English, as if someone else had come on to the line. "No," Emilio said angrily, "No, that's wrong. I got him onto the island which was all I promised to do. It's now up to you . . ."

In the pocket of that leather flight jacket, Jules's own cell phone started to vibrate. That was weird. He'd set Max's phone to ring silently, not his . . . *Shit*. He'd given Max the wrong phone.

He reached for it, but Emilio barked an order. "Hands on the steering wheel, where I can see them!"

He'd apparently thought Jules was going for a weapon. Which, come to think of it, was a damn good idea.

Emilio couldn't shoot Jules, because Jules was driving. The road was crumbling and narrow, with hairpin turns, and guardrails that had rusted through in places. It wouldn't take much to spin out and take a super-express route down the mountain.

No, Emilio couldn't shoot Jules. But Jules could shoot Emilio.

"Pull over," Emilio ordered, after he finished his conversation and closed his cell phone.

"I don't think so," Jules said, and floored it.

"Damn it," Max said.

It was not on Molly's list of words she was hoping to hear from him right now. Like, "Hooray!" for example. Followed quickly with, "We're safe, we can stop running!" And then, "Who wants barbeque for lunch, followed by chocolate cake?"

She'd ended the morning-sickness phase of her day, and entered the ravenously hungry part.

"I just lost all signal for my cell," Max said instead.

"Maybe we're getting too close to a tower," Gina panted. Running uphill clearly wasn't on her fun list, either.

They'd spent a lot of time running, ever since Molly'd gotten stitched up after her biopsy.

"What the hell is that?" Jones asked.

What was what? They skidded to a stop on the dusty dirt road. Molly bent over, trying to catch her breath as . . .

That was the unmistakable sound of an approaching

truck. It was still out of sight on the street ahead of them, and ten to one it wasn't an eighteen-wheeler with a shipment of festive paper plates and napkins for the local Wal-Mart.

"Oh, shit," Jones said.

From Molly's previous time spent in this part of the world, she knew that the sound of a truck—gears grinding, engine rumbling—meant only one thing.

Max spelled it out for Gina. "It's probably a troop transport."

Heading toward them.

The million dollar question was, whose troops were being transported?

The fact that a U.S. embassy had moved into nearby East Timor meant that there would also be U.S. Marines around to protect it, didn't it? So it wasn't entirely impossible to imagine that the truck might be filled with allies.

But Jones and Max were exchanging a glance that told Molly they weren't banking on that scenario.

"Can we hide and wait for it to pass?" Gina asked.

"Sounds like there's more than one truck coming," Jones said. "And they're going to be looking for us. They may not just drive past."

Besides, the houses were close together along this road, hugging the steep mountainside. On the other side of the road was sheer cliff. The view was amazing, but there was nowhere over there to hide.

"This way," Max ordered, and they headed back the way they'd come.

Because alternatives just weren't plentiful.

They'd recently passed what looked like a trail, heading off the road and up the mountain.

"That dead-ends," Jones barked, when Molly started toward it.

"How do you know?" she asked.

"I was out here last night." He wasn't even remotely

winded. Of course, he wasn't pregnant, with stitches in his breast. "There's another route we can take to that airfield," he said to Max. "It's not as direct. We'll have to go partway down the mountain and then back up, around the other side."

Going down sounded good.

Especially, as they continued to backtrack, the sheer cliff on their left turned into a steep, densely covered jungle. Max led the way up and over the guardrail, stopping to give Gina and then Molly a hand.

"Careful," he said, but Gina slipped. "Jones!"

He was right behind Molly. He held onto her tightly, as Max grabbed Gina by the back of her shirt.

"Oh my *God*!" Flailing, Gina went down on her bottom, knocking Max off his feet, too. But he didn't let go of her. He hung on as they both slipped and skidded, sliding quite a ways until Max managed to hook his elbow around one of the sturdier trees.

By this point, she was clinging to one of his legs.

"You all right?" Molly heard Max ask Gina.

"Oh my God," she said again.

Jones wrapped his hand around Molly's wrist, showing her how to hold tightly to his wrist, too, so that they were locked together. They began their descent significantly more slowly. "Wish I had a rope," he said.

"If I had a wish," Molly told him, "I wouldn't waste it on a rope."

"Good point," he said as they shuffled down the hill. "Wish I could have a half a dozen decades to grow old with you in a little house in some one-stop-sign town in, I don't know, maybe northern California?"

She laughed her surprise. "Really?" she asked. "I thought you hated the United States."

Jones shrugged. "I do." It was possible that admitting that embarrassed him. "That doesn't mean I don't want to go home."

And here she'd thought his push to go back to America had been pure selfless sacrifice. She liked it better this way, but there was no time to tell him that, because they'd caught up to Max and Gina.

Max was showing Gina how to hook her arm around the jungle vegetation if she started to slip again.

The fool was holding her around the waist, securely against him, and one of her arms was around his neck. They were practically nose to nose but he didn't take the opportunity to kiss her.

Instead, Max loosened his hold, looking up at Jones. "Which way?"

"I don't know," he admitted. "This is part of the mountain I didn't explore last night."

Max was not happy. "Me neither."

"I'm pretty sure we're north of Emilio's," Jones told him. "We head due south, we'll hit that cliff that looks down on the roof of his house. Our best bet is east. Away from the road."

East it was.

Max led the way, holding onto Gina the same way that Jones held Molly.

"Think you can go any faster?" Jones asked her.

Faster? Oh, Lord . . . "I can try," Molly said.

But slipping and sliding their way down the mountain was even harder than running uphill, and it wasn't long before she was out of breath. And Jones slowed their pace.

"Why don't you go for help?" Molly asked him, barely able to get the words out. God, her heart was pounding.

"Not a chance." He put his arm around her waist, slowing them down even more.

"Grady, please—"

"I'm not leaving you."

"But—"

"But nothing," he said. "Don't waste your breath."

*   *   *

Jules needed both hands on the steering wheel as he took the first hairpin turn on two wheels. The side of the car scraped the metal guardrail with an ear-splitting screech.

And Emilio clung to the grab bar, up above the door.

With his gun hand.

It was now or never, and Jules blessed Cranky Hank, the former Ranger who ran the firing range where Max's team regularly trained, who'd made Jules practice shooting with his left hand—over and over, until his eyes were ready to cross.

He reached for his weapon, trying to hold the car steady with his right hand, as they went skidding sideways down the mountain road.

It was easier said than done, and he quickly put both hands back on the wheel before they went into a roll.

"Motherfucker!" Emilio shouted—or at least the Italian equivalent.

His weapon fired, bullet shattering the passenger window behind Jules.

Jesus yikes! That had missed Jules's head by mere millimeters. He jerked the car hard left, directly into the guardrail as he stood on the brakes, because once they came to a stop—suddenly and unexpectedly from Emilio's standpoint—he'd be able to get his own weapon into his own hand and . . .

Okay—not part of his plan, this blasting through the rail and . . .

The car flipped as it went down the mountain, and Jules hung on for dear life.

As Emilio somehow managed to shoot at him yet again.

Sky.

There was too much brilliant blue sky ahead and Max tightened his grip on Gina, slowing them both down.

For about a half a second, he dared to hope that they'd

reached the road that snaked down this side of the mountain. But there was way too much sky for a mere road.

"Hold up," he called to Jones who, with Molly, was lagging quite a bit behind.

No, instead of finding the road, they'd come to the edge of the world.

Not really, of course. It just looked like it.

The jungle ended at a sheer cliff.

"Hold on to this." He anchored Gina to a sturdy tree, making sure she clasped her hands together, then cautiously approached the edge.

"Be careful," she called, anxiety in her voice.

Max moved even more slowly. He didn't want to scare her. God knows Gina scared him enough for both of them, back when she'd started sliding down the hill, up by the guardrail.

It was due to some pretty solid luck that his fingers had caught her shirt, and he'd managed to hang on to her.

Although, if he hadn't, he would have dived headfirst after her.

As it was, it had taken him far too long to hook onto a plant that didn't get uprooted. He'd had a clear and sudden vision of the two of them going over the side of a cliff, and him being unable to do a goddamn thing to save them.

It was amazing how fear could mask pain.

He'd gotten whacked directly in the balls by some errant branch, but he didn't feel a thing as he hauled Gina up and into his arms, as he lay there on the jungle floor, just holding her.

And shaking with terror.

The difference between dead and not dead had never been so hard to see. It was the slimmest of lines. Possible to cross at any given moment.

As Max now approached the edge of the cliff, he tested each hand- and foothold.

"Max," Gina called again.

"I'm okay," he called back. He had to make sure that the cliff didn't just look daunting from this perspective and . . .

Nope. There was no trail down. No obvious or easy route.

The view was breathtaking—the green of the jungle making the hills and valleys below look inviting, like they could jump and land with a bounce on its softness. The harbor town was a splash of color in the distance, the ocean beyond shimmering and blue.

The cliff curved around to the south—with no way to circumnavigate it in sight.

Max climbed back up the steep hillside to Gina. It was actually easier to climb up than down, because he could grab and hold on to roots and vines that he tested before trusting them with his full weight.

"This way," he said, pointing out a path that would parallel the cliff.

She reached for him, and he took her hand.

And once again they were moving.

Jules kicked out the battered driver's side window so he could crawl from the wreckage.

The engine was steaming and making that ticking sound that engines made when they cooled down after being too damn hot.

Emilio was gone. He hadn't been wearing his seatbelt, and he'd somehow departed the car—either involuntarily or by choice. Possibly when, plunging down that hillside, Jules had managed to remove his sidearm from his shoulder holster and discharge it.

His aim had been questionable, but he'd hit the son of a bitch, that much he knew. There was a spray of blood on the passenger side window.

And as far as Emilio's grand exit? Whether it had been on purpose or not, Jules hoped it had been at bone-crushingly high speeds.

Still he hadn't been under consideration for that FBI team leader position for nothing. He held his weapon now as he squeezed out of the window—which was much narrower than usual due to the partially crushed roof.

Damn, he was lucky he was vertically challenged.

His right leg wasn't working very well and instead of standing outside the car, he fell to the ground. The damn thing didn't hold his weight, didn't want to move at all. Like it was someone else's leg that was now attached to his body.

He crawled, using his elbows to pull him away from the car. Ow. Ow. Ow.

And Jesus, his head. Despite the airbag, he'd whacked himself something fierce. His brain felt scrambled, his vision funkatacious, all doubled and blurred.

But he was alive.

He knew he was alive, because every cell in his body hurt. His armpits hurt. His toenails.

But first things first. Warn Max.

He had to roll onto his back, which made him feel exposed, kind of like a turtle or a cockroach. But it was the only way he could dig for his phone.

He found it—covered with blood.

Son of a bitch, that was *his* blood. That bastard Testa had shot him.

Jules put his weapon down on his stomach, in easy reach, as he checked out the damage.

The bullet—small caliber, or he'd still be back in the car, in two very dead pieces—had caught him in the fleshy part of his side, going in, front to back. There was an exit wound, which was relatively good news.

Stopping the bleeding would be better news.

He applied pressure with his left hand as he wiped his phone off on the leg of his jeans with his right. God*damn* it, no wonder sitting up was as much of a challenge as walking. No wonder he hurt so freaking much.

He wished his head would stay attached to his shoulders. Damn, he was woozy. But okay. Okay. First things were still first. This wasn't his phone, it was Max's—which meant he had to call himself. He concentrated, trying to get his eyes to focus . . .

"They took the cell towers out. You won't get through."

Big ugly shit, on a big ugly stick.

"I guess it was too much to hope that you'd broken your neck," Jules told Emilio, turning his head to look—yes, it also would've been too much to hope he'd lost the damn thing in the melee—into the barrel of the other man's gun.

Gina recognized that sound. It was the sound of her nightmares.

Max was several steps behind her and he started shouting, "Get down, get down, get down!"

They were being shot at.

He was on top of her, shielding her, pushing her forward. "Go! Go!"

With Max right behind her, Gina ran.

Just moments before, she'd been so relieved. They'd finally come down off the mountain and onto a road that led them back to a cluster of houses.

But that road had curved to the right and . . .

Max and Jones had both said quite a few choice words.

Because they were back where they'd started. At Emilio's house.

And there was nowhere to go but forward. The road opened on to that village square—an empty, dusty marketplace surrounded by a knee-high wall, surrounded by other houses.

There was no one about—no one on foot, at least. There had been children playing there when they'd left Emilio's, but upon their return both the square and the streets were like a ghost town.

Until the shooting started.

Across the square there was a truck—no, two. One was smaller—a jeep—with some sort of machine gun mounted on it. It was bouncing toward them, making that awful ripping sound.

"Get them inside!" Jones shouted.

Max grabbed Molly—he already had Gina—and pulled them both with him into the shadows of Emilio's garage.

The ripping sound was louder then, as Jones fired back at the trucks, as he backed his way into the garage, as Max lowered the garage door.

Someone was screaming, and it wasn't until Max got in her face—"Gina! Were you hit?"—that she realized she was the one making all that noise.

So she stopped. Because God knows it wasn't helping.

"Are you hurt?" he asked her again, checking her, touching her, turning her around.

"I don't think so," she said. "Are you?"

Jones came out of the house—which was weird. She hadn't seen him go in. "Clear," he told Max.

"Good," Max gently pushed her toward Molly. "Get inside."

"We're fucked," Jones told Max. "There's no backdoor, remember? They've got us pinned."

"This place is built like a fortress," Max said. "There are worse places to be pinned. Let's get as much of this inside as we can." He was taking the guns from the back of Emilio's blue car, piling them into Jones's waiting arms.

"I can help," Gina said.

Max pulled a backpack out of the trunk. "Here." It was so heavy she staggered under the weight.

"Ammo," he said, "take it inside. Go!"

Gina handed it to Molly with the warning, "It's heavy," and Max gave her another. She was ready for it this time.

As she went into the house through that door, she realized that it looked like one you might find on a bank vault.

Or a bomb shelter.

Or your house if you were a super-paranoid gun smuggler and kidnapper and all-around baddie, and you wanted to withstand a siege against an entire army.

"Gina, are you . . . ?" Molly had blood on her hand. She touched the backpack again—there was even more now, on her fingers. Bright red.

Gina looked down at her own hands, at the pack she was carrying.

There was blood on hers, too. "It's not me," she told Molly.

Heart in her throat, Gina turned back to the garage, where, yes, Max was bleeding.

CHAPTER EIGHTEEN

"You're bleeding," Gina said again.

"I know," Max also said again as he surveyed the weapons and ammo they'd taken out of the trunk of that car. "I'm all right, though."

He'd taken the two women back into what he thought of as the hostage room as Jones, far more nimble without a bullet in his ass, did a closer look-see at the rest of the building.

From the quick glance Max had had of the lower level—kitchen and two living areas, one with a window and one without—Jones's eloquent description of this place was dead-on. It truly was re-in-fucking-forced.

Emilio had installed far more than a bunch of super doors in his narrow little two-story house. The few windows—all on the front of the structure—were encased with entry-proof bars.

At first glance that wasn't so different from many of the other houses on this street in this semi-well-to-do part of a piss-poor island. But unlike the other houses, these bars were not designed merely to discourage the casual burglar. These bars were meant to keep out the most determined intruders.

The walls were thick, too—three feet in some places. Even the interior walls. Which was unusual, to say the least.

Miniature security cameras positioned outside the house added a high-tech slant to its impregnability.

Gina got in his way. "*All right* is what you are when you're *not* bleeding." She was indignant.

And scared to death, Max realized. For him.

He gave her his full attention. "I'm mostly just bruised," he said. This entire scenario had to be a nightmare for her. God knows that he'd been sent on his own little time-traveling trip to hell when she'd screamed, back when the shooting first started. Instant cold sweat. The last thing Gina needed now was to think he was going to drop dead any second. "The bullet that hit me was almost completely spent."

But she still looked so worried. "I don't know what that means. Spent?"

"Think about the physics of firing a weapon," he explained as he went back to sorting ammunition: 9mm versus .44 cal. Grabbing the wrong ammo could have deadly consequences. An HK 9mm MP5 submachine gun was a formidable tiger of a weapon. But an MP5 with a backpack of .44 caliber bullets was about as formidable as a poodle.

"A bullet doesn't just follow its trajectory until it hits something, right?" Max continued. "Because what if there's nothing there to hit? You can't fire an assault weapon on the Jersey Shore and expect to hit someone in Spain, just because there's nothing but ocean between the two of you."

"Well, yeah," Gina said. "Obviously."

"A bullet travels until it runs out of energy," he told her. This was good. They were talking, and she didn't look so scared, and the topic wasn't anything that would add to the swirling chaos inside his head. He was able to sound cool. Calm. "But when it does, it doesn't just stop and drop, like in a Bugs Bunny cartoon. It keeps moving forward, but it's less and less effective. It's spent."

"So if the bullet that hit you was spent," she asked, crossing her arms, "why are you bleeding?"

"It was almost spent," he corrected her.

Gina got in his way. "Let me see."

"Later," Max lied.

She somehow knew. She always did have a highly honed and super-sensitive bullshit meter. "I want to see it now."

"Do you want me to just drop trou?" he asked. "Right here?"

She didn't say a word. She didn't have to. She just looked at him.

And that same heat that had always sparked whenever Max gazed for too long into Gina's eyes jumped to life. Instant meltdown, like stepping into a steam room.

It wasn't so much that he wanted to fuck her, except it was.

Except it wasn't.

It both was and wasn't, because really, when he had been told that she'd died, what he'd wanted more than life itself was for her to still be.

Just be.

Just Gina. Alive.

Except her being alive and breathing and standing right in front of him got all mixed up with sex and pleasure and guilt and the memory of the way she'd smiled and the sparkle in her eyes that had turned into such satisfaction when he'd . . . when they'd . . .

Right now she practically jerked her head away, breaking that eye contact, and Max—always good at helping his mental chaos come to a full boil—found himself wondering if she'd had this same instant animal attraction with the father of her unborn child.

He placed two Beretta M9s over by the 9mm ammo as gently as he possibly could. This was not the right time for *that* conversation.

She sighed and he was sure she was going to retreat—maybe go check on Molly. But she turned back to him instead. "Look, I'm sorry, but I just want to make sure you're really all right."

Christ. "Gina, it's going to look bad, you're going to

freak. You're just going to have to trust me. I'm not bleeding to death. I'm not going to die." He wasn't leaving her. Not in any way, shape, or form. "At least I'm not if you let me have a second to think and figure out what we're going to do next."

Saying that was dirty pool, but it worked. She backed down. "What can I do to help?"

"Go make sure that Molly's all right."

When they'd first come in here, Molly had made a beeline into the bathroom and closed the door behind her.

"She's all right," Gina told him now. "She's giving us privacy. You know, in case we wanted to say something heartfelt to each other. Like, thank you for quitting your job so you could rescue me."

She was a smart woman. Max wasn't surprised that she'd figured that out.

"In case you haven't noticed," he said, "I haven't quite managed to rescue you yet."

"Or: I'm sorry I still piss you off," she said.

He sighed his exasperation. "You don't piss me—"

"Or maybe even something like: I really didn't expect you to come at all," Gina said quietly.

Goddamn it, what could he say in response to that? "You thought I'd just, what?" he asked tightly. "Shrug it off? Because you're not my responsibility anymore?"

"Oh, great," she said. "The R-word. I was wondering how long it was going to take before I heard that one. I've *never* been—I've never *wanted* to be your responsibility. Is that really why you came all this way? Because even though I'm no longer your responsibility, you still feel—wait for it!—responsible for me?"

For the love of God . . . "Gina, how about we fight *after* you're safe?"

"How did you survive, Max?" She was very angry. "All those months, with me in Kenya? Didn't it drive you nuts, thinking I was maybe gonna get eaten by a wild animal, or . . . or . . . killed in some tribal dispute?"

Like her friend Paul Jimmo had been.

Max lost it. He felt himself just . . . snap. "Yes, it drove me nuts," he found himself shouting at her, part of him looking on in complete horror. "It made me freaking crazy!"

"Well, it shouldn't have!" she lashed back at him. "You wanted me to leave. You can't have it both ways, Max. You either have me in your life or you don't. And when you chose *don't*, you gave up the right to be driven freaking crazy! You gave up the right to—"

"*I* gave up?" he asked, disbelief dripping off every word. "*You* left *me*."

"No." Gina got in his face. "*You* left *me*. Do you have any idea what it was like—"

"To have to live with me?" he finished for her at high decibels. "Yeah, I do, Gina, because I fucking have to live with me! 24/7. And I'm sorry that I put you through it, too. Goddamn it, I'm sorry about all of it—*all* of it! And you want to hear something really fucked up? What I'm sorry about most of all is that I didn't go to Kenya and drag you home a year and a half ago!"

Okay, so that was probably something he never should have told her.

In the dead silence that followed, she was looking at him with the same amount of stunned surprise on her face that she might've worn if her father's schnauzers had suddenly started singing opera. In harmony.

But Jones came thundering down the stairs, saving them the further embarrassment of attempting to speak civilly after that conversational train wreck.

The really stupid thing was that Max had been wanting to apologize to Gina for a long, long time. He definitely owed her one, but Christ, that had come out really wrong.

What he'd really wanted to do was tell her that he was truly, honestly, sincerely sorry—about almost every single thing that had happened between them, over the past few years.

Well, almost everything.

The nights that he'd actually slept because she was there in his arms, the way she made him laugh, her insistence on reading aloud to him while he was in the hospital, that look she gave him from beneath her eyelashes, that smile right before she locked the door and . . .

Okay, he definitely felt sorry about all that, too, but it was a bigger, more complicated kind of sorry.

"The top floor is divided into five small rooms," Jones reported, and Max made himself pay attention.

Molly even came out of the bathroom to listen, which meant private time was officially over. Thank God.

"Two are in the front," Jones continued, "but only one of them has a window. Three in the back without—and one of those rooms has the same security monitor setup that's in the kitchen. Three screens, showing views both from exterior and interior cameras. The rooms are all smaller than they should be, but then I realized that the walls are seriously wide, even up there. Best I can think of is Emilio played host to more than one involuntary guest at a time and didn't want them communicating with each other."

Gina was still staring at Max, her eyes filled with tears.

Great. Good job, Bhagat. Make the girl—*Woman. Shit.* Make the woman cry.

"What kind of professional criminal owns a house that's built like a fortress," Max put voice to one of the important questions that they needed to be focusing on, "but doesn't have a backdoor or escape tunnel? Have you looked at his security cam setup?" he asked Jones.

He nodded, scratching the back of his hand with the stubble on his chin. "Yeah, I was going to mention that. That seventh exterior camera, right? You think—"

"Oh, yeah," Max said.

Emilio had seven security cameras in place outside of his

house. One on the roof, two showing different angles of the front of the house, one in the garage, two on the sides of the house. There was no need for one in the back—the building was built against that steep mountainside.

Yet there remained one last mystery camera. It showed what looked to be a dense patch of jungle in the middle of nowhere.

That camera had to be placed at the end of Emilio's escape tunnel. *Had* to be.

"What are you talking about?" Molly asked, trying to follow.

"We think Emilio *does* have some kind of tunnel out of here," Jones told her. "We just haven't found the damn thing yet." He turned back to Max. "Maybe you should look in the kitchen and living room—see if you can find it. Because I couldn't."

Boom.

"What was that?" Gina asked.

"Grenade," Jones answered, already heading toward the kitchen, Molly at his side. "They're going to have to do better than that. This place is solid."

Max followed more slowly, trying not to wince from the very literal pain in his ass. Gina was right behind him, watching his every move.

"So would you have dragged me home by my hair?" she asked him, her voice low.

What? Oh, wonderful. It figured that she had something to say about Max's "drag her home from Kenya" remark.

"Because I definitely wouldn't have gone," Gina told him, "unless you dragged me by my hair."

How could she joke about something like that?

"A chest thump or two would've been a nice touch," she added. "Nothing like a good alpha caveman chest thumping to make me totally hot."

"Okay," he was going to say, "you can stop now," but he had a sudden flash of memory—not of Gina, laughing on top of him, but instead that shroud-covered young woman who could have been Gina, lying in the airport morgue. It was all he could do not to fall to his knees and thank God he'd found her alive.

"Am I pissing you off yet?" she asked. "Oh, wait. It's *you* who's so good at pissing *me* off."

As he grabbed for the kitchen counter, she mistook his unsteadiness for pain.

"God, Max," she said, all sarcasm instantly vanished. "Are you okay?"

He nodded, wanting to reassure her, but afraid of the subhuman noises that might come out of his mouth if he tried to speak.

"I'm so sorry." Gina put her arms around him, and ah, God, it nearly did him in.

"I'm sorry, too." Max had to pull away from her, definitely pissed—at himself for putting that frightened look back on her face.

But he had to focus on the problem, and he scanned the room, looking for that escape route.

If he were Emilio, where would he have put it?

The man hadn't cut costs anywhere in this house—the appliances in the kitchen were all restaurant quality.

Max took a few more seconds to slow his breathing, to fully reemerge back into this world—the real world, in which Gina truly hadn't been lying there, dead on that table.

He forced himself to check the video monitors that were built into the wall—technology circa the early 1990s, when digital was fantastically expensive. All of the security cameras were still up and running, the three screens flipping from view to view to view. They all showed that the troops surrounding them were still keeping their distance. There was no sign of any damage from that grenade.

That was good.

He or Jones should probably go up to the second floor in

a very short while, and fire a shot or two dozen down into the dusty street. Make that army continue to stay back out of range.

Last thing they needed was some cowboy coming up to the windows, trying to dislodge those bars.

Not that it would be easy to do.

Max had never been on this end of a military takedown before, never mind that this particular military wasn't as powerful or well-equipped as the one he was used to working with. It was still impressive—all those soldiers and trucks. He knew more and more would be arriving with each passing hour.

And after the commanding officer got his men organized, one of the first things he'd do was knock out the security cameras. Provided he knew that there were security cameras that needed knocking out.

Max had to assume someone knew—that Emilio was still alive. It was highly likely that the man who'd built this house would be willing and eager to point out its vulnerabilities.

Which meant he'd also reveal the location of that freaking escape route—which, had they not underestimated the man, they would have thought to search for a half an hour ago.

Gina spoke—loudly enough for everyone to hear this time. "Why don't we just stay put until Jules brings help?"

Jones shot Max a look that asked, *You want to answer that, or should I?*

Max took it. He cleared his throat a few times as he figured out how to soften his response. "Jules . . . may not be able to get help," he told her. "He, uh, is probably going to have more trouble than we originally thought making it to the embassy. Those soldiers out there, Gina—they were shooting at us. That's not SOP—standard operating procedure. Firing on civilians without issuing a challenge or warning? No, someone high up their chain of command is involved in this, in the kidnapping, in all of it. Whoever they are, they also had the ability to take out whatever cell towers were on this island. These are some powerful people." He shook his head, knowing that however soft he made this, she could see the hard truth on his face.

She didn't mince words. "You think Jules is dead."

Think? "I hope not," Max said. "I think he's probably . . . in trouble." He cleared his throat again, watching Jones help Molly move the refrigerator on the off chance that there was a secret passageway behind it. That was ridiculous. The entrance had to be easily accessible. Still, they were being thorough. "But I hope not."

Gina took his hand. Squeezed it. "He's good, you know. People underestimate Jules because he's always making jokes. And because he's so good-looking. He's cute and he looks so young, so they think . . . But he's going to be okay."

"Yeah," Max agreed. There were tears in Gina's eyes again, but she was trying to smile, trying to stay positive. But try as he might, he couldn't smile, too.

The fridge wasn't hiding anything. Nor was the stove.

Jones got onto his knees, examining the bottom of the cabinet under the sink. "If I had unlimited funds," he was telling Molly, "and I were putting in an escape route, I'd put it in the least likely place. Keep my enemies guessing."

Boom.

Over on the monitors, wisps of smoke drifted across one of the screens.

"That one sounded louder," Molly said.

Max went into the other room, looking at the furniture Jones had already dragged away from the walls in his search. Again, it was obvious that money had been spent on this place.

"It's not," Jones reassured Molly, his voice carrying from the kitchen. "Don't let it get to you."

"This isn't your fault." Gina had followed Max, touching his arm to get his attention. "I know I said that you shouldn't have let Jules go with Emilio, but you were right. You didn't *let* him go. You wouldn't have been able to stop him."

Max nodded. Right. "I have that problem with all of my friends, don't I?"

"I hate that word," she said through gritted teeth. "I'm sorry, Max, but come *on*. Didn't I have, I don't know, even just *slightly* higher status than Jules?"

"Yeah," he said, unable to keep from noting her pointed past tense. So he used it, too, as once again his own temper flared. "You were the best friend I ever had. And as far as letting you go—honey, I was cheering you on when you walked out that door. I was—" He shut his mouth and turned around, and went back into the kitchen, because just like that, from out of the storm of his anger and frustration, he knew.

Clarity.

"Least likely place is up on the second floor," Max told Jones. "Listen—if someone's chasing you, and you run upstairs? They're going to take their time because they think they've got you cornered. It's upstairs. Gotta be."

Jones dusted off his hands as he stood up. He looked at Gina and then back to Max, clearly uncomfortable about interrupting their argument.

"You said the interior walls were thick," Max persisted. "He's probably got a staircase going through the house, and then tunneling down the mountain . . ." He pointed to that seventh video camera's jungle view as it came up on the monitor. "To here."

He glanced at Gina, who had an expression on her face that he couldn't identify. Ah, please God, don't let it be pity . . .

"It's just crazy enough," Jones said. "Expensive as shit, but maybe that's also what we should be asking. Where's the most costly place to put the entrance to an escape route?" He laughed his disgust. "Wish I had money to burn."

"You okay?" Max heard Molly ask Gina, as he followed Jones far more slowly up the stairs.

"Actually," he heard Gina say, "Yeah. I'm . . . Yeah."

"Jackpot," Jones called from the second floor. "Here it is. Fake freaking bookcase and everything."

Maybe—just maybe—their luck was about to change.

Emilio was all the way on the other side of the wreck and slightly uphill—close enough to the car to use it for cover.

"Hands where I can see them," he ordered.

Jules, sadly, had moved far enough away on the off chance that the car might explode. He was in a clearing—if you could call it that, considering the canopy of leaves and branches overhead completely blocked the sun. He'd always thought of the jungle as being dense—with the kind of underbrush that needed a machete to cut through. But since the sun didn't shine down here, there wasn't that much capable of growing. A few very undernourished ferns and some other plants that—with his luck—were probably the local equivalent of poison ivy.

He had nothing to hide behind, considering his ability to do more than roll was seriously limited. And in the time he'd take to roll to the nearest cluster of trunks and roots, Emilio would fill him with lead.

Jules dropped his cell phone, holding his right hand out and open. Think, *think*. Crap, his vision was starting to fade out around the edges—not a good sign.

But he wasn't dead yet. His weapon was heavy on his chest, hidden from Emilio by the voluminous sleeve of that leather flight jacket. All he had to do was grab it and . . .

Except, how was he going to walk out of here, with tunnel vision? Forget the tunnel vision, how was he going to walk on a leg that was useless and heavy? Broken in God knows how many places. Okay, whoa. Getting ahead of himself—

"Hands!" Emilio repeated. "Both of them out, right now!"

"My left arm's broken," he told Emilio with a stroke of genius. Part of him was aware that it was a miracle the man hadn't already shot him. But maybe the E-man had hit his head, too, so Jules's time delay seemed normal to him. "I can't move it. At all. Unless you want me to move it, you know, with my right hand . . ."

At which point he could grab his weapon and . . .

"Just don't move," Emilio ordered.

And Jules realized he must look to be in even worse shape than he truly was. He glanced down to see that blood stained his shirt and jeans, and even pooled beneath him and . . . Shit, he *was* in bad shape.

As far as Emilio . . . As the man got closer, Jules could see that he had blood on his face and neck. He must've broken his nose, because his shirt had been sprayed. His right arm was wrapped around his torso, like he was holding himself together. He'd probably injured his shoulder or collarbone. Or maybe he'd broken some ribs.

Either way, he was moving as if he were really hurt.

Good.

Because unless a team of Navy SEALs dropped from the sky to save his ass, it seemed likely Jules was going to die by Emilio's hand.

Okay, God. Send that helicopter. Any time now would be good . . .

But the only sound he heard was distant gunfire.

It was not a happy sound. The implication was that Max wouldn't be coming to his rescue in the very near future either.

Which meant that whether Jules lived or died was down to sheer luck. There was nothing left for him to do but grab for his sidearm—which would result in Emilio's shooting him immediately in the head.

Most likely before Jules could get his own weapon up and aimed.

The odds of his winning that kind of a quick draw, so to speak, were not in his favor.

It didn't help that his vision was blurring and he was so freaking cold. Shock from loss of blood.

Talking this guy into surrendering was definitely a long shot, but he couldn't just lie there and wait to die.

"Don't do this," Jules tried, working to keep from slurring. It was hard—his teeth were chattering. "Whatever you've gotten into, I can help you get out."

"You can help me?" Emilio laughed, limping slowly, painfully closer.

What was wrong with this picture?

There was something here Jules knew he should be paying attention to. This was more than just a situation to which he had never given much thought—a scenario that could and probably would result in his own death.

There were beads of sweat on E's upper lip, and his gun hand shook, but only very slightly as he continued to advance.

"I doubt you can help me," the man continued. "But I'm going to help you. Your associates aren't so lucky, I'm afraid. Once they fall into Colonel Subandrio's hands, they'll beg for the mercy of a bullet to the brain."

Colonel Who?

And okay. Jules so couldn't die now. He absolutely refused. That was way too melodramatic—like this guy had studied Evil Overlord technique, sitting at the feet of famous James Bond movies villains. It would be just too pathetic if this conversation with this idiot was the last thing Jules did on earth.

God couldn't be that unfair.

But then he thought of his ex-partner, Adam, who'd hooked up with Robin—Robin being the first person in years that Jules had been seriously interested in . . .

Yeah, actually God *could* be that unfair.

So okay. If Jules was going to go down, he was going to go fighting.

Still, he had to wait until Mr. Drama cleared the car before he went for his own gun. It wouldn't do to lose his one chance at a Hail-Mary shot because the son of a bitch ducked behind the fender.

"You don't know my *associates* very well," Jules told him, trying to keep Emilio talking, trying to keep himself alert. Jesus, he was cold. "I don't think Max has ever begged for anything in his entire life."

"So who is he?" Emilio asked, dragging himself even closer. "He's obviously more than a diplomat, as he told me he was."

Yeah, like Jules was going to say anything about their connection to the FBI to *this* prick.

And, it was obvious that Emilio didn't give a damn who or what Max was. He was just making noise, killing time. Which was fine with Jules. Every step Emilio took shifted the odds in Jules's favor. It shifted them infinitesimally, sure. But he'd take whatever he could get.

"Max is actually unemployed right now," Jules told him, keeping the conversation going. "Although he has a history of his boss refusing to accept his resignation letters. I think, though, after he kills you and Colonel Whosis and everyone else that you're working with . . . ? He's going to take some time off. Spend a month on the beach somewhere, with Gina."

"Ah," Emilio said. "The lovely Gina. Perhaps the Colonel will use Gina to help Max learn how to beg."

Fuck you. Jules clenched his teeth over the words. "Don't you feel really bad," he said instead, "when you have to kill someone? I mean, to waste a life like that?"

"That's the problem with you Americans," Emilio said. Blah, blah, blah. Jules stopped listening.

Because Emilio was close enough to pop Jules with a head

shot—he had been for quite some time. He was plenty close, plus he had the car to use as cover.

Unless . . .

It was entirely possible that, unlike Jules, Emilio hadn't spent time learning to shoot with his nondominant hand.

The winner buzzer sounded in Jules's spinning head.

What was wrong with this picture?

Even with a freaking concussion, Jules had figured it out. Emilio, who'd done everything right-handed up to this point—talk on the phone, brandish a handgun—was now holding his weapon in his left.

It was likely dude was low on ammo, too. So he had to get very close to make sure he didn't miss as he used his less-practiced hand to fire that so-called mercy bullet into Jules's waiting brain.

A brain that was finally done waiting, as, still talking, Emilio stepped around the front of the car to finish him off.

But Jules was ready. He rolled, reaching for his weapon, pulling it up as he squeezed the trigger once, twice.

And Emilio fell like a stone, two small round holes in the center of his very dead forehead.

Jules shot him again, just in case he was still seeing double.

Sometimes, when he shot and killed someone, he felt bad, like he felt right now. Except the thing that he felt bad about now was that someone else hadn't rid the world of this scumbag years earlier.

Okay. Breathe. Oxygen was good.

There wasn't enough time to celebrate his victory by falling unconscious. Keep it together, Cassidy.

Step one. Don't bleed to death. He maneuvered himself out of that jacket. His T-shirt was even harder to get off, but he succeeded. He tore it into pieces, using it as a bandage.

By the time he was finished, jacket back on and zipped

up, he was exhausted. His head was swimming worse than ever, and blackness was descending.

Still, he knew what he had to do. Appropriate Emilio's weapon. Pocket his own, along with his cell, which he had to search for by feel on the spongy jungle floor, because the vision thing was more and more cloudy with every second that ticked by. He had to find it. Because maybe someone would get those towers up and working . . .

His fingers bumped against it and he grabbed it, still sticky with his own blood.

Shivering in what he knew to be eighty-degree heat, Jules began crawling down the hillside one painful inch at a time, looking for the road.

CHAPTER
NINETEEN

So much for easy outs.

As Jones followed Molly up the dank, spider web–filled staircase and back into the house, he could just imagine the conversation between the overzealous soldiers and their superior officer.

"What part of ambush do you idiots not understand?"

"Sir, the door opened, sir! So we discharged our weapons, as ordered!"

"At which time the door was swiftly closed. And locked. No injuries, no dead, no prisoners."

"Sir, yes sir! No dead on our side, as well, sir! Perhaps crisp new uniforms and ten minutes of training don't make us real soldiers after all! Sir!"

Jones's heart was still pounding. That could have been ugly. The troops must've moved into place while they were in the tunnel, which was quite a flaw in the design of Emilio's security setup.

Of course, in a perfect world, surrounded by minions, a video screen at the door of the escape tunnel probably wasn't necessary. Because in a perfect world, cell phones still worked. A quick call to Igor in the kitchen and they'd know whether or not they were good to go.

With neither phones nor Igor, Jones had opened the door ver-r-ry carefully.

Max had anticipated trouble. He'd carried a mop with him that he'd taken from the kitchen.

As they'd traveled down the tunnel, Jones had thought Max had brought it to lean on—that he was hurt worse than he'd let on. But then he used it to clear the tunnel of the spider webs, so Jones had figured it was possible the brilliant and powerful Max Bhagat was a baby when it came to creepy-crawlies.

Of course when they'd opened that door—hatch really—Jones had discovered Max's real reason for bringing the mop.

He'd slowly stuck it out of the opening, like a head peering out from behind the hatch . . .

And it had been shot out of his hands.

The hatch was resealed.

They were safe.

Or trapped.

Depending on how you looked at it.

Of course, another no-win, no-way-out situation seemed almost no big deal to Jones. He was already smack in the middle of one with the pregnancy and cancer thing.

He hadn't known what to say when Molly had told him she'd felt the baby move. She was always telling him to be honest, but he knew damn well that in this case she wouldn't want to hear what he was thinking.

As in "Gee, and I was hoping all the trauma would trigger a miscarriage."

But okay. Molly was also always selling positive thinking, and since Jones couldn't manage honesty right now, he was trying hard to be optimistic to make up for it. Yes, they were safe here in Emilio's cozy little fortress. True, they were down to Plan C, but—yay rah rah, go team—in their version of the alphabet, C stood for siege. As in, go ahead and shoot at us, mo-fo's. Short of withstanding a direct attack with some serious artillery, they were assault-proof.

Their absent host had even done most of their prep work for them, bless his black heart.

Which meant, after they'd double-checked all the doors

and windows making sure they were still secure, after they'd shut down the AC and sealed all the air vents—just say no to poison gas—and filled the bathtubs, sinks, and every available container with water, as long as they kept an eye on those security monitors and made sure they weren't under attack . . .

They had a little extra time on their hands.

And *that* meant, after they'd both had a turn in that shower—thank you, Jesus—Max was finally ready to let Jones take a look at his so-called "it's just a scratch" of a bullet wound.

As Jones scrubbed up in the kitchen—how long had it been since he'd done that?—Molly and Gina helped by washing down the banquet-sized table. They also had water boiling, to sterilize the collection of knives and other kitchen utensils that he was going to need to de-bullet Max.

Eventually the generator—which they'd found housed down in the tunnel—would run out of gas. Until it did, they'd conserve.

They'd found a first-aid kit, but it was barely the size of a school lunch box, and the supplies inside had been mostly depleted. There were still several adhesive bandages, designed to take the place of stitches. Which was good because instead of surgical silk, someone had tossed in one of those mini sewing kits that were given out at fancy hotels.

The lack of real surgical thread worried him less than the absence of antibiotics. In this climate, with a bullet in his butt that had passed through his grimy jeans, there was a serious danger that Max would suffer from infection.

Emilio had spent a million dollars on security cameras, but apparently he couldn't throw a few extra bucks toward a more realistic supply of medical basics.

Go figure.

Clad in a white bathrobe that he'd already bled through, but looking more like his old self, thanks to a disposable razor he'd found in the bathroom, Max now searched the kitchen for Emilio's liquor cabinet.

"If you can't find anything," Jones told him, "sugar's a decent substitute. I'm assuming your intention is antibiotic rather than anesthetic."

Max didn't bother to answer. Stupid question. "After we're done here," he said instead, "we should do an inventory—go through every cabinet, every closet. See if we can't find a shortwave radio."

"That's a good idea," Molly said.

"I can't believe that all that time we were in Kenya, you never once helped out in the hospital tent." Gina's words were such a non sequitur that it took Jones a second to realize she was talking to him. Not just talking to him—bitching at him.

He closed his mouth over the "What the hell is *your* problem?" that had almost escaped.

Because he knew what her problem was. She was scared to death that Max was hurt worse than he was letting on. Plus she and Max had had an exchange of words, as Molly so politely called it, just a short time ago.

Jones didn't take Gina's less-than-sunny attitude personally. He knew she was also scared for Jules Cassidy—whom Max had described as being "in trouble."

Enough with the euphemisms. Max had been shot, he and Gina had had a rip-roaring fight, and Jules was surely dead.

Jules's "troubles" had reached an end. Help still might be on its way, but it wouldn't be coming from him.

No, if they wanted to be rescued, they were going to have to wait however long it took for someone in the Jakarta CIA office to realize that Jules and Max had fallen off the edge of the earth.

Which would probably be a while. The U.S. Government had a few other things on their plate this week.

And, it was entirely possible that no one would ever come.

Withstanding a siege was only possible with limitless food and water. Eventually their supply would run out.

And when it did, they would be forced to go to Plan D. D for death. As in his.

Okay, now he was working the honesty angle, but it was pretty bleak. He couldn't seem to do both honesty and positive thinking at the same time.

"He couldn't work in our camp clinic." Molly was defending Jones to Gina. "He didn't want anyone to know that he had medical experience. He couldn't risk someone connecting Leslie Pollard to either Dave Jones or Grady Morant."

Gina turned to him. "So are you a real doctor, or . . . ?" She made a face that was part shrug, part disgusted curiosity, and pure New Yorker. Scared to death and trying to hide it by being pissed off. New Yorkers were taught from infancy never to show any fear.

"I was a medic in the Army." Among other things. "I was trained to treat battle-related injuries—gunshot wounds are right up my alley."

"But don't medics just patch people up until they can get to a real hospital?" Gina's worry was showing.

"He spent two years running a hospital for Chai." Molly put her arm around the younger woman. "Which was the equivalent of working the ER in a city like New York or Chicago. He saved a lot of lives." She made sure Max was paying attention, too. "And before you say, 'Yeah, of drug runners, killers, and thieves,' you should also know that his patients were just regular people who worked for Chai because he was the only steady employer in the area. Or because they knew they'd end up in some mass grave if they refused his offer of employment. Before Grady came in, if they were injured in some battle with a rival gang, they were just left for dead."

Jones looked up to find Max watching him as he steril-ized a particularly sharp knife. "Me and Jesus," he said. "So much alike, people often get us confused."

"Mock me all you want—I'm just saying." Molly had on her Hurt Feelings face. It may have fooled Max, but Jones knew it was only there to mask her Relentless Crusader. She was lobbying hard for Max to be on Jones's side if they made it out of here alive. And she wasn't done. "Yes, Grady Morant worked for Chai for a few years—after the U.S. left him to die in some torture chamber. He's so evil, except what was he doing during those two years? *Oh*, he was saving lives . . . ?"

"I was practicing medicine without a license," Jones pointed out. "You just gave Max something else to charge me with when we get home."

When, not *if*. Even though he wasn't convinced that they weren't in *if* territory, he'd used the word on purpose. The look Molly shot him was filled with gratitude.

He gave her a smoldering blast of his best "Yeah, you can thank me later in private, baby" look, and, as he'd hoped she would, she laughed.

Max, meanwhile, had uncovered a bottle of rum. 151 proof. Yee-hah.

"Let's do this," he said, then turned to Gina.

"I'm not leaving," Gina told him before he could ask her to do just that. "In case you were thinking of *cheering me on*."

Gina was obviously referencing their earlier argument, and sure enough, Max closed his eyes as he sighed. "I'm sorry for losing my temper before."

"I'm not," she said. "I'm sorry I left you. I thought . . ." She laughed her disgust as she shook her head. "I was wrong. I should have stayed. I shouldn't have let you chase me away just because you were scared."

"Hail, Gina," Jones said. "Queen of the perfect timing."

"What?" she said. "I'm supposed to wait to say this?

Until when? Until we have some privacy—oh, except for the platoons of soldiers outside, some of whom have high-tech listening devices?"

"Maybe they don't," Jones said. "In this part of the world, there's not so much of the high-tech—"

Gina didn't care. "That's what you did, isn't it?" she asked Max. "Chased me away?"

"Can you at least let my patient get on the table," Jones said, "before you grill him?"

"Please," Gina said with a grand gesture, stepping back. "I didn't mean to slow down the process."

Max gave it one last try. "I'd rather you weren't in h—"

"No."

Max glanced at Molly.

"I'll catch her if she gets woozy," she assured him.

He just shook his head, no doubt recognizing that if there ever were a time to surrender, it was right now.

At least it was here, in their makeshift operating room. Dealing with the army that was gathering out on the street was a different story.

Max climbed onto the table and settled himself face down, head on his folded arms.

Jones lifted the edge of the bathrobe and . . .

"Oh my God," Gina breathed.

That was no mere *scratch*. That bullet was going to hurt coming out. And then he had to clean the wound.

"Oh my God, is right," Molly said, admiration in her voice. "Nice butt, Bhagat."

"Hey," Jones said, mostly because he knew she expected him to. As usual, the woman who probably had cancer was working to keep things upbeat.

Sure enough, she looked at him wearing her "What?" face, a picture of pure G-rated Sunday School innocence as she told Gina, "His wound really is very superficial. I mean, yeah, he's going to have a cute little scar . . ." She turned to Jones. "You have a very nice butt, too, honey."

"Oh my God," Gina said again, more faintly and Jones quickly looked over at her. She was living up to the reputation she'd gotten back in Kenya. *Get an extra bed ready for Vitagliano,* Sister Double-M would mutter when Gina came into the hospital tent to help. Right now she was green.

"Mol . . ." he warned.

"Yup, I've got her."

"Gina, come here and hold my hand," Max said through gritted teeth, as Molly pushed her into a chair, pushed her head down between her legs. "Jones, will you please goddamn tell her that I'm going to be fine?"

"Gina, he's going to be fine," Jones repeated. He kept the second half of that sentence to himself: *Provided that army outside didn't get hold of some demolitions experts and figure out a way to blow a hole in Emilio's assault-proof castle.*

Jules heard voices.

It was possible that they were good voices—the real kind, not the kind that were in his head that urged him to close his eyes just for a moment, to surrender, just for a short time, to the darkness.

He'd found it worked best to talk back to them—the inside-his-head voices. "We all know if I close my eyes, it's over."

Wouldn't it be nice for it just to be over? It's called eternal peace for a reason . . .

"*Shut up,* shut up. *Shut up,* shut up." He used it as a mantra. Or maybe it was more like a marching cadence. Right elbow out on the first *Shut up,* digging in, pulling him forward on the next. He mixed it up occasionally with the longer version. "*Shut* the fuck *up. Shut* the fuck *up . . .*"

But now the voices he heard were coming from an external source. Unless, of course, the inside-his-head voices' powers were growing stronger, combining forces with the double vision and the relentless pain. Unless they were now able to make him hallucinate.

In which case he was screwed.

Okay, that was so not Jules.

That was one of the voices, pretending to be him. He was *not* screwed. He refused to be screwed. He would just keep on ignoring them.

Because eternal peace sounded way too boring. He didn't want to be eternally peaceful. He wanted to be eternally on vacation in Provincetown with the man of his dreams. He wanted to be eternally loved, married even—with two kids and a dog.

That was just a myth, that kind of love. What he really wanted was to be eternally laid.

"Shut up," Jules said as he kept crawling, the sun now hot on the back of his head. "It is not a myth. And eternally loved comes with the bonus of being eternally laid."

Yeah, right. He didn't really *believe that, did he?*

"Stephen found it. Shit, I was going to tell Gina about Stephen, about going over to his place . . ."

After he'd gotten home from a recent trip to Los Angeles, Jules had finally gotten up the nerve to go over to Stephen-the-fabulous-but-no-longer-new-neighbor's apartment and ring the doorbell.

"I was going to ask him out to dinner," Jules said. "You know, on a date? Like, 'Hey, how've you been? I haven't seen you in a while. I was wondering if you were free tonight . . .' "

Except Stephen hadn't answered the door. Brian had. Brian the cop, who looked like a weird musclebound knock-off of Jules. Compact, cute, dark hair, brown eyes. Funny and friendly. And clearly head over heels in love with Stephen, who was so happy, too, that he glowed.

"So I stayed and had dinner with both of them," Jules told Gina, except wait. She wasn't there with him.

Regardless, she'd been right about Stephen. He *was* perfect.

It could have been Jules instead of Brian, packing to move up to Massachusetts to get married.

"I meant, he's perfect for Brian," Jules told the voices.

Jeez, it was hot. Why was he suddenly so freaking hot?

And why were the voices suddenly shouting at him, in a language he couldn't understand?

There were lots of them, talking all at once, talking to each other—which was a pretty powerful parlor trick, since the voices were part of him. They were his dark side, true, but since when had his dark side gone and enrolled in a Berlitz class without his light side knowing about it?

"Hey," Jules said to them, "if you don't speak English, I'm just going to keep on ignoring you."

But whoa, his voices suddenly had feet. Lots of them. Both bare and clad, in worn boots and sandals.

Feet and legs and . . . Jules tried to look up, but the sun was too bright.

One of the voices leaned down, turning from a shadowy shape into a blurred, doubled face. Asian—dark hair, dark eyes, killer cheekbones, Fu-Manchu mustache around a mouth that spoke. *"Sorry about your shirt."* But like a badly dubbed movie, his mouth kept on moving.

"Okay," Jules said. "You're definitely not real."

Another face—faces—appeared. *"Steer clear of that mean Peggy Ryan."*

"Not funny," Jules said. This was very, very not funny. That was what Robin, whom he'd cared very much about, had said to Jules the last time they were together—instead of good-bye. "Go away!"

The first face was back. *"I hope we can be friends again some day."*

Enough was enough. "Get the fuck away from me!" Jules shouted, and they all backed off. He reached for his weapon, fumbling to pull it free from inside that oven of a leather jacket.

And one of the feet came toward him, like his head was a soccer ball. He couldn't move, but so what. A hallucination couldn't hurt him—

Crunch.

Jules both heard and felt the connection, felt himself flung back, his body following his head. Which was probably a good thing.

New pain blended with old. Stars sparked and faded. But before the grayness turned to black, Fu-Manchu came back into view, leaning close. *"Goal!"* he said, like the TV announcer of an international soccer game.

Jules fought to speak. "American," he managed. *Embassy,* he tried to say, too. *In Dili.* But the world went black.

"This might hurt," Jones announced.

Might hurt? Might?

Forget about the implication that everything that had come before this hadn't hurt.

Max had his eyes closed, teeth clenched, sweat pouring off him.

Jesus H. Christ.

"On three," Jones said. "Ready? One, two—"

"Hold up." Gina's voice. Softer now, but close to his ear. "Max, it's really all right if you scream."

"No, it's not," he ground out.

"Yes, it is. And open your eyes. I read somewhere that it hurts less if you open your eyes. With your eyes closed, you focus on the pain and—"

Max opened his eyes. Gina was right there—her eyes, her face. She was looking a little pale, sitting in the chair that Molly had dragged over, holding both of his hands in hers.

"I don't need to scream," he told her.

"I made a bet with myself," she said, "that you wouldn't. Don't let me win."

What?

He tried to loosen his grip on her hands. He was squeezing her too tightly, but she wouldn't let him go.

He'd survived a lot in his life, and the past five minutes had been particularly hellacious. Still it was nothing—*nothing*—like the past few days.

"Three," he told Jones. "Just do it."

Mother of God! Max closed his eyes—he couldn't help it.

"Open your eyes," Gina urged him. "Come on, Max, *scream*."

"Come on, Max," Molly chimed in from somewhere down near the source of that pain. "We'll all scream with you."

"Don't want . . . to scare you. Ah, God, Gina . . ."

"No." Gina's voice shook. "You don't want to scare *you*. You don't scare me. Haven't you figured that out yet? You don't scare me at all."

"Almost done," Jones announced as the pain let up a bit.

Of course, then it was back, worse than ever.

"God," Max gasped again.

"You know, you were the best friend I ever had, too," Gina told him.

Still past tense. He opened his eyes and there she was. She had a scratch across her cheek that marred the smooth perfection of her skin, probably from their asinine flail through the jungle. It was mostly a welt—slightly pink and raised—although up this close, he could see several tiny beads of blood where the branch that had whacked her had broken the skin.

And even though she was fighting it, tears made her eyes luminous. One of them escaped and slid down her cheek.

Life—wonderful, abundant life. She was so filled with it, so beautifully alive, it was seeping from her.

It slipped through her lips as well.

"Although, I probably would've used different words," she told him. "More like *the love of my life*."

Maybe his confusion had something to do with the god-damn fire in his butt, but he had to ask because her tense wasn't clear. "Were?" he ground out. "Or are?"

Gina held his gaze with that same determination that had so impressed him the very first time he'd talked to her, over the radio of a hijacked airliner. "What do you care?" she asked. "Didn't you purposely not call and tell me that Ajay died so that I would leave you?"

"Almost done," Jones said again.

"Don't fucking say that unless it's true!" It was more of a howl than a scream, and yes, Gina was right. It scared the hell out of him.

"I played right into your hand," Gina told him. "Didn't I?"

"Yes," Max said through gritted teeth. "Yes, all right? I'm a selfish asshole—I told you that right from the start!"

"Is that what you tell yourself?" She was pissed. "That you're selfish? Is that easier to handle than the truth—that you're scared?"

"Goddamn it!"

"What would've happened, Max, if you'd let me in? What would've happened, if you'd given yourself permission not just to grieve for Ajay, but to share what you were feeling with me?"

"I don't know, I don't know," he told her. "Jesus, Gina. Jones, what the fuck . . . ?"

"Almost done."

"God . . ." Now he wanted to howl, but he fought it, and the words came out little more than gasps. "Damn . . ."

"Why are you so afraid to let yourself be human?" Gina asked. "That's why I love you, you know."

Present tense. Jesus, Jesus, present tense!

She didn't take so much as a breath as she kept going. "Because even though you try to hide it, I can see you in there. You're not perfect—no one's perfect. Shoot, Max, don't you know? I don't want perfect. I want you. I want the little boy who watched Elvis movies with his grandfather. I want the man who put his fist through the wall because he couldn't stop some bad people from hurting me. But you know what? I even want the man who makes himself so . . . cold and, and . . . distant, who blames himself for all of his so-called failures. I just wish you'd realize that human beings learn from failure. We learn and we grow and we let our mistakes go, because we know we'll do it differently the next time. If we're lucky enough to be given a next time."

Still holding his hands, she wiped her cheeks on the sleeves of her T-shirt, then added, "Are. To answer your question directly. You *are* the love of my life. And guess what? I've learned. If you can forgive me for quitting on you, if you can give us a second chance, I will not let you scare me away again."

Jesus.

"Got it," Jones said triumphantly. "Sorry, there was this one little piece of shit or fabric or something, but I finally got it. Ready for a little 151 cleansing action?"

"Yeah," Max rasped. Are. Present tense. If *he* could forgive *her?* Yet Gina was serious.

And, yes, he was ready for damn near anything now.

As Jones poured high octane rum onto his bullet wound, Max opened his mouth and roared. "Jee-zus Jee-zus *Jee-zus!*"

Just as they'd promised, Gina and Molly shouted and screamed right along with him, although Gina might've been laughing. It was a little hard to tell—she exploded into tears.

There was so much noise—even Jones was howling—they almost didn't hear it.

A voice. Over a megaphone. "Grady Morant."

Molly was the last to hear it, and both Gina and Jones hushed her.

"Grady Morant," it came again.

"Oh, God," Gina breathed as Max finally released her hands.

Jones quickly bandaged Max's wound, and moved to the sink to wash his hands. Max pushed himself up onto his hands and knees. "Has anyone seen my pants?"

"They're soaking wet," Molly informed him. "I tried to get the bloodstains out, but . . ."

"I'll get you something else." Gina vanished.

"Grady Morant, you are completely surrounded," the megaphone voice continued. "Surrender peacefully for the sake of your companions. Surrender peacefully, and no one will get hurt."

CHAPTER TWENTY

Gina ran an armload of clothes from what had to be Emilio's closet back into the kitchen, as the man with the megaphone continued to ask for Grady's surrender.

Molly and Jones had already gone upstairs to use Emilio's binoculars to peer out the window.

Max was over at the sink, splashing water on his face. "It's the moment of truth," he said, shutting off the faucet.

Gina dumped the clothes onto one of the kitchen chairs, then handed him the towel that was hanging on the refrigerator door.

"Thanks." He dried himself off. "This is where we find out who Emilio was working for. It's possible the soldiers who tried to kill us weren't acting on official orders. If not, whoever's in command out there might be willing to let us surrender to a special contingency from the American Embassy in Dili. If I can set that up, we're home free."

Gina nodded. But if he couldn't?

"If I can't . . ." Max met her gaze. Smiled ruefully. "No one can. And that's not just me being cocky."

"I know." She sorted through the clothes. "Do you mind wearing Emilio's underwear?" She turned back to him with the two different styles that she'd found. "You're about the same size. And they're clean. They were wrapped in a paper package, like from a laundry service."

Max gave her a look, because along with the very nice,

very expensive pair of black silk boxers she'd pilfered from Emilio, she'd also borrowed one of his thongs.

"What?" Gina said. It was definitely a man-thong. It had all that extra room for various non-female body parts.

"Don't be ridiculous."

"I'm not," she said, trying to play it as serious. "One, it's been a while, maybe your tastes have changed. And two, these might actually be more comfortable, considering the placement of your bandage and—"

He took the boxers from her.

"Apparently I was wrong." She turned away and started sorting through the pairs of pants and Bermuda shorts she'd grabbed, trying not to be too obvious about the fact that she was watching him out of the corner of her eye. To make sure he didn't fall over.

Right.

After he got the boxers on, he took off the bathrobe and . . .

Okay, he definitely wasn't as skinny as he'd been after his lengthy stint in the hospital. Emilio's pants probably weren't going to fit him, after all. Although, there was one pair that looked like they'd be nice and loose . . . There they were. The kelly green Bermuda shorts.

Max gave her another one of those you've-got-to-be-kidding glances as he put the bathrobe over the back of another chair. "Do I really look as if I've ever worn shorts that color in my entire life?"

She tried not to smile. "I honestly don't think you have much choice." She let herself look at him. "You know, you could just go with the boxers. At least until your pants are dry. You know what would really work with that, though? A bowtie." She turned, as if to go back to the closet. "I'm sure Emilio has a tux. Judging from his other clothes, it's probably polyester and chartreuse, but maybe the bowtie is—"

"Gina." Max stopped her before she reached the door. He motioned for her to come back.

She held out the green shorts, but instead of taking them, he took her arm, pulled her close.

"I love you," Max said, as if he were dispatching some terrible, dire news that somehow still managed to amuse him at least a little.

Gina had been hoping that he'd say it, praying even, but the fact that he'd managed to smile, even just a bit while he did, was a miracle.

And then, before her heart even had a chance to start beating again, he kissed her.

And oh, she was also beyond ready for that particular marvel, for the sweet softness of his mouth, for the solidness of his arms around her. There was more of him to hold her since he'd regained his fighting weight—and that was amazing, too. She skimmed her hands across the muscular smoothness of his back, his shoulders, as his kiss changed from tender to heated.

And, God. That was a miracle, too.

Except she couldn't help but wonder about those words, wrenched from him, as if it cost him his soul to speak them aloud. Why tell her this right now?

Yes, she'd been waiting for years to hear him say that he loved her, but . . .

"Are you . . . Did you say that . . . Do you think we're going to die?" Gina asked.

Max laughed his surprise. "No. Why do you . . . ?" He figured it out himself. "No, no, Gina, just . . . I should've said it before. I should have said it years ago, but I really should have said it, you know, instead of *hi*." He laughed again, clearly disgusted with himself. "God, I'm an idiot. I mean, *hi*? I should have walked in and said, 'Gina, I need you. I love you, don't ever leave me again.' "

She stared at him. It was probably a good thing that he hadn't said that at the time, because she might've fainted.

It was obvious that he wanted her to say something, but she was completely speechless.

"Okay," Max said. "Now I'm terrified that I, um, said it too late?"

His uncertainty turned his words into a question. "Am I too late?" he asked again, as if he actually thought . . .

As much as Gina enjoyed watching him squirm, she forced her lungs and vocal cords to start working again. "Are you . . . ?" She had to clear her throat, but then it really didn't matter what she said, because the tears in her eyes surely told him everything he wanted to hear.

She saw his relief, and yes, he was still scared, she saw that, too, but mixed in with that was hope. And something that looked a heck of a lot like happiness.

Happiness—in Max's eyes.

"Are you really asking *me* for a second chance?" she managed to get it all out in a breathless exhale.

He kissed her then, as if he couldn't bear to stand so close and not kiss her. "Please," he breathed, as he kissed her again, as he licked his way into her mouth and . . . God . . .

She could've stood there, kissing Max forever, but the man on the megaphone just wouldn't shut up.

Besides, she wanted to be sure that this was about more than just sex.

"Do you *want* me in your life?" Gina asked him. "I mean, need is nice, but . . ." It implied a certain lack of free will. *Want* on the other hand . . .

"Want," he said. "Yes. I want you. Very much. In my life. Gina, I was lost without you." He caught himself. "More lost, or . . ." He shook his head. "Fuck it, I'm a mess, but if for some reason you still love me anyway . . . If you really meant what you said, about . . ." There it was again, in his eyes. Hope. "Loving me anyway . . ."

"I don't love you *anyway*," she told him, her heart in her throat. "I love you *because*." She touched his face, his smoothly shaven cheeks. "Although now that you mention it, you *are* something of a mess, and I'm probably entitled to . . . compensation in certain areas. I mean, in any relationship, you need to negotiate a certain amount of compromise, right?"

He actually thought she was serious. "Well, yeah."

"So if, say, I were to point out how incredibly hot you'd look wearing that thong—"

Max laughed his relief. "Shit, I thought you were serious."

"Shit," Gina teased, "I am."

He cupped her face between both of his hands, and the heat in his eyes made her knees week. "I'll wear one if you'll wear one . . ."

He kissed her again, and this time it was pure sex. His lips were no longer soft as he claimed her mouth, as he dragged her close, closer, as she in turn clung to him, her fingers in his hair. She wanted to touch all of him—this incredibly healthy Max, with his muscular arms and broad back, with that hint-of-a-six-pack that had surprised her that very first time she'd seen him naked—in her motel room in Florida, what seemed like at least a lifetime ago.

Or if not quite a lifetime, it was—for Max—two bullet wounds ago. And Gina wondered, as she kissed him, if FBI agents actually measured the passage of time by their various injuries.

She wondered, too, if he knew that the hot bod so didn't matter to her. Skinny or fat, buff or flabby, she didn't give a damn. She wanted him healthy and alive, and preferably happy enough to smile at her—that was all she cared about.

Still, she couldn't get enough of touching him. His back, his arms, his shoulders.

And oh, he smelled so good.

Gina lost herself in his kisses—desperate, hungry, possessive kisses that she answered in kind. She lost herself in the touch of his hands, in the feel of his chest, hard against hers, as he pushed between her legs—more hard against her soft.

She felt the kitchen table against the backs of her thighs, felt his fingers on the button at her waist, and then, God, she was helping him. Peeling off her pants so he could lift her up and onto the table, so there was nothing between them. She wrapped her legs around him and he . . .

God.

How she'd missed him, missed this, and she tried to tell him but he was kissing her as if he were trying to touch her soul with his tongue.

It was possible he succeeded.

And all she managed to say was, "More . . ." and "Please . . ."

He was holding her up, so her backbone wasn't grinding against the hard wood of the table and it felt so good to be held like that—so unbelievably good as he kissed her and kissed her, as he drove himself hard, harder into her.

It was Max and it was sex, but it was unlike any sex she'd ever had with Max because he wasn't being overly careful. Not of his broken collarbone that had long since healed. And not of her.

She wasn't on top.

Gina knew he'd liked her on top because he knew she would be in control. Even when his injuries had healed enough to allow for other possibilities, he'd always been too tense, too hyperaware that she might feel pinned down if they had sex any other way.

Gina also knew he had been trying to make things easier, not more difficult, but unless she'd closed her eyes, more often than not she'd end up reminded of the hijacking, of the rape. It was there in his caution, in his constant checking to see that she was okay, in the way that he tried to hide the fact he was thinking of it. He was always thinking of it.

Always.

But it wasn't there now, between them. There was nothing between them.

There was only Max. Not pinning her down. Instead, anchoring her, holding her safe.

"Gina," he breathed as she strained against him, wanting him closer, even closer. "Are you . . ."

Don't ask if she was all right. Please don't ask . . .

"God," he exhaled, the word ripped from him. "It's too good. I can't . . . not . . ."

His sudden release was an incredible turn-on, and Gina came, hard and fast. It was a rush of blinding pleasure, made even more intense with the knowledge that he was feeling it, too.

"I love you," she gasped over the pounding of her heart, as he just held her there, still so tightly, as they both struggled to catch their breath. She couldn't remember if she'd told him that yet.

"Shit! Sorry!" That was Jones's voice.

Oh, God! Gina turned toward the very open kitchen doorway, the one that led to the hall, the one that didn't even have a door to close, should privacy be needed.

Max leapt into action, trying to cover up her nakedness with the bathrobe, with his own body.

But Jones wasn't standing there.

At least not anymore.

"Not looking!" he called from the hall. "Sorry, it's just . . . we could really use you upstairs."

The voice was still droning that same message over and over on the bullhorn. Funny how she'd stopped hearing it after a while.

"Although, Jesus, Bhagat, I better use some of that thread to stitch you up properly if you're going to . . . What?"

Molly's voice murmured, her words indistinguishable, as their footsteps faded away.

Gina started to laugh, completely, thoroughly mortified. "Oh my God," she said. "Did we really just do that?"

And—holy shit—they'd also done it without a condom. It was such a totally non-Max thing to do.

It was possible that he'd been lying when he told her that he didn't think they were going to die. Such things as protection and birth control were moot if they only had a few days—or hours—left to live.

As Max pulled on those hideous green shorts, he had both guilt and apology all over his face. He opened his mouth, but she stopped him.

"Don't you dare tell me you're sorry," Gina said, "because I'm not. Yes, our timing was . . . off, and we probably should have—"

"I love you, too," he said. "Is that okay to say? And yes, you're right, I was probably going to add that I'm sorry—"

"Yes, it's okay," she said, "but I'm not listening to the rest. La la la—"

"—that it happened like this, instead of someplace more, I don't know, romantic or at least private—"

"Are you kidding?" Gina said. "Doing it on the kitchen table is one of *the* big, all-time female romantic fantasies—right down to potentially being discovered by Fred and Ethyl. With the exception of actually being discovered, of course. Oh my God." She had to laugh.

Max was laughing, too, but as he checked his bandage, he winced.

Crap, she'd actually forgotten all about his latest bullet wound. "I didn't hurt you, did I?" she asked anxiously.

"Not even close." He kissed her as he grabbed one of Emilio's shirts from the pile of clothes. "I'm not going to wait for you, okay?"

She nodded. She definitely needed to get cleaned up. It was amazing that he wasn't freaking out about not having used protection—that postcoital shock and regret wasn't kicking in. "I'll be quick. I just have to . . ."

"Gina!" came a shout from upstairs. It was Molly. "I'm am *so* sorry, but we really need Max. Right now!"

Max kissed her again, and headed for the door. But before he went out of the kitchen, he turned back.

"Oh, yeah," he said, "there was one other thing I was going to say. I want you to marry me."

And with that, he was gone.

It was unbelievable.

Absolutely unbelievable. Molly was furious. "Whoever's idea it was to use a child this way—they ought to be strung up."

The people who lived in the neighboring houses had all been evacuated. Many of them stood back behind the line of soldiers, watching the drama play out.

Or not play out, as the case had been for the past several hours. But now one of the soldiers who spoke English had manned a megaphone, calling out for Jones to surrender.

And another of the soldiers had snatched one of the children—a baby of maybe eight months—out of the arms of her mother. He was using the child as a shield as he crossed the square, toward them.

The baby was screaming and reaching for her mother, who was also wailing, held back by several older women.

It would have been funny the way most of the civilians all instantly scattered. One moment they were there, the next they were gone. With the exception of the desperate young mother and her two companions, they all just vanished into the lengthening shadows of the afternoon.

But there was nothing even remotely humorous about a baby used as a human shield.

One of the soldiers approached the crying mother. He raised his weapon. And the woman fell to her knees—if not quite silenced, then silent enough.

"Hold your fire," the megaphone man said, both in English and in a dialect Molly could roughly understand. It was different from the language spoken on Parwati Island, where she'd spent several years. But it was close enough for her to recognize similarities.

"What's going on?" Max said as he came into the room. He was buttoning his shirt, and aside from one slightly sheepish glance at Molly and a quick attempt to straighten his hair, his attention was now fully on the situation unfolding.

"They're bringing us some kind of radio," Jones said, handing him the binoculars.

The window was one-way—mirrored on the outside. They could see out, but no one could see in. Still, Jones had told Molly that didn't mean there wasn't a sharpshooter somewhere across the square with a scope that was high-tech enough to see through it. Max apparently was thinking the same thing. He stood back and off to the side as he looked out through the bars.

"A radio?" Max said, his voice heavy with disbelief.

"Yeah," Jones said. "Don't get your hopes up. I think it's going to be a single-channel walkie-talkie. Our interpreter probably didn't know the word for it."

"Mmm," Max acknowledged him, binoculars trained on the military personnel clustered on the far side of the square. "They think they're out of our range. They must not know we've got some serious weaponry in here. I wonder . . ."

"Maybe they know we'd never use it," Molly suggested. "I mean, they must know we wouldn't shoot at the soldier, for fear of hitting the little girl."

"The baby's for us," Max told her, still looking through those binoculars. "We're supposed to believe that they won't fire at us when we open the door, if the baby is out there on the doorstep."

The soldier with the baby was getting closer, and Molly could see that he was indeed carrying something besides the child.

"I'm going downstairs," Max said.

"I am, too. I should be the one to open the door," Jones said.

"What if it's a bomb?"

Molly turned to see Gina standing just out in the hall—looking extremely worried, as if she'd already taken the return train, express, from Heaven. "This radio thing that they're so keen to give us," she clarified. "What if it's not really a radio?"

Max was shaking his head. "From what I can see, I doubt they have the technology to—"

"But what if they do?"

He looked at her, and Molly held her breath. But his answer wasn't patronizing or condescending, like, *Since everyone knows we just had sex, I'll pretend to respect you by answering as if your silly question is valid.*

Instead, he was honest. "That would be bad," he told her. "But we need to communicate with them, Gina. I don't see how we have a choice."

She nodded. "At least make sure it's really a radio," she said, "before you bring it inside."

"That won't be so easy to do," Jones told her.

Gina shot him a look. "Sure it will." She gestured to the window. "Shout down to the baby-stealer, and tell him send a message to the guys in charge, with that same radio that he's delivering. Have him tell them to repeat our message back to us over their megaphone. It should be something unusual, something that they wouldn't just say—like, you know, the lyrics of a song. Then we'll know it's really a radio." She frowned. "Unless he's wearing a second one . . ."

Max had the binoculars back up. "I don't see any wires on him. And I doubt they'd have miniatures—earpieces—when they obviously don't even have the money for body armor."

"Although," Gina said, clearly intent upon playing devil's advocate, "what if he doesn't speak English?"

*　　*　　*

The soldier who delivered the radio spoke just enough English.

Gina's strategy worked like a charm. The walkie-talkie was a single-channel short-range piece of shit—they couldn't use it to call for help. Max got it off the doorstep without being shot at and relocked the door.

The baby was taken back across the square and handed over to her weeping mother.

Everything was wonderful—including Gina's smile because Max had used lyrics from an old Elvis Presley song.

"Like a ribbon floats, Girlie, do you see," the words had been broadcast over the megaphone in stilted, accented English. Like a life-and-death version of the telephone game, most of them had been seriously misheard or misunderstood. "Dolly, sowing, goats, some things are men do be . . ."

But it was clearly close enough.

Everything was wonderful—except for the one thing that mattered the most.

The negotiation.

The CO—the army commander in charge of this operation—was following strict orders, that much was clear to Max within fifteen seconds of conversation with the interpreter. The CO wasn't a professional negotiator, and he told Max that he wasn't authorized to cut any kind of deal.

It was more than a lack of imagination on his part. The man clearly had a single goal—to save his own ass. There were people who played strictly by the book because they believed in the rules. But the CO did it because he was frightened.

Max spent about thirty minutes explaining—gently, so as not to frighten him further—that he was American and that he wanted to speak to someone from the American Embassy, and that yes, he knew there was no embassy here on Meda Island. He wanted to speak to someone from the embassy over on East Timor, in Dili.

Only to discover that the embassy in Dili had been shut down. Evacuated. Due to the increased terrorist threat, all personnel had been moved to a location deemed more safe.

Then came the worst news of all.

The commanding officer had been informed by his superiors that Grady Morant was the leader of a notorious terrorist cell, wanted both by the Indonesian and U.S. Governments.

And, oh, yeah, he'd also managed to let it slip that his orders were to shoot them—all—the moment they stepped out of the door, even with their hands up.

So much for no one getting hurt.

Now, maybe there were barriers due to language, but Max simply could not convince the CO that there was a serious misunderstanding.

"I want to speak to Emilio Testa," Max finally said.

"Who is Emilio Testa?" came the response.

Max looked over to find Gina watching him. She knew why he was asking. If Emilio was alive, then Jules probably wasn't.

"He's the man who lives in this house," Max said into the walkie-talkie.

There was silence, during which Gina spoke. Quietly. "If Jules isn't dead, if he's bringing help, he'd have been here by now, wouldn't he?"

Max couldn't lie to her. "Yeah."

The walkie-talkie squawked. "We know this man not, this Testa."

"That might be a lie," Max told Gina. "Or maybe not. Maybe Testa dealt with someone further up the chain of command."

"Are you prepared to surrender?" the voice from the walkie-talkie asked. It was clearly a selection right from the negotiation section of their translation book.

But was he kidding? If surrender meant opening the door and getting shot . . .

"I want to speak to an American," Max said. "Preferably someone from the Jakarta office of the CIA or the American Embassy. But I'll take—I'll talk to any officer of any branch of the U.S. Armed Forces. Any at all. Any American," he repeated.

"You are in no position to make demands," came the reply, also right from the book.

"Sure we are," Max said. "We've got enough food and water to last months." Not true, but if the officer didn't have access to Emilio Testa, then he didn't know that. "You really want to sit out there for that long?"

"The Colonel arrives tomorrow. As does the tank."

Max sat up. What the fuck?

"Did he just say *tank*?" Gina asked, wide-eyed.

"Please repeat," Max said into the walkie-talkie.

But he got only dead air. Whoever was on the other end had turned off their walkie-talkie.

No wonder their man wasn't a particularly skilled negotiator. He didn't have to be.

The colonel—whoever *he* was—was on his way. That was either good news or bad. They wouldn't know until he arrived.

As for the tank—no mystery there. That wasn't just bad news, it was freaking bad.

CHAPTER
TWENTY-ONE

"They might be bluffing," Molly said.

"They might not," Max said, meeting Jones's eyes. "You have any experience with . . . ?"

"Tanks?" Jones shrugged, trying to hide his fear. It had gone through him in waves when Max first brought him the news, and now it settled securely in his intestines. "Enough to know that there are two places I never want to be. Inside of one during a battle where the other guys have tank-busting artillery, and at the spot where the bastards who are inside of the tank are aiming its gun. I mean, yeah, this place is solid, but . . . A tank'll do some damage."

And wasn't *that* an understatement.

At that point, they split up—Molly and Jones going upstairs, Gina and Max staying down. The kitchen was their base of operations as they went through every cabinet and closet in the house.

Searching for a radio transmitter. Or anything else that might help them get the hell out of here in one piece.

A pair of ruby slippers? A magic portal to another dimension? A kit for a build-it-yourself helicopter with a special force-field feature that would keep them from getting the shit shot out of them when they took off from the upstairs window?

So far no luck.

They had, however, found a George Foreman grill and an espresso maker. A karaoke machine had created quite the false alarm since it looked rather radiolike. At least it looked more like a radio than the George Foreman did.

They'd found a copy machine and five boxes of paper. A year's supply of candles. An ancient box that claimed the device inside could make something called "Incredible Edibles," only it was filled with mint-condition baseball cards—including a Tom Seaver and a Ted Williams.

After setting that box aside—wouldn't it be nice to have Emilio help pay some of Molly's upcoming medical bills?— Jones moved into Emilio's bedroom, where he opened a cabinet to find a flat-screen TV.

The TV showed only snow when he turned it on, but there was a DVD player attached, plus three shelves of DVDs.

It seemed that Emilio had a thing for a porn star named Ruksana, who appeared on all the covers of her DVDs dressed as a Catholic schoolgirl, complete with her hair up in pigtails.

Molly, of course, caught him flipping through the various titles. "Let me guess," she said. "You're looking at these in order to get a better understanding of who Emilio is. So you can figure out where he might hide something like a radio. If he had a radio to hide."

Jones laughed. "Exactly." He couldn't have done a better job bullshitting his way out of that one himself. "I've discovered that Emilio's a lot like me. We both go for nice girls."

Molly looked at the cover of the DVD he was holding, and laughed. The English title was in small letters at the bottom of the picture—*Very Mischief Maiden in Big Trouble*. Apparently something had been lost in translation.

"If I ever write my memoirs," she said. "I will definitely use this title." She flipped the box over. "Who knew I had so much in common with 'the one Ruksana?' "

Jones looked at her. The mostly windowless house was dimly lit—they were using candles in an attempt to conserve the generator's gasoline. But Molly could bring light into the darkest room.

She smiled at him as she put the DVD back on the shelf. "So if you had a radio, where would you hide it?"

"I wouldn't have one," Jones told her, playing with a lock of her hair. She was wearing it up due to the heat, but as usual, tendrils escaped around her face. "You don't need a radio when you work alone. But if I had worked with someone that I needed to get in touch with, I'd've kept my radio in my car. Or in my boat or my plane."

"Do you think—"

"There's nothing in the Impala," he told her. "I went over it. A coupla times, before all the shooting started." He closed his eyes, trying to see the dashboard of that crappy subcompact that had been parked out on the street. The car that Emilio and Jules had driven off in. Jones had started to hotwire it when he'd thought Molly was inside of the white van that had left in such a hurry.

He tried to picture the glove compartment, to see if it had a lock on it that was more substantial than usual. But it was no good. He just didn't remember.

"What?" Molly asked.

"If I were Emilio," Jones told her, "I'd keep my radio in the car I always used when I was, um, not necessarily following the letter of the law. My less obviously identifiable car. Like the little Ford he took down the mountain."

"Shit." Molly rarely swore, but if there was ever a time for it, it was now. They'd sifted through just about every closet, drawer, or cabinet in the place.

No radio. At least none that acted as a transmitter.

But Gina came into the room, radiating excitement. "Hey, have you found any . . ." She saw them standing by the cabinet. "Great, this is exactly what I was looking for."

"Porn?" Jones asked.

"Honey," Molly said to Jones in her super-patient sitcom

wife voice. "Gina doesn't need porn to make *her* sex life more exciting."

"Oh, Mr. Pizza Delivery Man . . ." He pretended to be Gina, his voice all breathy and high-pitched. "Really? Right here in the kitchen? Even though my friends are upstairs? Okay! Wocka-chicka, wocka-chicka."

"Shut up!" Gina laughed, but she was blushing. "Give me a break, I haven't seen the man in a year and a half."

"So the first thing you do is jump him? Without even . . ." Jones realized what he was saying. Molly was looking at him. Oops.

"We just don't want you to get hurt," Molly told Gina.

"I'm trapped in a bunker disguised as a house on a remote island in Indonesia," Gina said, "surrounded by an army whose commander has been given an order to shoot to kill, even if we surrender. A tank is on its way, the intention being to blast us out of here."

"Point taken," Jones said. "So why are you looking for porn?" He took the DVD case from Gina. *Ruksana Visits Vatican City.* "Didn't Ruksana win some award for this one?" he asked. "Like most tasteless and offensive piece of shit of the year?"

"Oh, dear," Molly said as she saw it. "That's just *wrong.*"

"Open the box," Gina told him.

Aha. There wasn't a DVD inside. There was a computer diskette.

"We think it's some kind of backup file," she told them. "It was hidden in the pantry. With an old computer—one that was being stored there. Like someone got a laptop but didn't want to throw the old desktop away? I thought it was weird to hide a DVD back there, so . . . Of course it *is* porn, and I guess people who are into it hide it wherever, but I opened the box and . . ."

Molly had already taken one of the DVD cases from the shelf, opening it and . . . "Here's another."

Jones grabbed a stack and started searching, too.

"Max is setting the computer up in the kitchen," Gina told them. "If he can get it to work, we can try to see what's on these disks."

The computer was practically an antique, the monitor tiny by modern standards. It chugged slowly to life as Gina brought Molly and Jones back into the kitchen.

"Find anything else?" Max asked from atop his pillow. It hurt to sit, but if he kind of half perched, using the cushion, it wasn't too painful.

"The mother lode," Gina reported. "Ten more disks."

The contents of the pantry were spread out across the kitchen floor—everything from piles of old newspapers to a supply of dog food to a box of fliers—printed half in Indonesian, half in Portuguese—for what looked like a political campaign. They had to step over it all to get to the table.

"Does anyone else want tea?" Molly asked, crossing instead to the stove.

Gina put the disks down on the table near Max. "Yeah, I'd like some, too, but I'll get it." She touched the back of his neck as she headed toward Molly. It was the lightest caress, but it was both possessive and intimate, and Max suddenly became acutely aware that this very table was where they'd recently . . .

Okay. Anyone else in the room thinking about that? Max glanced at Jones, who caught his eye and tried not to smile and . . .

Yup, Jones was thinking about it, too.

"Sit," Gina told Molly. "Put your feet up."

"Thanks, sweetie." Molly came over to sit at the table, right across from Max.

Max pretended to be fascinated by the computer monitor, which was still giving him an hourglass icon. In his peripheral vision, he could see Jones moving a chair so that Molly could elevate her feet.

"My ankles have been starting to swell," Molly said. She was speaking directly to him. He couldn't not look up at her. Oh, man, was he actually blushing? "It's a recent development."

Wait. Swollen ankles were . . . ? Didn't she have breast cancer?

She smiled across the table at him. "Don't look so worried, Bhagat. It's normal. It's probably from the heat. I'm just supposed to be careful because, well, I *am* in my forties . . ."

Now Max was completely mystified.

Molly's smile widened. "What? You're looking at me like . . ." But then her smile vanished and she turned toward Jones. "You didn't tell him I was pregnant," she said. "Did you?"

"You're pregnant, too?" Max asked. He turned to look at Jones. "No, he didn't tell me that."

Jones rubbed his forehead as if he had a bad headache. "Mol, I thought it was private. Until we got the results of the biopsy . . ."

Molly was pissed. "You thought you'd be able to talk me into terminating this pregnancy—"

"I thought," Jones said, over her, "that after you spoke to another doctor or twenty, you might decide that saving your own life is a priority, at which point you might want the *privacy*—"

"What I *want* is this baby," Molly said.

Max met Gina's eyes from across the room. She had to be thinking the same thing he was—that they owed Molly and Jones an apology for fighting in front of them before. This was excruciatingly painful to have to sit through.

"I know you do," Jones told her grimly. "And I'm sorry, but I don't. God, Molly—"

"Well. I'm glad you finally found the courage to let me know that." Molly stood up. She was statuesque, always standing very straight, but now she drew herself up even taller. "Excuse me," she said to Max as she headed for the door.

Jones, meanwhile, was obviously frustrated. And pissed. "What I was about to say was: God, Molly, not if having it is going to kill you. Shit, Mol, don't—"

But she'd already left the room. He chased her, and moving too fast, had to leap over the bag of dog food. In doing so, he knocked over the box of political fliers. They went everywhere. "Ow, shit, fuck, sorry!"

"I'll get it," Gina said, coming to his rescue. "Just go."

But Jones stopped. He bent down and picked up one of the fliers, staring at the picture of the smiling candidate. "Shit," he said again. He flipped the flier over, clearly looking for the part that was in English. There wasn't any. "Molly!" he shouted. "I need you in here!" He looked up at Gina. "Go get her."

Gina didn't seem convinced that that was the best thing to do right now, but Jones was adamant.

"Tell Molly I need her to help me read this," he said. "She's better than me with languages." He turned to Max. "I think I know what this whole goatfuck is about. I think I know who's after me." He held up the flier. "See this guy? He paid Chai a serious chunk of change for me to kill his mistress."

"His name is Heru Nusantara," Jones told them. "I don't know what he's running for, but someone's obviously investing some money into his campaign."

"I don't think it's a campaign," Molly said. She was back sitting at the table, flipping over the flier. "I think it's just, I don't know, propaganda . . . ? It doesn't say what he's running for. At least not that I can tell. I mean, there are some similarities here to the dialects I *can* read, but . . ."

"You're doing way better than I could," Gina told her. The tea had finally steeped, and she poured it into two mugs. She brought one over to Molly.

"This part here has something to do with East Timor," Molly pointed to the top of the flier. She smiled wanly at Gina. "Thanks."

Gina got her own mug and sat down at the table next to Max, who was clicking and scrolling his way through the diskettes they'd found.

It was more than obvious that Molly was overheated, she was tired, she was upset, she was scared—Gina could relate. It had been one hell of a month, and it was far from over.

As if he could read her mind, Max, who had been resting his chin in his hand, shifted so that his arm was on the back of her chair. It was too warm in the kitchen for full contact, but he touched her anyway—with just a few of his fingertips, lightly against her back, the slightest pressure.

It nearly made her start to cry.

He was there. Beside her.

He loved her—somehow, he was finally at peace with that.

There was nothing more that she wanted—except maybe to live another hundred years with Max beside her.

Problem was, they only had enough food and water to last a few weeks. At most. And that wasn't taking into consideration this tank that was coming.

Still, Max was here. He wasn't just a voice on a radio, he wasn't just a figment of her imagination.

"There's something here about an American company coming in." Molly looked at Jones. "Doesn't East Timor have . . . I know it's not oil . . ."

"Natural gas," he said. "But no one wants to touch it because of the violence—the constant fighting on the island."

"It looks like this is saying this politician, Heru Nusantara, helped set up a deal with a company called Alliance Co.," Molly said. "The implication is it's going to bring jobs and money into the area—and make East Timor a proper part of Indonesia once and for all."

"Yeah," Jones scoffed. "Like that's going to happen. Someone's going to get rich, and it's not going to be the starving people of East Timor. That I can guarantee."

"There's also something about how the American embassy has come to Dili," Molly told them. "Obviously, they're there to support Alliance Co. The implication is that the American presence will create stability in East Timor."

"So what does this politician have to do with you?" Max asked Jones.

"Nusantara was one of Chai's . . . I don't know, business associates, I guess you would call him," Jones said.

Molly made a raspberry sound. "Says here he's bringing honesty and trustworthiness back to Indonesia. This whole thing is all about what a hero he is. Incorruptible. Hah. Heru, the hero of the people. Right."

"If that's the case," Jones said, "I can understand why he's looking for me. I have some serious dirt on him."

"Such as?" Max asked, his focus seemingly still on that computer screen. "You mentioned . . . his mistress?"

Jones nodded. "She was barely sixteen. And pregnant. Chai gave her to me and told me to kill her."

"Dear Lord," Molly said.

"I didn't, okay?" he told her sharply. "But thanks for the vote of confidence.' "

She looked as if she were going to cry. "I wasn't—"

"I know," he said. "Shit, I'm sorry." He rubbed his forehead. Looked at Molly from beneath his hand. "There are . . . things I never told you. Things I deserve to be . . ." He stopped. Started again. "Just let me . . . try to . . ."

Molly nodded, her face pale. Without her default smile, the lines on her face seemed pronounced. She looked exhausted.

And for the first time since Molly had discovered that lump in her breast, Gina realized that her friend could well be dying.

It was obvious that Jones, however, had been unable to think about anything else from the moment he'd gotten the news that Molly needed a biopsy. It was also clear that he thought of her illness as some kind of cosmic payback. Punishment for his sins.

There was sure to be a sin or two in the story he was going to tell them now.

Ever since she'd first met Jones, Gina had suspected his reputation as a dangerous man was not entirely trumped up. Still, this was not going to be easy to hear.

And it was going to be even less easy for him to talk about. Especially with Molly already upset.

But as Jones sat there, struggling to find the words, Molly reached out and took his hand. "Just tell the story," she said gently. "You know I love you. What's past is past. I'm not going to judge you—no one here is. We've all made mistakes."

Jones held her gaze for a long time. But then he nodded. "It was . . ." He took a deep breath, blew it out hard. "It was toward the end of my . . . association with Chai. I think this probably was the event that made him decide to jettison me. But it started, I think, when he noticed that I spent most of my time in the hospital. Saving lives. Not going out and . . ." He shook off the memory.

"I don't know, maybe I thought I'd sufficiently paid him back for getting me out of that prison. I really don't know what I was thinking. It was another . . . lifetime ago. But I'd definitely cut myself off from the, um, uglier aspects of his business. I'm pretty sure when this all happened, he was testing my loyalty." Jones laughed. "Apparently I failed.

"See, at the time Nusantara was . . . I don't know, mayor, I think," Jones continued. "Or maybe governor of . . . I can't even remember the island or town or whatever it was. It's a blur. But it was definitely two-bit and poor as shit. Still, he was running for reelection, and the race was tight. So I guess he thought he'd play the hero card. He had a connection—"

"Nusantara?" Max clarified.

"Yeah," Jones told him. "He was relatively tight with another one of the crime lords who operated on a neighboring island. This guy created a lot of chaos—he was heavy into pirating, which is a huge business here in Indonesia. Anyway, this was someone who was four or five tiers down from Chai. It was no skin off Chai's nose if this lower-level thug went out in a blaze of glory.

"So Nusantara set the thug up. He paid some hired guns to come in and blow the crime lord away while the guy was having a meal out on his patio. Only, whoops. Guess who came over for lunch that day, probably to try to talk him into staying away from the local fishermen. It was Nusantara's political opponent. Along with his wife and two young kids."

"Oh, Lord," Molly said.

"Yeah," Jones agreed. "It was a bloodbath. No one survived. Nusantara had made sure he couldn't be connected to the murders. He'd set up the gang he'd hired to do the shooting—these were not people who went quietly when apprehended by the police, so . . . They were all killed.

"He was home free. But when he found out there were children among the dead, he panicked. He made a phone call, which his mistress, Esma, overheard.

"He was squeamish about actually committing murder, which was lucky for Esma," Jones continued. "He didn't have a problem, though, farming out his various crimes. He came to Chai with the girl, told him he needed her vanished. Chai delegated the task to me."

He paused. Cleared his throat. "If I told you I never took a life because Chai gave the order, I'd be lying," Jones said quietly. He was looking at Molly. "I guess I always justified it—I was ridding the world of some bad people and . . . But this, I couldn't do. Except I knew if *I* didn't, someone else would. So I took advantage of semantics. The boss had told me to get rid of her, permanently. So that's what I did.

"I borrowed a seaplane," he said, "and I took Esma far from Chai's base of operations. I brought her to a village on this tiny island—I spotted their church from the air. I landed and motored into this cove, and we hiked up into the hills and . . .

"I told the village leaders that she was a widow—and that I had killed her husband. I said I'd found out that she was pregnant with his child, and now I didn't want her anymore. Instead of killing her, I was going to leave her with them. If I saw her again, I *would* kill her. And then I'd come back and kill all of them. I also told them if I came back and she was gone, I'd kill them all. I gave her some money, courtesy of Chai. Not a lot, but enough to give her a fresh start. I hiked back down to the plane, flew away and that was that."

Jones laughed. "Well, not quite. I guess I thought because I was, you know, Chai's favorite son—his pet American expat—I guess I thought that we'd both just have a good laugh about our differing definitions for 'get rid of her.' I told him that she was as good as dead. We'd never hear from her again.

"Long story short, Nusantara went apeshit. He wanted her dead, he wanted proof she was dead. I guess he was afraid she'd turn up again some day, with his illegitimate child in tow spouting accusations of murder." Jones shook his head. "Turned out Chai needed Nusantara's cooperation for a shipment of drugs that was going out. He needed the police to be far away from his drop point, so he had to keep Nusantara happy.

"Chai beat the shit out of me, which was . . . not completely unexpected. But I didn't tell him where I'd taken the girl. Not because I'm a hero," he said quietly, his words directed at Molly. "But because I'd anticipated something like this. I'd made a point to fly in circles after I left the island. I had no idea which island it was. I mean, I knew the general area, but . . . I told them this. Both Chai and Nusantara. And I knew Nusantara, at least, didn't believe me.

"It wasn't long after that, that I found out Chai was setting me up. He was going to sell me back to the U.S. as a deserter, which after being left for three years in that prison was a bad joke, but . . . Anyway. There you have it. Heru Nusantara—hero of the people—has blood on his hands. He must be planning to run for something big. Prime minister, president? What do they have in Indonesia? I never really paid attention."

"A president," Molly said. She must've squeezed his hand—she was holding it that whole time, because he looked at her. He tried to smile, but his eyes were haunted.

"It's like it was a whole different lifetime ago," he said quietly. "I hate even thinking about it." He exhaled hard, turned to Max. "So I guess Nusantara's cleaning all the potential skeletons out of his closet. What do you think? Am I crazy, or . . ."

"I think," Max said, still focused on that computer screen, "that Emilio recently sold information about the American Embassy in Jakarta, along with a crapload of weapons, to an extremely powerful al Qaeda operative who went missing back in 2001, from Afghanistan." He looked up as he popped the diskette out of the computer, put the next one in. "Guess he's not dead."

"We have to tell someone," Molly said.

"We could tell this colonel who's coming," Gina suggested.

Jones cleared his throat. "I *meant,* what do you think about—"

"I think you've figured out who wants you and why," Max interrupted him. "So far I've found a pretty solid connection between Emilio and Nusantara," he said. "Emilio was paid to distribute these fliers—which he didn't do very well, did he? Guess how much the going rate was for that particular job?"

"This ought to be good," Jones scoffed. "What, ten, twenty K?"

"How's a half a million dollars, U.S.?" Max asked.

"Shee-yit," Gina said. "Are you serious?" But then she understood. The money was really the first installment of a bounty for bringing Grady Morant to this island.

"Nusantara paid him that, directly?" Jones wanted to know.

"No," Max said. "There was a third party. Someone by the name of . . . Ram Subandrio. Ring any bells?"

Jones sat back in his chair. "Oh yeah," he said, and it was clear to Gina that the bells that were ringing weren't playing a happy song. "Remember how we're up Shit's Creek without a paddle, what with this tank coming and all? Well, the canoe just overturned. My old 'friend' Ramelan Subandrio used to work for Chai. He found him in the same prison where he found me—except Subandrio was on the other end of the ol' cattle prod."

Jones wasn't done. He dropped the final bomb, his voice grim. "And last I'd heard, he'd been made a colonel in some special branch of some kind of secret police."

CHAPTER
TWENTY-TWO

"Would you honestly tell me if you thought we were going to die tomorrow?" Gina asked as she and Max made dinner.

That is, if opening a can and giving them each a small portion of her old favorite, monkey stew, could be called making dinner.

They were rationing both their food and water, which seemed a little crazy. Unless, of course, the threat of that approaching tank was just a bluff.

"I don't think we're going to die tomorrow. I think this colonel's going to come, and I'm going to negotiate with him, and we're going to settle this peacefully." Max went over to the giant bag of dried dog food. He opened it, sifted through it, all the way to the bottom, no doubt to see if a radio was hidden inside. But as Gina watched, he sniffed it. He even crunched on a piece.

He smiled, no doubt at the expression on her face. Held out a handful.

She shook her head. "No, thanks."

"It's not bad."

"I'll wait until it's a necessity," she said, but she moved toward him, drawn by his lingering smile, by the warmth in his eyes.

The ever-changing light from the security camera monitors played across his face. Aside from the flickering candle on the table, it was the only light in the room.

He was obviously exhausted. And distracted by the contents of Emilio's closets, still spread out on the kitchen floor. She knew he was seriously unhappy with their current predicament. Being under siege was, by nature, a lack-of-control situation, and she knew Max well enough to know he found this maddening.

Gina was certain that even if she could talk him into skipping dinner and finding a room with a door and bed, he'd only sleep for a short time. He'd be up, just sitting—gingerly, because sitting hurt him worse than he was letting on—and staring at all the utterly useless things they'd found in those closets and cabinets.

He would sit and try to figure out what he'd missed. Or how he could use these relatively random household items to build a radio.

"Don't think I didn't notice that you avoided my question," she told him.

"I answered it," Max said, as she came close enough for him to take her in his arms, as he pulled her against him.

He was looking at her the way she'd always wanted him to look at her. As if he weren't afraid to let her know that he loved her. It was wonderful—or it would have been, if only they weren't surrounded by men with guns who wanted to kill them.

Gina looped her arms around his neck. She kissed him, unable to resist the temptation. His mouth was warm and sweet and no, she was not going to let him distract her this way.

"No, you didn't," she said. "The question was, would you honestly *tell* me. It requires a simple answer—yes or no."

He kissed her again—longer this time, lazily. As if the army outside didn't scare him to death.

Of course, maybe it didn't. Maybe it only pissed him off. Maybe she was the only one who was terrified. Maybe he'd never been in a situation like this before—he was usually the one on the other side of the megaphone.

"Maybe we should forget about dinner," Gina said breathlessly, "and just find a room with a door."

She pulled away, ready to drag him into the hall, but he didn't release her. "Yes, I'd tell you," he said, as if he knew that part of her urgency came from her fear that this was their last night together, their last night on earth. "I promise. And no, I honestly don't think we're going to die."

"We, you and me?" she asked. "Or we, all of us, including Jones—Grady. You know, old multiple-name-man, my best friend's husband?"

He gave her another smile, but it faded far too quickly. "Grady Morant is why we're here," he finally told her. Again, not quite an answer.

"He's a good person," Gina said. "He may have done some bad things—"

"Very bad things," he agreed.

"He had some very bad things done to him first," she pointed out. "He was left to die—to rot in that prison where some really nasty people tortured him. For three years, Max. Did you know—"

"Yes," Max said, "I do know."

Molly had told her a little—just a bit—about Jones's ordeal. Beatings, torture—both physical and psychological. It made Gina's skin crawl just to think about it.

"Do you think that excuses the fact that he then went to work for Chai?" Max asked her now.

Gina didn't hesitate. Chai had gotten Jones out of there, made the torture end. "Yes, I do."

Max nodded. "It's an interesting ethical debate."

"It's not an ethical debate." Gina pulled away from him, stepping over piles of newspapers as she went back to the counter where their plates of food were sitting. "It's a man's *life*."

"Yeah," Max said. "Believe it or not, I like him, too.

Which is saying something, because I didn't at first. I'm just not as sure as you are about the free pass for his previous life of crime."

"Please don't give him to the colonel and this Nusantara guy." Gina scraped the food they'd set aside for Molly and Jones onto the two other plates. It was more than obvious that they weren't coming down. And in this heat, the food wouldn't keep. Since they'd unplugged it, the refrigerator was only slightly cooler than room temperature. "If he says they'll kill him, they'll definitely kill him."

"He seems ready to make that sacrifice," Max pointed out.

Gina handed him a plate and a fork. "He loves Molly."

"That I believe," Max said. "He's willing to die for her."

"That's, like, butthead stupid," Gina told him. "Dying *for* someone? You want to be a real hero? Figure out a way to save both the person you love *and* yourself. And then spend the rest of your life working your ass off to keep the relationship healthy. I mean, dying is easy. Living's the real challenge."

Max nodded, as they both ate the stew, right there, standing up. It was cold and a little greasy. "The dog food's better," he said, and she laughed.

"Yeah, I bet." She licked her plate clean. "I was going to say, don't ever die for me, but I changed my mind—I'm just going to say, don't ever die."

Max smiled. "I love you," he told her, and this time he didn't look quite so pained as he said it. As if he weren't quite so appalled by the idea.

It was somewhat surreal.

"So what happened?" she asked him as he licked his plate clean, too. She hadn't done it to be suggestive. It just seemed the best way to handle both the lack of food and water for cleaning. And yet when Max did it, all she could think about was . . . finding a room with a door. Green Bermuda shorts had never been so alluring. She cleared her throat. "I mean, between me leaving, and you deciding that you want to, you know, marry me. What changed?"

"I missed you," he said.

Gina glanced at him as she wiped their plates and forks with a cloth. Her mother, the sterilization queen, would've been appalled, but then again, her mother had never been under siege. "That's it? No near-death revelation, where Abraham Lincoln, Walt Whitman, and Elvis pushed you away from the light and told you, in three-part harmony, to go find me? I mean . . . how *did* you find me?"

Max's smile widened, and if she pretended not to see the current of tension that was wrapped around him, she might almost believe that he would be happy to stand there, forever, just gazing at her.

"Why did I think I could live without you?" he wondered aloud.

Those were words she'd never thought she'd hear outside of her dreams. Her heart skipped a beat, and his smile made her go into freefall. God, she just could not get used to the way he was letting himself look at her.

"Well, yeah, that's what I've been telling you for years." Gina crossed her arms, leaned back against the counter. From where she was standing, she had an excellent view of that kitchen table. That, plus Max's smile and his plate licking and his eyes and his hands and his mouth and his green shorts and his everything made it impossible for her not to think about sex. And it would just be too embarrassing if Molly or Jones came down here to find them going at it again. "How *did* you find me? Did Jones call you, or . . . ?"

"No, actually." Max leaned back against the counter, too, careful of his posterior, wincing slightly, but trying to hide it, of course. "I was . . . already in Hamburg."

"That terrorist bombing," Gina said. "I saw it on the news. The TV worked when we first got here—before the

Army of Darkness out there shot down the sat-dish. That *was* why you were in Germany, right?"

"Sort of." He paused for a very long time, then said, "They had your name on a casualty list of people killed in the attack."

Gina stopped leaning back. "What?" she whispered, horrified.

"I went to Hamburg to identify your body," Max told her in his dispassionately cool negotiator voice. But the look in his eyes, on his face was neither dispassionate nor cool. "It turned out this other woman had your passport. When you ditched it at the forgers, the terrorists responsible for the bombing picked it up and . . ."

Gina couldn't breathe. "I didn't want Emilio to know which one of us was Molly," she told him. She couldn't believe this. "Max, my God, you actually thought I was dead?"

She saw the answer in his eyes as he nodded.

"It was a near-death revelation of a different kind. They had you out on this table and . . . I had to go into this room—a morgue, I guess, right at the airport and . . ." His voice shook. It actually shook. "Only it wasn't you, so . . ."

But he'd thought it was. He'd been told . . . She moved toward him, and he pulled her into his arms. He just held her, tightly.

"For how long?" she whispered, and he understood.

"It was around twenty-four hours between the time I got the news and the time I found out it wasn't you." He forced a smile. "It was a very, very bad day."

"I'm so sorry," Gina said. But oh, God. "My parents?"

"They know you're alive," Max reassured her, touching her face, as if he still couldn't quite believe she wasn't dead.

She knew, somewhat, how he was feeling. She'd sat beside him, touching him, just content to be near him, for days on end in the hospital, after he'd almost died.

"Jules made sure they were kept informed as we went,"
Max continued. "Until, you know, we lost cell phones."

Jules.

It was obvious that Max was thinking about him, too.
The muscle jumped in his jaw as he clenched his teeth.

"Gina," he said, pulling back even farther, taking her
hands. "I know you said you love me. All of me and . .
Just last night I was talking to Jules and I told him that I
was afraid of hurting you. That I didn't want you to . .
have to live in my life, in my world, with all my . . . bullshit
and . . . I can't promise you that it won't be awful. I can
only promise you that I'll try. You accused me, once, of not
trying and . . ." He nodded. "You were right. But you also
always said that I . . . didn't talk to you, and . . ."

"I was wrong about that," she said softly, lacing their fingers together.

"I talked to you more than I ever talked to anyone,"
Max admitted. "I'm not, you know, like Jules. He could
really . . . go. Really get pretty intensely personal, pretty
quickly. I was sitting there last night, thinking, thank God
he's gay—otherwise the two of you would've run away together, years ago. I just . . . There are some things I can't
talk about very easily. So if that's what you want—"

Gina had to laugh. "When I met Jules," she told Max, "I
was already in love with you. It didn't matter if he was gay
or straight or whatever. I love you. What I want is *you*.
And please stop talking about Jules as if he's dead. We
don't know that."

Maybe not, but Max strongly suspected it. Gina could
see that in his eyes.

"I've loved you for a long time, too," he admitted.
"Probably since you asked me if I was the janitor." He
laughed softly, shaking his head.

"What? When did I . . . ?" She had no idea what he was
talking about.

"It was one of the first things you said to me, over the

radio, while you were on that hijacked plane," Max told her. "I asked if you were okay, and you asked me if I was the airport janitor, because that was a really stupid question. Considering the circumstances."

"I don't remember that."

"I do," he said. "I remember thinking that you were the most incredibly courageous woman on the planet. To do what you did. To survive what you survived, and then still be able to make jokes and . . . To not be afraid to live." He paused. "To forgive me for letting it happen."

"You *let* it happen about as much as I did," Gina told him. Please God, don't let him start with this again.

"I know. But that didn't keep me from wanting a do-over. There were things I could have done differently during the hijacking. Not *should* have done—it was a crapshoot, I know that. I *knew* it." He looked down at their hands, fingers intertwined. "I wasted so much time running what-if scenarios in my head. What if I'd done *this* differently, what if I'd done *that* instead . . ."

"If you'd done any of it differently," Gina pointed out, "I might've been killed, instead of—"

"I know," Max said again. "I do know that. I did know it. Logically, rationally—it all made sense. But I just couldn't let it go." There were actually tears in his eyes. "And then . . ." He forced the words out. "Then I was told you were dead. Killed by a terrorist bomb in Hamburg."

He swallowed. "I think, before that, I was just waiting for you to come back. I think I expected—that I counted on—you having the sense and, and . . . *vision* I guess, to shove your way back into my life someday. And suddenly, a bomb went off, and someday was gone. *You* were gone. Forever."

"Oh, Max," she breathed.

"And none of it mattered anymore," he whispered. "None of it. What I should have done four years ago, what I could have done . . . The only thing that mattered was what I *didn't* do last year, when I had the chance. Which was tell you how much I loved you, and to admit that I wanted you in my life—if you were crazy enough to put up with me."

Gina couldn't say a word because her heart was jammed so tightly in her throat. What she could do, and she did, was bring his hand to her lips and kiss him. His fingers, his palm. He cupped her cheek, and when she looked up at him, he had so much love in his eyes, it took her breath away.

Love, plus heat. Desire.

It embarrassed him a little, or maybe he thought it was inappropriate, because although he smiled, it was rueful and he looked away.

"You know, I love it when you look at me like that," she whispered.

He met her eyes again and . . . Oh, yeah, it was definitely time to find a room. With a door. The bed was entirely optional.

Except . . .

"Oh, shoot," Gina said. "There's something I have to tell you."

But she didn't get a chance, because the light from the security camera monitors flickered and then faded completely away.

"It's the generator," Jones reported, speaking softly because his wife was still sleeping in the other room. "We're out of gas."

He could see that Gina was relieved that this wasn't something the army outside had attempted—some simultaneous attack on all of the security cameras at the exact same moment, in advance of some other far more violent and catastrophic nighttime assault.

"I don't think they even knew we had security cameras."

Max used the binoculars to look out the second-story window at the army camped at the edge of the square.

Making a run for it under cover of darkness.

That was the most viable of the many options and suggestions they'd come up with today as they'd brainstormed ways either to escape, or get noticed by friends or allies.

Some of the ideas were silly, thanks to Molly, who, despite being upset with Jones was still trying to keep the mood upbeat.

They had boxes and boxes of copy paper. They could make thousands of paper airplanes with the message, "Help!" written on them and fly them out the windows.

Could they try to blast their way out of the tunnel? Maybe dig an alternative route to the surface? It seemed a long shot, worth going back in there and taking a look at the construction—which Jones had done only to come back out, thumbs down.

Two of them could create a diversion, while the other two took the Impala and crashed their way out of the garage.

At which point the Impala—and everyone in it—would be hit by hundreds of bullets.

That one—along with taking their chances with the far fewer number of soldiers lying in wait at the end of the escape tunnel—went into the bad idea file.

Molly had thought that they could sing karaoke. Emilio had a Best of Whitney Houston karaoke CD. Their renditions of *I Will Always Love You,* she insisted, would cause the troops to break rank and run away screaming.

Except the karaoke machine was powered by electricity, which they were trying to use only for the computer and the security monitors, considering—at the time—that the generator was almost out of gasoline.

Yeah, *that* was why it was a silly idea.

It did, however, generate a lot of desperately needed laughter.

At that point, Gina had suggested using some of their firepower to try to get attention. If they kept firing their weapons—either into the air or down into the street—maybe someone would come to investigate. Or mention to someone in the nearest American Embassy that a full-scale battle appeared to be taking place on Pulau Meda.

Or—better yet—they could fire their weapons in a rhythmic pattern.

Gina apparently had a friend who was a SEAL who'd set off explosives to blow in the pattern of "Shave and a Haircut"—bump bah-dah bump bump—in hopes that some of his buddies would hear it and find him.

They could do something here, she'd suggested, that would be undeniably identifiable as American. Such as "Take Me Out to the Ball Game," or "The Star-Spangled Banner" or "Hit Me Baby One More Time." It would be like taking part in the world's most violent percussion section.

Of course, SOS in Morse Code had less flair, but that could work, too.

Or maybe, Max had said, when the colonel arrived, they could surrender the disk with the info on the impending Jakarta American Embassy attack. He'd used the computer to insert a "we are here" message on the disk. With luck, it would get into the right hands.

But luck hadn't been on their side so far, Jones pointed out. They were going to have to start thinking about ways to use him as a bargaining chip.

Molly had jumped on top of that, assuming he'd meant that Max should start thinking about surrendering Jones to the colonel. It was an option she wanted Max to promise he'd never consider.

Of course, Max wasn't about to make any promises he couldn't keep, so Molly had made her second dramatic exit of the day.

Jones had followed.

Furious with him, Molly had refused to talk. She had, however, taken him to bed where the sight of that bandage over her biopsy stitches put an additional weird spin on things.

Afterwards, she'd cried, which damn near broke his heart.

She'd fallen asleep just before sundown, holding tightly to him as if she were never going to let him go.

But now it was dark, and their most viable option—making a run for it under cover of darkness—was no longer a possibility.

Because someone out there was on top of the situation, and there was no darkness. Three jeeps had been moved into the square. Engines running, the vehicles' bright headlights were aimed at the front of the house. They had their fog lights lit, too, which meant that shooting out the lights would require not just six well-aimed bullets, but twelve. Which was a crying shame.

Max had been keeping an eye on the security monitors, and he told Jones that someone down at the end of the escape tunnel had done something similar, although it had been hard to see if there was more than one jeep down there.

And as far as the security cameras went . . .

Now that they were gone, he and Max were going to have to use the old-fashioned method of keeping an eye on the army that had them surrounded.

"You want to take the first watch, or should I?" Jones asked him now.

Max was holding the binoculars, but he wasn't looking through them anymore. He was staring at the wall, frowning slightly.

Okay. It was possible the man was starting to hallucinate from lack of sleep, so Jones decided for him. "I'll take it first," he said. "I'm not that tired." He looked at Gina. "Make sure he really sleeps."

But Max didn't relinquish the binoculars. "Wait," he said. "Whoa. I think I know how to get us out of here." He looked at Gina. "All of us."

Max turned back to Jones. And it was clear he wasn't losing it. He may have been tired, but he was alert and completely, solidly there. "I need to get the commander back on the walkie-talkie," he said. "Help me wake him up."

"Molly. Mol."

She awoke to find Gina gently shaking her, light from a candle making shadows dance around the room and across her somber face. Molly clutched the sheet to her, aware with a flash of fear that Jones was no longer beside her in the bed. "What's wrong? Where's Grady?"

"Nothing's wrong," Gina reassured her. "He and Max are going to stir things up by shooting some of our guns. I didn't want you to wake up to that sound and think we were under attack."

Her relief was short-lived as the ripping sound of automatic gunfire exploded around them. Even though Molly was expecting it, it made her jump. And it still made her crazily anxious. What a terrible noise. She grabbed for Gina's hand, and they sat there, just holding onto each other, trying not to flinch.

She knew that Gina hated the sound, too.

But Max and Grady were sending an SOS—she recognized the pattern.

Gina caught her questioning look and nodded. "Two birds with one stone," she shouted over the racket.

There was silence then. Just for a moment, and then Max and Jones repeated the entire sequence.

Molly could only imagine how loud it would have been with the door open.

"What's going on?" she asked Gina when, once again, the sudden silence seemed to ring around them.

"Max is going to try to negotiate again with the commanding officer," Gina told her. "You know that information he found on Emilio's backup disks about the attack on the embassy?"

The American embassy. In Jakarta. Molly nodded.

"He's not going to hand over the information on disk," Gina told her, "and pray it gets into the hands of someone who'll be able to decode his 'send help' message. Instead, he's simply telling the CO that we have information about an impending terrorist attack. If the commander wants the details, he's going to have to bring in American authorities to help negotiate our little standoff here."

Dear Lord.

"Once we get the Americans involved, then hopefully this shoot-on-sight-even-if-we-surrender thing disappears," Gina continued. "Grady'll be arrested, sure, but he'll be in American custody. Which is way better than dead."

Molly nodded. It was.

"Basically, Max is giving this CO a choice," Gina told her. "If he hands Grady over to the Americans, Nusantara and his mystery colonel are going to be pissed, right? But if he sits on this info about a terrorist attack and the embassy is hit . . ."

"Innocent people could die," Molly said. She *hated* this.

"Yeah," Gina agreed. "That's what Max wants him to be thinking. As well as the fact that his knowing about it in advance, yet doing nothing, *will* get out. The interpreter will know, as well as his aides . . . People will find out, and fingers'll be pointed. They always are. And they could well point at the colonel and Nusantara, too. That's what Max is telling this guy, right now—to contact Nusantara and tell him this. As far as damage control goes, he's going to have to make a choice. What could hurt Nusantara's political career more? Accusations of murder from a nonreputable felon or the fact that his private agenda kept him from stopping a terrorist attack?"

Nonreputable felon.

Gina had always been good at reading Molly's mind. "You know that I don't think that's what Jones is, right?" she said. "I'm just trying to make it sound as if—"

As if on cue, Jones stuck his head in the door. "We're too late," he said flatly. "The attack on the embassy went down yesterday."

"There's gas in the Impala," Jones pointed out.

Molly looked at him. "But who's going into the garage to get it?"

"Look, Mol—"

"Don't 'Look, Mol,' me!" she shot back at him. "You told me yourself that the garage isn't reinforced. It's dangerous just to open that door. If someone goes out there . . ."

"Guys," Max said mildly, as he ran the binoculars over the surrounding army. They were settling back in, going back to sleep.

"I was just saying," Jones said. "There's gas in the Impala, and we need gas to power up the generator . . ."

They were all up in the second-story front room, down on the floor, out of range of the window. All except for Max, who was standing off to the side, over by the door.

During the last negotiation session, Jones had gone into the bathroom and taken the mirror off the medicine cabinet. He'd managed to set it up so they could use it to see out the window—while sitting safely out of range of a sniper's bullets.

"If we could get the computer up and running," Jones continued now, "maybe we'll find something else on one of those disks."

"Maybe I should be the one to get the gas," Molly said.

Damn. If Max had four perpetrators completely surrounded, he wouldn't be sitting back and taking a nap.

He'd have them on the radio, talking. He'd be keeping
them awake and jumpy. Keeping the noise level up to a
pretty continuous racket, either by blasting cacophonic
music or other jarring sounds through loudspeakers, or
with repeated and random small arms fire.

This mutual slumber time was ridiculous.

Unless, of course, there really *was* a tank on its way.

"What, *you're* going to siphon the gas from the car . . . ?"
Jones asked.

"I do know how to do it." Molly sounded insulted that
he should think otherwise.

Max looked at the jeeps, with their headlights blazing.
He judged the distance, tried to do the math. Twelve lights.
How long would it take, from the moment of that very first
shot? Twelve shots, divided by two shooters . . .

"We can help, you know," Molly implored Jones, and
Max as well. "Gina and I. It's not as if we're . . . we're . . .
sacks of potatoes, just sitting here waiting to be rescued by
the menfolk. We have skills, too. I happen to have been
taught to siphon gas in a third-world country by a nun
with a lot of rage issues after losing funding. She could
probably even teach *you* a thing or two about black market scamming."

But what if they had three shooters . . .

"How are you at target shooting?" Max interrupted her.

Molly blinked at him. "You mean, with a gun?"

"With a rifle," he said.

She shook her head. "Use of killing-sticks is not one of
my skills. I *am* really good, though, at popping balloons
with a dart. Oh, yes, and annoying my husband. I'm *really*
good at that."

"Gina?" Max asked, even though he knew the answer.

"Sorry," Gina said.

"You don't annoy me," Jones told Molly. "You terrify

me. Come on, you need to go back to bed. You're pract
cally falling over. How can you make jokes when . . ."

As Jones and Molly argued their way out of the room
Gina inched closer. She sat on the floor beneath the wir
dows, her back against the wall.

Using her foot, she dragged over the pillow that Max ha
been using earlier, putting it beside her—a silent invitatio
to come and sit. "What are you thinking?"

Max shook his head. "That we could shoot out th
lights, but it won't work. There's too many of them. I'r
good, but I'm no Alyssa Locke." He glanced down at he
"She's a sharpshooter. Did you know that?"

Of course she did. Alyssa had helped with the takedow
of the hijacked plane. She was one of the snipers who too
out the terrorists in the cockpit, where Gina was bein
held.

Gina was intimately acquainted with Alyssa's deadly ac
curacy with a rifle.

Her eyebrows were raised. "You bring up your forme
girlfriend, because . . . ?"

Max shrugged, looking out through the binoculars again
"We could use a marksman. I'm decent, but . . . Althougl
even Alyssa would take too long—twelve shots? Even if sh
could do it relatively quickly, once the lights went out—
after all that noise? Sneaking past the troops is one thing
when they're sleeping. Wide awake . . . That would be .
challenge. Maybe we could dress in Emilio's clothes, try t
make it look as if we're all in uniform, try to blend in . . .'
He shook his head, handing the binoculars to her. She wa
closer to the floor, and his entire leg was starting to stiffer
up. "There's got to be a way out of here, but that's not it."

Gingerly, he lowered himself down beside her, onto th
pillow. "I guess we're on first watch," he said from be
tween clenched teeth as he tried to find the right balance o
pillow and air.

"I'm sorry I can't shoot like Alyssa Locke," Gina said. She sounded far more annoyed than sorry. Annoyed with him for bringing her up.

Jealous, even.

Good. Better she was jealous than scared to death about the coming dawn.

Max reached over and took her by the chin, turning her so that she faced him. She had such beautiful skin, so soft. He leaned close.

Kissed her.

She resisted—for about a tenth of a second. Many, many tenths of seconds later, he was the one who finally pulled back.

First watch meant *watch*—which meant his eyes needed to be open. He used the mirror to look out the window. Everything was exactly the same. No movement, no change.

"God, I hate that you can do that," Gina said after she'd caught her breath. "You're just too good at kissing. It should be illegal. You get me all pissed off by talking about your old girlfriend and then you're like, *kiss me,* and I'm all *no, no, yes, yes, yes.*"

"She wasn't really my girlfriend," Max told Gina. "Alyssa. I loved her, yeah, but I didn't really *love* her. Not the way I love you. I was attracted to her, but it wasn't . . . And I stayed away, because she was working for me. You know, bad policy to sleep with subordinates? Anyway, I knew I had to keep some distance, and I did. It just wasn't that big a deal for me.

"But when I tried to stay away from *you* . . ." He laughed. "Any other woman in the world, I could walk away from. But not you."

"Well, yeah," Gina said, her annoyance visibly fading. "Because I chased after you."

"No," Max said. "It was more than that. You know that couples counselor we visited?" He glanced at her.

Gina nodded. "Rita."

Max nodded, too. "After you left the room, she asked me what I was so afraid of." He glanced at her again. She was definitely no longer annoyed. In fact, she looked downright stunned that he'd brought this up.

"I've had a lot of time to think about that and . . . I'm not trying to make excuses, but . . . In my world," he told her quietly, "it doesn't pay to love something or someone that much. It's too . . . risky. You love it, you'll lose it. So there you were—scaring me to death. Being with you seemed wrong for all kinds of reasons, so I built those reasons up, in my head, into huge problems—so I could pretend that the biggest problem wasn't really me being terrified. And then, there was Alyssa—beautiful and smart. Strong enough to deal with all my bullshit. And best of all I loved her, but I didn't love her too much. I knew I could live without her.

"I asked her to marry me because I thought it would keep me away from you," Max confessed. "Because I was afraid of how much I loved you." He cleared his throat. God, there was a time in the not-so-distant past when he would have done anything to keep Gina from knowing the truth. And now here he sat, just blurting it out. "I just wanted you to know that."

They sat in silence for several moments.

"Feel free to kiss me," Gina said. "Any time you have the urge."

He had to laugh. "Yeah, well, I'm supposed to be on watch."

"Watching what?" she said. "They're not going to move until that tank arrives."

"Still," he said.

"Have you ever tried making love with your eyes open the entire time?" Gina asked.

He looked at her.

"What?" she said. "I'm just making conversation."

"Right." Max glanced at her again, and she gave him that smile. That promise-filled, next-stop-heaven little smile, and he knew that *she* knew he was actually thinking about . . .

"Ow," he said, knowing that there was only one way to put on the brakes. "My leg's really hurting."

"All right," Gina said. "You win. I mean, I *could* say I'll kiss it and make it better, but I won't."

Yeah, okay. Max nodded. "Good plan. To not. You know, say that."

He wanted to laugh. It was so screwed up—this feeling of total contentment.

They were in serious trouble here. If that tank wasn't just a bluff—and his gut was telling him it wasn't—he was going to have to consider throwing Grady Morant to the wolves.

If he did that, Gina would never forgive him.

They sat in silence for about twelve seconds this time.

"Can I tell you a funny story?" Gina asked. She didn't wait for him to say yes or no. "It's about, well . . . You know the whole age-issue thing?"

"The age-issue thing," Max repeated. "Are you sure this is a funny story?"

"Does it still bother you?" she asked. "Being a little bit older than me? And it's more funny weird than funny ha-ha."

"Twenty years isn't exactly 'a little bit,' " he said.

"Tell that to a paleontologist," she countered.

Okay, he'd give her that one. "Just tell me the story."

"Once upon a time, when Jones first came to Kenya," Gina said, "I didn't know who he was. Molly didn't tell me, and he came to our tent for tea, and . . . Maybe this isn't even a funny weird story. Maybe it's more of an 'I'm an asshole' story, because I immediately jumped to the conclusion that he was there because he was all hot for me. It never occurred to me—it never even crossed my narrow little mind—that he might've been crushing on Molly. And she's only maybe ten years older than he is. I remember sitting there after I figured it out, and thinking, *shoot*. People *do* make assumptions based on age. Max wasn't just being crazy." She smiled at him. "Or at least not crazier than usual. I guess . . . I just wanted to apologize for mocking you all those times."

"It's okay," Max said. "I just keep reminding myself that love doesn't always stop to do the math." He looked at her. "I'm trying to talk myself into that. How'd I sound? Convincing?"

"That was pretty good." They sat in silence for a moment, then Gina spoke again. "Maybe I could get a T-shirt that says, 'I'm not his daughter, I'm his wife.' "

Max nodded as he laughed. "Yet still you mock me."

"Yeah," she said. "Because I really don't care what other people think, and I don't think you should either."

He watched the night, reflected in that mirror. "So, was that wife comment a roundabout way of telling me that you'll marry me?"

"Hang on." Gina took the binoculars and crawled over to the door. Standing up, she looked out the window, adjusting the lenses. "I'm just making sure we're not going to be interrupted again," she explained.

"You were going to tell me something important," Max remembered.

"Yeah, and it's kind of weird and complicated," she said.

"Are you pregnant?" he asked.

Gina was clearly surprised. "How did you . . . ? That's kind of part of it, but I don't really know if . . ." She crawled back into the room, sat down beside him again. "I don't know for sure, but yeah, I guess I could be."

Max nodded. Don't be jealous, don't be jealous. "Don't get mad, but when I was trying to find you, I searched your hotel and . . . There was a receipt from the clinic where you had that pregnancy test."

Now she was looking at him funny. "I *meant* I could be pregnant because when we, you know, in the kitchen . . . ? Hot sex, no birth control?"

"But . . . You had a pregnancy test. In Germany."

"I didn't have a test because I thought I was pregnant," Gina told him. "I *knew* I wasn't pregnant."

Okay, he was really tired, but this definitely didn't make sense. Max knew he should be relieved, but he was too confused. "So why'd you have the test?" he asked her.

"You really thought I was pregnant?" she asked, realization dawning. "You thought . . . ? God, Max, who'd you think the father was?"

He shook his head. "I don't know. It didn't matter. I mean, unless you still loved him, which it seemed as if you didn't, so . . ."

"God," she said again. She turned to look at him. "How many people have *you* slept with since I left for Kenya?"

Was she serious? "You mean you couldn't tell from the kitchen table thing?" he asked.

"Zero?" she asked. "Because I just spent over a year with absolutely zero sex, which would make my pregnancy pretty special. And for the record, the kitchen table thing *rocked*. I hope we don't have to go without sex for another year before we can do that again."

He had to laugh. She totally cracked him up. "It was over pretty quick," he pointed out.

"I love quick," Gina said. "And come on, I'm getting jealous here. Was it zero sex last year for you, too?"

"Yes," he admitted. "I love you, you weren't there— what was I going to do?"

"Are you actually *embarrassed*," she asked, "because you weren't some kind of man-ho and—"

"No," Max said. "I'm embarrassed that it took me an

entire fucking year and a half and the worst scare of my life to figure out that I can't live without you."

Gina's eyes were shining—she looked amazingly happy, considering they were surrounded by an army of people who wanted to kill them.

"Actually," she said, "it took you an entire non-fucking year and a half. Here's the deal with the pregnancy test, okay? When Molly found out *she* was pregnant but that she might have breast cancer, I did some research, because I knew that Grady was flipping out. He really wants her to have the full treatment—chemo, radiation—as soon as possible, which she can't do until after she has the baby. Unless she terminates the pregnancy.

"I read about something called a 'gestational carrier,' where a third party, me for example, would carry the baby to term for the parents. It's different from being a traditional surrogate, because the baby—both the egg and sperm—would be Molly and Grady's. I'd just provide the uterus and, well, nine months of my life. At first I thought they could take the baby out of Molly and, you know, just transplant it, but that's not possible. Maybe someday they'll have that technology . . .

"Still, one of the things that was freaking Molly out about the idea of chemo and radiation was that afterwards, she might not be able to have a baby," Gina continued. "The whole process might send her into early menopause or God knows what. Anyway, I wanted to give her as many options as possible, so I offered to be her gestational carrier—if she ever wants or needs one. I just thought it would lighten her burden, even just a little, if she knew I'd be there to help if . . . God forbid, you know?

"Pregnancy tests are necessary for gestational carriers, along with a clean bill of health. Makes sense, right? So I went to the clinic when Molly did, had a checkup, got the ball rolling. Although, while I was there, the doctor told me it was a little early. They recommend cancer patients wait a certain number of years after they're clean, before having children."

Gina took a deep breath. "So. I made Molly a promise. Which means there's a chance that in a couple of years we'll have to add the lines, 'and she's pregnant with her best friend Molly's baby' to that funky T-shirt I'm going to be wearing."

Max didn't know whether to laugh or cry. He managed to do neither. "I'm good with that," he said. "And by the way, I think I love you now more than ever."

She leaned her head against his shoulder. Now she was the one trying not to cry. "Can I ask you one more thing?"

"Sure," he said. He couldn't imagine the question that was coming. Knowing Gina, it was bound to be a good one.

"Did you ask me to marry you only because you thought I was pregnant?" she asked. "With someone else's child?"

Oh, shit.

Max knew he had to tell her the truth.

"No," he said. "I asked you because I love you." He paused. "And because I thought you might be pregnant with someone else's child, and I didn't want you to have to deal with that all alone. And because it really didn't matter who the someone else was, but I kind of hoped that it was someone that you liked at least a little, rather than someone that you didn't like at all. And I also hoped that, either way, you would know the only thing that really mattered to me was that you were safe and alive and in my life."

She was silent several long moments. But then she spoke. "Good answer," she said. "If we die tomorrow—"

"We're not going to die tomorrow," Max told her.

"Yeah, but if we do," she said, and he knew she believed it was a real possibility, "at least we had tonight."

She used her toe to push the door, and it closed with a click.

She gave him the binoculars. Along with her trademark smile.

"Gina," he said.

"Shhh. I have to check your bandage," she said, her fingers unfastening his pants. "I'll be gentle, I promise."

And Max discovered that keeping his eyes open was, indeed, something of a challenge.

CHAPTER
TWENTY-THREE

Jules had *the* most godawful hangover of his entire life.

The first thing he saw when he opened his eyes was light. Too much of it.

Candles, in what was no doubt meant to be a romantic arrangement, but somehow they seemed way too bright. He had to keep his eyes mostly closed. Slits, to keep his brain from splitting.

There ought to be a way to say that so it rhymed more perfectly, but his head was throbbing and his stomach— God, he hurt. His entire side was on fire.

He was in a room he didn't recognize, in a bed he couldn't remember seeing before. What the hell was wrong with him? He'd given up this sort of behavior shortly after college.

Voices. Laughter, distant—as if from another room, or maybe . . . Outside? Was the party still going on?

Someone stirred beside him in that bed, and he turned his head, but God*damn*, it hurt so much he had to close his eyes until his brain settled back into place.

Slowly, he opened his eyes, just the narrowest bit . . .

Who the hell was . . . *she*?

He opened his eyes wider, which nearly caused his head to break in two, but he had to look more closely because there was definitely a girl in bed with him.

Yes, she was probably the most beautiful girl he'd ever seen, with long dark hair and delicate Indonesian features, but on top of being female, she was also maybe sixteen at the very most and . . .

His memory returned with a whoosh that hurt like a son of a bitch.

He remembered this girl, leaning close, concern on her pretty face as she spoke to the men who were carrying him. Her words were in a language Jules didn't understand.

She pushed his hair back to look at his face, chattering away, as they put him on this bed. She was giving orders to the men, no doubt. But then she saw that his eyes were open. Or at least more open than they had been. And she smiled.

"You'll be all right now," she said in close to perfect American English.

He remembered feet. Faces. An Indonesian man with a moustache and goatee.

The accident, the car crashing down the steep hillside.

Emilio.

Falling dead.

Emilio, not Jules. The pain he was feeling now was proof that he was still quite alive.

He'd broken his leg and hit his head in that not-quite-accidental accident. He'd taken a bullet from Emilio's gun.

Yeah, that was why he hurt so much.

He remembered Max. Back in Emilio's garage. Max would be worried about him.

That is, if he and Gina and the others had managed to avoid Emilio's trap.

If they weren't already dead.

Jules realized that the leather jacket was gone, and with it his cell phone and sidearm. His pants were missing, too. He was even wearing someone else's underwear.

God, he hoped Junior Miss Indonesia over there hadn't been the one playing with him, like a giant Ken doll. Not for his sake, but for hers. What was she doing, in bed with him, anyway?

Okay, she was sleeping. On top of the sheet that covered him. Close at hand, in case he awoke.

She was babysitting him, he realized, much to his relief.

He reached out to touch her, to nudge her awake, but the movement made him hurt like a bitch. Although he didn't quite scream, the sound that came out of his mouth was pretty damn close.

It did the trick. The girl sat up, wide-eyed.

"Hey," he rasped through a throat that was dry, through lips that were split and swollen. Had someone actually kicked him in the face? "May I borrow your telephone?"

She started to speak, loudly and rapid-fire, in that language he didn't understand.

Ah, crap.

That memory he had of her speaking to him in clear, precise English must've been a hallucination.

"My name," he said slowly, hand on his chest, "is Jules Cassidy. I need—" he made the international hand signal for telephone, which was very similar to the ASL sign for "I love you" held up to one's ear "—a telephone?"

Maybe if she had paper and a pen, he could draw one for her.

God, his head hurt. Just what he needed—to play Pictionary with what felt like a fractured skull, for life and death stakes.

An older woman came into the room, carrying a tray with a glass of what he hoped was potable water. She set it down near his bedmate, who was still rattling on.

The girl held the glass out for him so that he could drink.

And then she surprised the hell out of him.

"I'm sorry, Mr. Cassidy," she told Jules in crisp perfect English. "We don't have a landline, and the cell towers are apparently still out."

"Man, you should be asleep," Jones said, as Max came into the room where he was keeping watch.

Dawn was coming. It was a matter of minutes, maybe a half hour, before the sky would turn to pewter instead of black.

"Or at the very least," Jones added, "showing Gina how much you love and worship her."

"She's asleep," Max told him. He'd slipped out of bed as soon as her breathing had turned steady. He'd . . . worshipped her quite nicely before that. Not that he was going to tell Jones about it. But shee-yit, as Gina might've said.

Max found himself grinning into the darkness.

"You *do* love her, right?" Jones asked from his seat beneath the window. He threw Max the pillow, so he could sit, too. "Message from Molly: if you're just fucking around with Gina, you better stop right now. If you hurt her, I'll fucking make you sorry you were born."

Message from Molly, huh?

"I'm paraphrasing," Jones told him.

"I love her," Max said, as he sat down. Ouch.

"Yeah, it's actually kind of obvious," Jones told him. "But I promised Molly I'd do the tough guy threat thing. She's awesome, by the way. Gina. You're one fucking-go-lucky son of a bitch."

Max just shook his head. There must've been a military training course in Creative Swearing that, as a civilian, Max hadn't been required to take.

"So, you're actually human," Jones said. "And, as far as total bastards go, you're . . . okay. Imagine my surprise."

"Yeah," Max said. Although wasn't that supposed to be his line?

Gina was right—Jones was, if not quite a good man, a decent one. It was interesting, too, to see how quickly he'd morphed back into a highly efficient professional soldier.

There was a saying in the counterterrorist world: "Proper training is permanent training."

But Max wasn't at all surprised by that. His years of experience with operators from all branches of both the military and the civilian sector had provided him with his own adage. "Expect the absolute best from everyone, and prepare to be surprised at how far they'll surpass those expectations."

"If this colonel who's coming," Jones said, getting down to the serious stuff without any further small talk, "is the colonel I think it is . . ."

Max waited.

"It's important," Jones said quietly, "when you turn me over to him—his name is Ram Subandrio—that I'm already dead."

Max cleared his throat. "I don't think—"

"Yeah," Jones said. "Well, I don't think either. I know. And I've been figuring out the best way to do this. To make it . . . easier for Molly . . . But, fuck. It's not going to be easy whatever way . . . All I know is that I'm going to need you to do it, because I'm a fucking coward, and I won't be able to do it myself."

Christ. "Look," Max said. "Grady. Maybe—"

"Here's what I think we should do," Jones told him. "You should walk me out there. Get me out of the building. We can tell Molly and Gina to go into the escape tunnel, so they won't be able to watch. I'll have my hands up as you take me into the square. You'll have a weapon and—"

"Tell me about Subandrio," Max said. "If he is the colonel who's coming, he's the man I'm going to be talking to."

"He's a fucking maniac," Jones said. "Chai found him in the same prison where he found me. Only he was working there. By choice. Will you just promise me—"

"I'm not going to kill you," Max told him. "We'll figure something else out."

Jones was silent. "Like what?"

"Jesus. Like, anything."

Max couldn't see the other man's face clearly from where

he was sitting, but he could see that Jones was shaking his head.

"How about if I told you that Subandrio will strip the skin from my body to get me to tell him where I brought Nusantara's mistress," Jones said, his voice low. "What if I tell you he'll keep me alive for weeks? Months. Kill me just a little and then let me heal. What if I tell you that as long as I'm alive, he'll try to get to Molly. Gina, too. He'll have me, and he'll still blast a hole in this house with his tank, so he can peel the skin from them—in front of me, to make me suffer even more. And you, you're not immune to this, either, friend. He'll make you watch as he tortures them, too. He'll cut my baby out of Molly's body—you want to watch him do that? Believe me. He's done it before. He's probably looking forward to it."

God.

"I don't know," Jones's voice shook as he continued. "It's entirely possible that Subandrio will torture Molly and Gina anyway. Even if I'm dead. The kindest thing might be just to make sure the end comes quickly for them."

"Maybe it's not this Subandrio who's coming," Max said.

"Yeah," Jones scoffed. "And maybe Molly doesn't really have breast cancer."

"Maybe she doesn't."

"Right." He laughed, and it was an ugly sound.

Max exhaled hard. "Grady, look, I know you're scared, but I'm not going to—"

"You're a fool—still believing in miracles. Thinking . . . What? I don't know what I'm talking about?"

"No," Max said, but Jones wasn't listening.

"I'm a coward, I'm less than," he ranted, "because I *let* myself be broken? Jesus, you're a fucking arrogant prick! You think you're better than me. You think *you* wouldn't have broken in that prison, don't you? Three years of torture—shit, you could do that standing on your head, couldn't you? Well, fuck you, Bhagat. Despite what you think you're human, too. And just like every other man on this planet, you've got a breaking point."

"Look, Grady," Max tried.

"You really want to find out where yours is? Let them slice the skin off the bottoms of your feet. Let them whip you til you're one more flick of their wrist from dead. No fucking problem. You're indestructible. Your goddamn self-righteousness will keep you alive. But wait. What about when they bring Gina into the room? How you feeling then, champ? Having to watch them rape her, hear her scream and be unable to move, let alone help her? How'd you like to sit through that? Because you're going to have to."

Silence.

Max didn't know what to say. Like, *Yeah, actually, I've done that*. Hearing Gina scream, being unable to help her.

He hadn't realized, while he was living through it, while he was suffering from the aftereffects, that there was a name for it.

Torture.

In his life, he'd only had one experience that was more horrific.

And that was believing Gina was dead.

Jones stood up. Right in front of the window.

"Get down," Max ordered him.

But he didn't. He just walked upright, out the door. "Finish up my shift," he said. "Let me know when you've finally run out of options. I'm going to go spend the rest of my life with my wife."

Jules looked from Dr. Dewi Ernalia to her three gorgeous brothers and back, praying that they were going to believe him.

Hell, if anyone deserved to be skeptical here, he should

be first in line. This skinny little girl supposedly had a medical degree from Tufts University?

Of course, she *had* set his leg and stitched him up, so it was probably better to believe the degree thing. The alternative was slightly less confidence-inspiring—that she was a precocious teen working on her ER Surgeon Girl Scout badge.

As Dr. Ernalia's trio of brothers gathered at the foot of the bed, she'd told Jules that she was the only doctor on this side of the island, and this little cottage without electricity was the closest thing there was to a hospital for miles.

She was worried because brother number one had told her there were terrorists holed up in a house farther up the mountain. Brother number two apparently reported that rumors were afoot that the military was bringing in a tank to blast those terrorists out.

Which meant, according to the Doc's experience, that there was a potential for some serious casualties.

Yeah, no kidding.

And the worst of those casualties were going to be Max, Gina, Jones, and Molly. Those were no terrorists, holed up in that house. Those were Jules's friends.

Of course, the doctor told him, the potential for serious casualties would be even greater if the Americans were involved.

But apparently the Americans were being kept away because it was believed that these terrorists were part of a cell that had attacked the American embassy in Jakarta—where a beloved statesman from Pulau Meda had been killed. If the Americans became involved, they would take the terrorists into custody, instead of dishing out immediate and just punishment.

"I'm an agent with the American Federal Bureau of Investigations," Jules told them, wishing he was wearing something more dignified than borrowed underwear—a pair of boxers bearing the logo for the Boston Red Sox. They were pinned precariously together on one side, to accommodate the splint on his lower leg. "I came to Pulau Meda investigating the kidnapping of two American women." He waited while the Doc translated for her brothers.

And then he waited even longer, while another man came into the room. He was another of the young doctor's brothers—these people could not look more like siblings if they tried. They were all exotically beautiful.

There was more discussion, lots of gesturing, many furtive glances in his direction.

Dr. Ernalia finally quieted them down. She turned back to Jules. "My brothers want to know," she asked him, "whether you killed Emilio Testa."

Jules looked at that row of faces at the foot of his bed, and he could not read them. Not even slightly. Blank expectation. That was all he got. This family could have been the most successful team of Texas Hold 'Em players in the world.

And gee, he really hoped Emilio Testa wasn't a good friend of theirs.

Molly awoke to find herself alone in the bed.

But she wasn't alone in the room. Jones was hunkered down on the floor just inside the door, a shape in the darkness, watching her.

"Hi," she said groggily, pushing her hair out of her face. "What's happening? Is your shift over already? Is it time for me to take a turn?"

"No, it's . . . no," he said. "I'm sorry I woke you."

"You didn't." There was a candle on the table next to the bed, and she found it by touch, found the matchbook. The light didn't quite reach as far as the wall, though. It didn't make it any easier to see his face. "What are you doing over there?" She propped herself up on one elbow.

"You're so beautiful," he whispered.

"If that's the beginning of an apology," she told him. "I accept. You're forgiven."

"I am sorry," Jones said. "I should have stayed away from you. I never should have gone to Kenya."

While Molly hadn't been looking forward to this conversation, she'd been expecting it. Jones's spirits had taken a real nosedive when he'd found out that Max couldn't use their knowledge of the planned terrorist attack on the Jakarta embassy as a bargaining chip, because the attack had already happened.

It was possible he'd been chugging along in dire situation mode, but that Max's idea had given him real hope.

Hope that had quickly been dashed.

"Well," Molly said now, "okay. Maybe if you'd skipped the Kenya trip, neither of us would be right here, right now—"

"Damn straight."

"—but you have to know that I wouldn't trade the past four months with you for anything," she told him fiercely.

"You'd really rather die," he said flatly. "For four lousy months of living a lie?"

"No," she said. "I'd really rather *not* die, thanks. And what exactly was the lie? Your name? Your fake accent? Big deal. Stop beating yourself up for making me the happiest woman in the world. Well, except maybe for Gina, when she was on the kitchen table . . ."

Jones didn't laugh. He didn't even crack a smile. He put his head down, resting it on his folded arms.

"Come on," Molly said. "What's with this defeatist attitude?"

She pulled back the sheet, took the candle from the table, and with it, crossed the room. Naked. With all of her forty-something jiggles, and that maybe-she-just-ate-too-much-chocolate-cake of a soft, round belly that didn't quite look pregnant yet. With her breasts expanding by the minute.

She'd always been full figured, but pregnancy was turning her into a burlesque star anomaly. At least it felt that way.

But when Jones looked at her, she felt beautiful. Sometimes even svelte. And always unbelievably sexy.

Even despite the bandage covering her Frankenstein-looking biopsy stitches.

Problem was, he didn't want to look at her right now. He was frightened and angry, and he had no room in his soul for anything but his misery and self-loathing.

"I should have died years ago," Jones said, as she sat down on the floor, next to him. "I think I was probably supposed to, but I was too much of a son of a bitch to realize it."

"If you were supposed to die," she pointed out, "then you would have. Assuming there's such a thing in life as *supposed to*. But okay, let's run with that. When were you supposed to die?"

"When I got that infection," he told her. "I almost did die."

Molly nodded. She remembered.

She'd first seen his souvenir of that event—a new scar in his vast collection—on their wedding night. It was on his back, jagged and still angry looking, long after he'd been injured.

Stabbed, actually.

He'd told her that he'd gotten that scar while on his way to Africa. Years earlier.

It had happened right after Molly had left Indonesia, in fact. After she'd been shot, and he'd been beaten half to death. After they'd both messed up their lives and their relationship by mistrusting one another.

Jones had gotten aboard a ship heading east, intending to do whatever it took find her, to grovel and beg for forgiveness.

But Chai's men had tracked him down. They'd found

him and nearly killed him, and as he fought for his life, he'd been stabbed in the back.

And it was then, as he crawled off that cargo ship in Sri Lanka, bleeding from a knife wound that would damn near kill him a second time when it became infected, that he came to the realization that Chai would not rest until he was dead.

He could not hide, he could only run. And if he continued on to Africa, he'd told her, he knew he'd lead that son of a bitch right to Molly, putting her into terrible danger.

Jones had vowed then and there that he would not make that mistake again.

Molly knew he was thinking about that now. "You weren't supposed to die," she told him. "Stop blaming yourself—this isn't your fault."

"Yeah," he said. "You're not going to convince me of that. Damn it, Mol, I feel like I've killed you. One way or another. If you survive this ordeal, well, *shit*! Then it's time to battle cancer—except, if I'm alive, where am I? It's hard to hold your hand from jail." His voice shook. "If I hadn't come to Kenya, then I wouldn't have gotten you pregnant, and you'd be worrying about your own health, instead of the freaking spawn of Satan inside of you!"

"Wow," she said. "That was pretty harsh."

"God, I'm sorry," he whispered. "Do you think he heard me? Shit, it's probably better that I'm . . . I would've made a lousy father—"

"No," she said, purposely ignoring his defeatist verb tense, focusing instead on the fact that, for the very first time, Jones had acknowledged the life—their baby—that she was carrying as a person. "I don't think he even has ears yet. And if he does, his English needs work. I *meant* that was harsh on *you*. I mean, come on. If I'm carrying the 'freaking spawn of Satan,' what does that make you?"

Jones turned to look at her. "You're naked," he said, as if the fact had only just registered.

"This is how it starts," Molly said, with an exaggerated sigh. "The beginning of the end. At first it's all, 'Ooh, you're naked!' " She put a lot of excitement into her voice. "Then, after just a few months of marriage, you turn around, and it's 'What, are you naked? Again?' "

He finally smiled. "That's not how I meant it," he said. "I'm just . . . Mol, I'm scared shitless."

"That doesn't mean we should just quit," she told him softly.

And then there it was. Again. The baby. Moving.

Molly took her husband's hand, placed it on her belly. "Do you feel it?" she asked him.

"I don't know," he breathed. He looked at her, searchingly, as if eye contact would help him feel what she was feeling.

"It's this . . . flutter. Like something's almost . . . flying around inside of me. Like my dinner is doing a little happy-dance."

"That?" he asked.

Molly smiled. "Yes," she said. "Isn't that amazing?"

"Jesus," he said. He had tears in his eyes. "Holy God. That's . . ."

"Our baby," she said.

"Jesus, that's incredible."

"There's someone inside of me who's alive, Grady. Someone who wouldn't exist if you didn't love me, and I didn't love you. It's amazing. It's fantastic. We did this. You didn't do it, I didn't do it—we did it together. Think about that. If we can do something like this, then surely we can handle some of these other mundane problems that we're facing."

He laughed at that. "Mundane problems? Like surviving a tank attack? And beating cancer? God, I love you."

"Good. Hold that thought. Let's find Max," Molly suggested. "See if he's come up with any more ideas for getting us out of here alive."

"Can we just . . . sit for a minute?" Jones asked her. "I just want to . . ."

He wanted to feel the miracle of their baby moving around inside of her again.

And Molly knew at that moment, that if this baby turned out to be a girl, she was going to name her Hope.

Providing, of course, that her daddy agreed.

CHAPTER
TWENTY-FOUR

Gina couldn't believe what she was hearing. "Should I be worried," she said, "that Grady's alone, in the other room, with Molly, right now?"

Max shook his head. "I don't think he could really do it. I think he was trying to see—if it came down to it—whether *I'd* be willing."

" 'Kill my wife for me, will ya?' " Gina shook her head. "That's nuts."

"No, it's not," Max said as he gazed out the window through the binoculars.

In just a short amount of time, the sun had climbed into the sky. It was already incredibly warm, and getting warmer.

"He's lived through something awful," Max continued, still not looking at her. "Really unbearable, I think. He was talking about it, just a little, and . . . I don't know for sure, but I think it hurt him more to watch other people being tortured than it did to be tortured himself. I think his captors knew that and used it against him. I've heard some really chilling stories about the prison he was in. Stories about men being forced to watch as their wives and children were systematically raped and murdered." He looked at her. "I can relate, to some degree."

Gina reached for him, and he took her hand. But then the walkie-talkie crackled.

"Grady Morant," a voice said through the static. "How nice of you to come all this way to talk to me again."

Max keyed the button. "Is this Colonel Subandrio?"

"You recognized me, you foul shitrag, did you?"

There was name calling and then there was name calling. Gina made a face at Max, trying to pretend that she was freaked out by the colonel's nasty compound word, rather than the fact that she could well be listening to the voice of the man who was going to kill her.

Painfully.

While Max was forced to watch.

"Do you hear that sound?" the colonel continued. "That is the sound of the approaching tank that is going to blow you to hell."

"I don't hear it," Gina said. "Is he bluffing?"

"Listen," Max told her. "It's a low pitched rumble."

Oh, God. There really was a tank.

"For the record," Gina told him, "I'd rather take my chances with the torture. As long as we're alive, there's a chance that we'll stay alive. If you—"

Max kissed her. "I know," he said. "I'm with you on this. Now, shh. Let me talk to this guy."

He hit the button.

"Sir," he said. "My name is Max Bhagat, I'm an American citizen and a top-level team leader in the FBI. We've never met, but I was told by my superiors that you would be coming here to discuss the situation regarding Heru Nusantara and Grady Morant. Right now, sir, I'm going to have to ask you to hold, because I'm receiving an incoming radio message from President Bryant."

He cut the connection.

Wow. "Liar, liar, green pants on fire," Gina said.

"Speaking of pants," Max said, "I need mine. I don't care if they're still wet. Will you get them for me? And see if Emilio has a jacket and shirt that'll fit me. Oh, and a tie without hula girls on it. Now, please."

Gina scrambled. And as she went down the hall, she heard Max shouting for Molly and Jones.

* * *

Jules was the new hero of the day.

Apparently, the discovery of Emilio Testa's dead body meant it was party time in Dr. Ernalia's house.

Her brothers had towed Emilio's battered car into their yard, and were already starting to strip it down so they could sell the parts. It was their final act of revenge against a long-despised enemy.

"I need to get to a telephone," Jules said again. "And I could use something to wear."

The doc said something to the three brothers who were still inside the house, and they all started taking off their clothes.

"Okay, whoa," Jules said.

But the young woman was already stopping them—after taking her youngest brother's Hawaiian print shirt and her mustached brother's black shorts. She issued a command, and the other brother took a knife to the shorts, cutting them so Jules wouldn't have to pull them on over his splint.

The doctor and her youngest bro helped him into the shirt and pinned the shorts onto him, while mustache went into the other room and returned with a pair of crutches.

"My brothers think the nearest phone is down at the harbor, at the police station," she informed him. "And we also think if that phone isn't working, you could rent a seaplane and head for Soe or Kupang. My brother, Daksa, suggests that you avoid Dili. Rexi'll give you a ride to town in his Mini."

God, his head was still pounding. Standing up was a challenge, forget about balancing on crutches.

But he'd already wasted far too much time unconscious.

Jules started for the door, but two of the brothers came back inside, shouting about something. And holding . . .

"I know you'd prefer a telephone," Dr. Ernalia said, "but would a radio do? Umar found this shortwave in Emilio Testa's car."

* * *

"We'll need rope," Max said as he straightened his tie.

"I saw some in the kitchen," Gina said, and thundered down the stairs.

"Hey," Jones called after her. "New York, I'm not done with your lesson here—"

Molly took the submachine gun from his hands. "Always keep the muzzle pointed down and away from other people," she recited as she did just that. "Do this . . . and . . . pull the trigger. Fire out the window, down into the street, not up into the air because someone might get hurt. Don't fire in the house. It's not just bad luck, like opening an umbrella, but the walls are reinforced so the bullets will bounce off and we could end up like Max did, with one in our butt. Or worse. Extra ammo's in the backpack. Fire the weapons for a count of four, no more, then get the hell down." She gazed at him. "Hon, if I've got it, Gina's got it."

What a crazy sight—Molly, cradling a firearm. Jones resisted the urge to check out the window to make sure that it wasn't snowing. It wasn't quite July, but that cold day sure seemed to have come early. As far as hell freezing over went—he prayed he wasn't going to get the chance to verify that. At least not for a long time.

He turned to Max. "I still think they should go into the escape tunnel until it's over."

"Excuse me," Molly said, waving. "This half of the *they* you're talking about is standing right here. We're ready and willing to help, although I'd like to point out that usually when group A opens fire on group B, group B tends to turn around and shoot back. Isn't that a problem since you're going to be standing right in the middle of the square?"

Max had been fixing his hair, but now he pushed the mirror back into place. "Actually," he told her. "The very first thing they'll do is dive for cover. From what I can tell, there's only one person invested in this operation, and it's Colonel Subandrio—who's definitely working for Heru Nusantara. Everyone else is far more interested in not getting killed." He turned to include Jones in his pep talk. "We're going to use this to our advantage."

"Here's the rope." Gina was back.

"Good," Max said. "Cut it into three pieces. Tie one around each of Grady's wrists and loop the third around him loosely—we want it to look as if he's tied up, but we don't want to make it hard for him to get his hands free, okay?"

He put on Emilio's suit jacket, checking all the various weapons he had hidden in his pockets and at the small of his back as Jones held his hands out.

"Let's talk tank," Max said.

Jones had had an opportunity to examine the tank in question through the binoculars. "It looks like it's something that might've been made in Russia in the late 1980s. The crew definitely has a limited visual of what's going on outside. They rely on radio contact for both directions and orders."

"Good," Max said.

Molly put down the weapon and helped Gina with the rope. She caught Jones's eye. "Admit that you're enjoying this—two women tying you up . . . ?"

"I'm too scared to," he told her. "But after this is over, if we live, would you mind very much doing this again? Just the two of us, though. I mean, Gina's cute, but if we invite her, we'd have to invite Max and that would kind of ruin it for me."

Molly laughed, but there were tears in her eyes. Probably because she knew how goddamn hard it was for him to make a joke about any of this.

"We'll need something that looks like blood." Max was either not paying attention or purposely ignoring their conversation.

"I've got it handled," Jones told him, turning the knots to the inside of his wrists.

"There's catsup in the fridge," Gina volunteered.

Catsup not only looked like catsup, but it smelled like catsup. That wasn't good enough. If this was going to work, if they expected to fool Ram Subandrio, it had to look real. Subandrio had seen a freaking river of blood in his life.

"Do you want me to get it?" Gina asked him.

"Oh," Jones said. "No. Thanks. We'll have to go out that way, so . . . Might as well keep it fresh." He looked up to meet Max's eyes. "Let's do this."

Molly stood there, looking significantly less ferocious without the weaponry. She was so worried she was practically wringing her hands. But still, she managed to smile for him. "Thank you for loving me enough to take this chance," she told him.

"Yeah," Jones said. "Well." He didn't want to tell her, but he and Max had a backup plan that she would've hated, had she known about it. "If something goes wrong, hide in the tunnel. Maybe they won't find the entrance."

"If the baby's a boy," Molly said. "I think we should name him Leslie."

"*What?*" This was only the first of all the disasters they had to survive, but she was already thinking of names for the baby? But, shit, surely she could come up with something a little more . . . normal. When he was growing up, he'd always wished for a name like John or Jim. Tom. Dan.

She was smiling at him as if she knew exactly what he was thinking—which, come to think of it, she probably did.

Jones realized she'd started a little early with that diversion she was supposed to create, pulling him out of a future where he was dead and she was hiding in that tunnel, and into one where they had a baby who needed a name. "I've always been fond of David," he said, because he wanted that second version of the future so badly he could almost taste it.

But then, across the room, Max picked up the walkie-talkie. "Here we go."

Max was one heck of a talented liar.

Gina watched him as he spoke into the walkie-talkie, as he ordered the interpreter to let him talk directly with Colonel Subandrio.

Wearing a tie and jacket with that crisp white shirt, he looked more like the Max she'd first met four years ago.

Although a jacket and tie with jeans and sneakers—that was something she never thought she'd live to see. But Emilio's pants didn't fit him.

He caught her looking at him and, as he waited for the Colonel, he said, "I wish I had a real suit."

"You look good." Gina tried to smile through her fear. "Please don't die today."

"That would be bad," he agreed, and then the colonel's voice came through.

"We've picked up no radio signals from this area," the man said, just jumping right in. "If you think—"

Max held down the talk button, and the walkie-talkie squealed.

"Colonel," he said, when the squealing stopped. "Surely you know that the United States' latest comm system doesn't use conventional radio waves. It was down for a while, but we managed to get it back up and running. I've since spoken to President Bryant, as well as his top advisors in Indonesian affairs. I have been briefed on this situation completely. I understand fully why the matter is of utmost importance to Mr. Nusantara, and why it's in need of being handled immediately."

Max didn't take a breath. "I've apologized to the President, and I wish to do the same to you, sir. When I became involved in what seemed to be a mere kidnapping, I didn't realize Grady Morant was wanted on so many different counts, both by your government and ours. Please pass along my apologies as well to Mr. Nusantara, and reassure him that President Bryant and the United States of America remain in full support of his candidacy. We believe he's the best man to lead this country, despite his past indiscretions. President Bryant, and myself as well, are prepared to do whatever we can to ensure Mr. Nusantara's election."

And still, he allowed no opportunity for the colonel to get in a word edgewise. "With that said, sir," Max continued, "please be advised that I've been ordered to sidestep the American embassy, and surrender Grady Morant directly to the Indonesian authorities, of which you are their representative. Are you prepared to take him into custody, Colonel, or do you need to make arrangements to transport him off the island?"

Max released the talk button, and Gina held her breath.

"Here's where we find out," Max told her, told Molly and Jones, too, "if Nusantara really is behind all this."

But there was only silence from the other end.

Jones had the binoculars. He was looking out at the tank. "No movement," he said. "They're just sitting there."

"Why is he taking so long to answer?" Gina asked.

Jules's head was throbbing as he attempted to communicate to the moron at the CIA office in Kupang.

"Yes, I know everyone's on standby," he said, "but isn't this *why* they're standing by? To be ready to help in the event of a situation?" Enough already. "Let me talk to your superior. Over."

"I'm it right now. We're stretched thin. Are you reporting a terrorist situation? Over?" The voice on the other end of the radio suddenly sounded as if he'd woken up.

"Affirmative." When Jules died, he was going to hell. He'd

cinched it now by lying. Except maybe this wasn't really a complete lie. "I've had numerous reports of a terrorist cell pinned down in the mountains here on Pulau Meda. Are there any aircraft carriers in the immediate vicinity? Over."

"Sir, these airwaves are not secure. I can't disclose that information, over."

Yeah, as if every hostile government around the world didn't have access to satellite images pinpointing every American naval vessel on the planet.

"I need at least three choppers filled with Marines to meet me here on Meda Island, ASAP," Jules said. "Can you please get that for me? Over."

There was a pause. It was the kind of pause that came in front of a negative response.

And crap, he'd started bleeding again. No wonder he was so dizzy.

The radio crackled. And here it came . . . "I'm sorry, sir. Can't do it. Over."

"Very good," Max said. "Thank you, Colonel. I'll bring him on out." He turned off the walkie-talkie.

It was the moment he'd been praying for. And dreading, at the same time.

Molly was crying, but only because Jones had already gone downstairs. He'd stood up the moment that the colonel had announced he was ready to take Grady Morant into custody. He'd asked Molly to stay up here, and he'd kissed her good-bye, then he'd gone into the kitchen to make himself look dead.

Now it was Max's turn to go.

Gina was fighting hard not to cry, too.

"Keep the door closed," Max told her, holding her close. "It'll lock when I shut it behind us. Don't open it for anything."

She nodded. "Except for you. I'll open it for you."

"Not even for me," he said. "I don't know what I'm

going to have to say to the colonel to convince him we're on the same side. If Jones is right about him, he might demand that you and Molly be arrested, too. And we definitely don't want that. So don't open the door for me."

"How about if we have a code?" she suggested, her fingers in his hair, her body soft against him. "If you say it, then I'll know it's okay to let you in."

"Do you know that one of the things I love the most about you is that you're really smart?" Max told her.

Gina smiled, but he knew that it was forced. She wanted to stand here, holding him forever. He knew, because he wanted that, too.

Unfortunately, it wasn't an option.

Max kissed her and she clung to him because she knew this was it. Neither of them had dared to say it, but they both were well aware that this could be their last kiss.

Ever.

"The code is an Elvis song," she pulled back to tell him. "Any Elvis song. You sing me an Elvis song and I will open that door. If not . . ." She shrugged.

Max laughed. "You just want to hear me sing."

"Absolutely. And if you dance, too . . . Well, there's no telling what'll happen after that door is open." She pushed him into the hall. "See you in a few, Wild Thing."

As Max went down the stairs in search of Jones, he realized he was grinning his ass off.

And instead of worrying about the coming face-to-face with Colonel Subandrio, he was mentally reviewing all of his favorite Elvis songs, trying to figure out which one was going to make Gina's smile the widest.

It was possible he was enjoying himself a little too much.

Christ, he was a twisted mess.

But it didn't matter. He knew that Gina loved him anyway.

* * *

The gunshot from the kitchen startled Molly.

She'd been waiting for it, dreading it, but it still made her jump.

Gina reached over and took her hand. "This is going to work," she said.

"I know," Molly said, trying to sound as if she believed it, too. "I trust Max. He was incredible, talking to that colonel. I almost believed him—that he was willing to hand over Grady."

She crawled closer to the mirror, angling it so she could see the street in front of the house.

They both heard the door shut, and now Gina came over to look, too.

"Oh, Lord," Molly breathed.

Max was carrying Jones in a fireman's hold, over his shoulder.

Jones's head was hanging down, and as Max moved slowly away from the house, she caught a glimpse of his face.

It was covered with blood, his hair matted with it.

"That's not catsup," Molly said, panic rising. "Dear Lord, Gina. What did Max do?"

Max reached the halfway point.

He'd mentally marked a spot in the square that was almost exactly equidistance to both the house behind him and the barricade of jeeps, trucks, and that massive tank in front of him.

The fact that he'd made it that far without being filled with bullets was at the very least, a small victory.

Add the fact that, in addition to Jones, he was also carrying a compact little .22 caliber pistol. It was right in his hand, in full view of his entire audience.

Of course the range on that thing was similar to a pea-shooter.

He kept moving forward.

Walking was challenge enough with his bullet wound, forget about adding 190 pounds of dead weight into the equation.

But he was moving. He was getting the job done.

Except, so much for the suit and tie—he'd already sweated through it. Jones, the bastard, had also bled all over it.

The morning sun was ridiculously hot. It had rained last night, but the moisture had evaporated hours ago.

Max could see Colonel Subandrio, peering out from behind the tank, looking much as Jones had described him. A short, heavyset man, with one of those faces that seemed to swallow his neck and puffy cheeks that went all the way down to his shoulders.

Max kept going, one painful step at a time.

Gina followed Molly into the kitchen.

"That was blood," Molly said. "Max shot Grady!"

"No, he didn't," Gina said, even though she wasn't quite convinced that he hadn't. Was this what the two men had been discussing, so quietly and seriously, while they'd sent Molly and Gina down to the weapon pile, to select guns that they felt comfortable holding?

What if there had really been two plans—one that Max and Jones told Gina and Molly, and one in which Max actually did deliver Grady Morant to the colonel?

"Oh, dear Lord," Molly breathed. There was definitely blood on the kitchen floor, on the table, smeared on the knob of one of the cabinets.

Blood even tinged a bowl of water that sat near the sink.

As if someone had rinsed their hands after committing a grisly murder.

"Grady said they had to make it look real," Gina reminded Molly, reminded herself.

Max wouldn't do something like this.

Would he?

Molly broke down into tears. "I'll kill him," she sobbed. "I'm going to kill him!"

"Molly, wait. Where are you going?" Gina called, as Molly turned and ran for the stairs.

"Halt."

The order finally came, and Max was nowhere near close enough. But he stopped, because the last thing he wanted was to piss off the colonel.

The man was still peering at them from the far side of the tank, about twenty yards away, standing among several other officers.

"Drop your weapon." The order came from the man who'd been in command of this debacle before Colonel Subandrio arrived, courtesy of the interpreter.

"We're all on the same side," Max reminded them. "Morant wasn't keen on a reunion with you, Colonel. He resisted, and . . . Well, I was told he was wanted, dead or alive, so I decided to make containing him easier on everyone."

Gina dashed up the stairs after Molly. "Whoa," she said, going into a crouch as she entered the room. "Wait. You don't know—"

But there, out the window, she could see Max tossing Jones onto the dusty ground.

He landed completely bonelessly, absolutely lifeless.

Dear God . . .

"It's an act," Gina told her friend, told herself. "He's not really dead. They're just trying to convince the colonel. Mol, lookit, there was a knife downstairs. I think he used it to cut his hand—see, he's got something wrapped around his palm. And if Max *had* shot him, there would have been a spray of, you know, blood. On the wall or . . . somewhere . . ."

Max was talking. She could see that from the way he was standing.

She could see the ugly little colonel, unwilling to come out from behind the shelter of that tank, probably because Max was holding a gun.

And then she saw Max turn away from the colonel. He pointed that weapon at Jones and . . .

Boom!

The gunshot echoed, and Gina and Molly both crouched there, stunned.

And then Molly completely lost it.

Holy Jesus!

Max, that motherfucking psycho, had actually shot him.

Right in the fucking leg.

Jones had to use every ounce of self-control he had—and some he didn't know he had—not to shout or scream. He didn't so much as move.

The pain was like a flame, and he focused on breathing shallowly and slowly. Colonel Subandrio would definitely notice if the dead man started gulping for air.

"He's dead," he heard Max tell Subandrio. He heard the sound of Velcro, too, as Max holstered the .22 and buddied up to the man. "It's nice to finally meet you, Colonel. I've heard a lot about you. You've certainly caught President Bryant's eye. He mentioned meeting you in Jakarta."

"We've never met," the man said, in that oily voice that Jones still heard in his nightmares.

"I must've misunderstood him," Max covered effortlessly. "He mentioned a trip to Jakarta—it must be something he's planning. He mentioned your name—it must've been that he wanted to meet you. Forgive my confusion. It's been a rough couple of days, tracking Morant down and . . ." He laughed. "I'm sure you know what that's—"

"Max! You bastard!"

What the fuck? Jones discovered new reserves of control

as he stayed completely still. That was Molly's voice. Thin and distant, but completely clear.

"I'm going to kill you!" she shouted. "I'm going to kill you! You promised you wouldn't hurt him! You promised!"

Did Molly actually think . . . ?

"Molly, come on, stop it! Get back from the window."

But Gina took a step back as, sobbing uncontrollably, Molly picked up one of those submachine guns that Jones had showed them how to fire.

"Okay," Gina said to the least violent person she'd ever met in her life. "That's enough. Put the gun down. Right now. Molly, look at me. Look at me. Have faith in Max, okay? You've got to have faith in Max!"

"That was his wife," Max explained to the colonel. "I had to knock her out before getting hold of Morant. I guess she regained consciousness."

Colonel Subandrio bought it.

Max didn't know whose idea it was to shout like that from the window, but it was beautiful.

Because it made the colonel come out from behind the tank.

The spineless CO was right behind him, eager to prove that he wasn't spineless. The interpreter, clutching the walkie-talkie, was behind *him*.

Max nudged Jones with his foot. "Grady Morant doesn't seem so dangerous anymore, does he?"

"He was guilty of some terrible crimes," the colonel said. "He won't be missed." He came closer, glanced across the square at the house. "Well, except for his . . . wife, you say?"

Ah, shit. This was the type of game where information was never willingly volunteered, and he'd just tossed Subandrio one hell of a bone.

Jones didn't move, but Max could feel his anger, radiating upwards.

Meanwhile, the colonel moved closer. "He usually doesn't marry them. He usually just kills them when he's through with them. At least that's what he did with my sister. We never found her body."

The lying sack of shit.

Jones didn't move. He didn't jump up shouting about shit-eating liars, and that the first place he'd look for the asswipe's dead sister was in Subandrio's own flower garden, beneath the roses.

But here was a dark thought: It was possible that Max might believe Subandrio. A colonel in a fancy uniform, versus a confessed former associate of a murdering drug lord . . . What if Max actually thought . . .

But Max was making the proper condolence noises, as the man Jones had watched torture children in front of their weeping parents brought the conversation back to Molly. "I'd like to meet her, this wife of Morant's."

It was going to be hard for him to do that—from *hell.*

Max skillfully segued away from the topic. "I don't think we'll convince her to come out until the helicopters arrive," he said.

His words weren't quite a lie. Max had simply omitted the fact that they hadn't yet contacted the Marines who flew those choppers. But they would—as soon as they got their hands on a radio.

"Helicopters?" Subandrio inquired.

"Standard procedure," Max told him. "They should be here any minute. They're coming from a carrier just east of Meda Island. Is that east?"

Jones's eyes were closed, so he didn't see Max pointing up toward the mountain, but he knew he'd made the gesture.

It was their signal. And sure enough, Molly and Gina opened fire from the window of the house.

As Jones erupted back to life.

"Look out!" Max shouted, as he tackled the CO. His shoulder connected with the man's chest, and they both went down, down into the dirt. He scrambled to restrain him, his weapon drawn—not the wimpy little .22, but a limb-ripping .44—while making it look as if he were shielding the CO from an attack.

Jones was on top of the colonel, like some kind of zombie gone mad. The whites of his eyes stood out in his blood-covered face, as he dragged Colonel Subandrio with him at gunpoint, so that his back was against the tank. Good plan.

"Hold your fire," Jones shouted as the shooting finally ended.

Max scrambled to his feet beside him, using the CO as a shield, sidearm at the man's throat. "Hands where I can see them," he ordered. Jones told the colonel the same thing in more colorful language.

The interpreter was flat on his face in the street, and Jones kicked a spray of dirt in his direction. "Hey, you! Tell them to hold their fire, or I'll kill him and then I'll fucking kill you, too!"

Fire the weapons for a count of four, no more, then get the hell down. Jones's voice rang in Gina's ears, along with the ringing that came after four solid seconds of high-decibel destruction.

She pulled Molly down with her, beneath the window, their backs to the wall.

"He moved, did you see that?" she asked Molly, who nodded, tears still streaming down her face.

"I thought he was really dead."

"I know," Gina said, holding tightly to her friend. "He's okay. They're both okay."

So far.

But it wasn't over yet.

Colonel Subandrio was playing the disdainful courage card, while Max's hostage had definitely wet his pants.

"I should have known better," the colonel told Jones. "You don't really think you'll get away from me, do you? Two men against hundreds?"

Jones pressed his weapon beneath Subandrio's chin as he went through the man's pockets, tossing a knife, a billfold, and a pearl-handled revolver onto the street. "Where's the radio to contact the tank?"

"I don't have it," the colonel said, although his gaze flicked briefly to the interpreter.

Okay.

"And if you think—"

"Shut the fuck up." Jones moved his gun up to the colonel's ear.

"Order your troops to stand down," Max ordered Subandrio. "Order the tank personnel to open the hatch and evacuate. Now."

"I will not," the colonel scoffed. "Drop your weapons or I'll order the tank to fire on the house. All I have to do is give the command to—"

Max looked at Jones.

Who didn't so much as blink as he pumped a pair of bullets into Subandrio's head.

He lowered the former colonel almost gently to the ground.

Max focused his attention on the CO, who may have soiled his pants yet again. "Order your troops to stand down. Order the crew of the tank to open the hatch and evacuate. Quickly." It was just a matter of time before one of the hundreds of soldiers surrounding them decided to play hero.

The CO stared down at Subandrio's body and then up as Jones stepped closer.

"Do it now," Jones said.

CHAPTER
TWENTY-FIVE

Jules was too late.

As Rexi Ernalia's Mini skidded to a stop, Jules saw a body lying in the square, near what was, indeed, a very large tank.

He scrambled from the car, jarring his leg and making himself damn near puke. But there was no time for that—he pulled himself up on the crutches and hobbled a little bit closer and . . .

It wasn't Max. It wasn't Jones.

It was a little toad of a man in a fancy uniform, looking even uglier than he'd started the day, with half his head gone.

The house across the square, however—Emilio's house—was still in one piece. It was clear from the position of the troops that this was where the "terrorists" were "holed up."

Apparently Max and Co. hadn't managed to leave after Jules had taken his fun ride down the mountain with Emilio.

"Who's in charge here?" Jules shouted now.

And no one answered. Of course, he *was* speaking English.

He heard that small-car-backing-up whining sound and looked to see Rexi flash him a peace sign as he pulled away. Hey, thanks, pal. Not, of course, that Rexi could have helped with Jules's translation problem.

It was wild—almost as if he were on the set of a movie.

As if the soldiers strategically positioned around the area were all actors taking five, muttering together and scratching their armpits, having a soda or cigarette.

A man who looked to be an officer finally approached him. "American?" he asked.

"Yes," Jules said, but the fellow launched into a long explanation, complete with gestures toward the body, the troops, the jeeps, the tank, and the house. He pointed to the road going up the mountain, pointed to the road going down.

And it was all totally not in English. Or even Spanish, which Jules also spoke quite well.

"English, please," Jules said when he could finally get in a word edgewise. "Does anyone here speak English?"

Again the officer pointed to the tank.

Which, seemingly on cue, roared to life.

Perfect.

"Tell your men," Jules mimed the words as well, pointing to his mouth and then the array of soldiers, "to stand down." Okay, how was he going to communicate *that*? He tried again. "To hold their fire." He pointed to the man's weapon, pretended he was firing something similar, and then made a giant *no* gesture.

The man seemed pleased to have something to tell the troops.

Except, what about the tank? Who was going to tell them?

As Jules headed toward it, it moved backwards a bit, then jerked to a stop. It moved forward, then stopped. And then the gun turret turned all the way to the right and all the way to the left, as if someone were testing its operating system.

He was right alongside of it now, except how the heck did you get the attention of soldiers inside of a tank?

Knock on its side?

It started moving again. Very slowly. Heading directly for Emilio's house.

It wouldn't take too many direct hits from a tank—particularly at a close range—to turn that place to rubble.

"Hey," Max said to Gina. "Look out the window."

She and Molly were lying on their backs on the floor in the upstairs room in Emilio's house, completely cried out.

Max's voice, coming in clearly over that walkie-talkie had been the sweetest sound Gina had ever heard.

Molly had grabbed it and apologized for threatening to kill him, but had he actually shot Grady out there in the square?

Jones had grabbed the walkie-talkie from Max and reassured her that although, yes, Max had shot him, it was extremely superficial. Max had very good aim. Everything vital was still right where it was supposed to be.

Part A of the plan was a tremendous success. Max and Jones had gotten complete control of the tank. Part B was a little problematic, since it ran on the assumption that there would be a radio in the tank.

There was not.

Nothing more, at least, than the same sort of walkie-talkie they already had.

So now the new plan was to maneuver the tank in front of the house, like a giant guard dog.

Sooner or later, help would come.

And until it did, they'd be in possession of the biggest gun on the island.

However, Max had told Gina that he was betting help would arrive on the sooner side. Especially considering they'd taken the CO and his interpreter hostage.

But now Max wanted Gina to look out the window.

"The cavalry has arrived," he told her.

Someone was standing directly in front of the tank. Whoever he was—a boy, dressed like a surfer, on crutches—was holding one hand out in front of him like a traffic cop signaling *halt*.

The tank, of course, had rolled to a stop.

And Gina realized this was no ordinary surfer, this was Jules Cassidy.

Jules was alive!

And here she'd thought she was all cried out.

Max laughed as he peered out through the slit that passed as a windshield for the tank. "He has no idea that we're in here," he said.

Damn, Jules looked like he'd been hit by a bus.

"Jesus, he has some balls." Jones turned to the interpreter, who still didn't quite believe that they weren't going to kill him. "Open the hatch."

"Yes, sir." He poked his head out.

"Do you speak English?" Max could hear Jules through the opening.

"Yes, sir."

"Tell your commanding officer to back up. In fact, tell him to leave the area. I'm in charge of this situation now. My name is Jules Cassidy and I'm an American, with the FBI. There are Marine gunships on their way, they'll be here any minute. They have armor-penetrating artillery—they'll blow you to hell, so back off."

"Tell him Jones wants to know if the gunships are really coming, or if that's just something he learned in FBI Bullshitting 101."

The interpreter passed the message along.

As Max watched, surprise and relief crossed Jules's face.

"Is Max in there, too?" Jules asked.

"Yes, sir," the interpreter said.

"Well, shit." Jules grinned. "I should've stayed in the hospital."

"I hear helicopters!" Gina's voice came through the

walkie-talkie. "I can see them, too! They're definitely American!"

Max took a deep breath, keyed the talk button. And sang. "Love me tender, love me sweet, never let me go . . ."

Jones sat in Emilio's kitchen with his arms around Molly.

She'd helped him clean out his various injuries, and satisfied herself that he didn't still have a bullet in his leg from Max's .22.

"Did you know he was going to do that?" she asked. "Shoot you?"

"No," he said. "It was inspired, though."

"I thought he'd really killed you," Molly told him. "It was the first time in a long time that I've been that angry. Angry enough to hurt somebody."

"Welcome to my world," he told her. "Must be the hormones."

Molly laughed, but it sounded a little grim. "That's the last time you're going to say that. Ever." She was looking around. "You know, we're alone."

"Yup." Jones knew where she was going, and he really didn't want to have this conversation. He tried to steer in a different direction. "Why? You want to give the old kitchen table a go?"

She laughed, but her smile faded to serious far too quickly. "I know you told me before that you made a deal with Max but—"

"Nothing's changed," Jones said quietly. "If anything, I owe him even more now."

"Hasn't it occurred to you that he's purposely off dealing with the Marine captain to give you a chance to slip away?"

"So what if he is?" Jones countered. "I gave him my word. And Mol, we talked a little bit in the tank, about me trying to cut a deal. Info on Heru Nusantara in exchange for a clean slate. A chance to go home. Raise this baby with you."

"It just seems . . . risky."

"Any riskier than waiting to start chemo until after the baby is born?"

"Fair enough," she said.

They sat silently for a moment, then Molly cleared her throat. "Do you maybe want to talk about—"

"Were you watching?" Jones asked. Again he knew exactly what she was thinking. About when he'd killed Ram Subandrio.

"No," she said. "I mean, I *was,* but I didn't see it. It was just . . . one minute he was there, and the next he was on the ground."

"That's pretty much how it works."

"Does it bother you?" Molly asked.

"You mean, do I feel guilty killing him? No. I once watched him murder a two-year-old. I think when Max and I went out there, I was actually kind of hoping it would go down the way it did."

"Knock-knock." Gina poked her head in the door.

"Come on in," Jones said. "We've got all our clothes on for a change. Oh, wait, it's *you* who gets it on in the—"

"Okay," Gina said. "Am I ever going to live this down?"

"Eventually," Molly said. "But Max singing you old Elvis songs over the walkie-talkie? Honey, *that's* going to be impossible to kill."

"I think it's sweet," Jones told her.

"The singing or the kitchen tabling?" she asked.

"Both," he said. "Seriously, Gina. He's all right. I always hated him for making you so unhappy, but . . . he's a good guy."

Gina nodded. "He's really thoughtful, and considerate and . . . Speaking of which. He asked me to give this to you." She handed Molly a cell phone. "He said to tell you that the Marines set up temporary towers, and that it's currently seven forty-seven A.M. in Hamburg, and the clinic opens at seven, so . . ." She handed her a piece of paper, too. "The phone number is on there. Ask for Dr. Bloom."

"They're not going to give me the biopsy results over the phone," Molly said. "Are they?"

The test results that would tell them whether or not Molly had cancer—and just how bad it was. Jones was glad he was sitting down.

"We weren't sure," Gina said. "Max sent someone from the Hamburg office over to talk to them and explain what's going on. Dr. Bloom is waiting for your call. He knows you're out of town in kind of a major way."

She hugged Molly and started to leave.

But Molly caught her hand. "Stay, okay?"

Jones took the phone and paper from her and dialed.

Marine Captain Ben Webster was pretty laid-back for a guy who looked as if he could bench press the entire Western Hemisphere.

He seemed fine with the fact that although he and his Marines had been sent to Meda Island to kick some terrorist ass, they'd instead been left to clean up after a confusing incident in which a high ranking Indonesian military officer—Colonel Subandrio—was apparently linked to a kidnapping and murder, as well as gunrunners and terrorists.

Max had made sure Emilio's computer disks were secure. The Marines were settling in to guard the house—at least until a team from the Jakarta CIA office could arrive to search it more thoroughly.

"Excuse me, Mr. Bhagat. I'm sorry to bother you, sir."

Max looked up from his conversation with Webster to see one of the Marine medics standing nearby. "What's up, Corporal?" he asked.

"Your associate, Mr. Cassidy, sir? I've been recommending that we get him back to the ship's hospital," the earnest young man said. "His leg needs to be properly set. Yes, it's splinted, but it's got to be killing him. In addition, he's lost a lot of blood from that gunshot wound, plus he's had a head injury. They can be real tricky."

"Good," Max said. "Get him over there."

"Yes, sir, that's the problem. He won't go. He insists that he's got to talk to both you and Cap'n Web."

Speak of the devil. Jules came hobbling over.

He held out his hand. "Captain Webster, once again, it was a pleasure, sir. Your men and women think very highly of you." The two men shook. "I didn't want to leave without thanking you," Jules told him.

"I should probably be thanking you," Webster said with a smile. "My people are glad to be on shore for awhile. We've been ramped up and ready to go ever since the word came down about the dirty bomb plot. We were hoping we'd get ordered back to San Diego, and for a while it looked like that was going to happen. Of course, then when the embassy in Jakarta was hit, we were way the hell over here—too far away to help."

Jules turned to Max. "I'm not sure if you heard, sir, but there were only a few casualties in that attack."

"It's been frustrating," Webster admitted. "But it's not every day we get an order direct from the White House."

A what? Max looked at Jules.

"Yes, well . . ." Jules met his eyes only briefly.

"I'd love to chat more," Webster continued, "but you know, Barney here, he's a smart kid. If he says you need to get to the hospital, then you should get going."

"Thanks again, sir." Jules shook his hand again.

"You're welcome again," the captain said, his smile warm. "I'll be back aboard the ship myself at around nineteen hundred. If it's okay with you, I'll, uh, stop in, see how you're doing."

Son of a bitch. Was Jules getting hit on? Max looked at Webster again. He looked like a Marine. Muscles, meticulous uniform, well-groomed hair. That didn't make him gay. And he'd smiled warmly at Max, too. The man was friendly, personable. And yet . . .

Jules was flustered.

"Thanks," he said. "That would be . . . That'd be nice. Would you excuse me, though, for a sec? I've got to speak to Max, before I, uh . . . But I'll head over to the ship right away."

Webster shook Max's hand. "It was an honor meeting you, sir." He smiled again at Jules.

Okay, he hadn't smiled at Max like that.

Max waited until the captain and the medic both were out of earshot. "Is he—"

"Don't ask, don't tell," Jules said. "But, oh my God."

"He seems nice," Max said.

"Yes," Jules said. "Yes, he does."

"So. The White House?"

"Yeah. About that . . ." Jules took a deep breath. "I need to let you know that you might be getting a call from President Bryant."

"Might be," Max repeated.

"Yes," Jules said. "In a very definite way." He spoke quickly, trying to run his words together: "I had a very interesting conversation with him in which I kind of let slip that you'd resigned again and he was unhappy about that so I told him I *might* be able to persuade you to come back to work if he'd order three choppers filled with Marines to Meda Island as soon as possible."

"You called the President of the United States," Max said. "During a time of international crisis, and basically blackmailed him into sending Marines."

Jules thought about that. "Yeah. Yup. Although it was a pretty weird phone call, because I was talking via radio to some grunt in the CIA office. I had him put in the call to the President for me, and we did this kind of relay thing."

"You called the President," Max repeated. "And you got through . . . ?"

"Yeah, see, I had your cell phone. I'd accidentally switched them, and . . . The President's direct line was in your address book, so . . ."

Max nodded. "Okay," he said.

"That's it?" Jules said. "Just, okay, you'll come back? Can I call Alan to tell him? We're on a first-name basis now, me and the Pres."

"No," Max said. "There's more. When you call your pal Alan, tell him I'm interested, but I'm looking to make a deal for a former Special Forces NCO."

"Grady Morant," Jules said.

"He's got info on Heru Nusantara that the president will find interesting. In return, we want a full pardon and a new identity."

Jules nodded. "I think I could set that up." He started for the helicopter, but then turned back. "What's Webster's first name? Do you know?"

"Ben," Max told him. "Have a nice vacation."

"Recovering from a gunshot wound is not a vacation. You need to write that, like, on your hand or something. Jeez."

Max laughed. "Hey, Jules?"

He turned back again. "Yes, sir?"

"Thanks for being such a good friend."

Jules's smile was beautiful. "You're welcome, Max." But that smile faded far too quickly. "Uh-oh, heads up—crying girlfriend on your six."

Ah, God, no . . . Max turned to see Gina, running toward him.

Please God, let those be tears of joy.

"What's the verdict?" he asked her.

Gina said the word he'd been praying for. "Benign."

Max took her in his arms, this woman who was the love of his life, and kissed her.

Right in front of the Marines.

CHAPTER
TWENTY-SIX

As the plane touched down at LAX, Molly held Jones's hand.

"You okay?" she asked.

He'd been glued to the window, watching Los Angeles grow larger and larger as they'd approached the runway, but now he looked up. "I think I'm still waiting for the squads of MPs to surround me, locked and loaded, and order me face down onto the ground."

"That's not going to happen," she told him.

Jones nodded. He even managed to smile at her.

But he didn't believe it.

And sure enough, as the announcement came to stay seated until the plane reached the gate, one of the flight attendants approached.

"Sir, we just received a message from airport security, asking you to remain on board until the rest of the passengers have deplaned," she said.

Jones glanced at Molly. *Here we go.* "Thanks," he told the woman.

But Molly leaned forward. "Excuse me," she said. "Is there a problem?"

The attendant's smile was sunny. "Not at all. Apparently

the gentleman who's meeting you wants to make sure he doesn't lose you in the crowd."

"See," Molly told him. "It's nothing."

But he didn't believe it.

"Whatever happens," Jones told his wife, "you get on that flight to Iowa tomorrow, okay?" He'd wanted her to visit her mother first thing—as well as her mother's doctor.

"Okay," she said, clearly humoring him.

"I'm serious."

"I know." She kissed him. "Hey, Byron's awake."

Byron?

"No?" she asked, obviously teasing him.

Jones shook his head. But he clung to the last shreds of his patience while the plane slowly emptied out by pressing his hand against Molly's stomach, trying to feel their baby dancing.

"Excuse me—Mr. and Mrs. Jones?" The man coming down the aisle was an FBI agent. Had to be. Dark suit, conservative tie—he wore the clothes and walked the walk. "My name's George Faulkner. I work with Max Bhagat. He's sorry he couldn't be here himself. He wanted to make sure everything was going smoothly, and that you have everything that you needed."

"Thank you," Molly said for him, because even though Jones shook the man's hand, he still didn't believe it. "We do."

There was no way that he was going to walk off of this plane unchallenged.

But Faulkner was carrying a briefcase and he opened it now, taking out what looked like all kinds of documents. "These are for the two of you." He handed them over.

Passports. Drivers licenses. Birth certificates. Social Security cards. Military documentation giving an honorable discharge dated today, for a Sergeant . . .

His new name, which was on all of the other documents as well, was William Davis Jones.

Faulkner was saying something that Jones didn't hear, but Molly was nodding, apparently paying attention.

"Back pay," she told him, as he looked questioningly at the envelope Faulkner was handing him.

Jones opened it and . . . Shit. He wasn't expecting this.

He was expecting his cheek ground into the pavement. Hands cuffed behind him as he was wrestled into a waiting cop car.

He looked at the rather large number on that check again and . . .

He still didn't believe it.

Molly had gathered up her bags and books, and Faulkner took their luggage down from the overhead rack. Jones followed them out of the airplane as the flight attendants smiled and said good-bye.

The walkway to the gate was like something out of a science fiction movie—it had been a long time since he'd been at LAX. The gate itself was blocked off from the rest of the terminal, with temporary walls leading down to the luggage area—like something that might be set up to lead cattle to slaughter.

Faulkner was talking about a car that was waiting for them, chatting with Molly about her due date and recommending restaurants near their hotel.

Molly took Jones's hand. "You okay?" she asked again.

He nodded, but he was lying and she knew it. She didn't let go of him.

"We don't have any checked luggage," she told Faulkner.

"I know," he said, "but I need you both to come over here and . . ."

And here it came. Jones took the envelope with the check for that so-called back pay out of his pocket and handed it to Molly. "You better take this," he said as he went around a corner and braced himself for . . .

A military band?

Playing "Stars and Stripes Forever . . . ?"

With a huge banner, that said, WELCOME HOME, SGT. JONES.

"Sorry for the subterfuge," Faulkner shouted over the trumpets and tubas. "Max wanted to make sure you got the message." He shook Jones's hand, Molly's too. "Car's right outside—whenever you're ready. If you need anything else, just give me a call."

And he was gone.

Leaving Jones and Molly standing in the Los Angeles airport. They were surrounded, not by military police with weapons drawn, but by other travelers who were giving him a round of applause.

Some of them even shook his hand, thanking him for his service.

As the band kicked into "America the Beautiful," Molly tugged on his arm. They went out through the automatic doors and over to the waiting cars, where, yes, one of the drivers held a sign saying JONES.

The California sun was warm on his face as he gave their bags to the man.

"Where you folks traveling from?" the driver asked.

"Kenya," Jones told him. "Via Jakarta and Hong Kong."

"Mmm," the man said. "Sounds like a nice trip. Still, nothing beats coming home."

"Yeah." Jones climbed in beside Molly. "Nothing beats coming home."

"You okay?" she asked him again.

"Yes," he said. "I am."

And this time she believed him.

EAST MEADOW, LONG ISLAND
JULY 16, 2005

So far so good.

Max was standing over by the bar, looking as if he were holding his own with Gina's two oldest brothers. It was hard to say, though, whether they were grilling him, or protecting him from the rest of the family.

It took a brave man to come into Anthony's Italian Restaurant's function room and meet the entire extended Vitagliano family all at once.

Max looked calm and cool, as usual. God only knew what he was thinking—especially after meeting the Great Aunts, Lucia and Tilly—who wanted to know what part of Italy the Bhagats came from. And then there was Uncle Arturo, who kept asking him how much an FBI agent earned each year.

Gina caught Max's eye, and he smiled, thank goodness. But then she had to turn away because the waiter was finally beside her. Thank *God*.

But he was holding a tray of champagne in elegant flutes.

"I'm sorry," she said. "About a half hour ago, I asked for a ginger ale. Will you get that for me, as soon as possible?"

He murmured something unintelligible as he headed . . . not to the bar, but into the crowd.

Shoot.

She had to get something into her stomach soon or this engagement party would turn into a total disaster.

But if she went toward the bar, she'd have to stop and chat with Father Timothy, and her cousins Mario and Angela, and Mrs. Fetterson who'd lived next door to Gina's grandparents for forty-five years . . .

"Gina!" Her mother waved to her from the corner, where she was arguing with Rob and Leo's wives—the wicked sisters-in-law—over the best place on Long Island to hold a wedding. "Debbie says La Maison has openings in December 2007 . . ."

"Just a sec, Mom . . ." Gina took a wide berth around them. Escape, escape . . . God, *where* was the ladies' room?

She felt a hand at her waist and looked up to find Max beside her.

"Are you all right?" he leaned close to ask her quietly.

She shook her head, completely unable even to speak.

But he steered her toward the kitchen, and—yes!—there it was.

She ran for it, praying that unlike most ladies' rooms on the planet, there wasn't a line.

There wasn't.

But she nearly knocked over a pretty African American woman as she lunged for the only open stall.

"Gina?"

Oh, shit—the woman she'd hip-checked into the sinks was none other than Alyssa Locke.

Max had told her that both Alyssa and her husband Sam were in New York City this week, and Gina had invited them to this party her parents were throwing to celebrate their engagement. Jules wasn't able to attend, nor were Molly and Jones. She'd thought it was only fair to have *some*one that Max knew there in the restaurant.

"Hi," Gina said, as she locked the door behind her. "Alyssa, right?"

"Yes, how are you?" Alyssa said. "Congratulations."

"Oh," Gina said. "Thanks . . . Excuse me—"

There was just no way to barf quietly.

Still, she probably could have gotten away with a cheerful comment about shellfish allergies, and a warning to be careful of the gourmet ravioli that was apparently stuffed with shrimp.

It might've worked, if she hadn't had one of those head-rushes of dizziness, the kind that happened sometimes when she stood up too fast, except this time it happened when she was trying to sit down.

The end result was that she connected with the floor much too quickly and much too hard, and with way more than just her rear end.

* * *

Max leaned against the wall by the ladies' room door, trying to be invisible so that Gina's Uncle Arturo wouldn't ask him for a job.

He looked at his watch. How long had she been in there? Gina's brother Leo had been telling him about this really awful stomach virus that was making the rounds at work.

The door opened, and he straightened up, but it wasn't Gina.

"Max! Get in here!"

It was Alyssa. She pulled him into the ladies' room where . . .

Gina was on the floor in one of the stalls. The door was locked, so he went underneath.

She was pushing herself up. "Oh, gross, my face was touching the floor."

Max helped her so that she was leaning against the wall. "What happened?" He unlocked the door and pushed it open.

"Sorry, this ladies' room is temporarily closed," he heard Alyssa stop people from coming in. "There's another upstairs. Sorry for the inconvenience and excuse me, would you mind standing out here for just a minute and . . . ? Thank you so much."

"I'm okay. I just . . . I shouldn't have skipped lunch," Gina said.

Alyssa appeared with a handful of wet paper towels and a handful of dry ones, too. "I'm going to go in search of some saltines or oyster crackers," she told them. "And ginger ale. That usually helps." She vanished.

"Are you really okay?" Max asked.

Gina nodded, wiping her mouth with one of the wet towels. "You know how you've been trying to talk me into going to law school?"

He nodded. He was no longer talking up NYU—that would be too far away. But there were plenty of good schools in D.C.

"Do you really need me to get a graduate degree?" she asked. "I mean, is there some FBI Wives Handbook that requires a Masters or better?"

"Of course not," Max said. "It's just . . . I work long hours and I'm out of town a lot. I just . . ." He made himself just say it. "I don't want you to get tired of me. You've always seemed so . . . restless. Going to Kenya and . . . Do you want me to get the car and take you home?"

Gina shook her head. "I'll be okay when Alyssa gets back with the . . . God, I'm pretty sure she's figured it out. Thank goodness she was in here and not my sister-in-law Debbie, the biggest gossip in the universe."

He was having trouble following her. "Figured what out? Gina, if you're not feeling well, we should really just go."

She seemed to want to stand, so he helped her to her feet. "I didn't find what I was looking for in Kenya."

"What *are* you looking for?" Max held onto her as she went to the sink. She still seemed so shaky.

She looked at him in the mirror as she washed her hands. As she rinsed out her mouth.

"This," Gina said. "Look at you. Ready to catch me if I fall. Standing beside me." She dried her hands, tossed the towel into the garbage. "I know you want to protect me from all the bad things that can happen in life, and I know it drives you crazy to think about all the awful things that could happen, but most of them are things we can't control. But what you *can* do is stand beside me when the bad things happen. That's what I want to do for you, too."

Max nodded. What was this leading to? He just waited for it. Whatever it was, it was coming.

She dug in her purse, coming up with a pack of mints. She put one in her mouth, held the pack out for him. He shook his head.

"You know, for a really long time I've felt this . . . responsibility to live a life of meaning," Gina told him. "Like, I must've survived that hijacking for a reason. But lately I've been thinking I've been looking too hard. *Meaning* doesn't mean I have to go to Kenya or become Mata Hari or Mother Teresa. Or even Ally McBeal. All I have to do is live well. Be happy.

"And that's what I'm doing," Gina said, turning to look at him, "when I'm with you."

"If we're still talking about you not wanting to go to law school," Max said, "you don't have to convince me. If you don't want to—"

"I was thinking," Gina said, "that I might want to be a stay-at-home mom."

And suddenly it all made sense.

Gina didn't have her brother Leo's stomach virus.

She was pregnant.

Holy God in heaven. Max went into freefall. Chaos. Terror.

"Are you sure?" he asked.

"No," she said, but she shook her head yes. "I haven't taken a home test yet, but . . . I know."

"Wow," he said. "Wow." He was going to be a father. "I don't know how to be a father. Not a good one. I mean, I know how to be a great bad father . . ."

"Are you kidding? You were amazing with Ajay."

Ajay had died. And Max still hadn't gotten over it.

"I know what you're thinking," Gina said, pulling him close. "Another person to love, another person to lose, right? Remember what I was just saying, about the lack of control thing? Here's the deal: As parents, you do everything you can possibly do to keep your children safe, with the knowledge that there are things we can't control. If something happens to our kid, Max, it won't be because we failed to protect her. It'll be because, well, life happens."

Life happens.

"Are you completely freaked out?" she asked him.

"No," Max said, but quickly recanted. "Yes, but it's a good kind of freaked out."

Gina laughed. "Good answer," she said, and kissed him. Life happens.

Chaos swirled around him—it always would. But Max held on tightly to this incredible woman who had brought light and laughter into his life.

"You want to go break the news to my mother that December 2007 isn't going to do it for us in terms of a wedding date? I mean, unless we want to work the baby in as flower girl . . ."

Life had indeed happened to Max, and her name was Gina.

PARTNERS—AND LOVERS—
SAM STARRETT AND ALYSSA LOCKE
ARE BACK IN ACTION IN
AN EXCLUSIVE SHORT STORY!

Sam Starrett's daughter had finally surrendered and fallen asleep when the telephone rang.

He closed her bedroom door as silently as possible and paced down the hall toward the living room, where he'd last seen the cordless phone.

Yesterday, three-and-a-half-year-old Haley had missed her nap and their dinner had been loud and far more tearful than dinosaur-shaped mac and cheese warranted. Apparently, without an afternoon rest, having to choose between green beans or peas as a side dish was a tragic dilemma of astronomical proportions.

Sam, always good at creative solutions, thought he'd solved the problem by heating up both vegetables.

At which point Haley wept inconsolably because the spoon she wanted to use was in the dishwasher.

It was then that Sam understood. As a former Navy SEAL and one of the top counterterrorism experts currently working in the private sector, he recognized that he was caught in a dread no-win scenario. He realized that even if he hand-washed the spoon, there would be something wrong with the fork, or the color of the napkin, or maybe even the brand of parmesan cheese he and his wife, Alyssa, kept in their fridge.

It was obvious that the real problem wasn't with the peas or the spoon or the cheese. Haley missed her mother—Sam's ex-wife, Mary Lou—and that, plus lack of a nap, had locked them into orbit around the Planet of Inconsolable Unhappiness.

Sam could totally relate. He, himself, was struggling hard to keep from joining his daughter there because Mary Lou wasn't the only one out of town. Just over a week ago, Alyssa had gone OCONUS.

A diplomat on a peace-keeping mission to Kazbekistan— a third-world terrorist hotbed nicknamed "the Pit"—had contacted Troubleshooters Incorporated, the private security company where Sam and Alyssa both worked. Former Senator Eugene Ryan was adamant about not showing up in the battle-weary country surrounded by heavily armed, dangerous-looking "bruisers" as guards. At the same time, he wisely didn't want to go in without adequate protection.

And so he'd requested Alyssa join his security team.

In a country that wasn't exactly known for its equal rights, no one would expect a woman to be an expert sharpshooter and total kick-ass bodyguard despite her lack of height and bulk.

Sam had desperately wanted to go along—but his goal was not to keep Ryan safe. No, he wanted to watch his wife's six. But he was the exact physical type that the former senator didn't want along for the ride. Not to mention the fact that he'd promised his ex-wife that he'd watch Haley this week. . . .

And so he'd driven Lys to the airport and kissed her good-bye, working overtime to keep her from noticing his tightly gritted teeth.

It had to happen sooner or later, but as he'd watched her walk into the terminal, he had to admit that he'd been hoping for much, much later. But here it was. For the first time since they were married, Alyssa was off on a dangerous assignment without him. And it would be another week, at least, before she came safely home.

So last night, as the green beans and peas were both heating in the microwave, Sam had sat down with Haley on the floor of the kitchen and told her it was obvious there was nothing to do but go on and have a good ol' cry.

"Why are you crying?" she'd asked.

"Wah," he'd said. "The Dallas Cowboys lost the football game last week."

His pretend sobs had made her giggle, at least for a little while.

Still, the entire rest of the evening had been filled with the potential for an all-out meltdown.

The first few days had been fun. An entire week at Daddy's was a novelty for Haley, who'd never spent more than a weekend away from her mother. Sam knew it had been exciting for her, too, to look at the pictures from the brochure and imagine Momma and her new husband having a romantic vacation aboard a cruise ship.

As for Sam, he'd appreciated the distraction—what was Alyssa doing right now? Was she in danger? Was he going to have to wait another five days before she had a chance to call him again?—as he took his tiny blond daughter to the zoo and over to Old Town San Diego.

But today, over their Cap'n Crunch and orange juice, Sam and Haley had started counting the days on the calendar—four—until Mary Lou came back home.

Four days was definitely doable, provided they didn't miss any more of those very important naps.

If he could convince her to fall asleep. He'd just sat with her for over an hour, holding her hand.

The phone shrilled again as Sam searched for it among the pile of toy cars and dolls on the living-room rug. He loved his little daughter dearly, but please, sweet Jesus, don't let her wake up yet.

He managed to find and grab the cordless phone before it completed that second ring. "Sam Starrett." Shoot, he must be tired. This was his home phone, and here the correct greeting was "Hello."

The woman on the other end didn't seem to mind. "Please hold for Mr. Cassidy," she said.

Well, la di dah. Lookie who got himself a secretary.

Sam had left a message for Jules Cassidy just yesterday, asking for an update in the FBI's search for a serial killer known as "the Dentist." He and Lys had handled a missing person case last year which hadn't ended happily. They'd found the young woman they were searching for—or rather, they'd found what was left of her after the Dentist worked her over.

They'd also discovered that the Dentist had been posing as a ski instructor in New Hampshire, using the alias "Steve Hathaway."

Alyssa—normally tough as nails—had been unusually upset when they'd found the body, even though the murder had occurred six months earlier. She'd taken it personally— so Sam had started getting regular updates on the case from Jules, her friend and former partner from her FBI days.

It was obvious to Sam that, after seeing that dead girl, Lys wanted to kick the Dentist's ass straight to hell where he belonged. She was afraid—and rightly so—that it was just a matter of time before the killer targeted his next victim.

After months of no progress, a man had recently surfaced in a resort town in Colorado who fit Hathaway's description. Sam was hoping the FBI agents working the case would locate the Dentist's grisly souvenirs from his victims and have enough evidence to take him into custody before Alyssa returned.

Giving her that news would be a wonderful welcome-home present—a thought that made him smile. Forget about flowers and chocolate. His wife wanted a psycho-killer behind bars.

She was different from most other women, no doubt about that. Which was not to say she didn't love chocolate . . .

Ah yes, Sam missed her very much.

There was a click, and Jules finally came on the line. "Sam."

"Hey," Sam greeted him, genuinely glad to hear Jules's voice. Five years ago, if someone had told him that he'd be happily married to his old nemesis Alyssa Locke, and best friends with *her* best friend—an openly gay man—Sam would've laughed his ass off. But obviously a lot could happen in five years. "Thanks for calling me back, *Mister Cassidy*."

There was the briefest pause, then Jules said, "I guess you're not watching TV."

"What? No. I've got Haley for the week and anything besides *Sesame Street* is too intense for her," Sam said, as he now began searching for the remote control beneath the Spider-Man and Powerpuff Girls coloring books that covered his coffee table. Haley got nightmares. It was Big Bird or a Disney DVD or the TV stayed off. Although it was possible that too much Big Bird was now giving Sam nightmares.

When he actually slept, that is.

"Sam, hang on a sec." Jules put his hand over the receiver as he spoke to someone else on his end. Usually irreverent and upbeat, he sounded serious. Hell, he was calling Sam *Sam* instead of SpongeBob or Pollyanna or one of those other humiliating nicknames that he usually used.

"What happened?" Sam asked as Jules came back on the phone. He answered his own question. "Another dead woman without teeth in Colorado."

"This isn't about the Dentist," Jules told him, as Sam found the remote and aimed it at the TV. "Listen, do yourself a favor and don't turn on the news."

Too late. Sam had already flipped to CNN where . . .

"Oh, shit," he breathed, sitting down heavily on the sofa.

Peacekeeper Attacked was the headline that hung over

the anchor's right shoulder, along with a picture of Eugene Ryan. ". . . in northern Kazbekistan, where the former senator's helicopter was believed to have been shot down."

Oh, God, no . . .

"We just received confirmation," Jules told him, "that one of Eugene Ryan's helicopters was hit by a shoulder-fired missile, just north of Ikrimah, which is a city in the northern province of—"

"I know where Ikrimah is," Sam interrupted him. " *One* of . . . ?" How many helos were transporting Ryan's delegation? Jesus, he couldn't breathe.

On the TV, the news anchor was now delivering a fluff piece on a pie-eating contest, a big smile on his face.

"One of two," Jules delivered the grim news as Sam hit the mute. Which meant there was a fifty-fifty chance Ly was on the helicopter that went down.

In flames.

"Before we lost radio contact," Jules continued, "the second chopper reported that there were definitely casualties but we don't know how many and we don't know who."

"Before," Sam repeated. "You lost . . . *radio contact?*"

"I am *so* sorry," Jules started, but Sam cut him off.

"Fuck sorry!" Sam winced, looking toward the room where Haley was sleeping. He lowered his voice, but it came out no less intense. "I don't want sorry. I want the information that you've—"

"We don't *have* any information." Jules raised his voice to talk over him. "All we have is speculation. Rumors. You know as well as I do what good that—"

"What are the rumors?" Sam asked.

"Sam," Jules said. "You *know* rumors are just—"

"Did the second helo go down, too?" Sam had to know.

"No," Jules said, but then added, "Not exactly. What we think happened, and, sweetie, breathe. This is mostly guesswork. Even though we have a few people who claim to be eyewitnesses, we have only their word that they were actully there. So yeah, they reported that after the first chopper crashed, the second swung back around to assist the survivors. According to these unreliable sources, it apparently landed, going out of view, behind several buildings. Then, allegedly, there was a second big explosion."

"And?" Sam asked tightly.

"And nothing," Jules said. "It's all speculation. You know as well as I do that this could be nothing more than one of the local warlords planting disinformation—"

"There was an *and* in your voice," Sam insisted. "God damn it, Jules, tell me all of it."

Jules exhaled hard. "The attack happened shortly before sunset. There've been unconfirmed reports of a fierce firefight in that area pretty much all night."

Sam was going to be sick. "So, best-case scenario is that my wife is on the ground in a hostile part of Kaz-fucking-bekistan, engaged in a gun battle with people who don't just want to kill her for being American, but who want to kill her slowly, on camera, broadcast over the Internet."

Worst case was that Alyssa was already dead—that she had been dead for hours.

"Who's going in after them?" Sam demanded.

"I don't know," Jules said. "Look, I'm going to make some phone calls, see what I can find out, okay? It may take me a while."

"Jules," Sam started, but he didn't have to say it. Jules said it for him.

"I'll call you back as soon as I hear anything. Good news or bad."

"Thanks." As Sam hung up the phone, the news anchor made a joke about a pop star who was getting married. It was absolutely surreal.

How could anyone laugh when Alyssa might be dead?

He turned off the TV, but then turned it back on, flipping to the other news stations and then back, hoping for something, anything that would let him see just what Alyssa was up against.

If there were any way to survive this, Lys would find it. Of that Sam had absolutely no doubt. She was strong, she was skilled, and she had the heart of a warrior.

But if her team was badly outnumbered by their attackers, if it was a handful against several hundred, they would soon be overpowered. And all of the skill, strength, and heart in the world wouldn't keep her alive.

Sam splashed water on his face, then dried it with his towel. It was one of the blue ones that he and Alyssa had picked out when they'd moved into this little house together, a few weeks before their wedding.

"Blue is all about serenity and tranquillity," she'd told him as they stood in the department store, when he'd suggested they get brown because it would hide the dirt and stains.

But she was serious, which had surprised him. For someone so down-to-earth and practical, as they'd decorated their house she'd paid a lot of attention to the mood created by color, as well as something called Feng Shui. Which was all about furniture placement and good vibes and all kinds of touchy-feely New Age voodoo.

Of course, maybe there was something to that Feng Shui crap, because Sam had never been happier and more at peace in his entire life than he had this past year, living here.

Then again, he'd be beyond ecstatic living in a cardboard box, as long as Alyssa was with him.

Please, God, keep her safe.

Sam took a deep breath, then opened the bathroom door.

The phone rang again, and Joan DaCosta, the wife of SEAL Team Sixteen's Lieutenant Mike Muldoon, picked it up out in the living room.

As the news of the downed choppers spread, friends and

relatives were calling him to find out details and offer their support. But it had quickly gotten overwhelming. "I'm sure Alyssa's all right. I'm sure she's fine . . . ," they reassured him. But they wanted him to say it back to them, too.

And the truth was, as optimistic as he usually was, in this case, he wasn't sure about anything. And no one *really* wanted to hear how he was scared shitless, and that this sitting still and waiting for news was driving him freaking nuts.

No one, that is, except for Joan and Savannah and Meg, the long-suffering wives of his three best friends from his days as a Navy SEAL.

Meg Nilsson—Johnny's wife—had been the first to arrive. She'd just opened his front door and walked inside his house, God bless her, announcing, "Hey, it's only me. I didn't ring the bell—I didn't want you to think I was someone bringing you bad news."

She'd brought her two daughters—Amy, a teenager from her first marriage, and four-year-old Robin, who had Johnny's eyes.

Amy possessed a maturity and sensitivity far beyond her years. She'd ushered both Robin and Haley outside, where she kept them occupied and entertained. Even now, hours later, Sam could hear their laughter from the backyard.

Shortly after Meg arrived, Chief Ken "WildCard" Karmody's wife, Savannah, pulled into the driveway. Mikey's Joan was right behind her.

They'd each given him a hug and told him they weren't going to let him go through this alone.

"Joan'll let me know if it's Jules on the phone, right?" Sam asked now, as he went back into the kitchen, where Meg and Savannah were sitting together at the table. At first glance they seemed to be unlikely friends.

Savannah was a high-powered attorney who had just made partner and opened a law office in San Diego, after years of a bicoastal marriage. She came from money and

worked not because she had to, but because she wanted to.
Sam suspected though, if and when the time came to start
a family with Kenny, she would throw herself into it with
the same wholehearted devotion.

Kind of the way Meg did. A brunette to Savannah's elf
princess blonde, Meg Nilsson worked part-time from a
home office. Her standard uniform was very different from
Van's lawyer clothes—T-shirts and shorts, sneakers on her
feet—better for chasing after Robin.

Sam knew for a fact that it wasn't easy for Meg and John
to make ends meet on John's salary.

And yet Savannah and Meg were friends. They both
loved their husbands—who willingly traveled to war zones
and other places that were hazardous to one's health.

They both knew that their husbands might be injured or
even killed in the line of duty at any given moment.

They knew what it felt like to carry around that anxiety,
to live for those overseas phone calls that usually came in
the middle of the night. "I'm sorry it's so late, but I finally
have cell service—it's weak, but it's there—and I'm not sure
when I'll get it again . . ."

Four days ago, before the helo crash, he got a call like
that from Alyssa. And for five minutes while he spoke to
her, he could breathe again. She had been safe, and he
knew it.

For those five minutes.

It ended far too quickly, and as soon as he hung up the
phone the anxiety came screaming back.

Alyssa had been scheduled to be away for just a short
time. SEALs, however, often went out for months. Sam absolutely couldn't imagine living like this for more than a
few weeks.

"Jules said it would be a while before he called again,"
Meg gently reminded him.

"Have you tried cleaning the refrigerator?" Savannah

suggested. "I've found it helps a little if you just keep moving."

Sam sat down, wearily rubbing his forehead. Jesus, his head ached. "I did the fridge the night Alyssa's flight left," he said on an exhale. "Then, in the morning, I took an axe, went out in the yard and removed this old stump we'd been talking about getting rid of." He'd chopped the crap out of it in about four hours.

"I usually stick to cleaning out closets." Savannah was impressed. "I've never tried anything that involves an axe."

"I have," Meg said dryly. "Don't bother. It doesn't help."

Nothing helped.

"If you want," Savannah suggested, "we could help you organize your closets. It'll keep you busy. And you'll also win big bonus points when Alyssa comes back."

When Alyssa comes back. They were sitting there, all three of them, pretending that *if Alyssa came back* wasn't what she really meant.

God, he hated this. But the alternative was sitting in his kitchen by himself. Or trying to fool Haley into thinking everything was all right, and sneaking into the bedroom every ten minutes to turn on CNN, to see if there was any new information that made it to the cable news station first.

So he told Savannah, "I did the closets on the second night. It took a while, but I wasn't going to sleep, so . . ."

"It's amazing, isn't it?" Meg asked, clearly working to keep the conversation going. "Just how much junk two people can accumulate in a short amount of time?"

"Yeah," he agreed. "I found this old hat—a baseball cap—that I thought I lost years ago and—" He broke off. "I can't do this. I'm sorry, I can't stand it. I'm just sitting here, so freaking helpless—I can't do a thing to help her. Even if I got on a plane . . ." It would take him at least forty-eight hours to get to Ikrimah. He closed his eyes.

"Right now, she could be dying. Right now. Right *now*. And I can't help her."

Meg took his hand. "I know," she said quietly. "It's hard, isn't it?"

Sam looked at her, and he knew that *she* knew exactly what he was feeling. "How many times have you done this?" he asked.

"Thought John might not be coming home?" she clarified. She didn't wait for him to respond. "There've been, oh, I guess three or four times somewhat similar to this situation. But, you know, every time he's out there and there's some news report about a helicopter crash or a suicide bomber or . . ." She laughed as she shook her head. "Believe me, there's a lot of prayer involved when you're married to a SEAL."

"And a lot of really clean refrigerators," Savannah added.

"Pristine closets."

"Well-gardened yards . . ."

"You see, John knows where he is when he's on an op," Meg told Sam. "He knows when he's safe and when he's at risk. But all I know is he's somewhere dangerous and . . ." She shrugged. "It sucks."

No kidding. "I had no idea," Sam admitted. "Before this, I just . . ." He shook his head. When he'd gone wheels-up with the team he'd understood that it was no picnic for the wives, girlfriends, and significant others they left behind. But he'd had no clue just how awful it could be.

Joan appeared in the doorway, cordless phone in her hands. "That was Mike," she told them. "The Team's training exercise'll be over in an hour. He and John and Ken'll bring dinner when they come."

The phone rang again, and Joan retreated toward the living room. "Starrett and Locke residence," Sam heard her say. But then she gasped. "Oh, my God!"

Sam was up and out of his chair, and he nearly collided

with her as she came racing back into the kitchen, thrusting the phone at him.

"Jules," he said as he clasped it to his ear. Please God, let this be good news. "What's the word?"

"It's not Jules," Joan said, but he waved for her to be quiet, because all he could hear was static, and then . . .

"Sam, it's me—I'm all right," Alyssa said—beautiful, wonderful, vibrant, and so-very-alive Alyssa—her voice suddenly clear as day.

"It's Lys," Joan announced, which was good because try as he might, Sam couldn't get the words out.

"Ah, Jesus, thank you, God," was all he could manage, and even that was little more than a whisper.

Meg and Savannah both leapt to their feet. Meg pulled one of the kitchen chairs behind him, and Savannah tugged him back into it, Joan pushing his head down between his knees—as if they thought he might actually faint.

"Hey!" But, shit, he *was* dizzy and on the verge of falling out of the chair, so maybe they were onto something there. But before he could thank them, they all left, hurrying out into the backyard to give him privacy.

"The SAS came in and . . . Gordon MacKenzie, remember him?" Alyssa asked him. "His team pulled us out. He remembers you—he wants to know what you think of his SAS boys now."

Gordon MacKenzie . . . ?

"Gordie told me his SAS team did some training exercises with SEAL Team Sixteen, back a few years," Alyssa continued as Sam desperately tried to regain his equilibrium. "He said they learned a lot from you—that you used to rate them on a scale from one to ten. But you never gave them anything higher than an eight."

Yeah, he remembered that. MacKenzie had gotten in his face and accused him of being a hard-nosed asshole. Actually *arsehole* was what he'd said in his quaint Scottish accent. Sam had countered by standing his ground and saying he'd give them a ten when they fucking deserved a ten. And no sooner. Maybe they'd earn it next year, he'd told Mac-Kenzie when the exercise had ended.

"Sam, are you still there? Can you hear me?" Alyssa was saying through the phone.

"Yeah," he said. "Yes. Lys, are you really all right?" Frickin' Gordie MacKenzie's team had helped save Alyssa's life. Next time he saw the dour bastard, he'd kiss him on the mouth. "Where are you?"

"The helo just landed on an aircraft carrier," she said. "We're safe." She sounded exhausted, and she exhaled hard. "Those of us who made it out alive."

"Are you hurt?" he asked, heart in his throat.

"Just a little tired," she told him—she always had been the queen of understatement. "Well, yeah, okay, I could use a few stitches—just a few, don't get upset, I'm fine. We're pretty dehydrated, though. They've got us all on IV drips."

"I am so freaking glad to hear your voice," he told her, and she laughed. "You have no idea . . ."

"Yeah," she said. "Actually, I do. Although, don't be jealous. I have to admit, as glad as I am to talk to you, I was even more glad to hear Gordie MacKenzie's voice this morning."

No kidding. "Tell Gordie that I love him," Sam said.

Alyssa laughed again. "Those aren't the three little words he's longing to hear from you, Sam. Seriously, what they did was . . . It was remarkably courageous. We were trapped and . . . I honestly didn't think anyone was coming for us—that anyone would be able to . . . I thought . . . It was bad," she said quietly.

Sam had to put his head back down between his knees. Alyssa, who never gave up, who wouldn't dream of quitting, had honestly thought she wasn't going to survive.

"He doesn't need me to give him a ten," Sam told her. "He knows."

"Still . . ." There was a storm of static. ". . . ignals fading—I have to go. Sam—"

"I love you," Sam told her. *Thank God, thank God, thank God . . .*

"I know." Alyssa's voice was fading in and out, but he could still make out her words. "There was a point where it would have been easier to, you know, just . . . have it over and done, but . . ."

"Thank you," he said, hoping she could still hear him. "For not giving up."

"How could I?" She sounded as if she were a million miles away. "You were with me, you know. Every minute. I could feel you by my side." Sam could just barely hear her laughter over the static. "Ready to give me shit if I so much as faltered. Gordie told me you have a permanent spot on his shoulder, too—whispering into his ear. And here you thought you were taking it easy, sitting around the kitchen with your feet up."

Taking it easy. She had no idea.

"I love you," he heard her say right before his phone beeped.

He looked at it and, yeah, the signal was gone.

Sitting around the kitchen . . . He'd been on dozens of dangerous missions. He'd risked his life more times than he could count.

None of it had been as hard as the past few hours.

Sam dialed Jules Cassidy's phone number, left a brief message. "Alyssa called. She's all right."

Through the kitchen window he could see Meg and Joan and Savannah out in the backyard with Haley and the other girls.

Sam punched Johnny Nilsson's cell number into his phone. The SEAL lieutenant was still out on a training exercise, so he left a voice mail. "Alyssa's safe—I just got off the phone with her. But that's not the only reason I'm calling. I think it would be smart if you brought your wife an armload of flowers when you came home," he told his friend. "Tell Mike and Kenny, too. Not just tonight, but every night for the rest of your lives."

It was already a half hour past Haley's bedtime when Sam sat on the edge of her bed. He'd promised she could watch a little bit of the football game with him, only it had started later than he'd thought.

"You want Duck or Hippo in there with you tonight?" His daughter frowned, and he quickly added, "Or both, on account of it being a special occasion."

"Because Alyssa's okay?" Haley asked.

"Yeah," he said, smiling into her anxious blue eyes. "And because she'll be home the same day as your mama."

Haley nodded, taking that in. "Amy said we had to stay outside in case you wanted to cry and say bad words," she told him. "Did you?"

"I think I said a few," Sam admitted. "And, yeah, I might've cried a little."

Haley nodded, so seriously. "If you want, I could put my fingers in my ears, like when the fire truck goes by."

Sam struggled to understand. "You mean . . . so you won't have to hear me cry? Haley, I'm not going to—"

"In case you say more bad words," she explained.

"I won't," he told her, struggling now not to laugh. "How about giving me a hug and kiss good night, Cookie Monster?"

"Sometimes there's nothing to do but have a good ol' cry," she said, repeating his words from the night before. "If you want, I could cry, too."

"No." Sam smoothed back her hair and kissed her on the cheek. "Thank you, but no." He tucked both Duck and Hippo in with her.

"If you want," Haley suggested, clinging to his fingers, "I could hold your hand. Keep you company until you fall asleep. I'm not very tired."

But her eyes were all but rolling back in her head. Amy had done quite a job, running Haley back and forth across the yard playing Tag and Red Light Green Light and Follow the Leader and other games Sam didn't even know the names of.

He'd keep that in mind tomorrow. Maybe they'd take a ride over to Coronado, buy a kite, and run up and down the beach a few thousand times.

"I love you, Haley," he whispered, but she was already asleep.

Sam left her door open a crack and went into the living room, where he turned on the TV and watched the football game right to the bitter end.

He then watched the news, where the anchors solemnly reported that five members of Eugene Ryan's delegation to Kazbekistan had died when their helo was shot down.

Five families had gotten the kind of phone call he'd been dreading. They had been given the message Meg and Savannah and all of the other wives of the SEALs in Team Sixteen prayed they'd never receive.

Their husband, wife, son, or daughter was never coming home.

It was entirely possible that any tears that Sam may have shed were the result of the Cowboys losing the game.

But probably not.

Read on for an exciting sneak peek
at Suzanne Brockmann's
new action-packed adventure

INTO THE STORM

Available in hardcover from Ballantine Books

Lindsey Fontaine knocked on her boss's door. It was ajar, so she pushed it open, peeking in. "You wanted to see me, sir," she started, but then realized there was someone in a Navy uniform sitting across from his desk. "Oh, I'm sorry."

"No, come on in, Linds." Her boss, Tom Paoletti, waved her into the room. "You've met Mark Jenkins, haven't you?"

"Not officially," Lindsey told him. She'd seen Jenkins earlier this morning. Hanging out at the new receptionist's desk.

Reading rank wasn't one of her strengths, but Tom was a former Navy SEAL. His company, Troubleshooters Incorporated, did a great deal of business with the government, including the military. Which meant lots of uniforms walked through their door.

The very young man—Jeez, were they really taking them this fresh out of diapers these days?—pushing himself to his feet while favoring his left side was a Petty Officer, First Class.

And oh, yes, he was definitely First Class—in more ways than one. Extra cute, with muscles.

But wait. His rank meant he'd been in the Navy for a number of years, because petty officers started at third class and worked their way up to first. And *that* meant he couldn't be as young as he looked.

Shame on her for making assumptions. She should've known better—as someone who still got carded. At the movies. When she went to see an R-rated film.

Lindsey knew firsthand what a pain in the butt it was to look far younger than her years.

"Nice to meet you," Jenkins said as he shook her hand.

Good grip. Solid eye contact. Pretty, *pretty* hazel eyes. Great smile. Cute freckles. And not too tall, either. She liked him already.

Except for the fact that he was clearly infatuated with Tracy Shapiro, Troubleshooters Incorporated's remarkably inept new receptionist. Of course, most men seemed to turn into idiots around women who looked like Tracy, the brainless hair-do.

Not that Lindsey had exchanged more than a casual greeting with Tracy, who'd started working there just a few days ago. But there was no doubt about it, Tracy had set Lindsey's Brainless Hair-Do-o-meter clacking right away. It might've had something to do with Tracy bumming five bucks for lunch off of Alyssa—after flat-out flirting with Alyssa's husband, Sam.

But okay, to be fair, it wasn't the flirting-with-Sam part that was a problem. Alyssa had to be good and used to that.

The real Hair-Do Action came from Tracy lamenting her lack of money for lunch, accepting a fiver from Alyssa with only the vaguest of promises to pay it back and then, without taking a breath, launching into an explanation of how she'd seen the shoes she was wearing on sale, and she just had to buy them, and could they believe she'd actually gotten them for only three hundred dollars?

When Lindsey came to work, she wore sneakers or clunky-heeled boots, bought on sale for $29.95, so . . . No. She could not believe that any pair of shoes, even those made by mermaids off the coast of Sicily, could be worth three hundred dollars.

"Jenk found Tracy for us," Tom Paoletti told Lindsey now. "They were friends back in high school."

"Ah," she said. *They were friends back in high school* was guy code for *Jenk had always wanted to jump her bones.* Apparently, he hadn't given up trying. He no doubt thought helping her get a job might work. "That explains it."

Oops, she probably shouldn't have said that aloud.

"I mean, I'm sure she's just . . . feeling her way, first days and all," Lindsey added, putting on what she hoped would be perceived as an optimistic expression. "I mean, we've all had 'em, right? First days . . . Kind of scary . . . Kind of overwhelming . . ."

"Absolutely," Jenk said, flashing her a grateful smile.

And first days of work had to be doubly hard for Tracy, who'd apparently been intercepted midway through her quest to see the Wizard and finally get a brain.

"Have a seat," Tom ordered in that easygoing way he had of making a demand sound like an invitation.

She sat. Jenkins sat too.

"We're going to be playing the part of Red Cell—the terrorists—in a training op with SEAL Team Sixteen," Tom told her now. "Jenk is going to be liaison as we work out the logistics."

"Really." Lindsey looked at the SEAL. "How . . ." *Convenient,* she was about to say, since his being liaison would give him even more access to Tracy. Except, Tracy was not a multitasker, and his distracting presence would be far less convenient for everyone else in the office. She, for one, was extremely tired of answering the phones because Tracy had managed to screw up the voice mail system again. "Interesting," she said instead, because they were both waiting for her to finish her sentence.

Day-am, the freckles across Jenk's nose were positively

adorable, especially when he frowned. Combined with those hazel eyes, rimmed by thick, dark lashes . . .

He was beyond cute, but it was probably in a way that he himself hated. Baby-faced cute. His mouth tightened slightly, because he misunderstood her comment. *Interesting.* . . . "I'm twenty-eight years old."

"Oh," she said. "No, I wasn't—"

"You were wondering," Jenk said. "I could see that you were wondering, so . . . Now you know. I'm old enough to vote."

"Actually, I wasn't wondering." Lindsey glanced at Tom, who smiled, apparently in no hurry to talk about that training op. Red Cell. That was going to be some kind of fun. "I mean, I was earlier, but then I did the math, figuring that you probably went to college and then . . . I had you at more like thirty, if you want to know the truth."

She'd surprised him. "You really thought . . . ?"

She shrugged. "Hey. Without makeup, I look about twelve."

He looked at her—really looked.

"Being flat-chested helps with the illusion," she said. "I'm five feet and three-eighths-of-an-inch tall—you better believe I count every eighth. I'm also the same age as my bra size. 30A. The A is for my four-oh average at UCLA, which I attended before my seven years with the LAPD." She smiled at him. "I'm one of Tom's best bodyguards, by the way. I specialize in the protection of people who might not want their friends, business associates, and/or enemies to know they're being protected. Because I could tell that *you* were wondering." She'd stunned him, so she turned to Tom who was now flat-out grinning. "Red Cell, huh? So you called me in here, boss, because you want me to play the part of Dr. Evil, the terrorist mastermind, right?"

She liked Tom for a lot of reasons, but particularly because she made him laugh. Some people didn't get her sense of humor, although Cutie-pie Jenkins seemed to be on the same page after he'd shaken off his shock.

"Sorry, I'm the terrorist mastermind of this one," Tom told her. "It was a direct request from Admiral Tucker."

Ah. "Which makes me . . ." She let her voice trail off. "Mini Me?"

Tom laughed again. "Tempting, but no. Not quite."

Uh-oh. "Please don't say that I'm . . ."

He spoke in unison with her. "The hostage."

Lindsey stared at him.

"Someone's got to be the hostage," Tom pointed out, undaunted by her scathing disbelief.

"Yeah, but come on. How realistic is it for the hostage to weigh only ninety-two pounds?" she leaned forward to argue. "Don't you want to give the SEALs a challenge?" Lindsey turned to Jenk. "Tell him you want a challenge. Tell him you want, I don't know, Sam Starrett to play the hostage. What is he? Six-and-a-half feet tall? Two ten? Now if only he had a heart condition, too, he'd be a perfect hostage."

"This time it's going to be you," Tom told her.

She knew when to stop pushing, so instead she sighed heavily. "All right." She stood up.

"We'll talk more later," Tom said, four little words made even more intriguing by the gleam in his eyes. Was it possible she was going to be more than the hostage? Suddenly this was back to maybe being fun.

Maybe.

"I just wanted you to meet Jenk," Tom continued. "If he needs help with the scheduling—or really anything," he added, addressing Jenkins directly, "he's going to come to you, Linds."

Oh, good. She was going to get to be the secretary, as well as the hostage, helping out with scheduling. Whoo-freakin'-hoo. She would have complained that she never saw Tom assigning Sam Starrett to help out with the scheduling—except for the fact that Sam was bitching about Tom giving him a similar task just last week.

"I was thinking it might be a good idea to have the two teams meet, sometime in the next week," Jenk suggested. "Maybe over at the LadyBug Lounge?"

"Really?" Lindsey was skeptical. "That doesn't seem very realistic. Meeting in advance, at a bar?"

"This is a silver bullet assignment," Jenk informed her, then translated. "Just short of R&R. Or it was supposed to be. Before Admiral Tucker got it into his head that it would be a kick to pit Tommy here against the new CO of Team Sixteen."

Lindsey looked at her boss. "Your old team versus your new?" she asked. "That's gotta suck. For your old team." She turned back to Jenk. "We are *so* going to kick your butts."

"Yeah, I don't think so. We're SEALs. And—no offense, Tommy—Commander Koehl's a good CO, so—"

"The poor guy," Lindsey said. "Because, like, isn't Team Sixteen still referred to as 'Tom's Team'? I mean, that's gotta sting. He's been there, what? At least a year already. That must be frustrating. And now if he loses—*when* he loses—"

Tom interrupted. "Training ops are not about winning and losing. They're about learning. About improving."

Lindsey looked at Jenk, who was looking back at Lindsey with an expression equally disbelieving. Not about winning? Who did Tom think he was kidding?

"And yes," Tom continued. "This *was* supposed to be fun. So let's see if we can't find the time for that social event. Don't forget to invite Lew Koehl. Let's try to downplay the winning and losing thing. Starting right here and now."

Lindsey looked over at Jenk again. "I'm down with learning," she said, even as she gazed pointedly at the spot where his rear was planted in that chair, making a tiny kicking motion with her foot.

"Totally into improving," he agreed, shooting her back a discreet L for loser, shaped with his thumb and forefinger, out of Tom's line of sight.

Lindsey couldn't help it. She laughed, covering it quickly with a cough.

Tom, of course, wasn't fooled. He rubbed his forehead. "I'm serious, people. This is going to be . . . at best, difficult. Both for Commander Koehl and for me. I want you working together. Let's turn this into a win for everyone." He smiled tightly. "Except maybe Admiral Tucker."

"We should look at a calendar," Jenk told Lindsey. "And exchange cell phone numbers."

Those words coming from those lips should have made her heart beat harder. Mark Jenkins wanted her phone number. He was cute and funny and smart—and tremendously flawed. He had, after all, the hots for the Hair-Do. And his wanting Lindsey's number was purely work-related.

No doubt about it, he was Lindsey's type. Perfectly, cleanly out of reach, unless, of course he got a little drunk and ended up going home with Lindsey as his solid second choice.

Oh, yeah, if she played her cards right, she could get totally skewered by this one.

Jenk sat in silence as Izzy drove them over to Tom Paoletti's house.

That hadn't gone the way he'd hoped it would.

In his fantasy version, he'd walk into the Troubleshooters Incorporated reception area to find that Tracy was finally getting the hang of manipulating the voicemail system. She'd smile at him, holding up one perfectly manicured finger, asking him to wait just a sec as she flawlessly connected the caller who'd requested operator assistance.

Then she'd smile at him again, thanking him for helping her find this wonderful job.

He'd remind her that he'd promised to take her to the furniture store with his truck, to pick up the dinette set she'd gotten on sale. He'd also promised he'd help bring it up to her second-floor apartment, help her put it together.

She'd suggest they go that evening, right after work. At which point he'd tell her he was babysitting for little Charlie Paoletti, and her eyes would widen the way Lindsey's had.

Izzy glanced at him now. "Dude, I hate to break it to you, but your girlfriend wants to jump me."

What?

Izzy nodded. "It's true."

"Why do people say *I hate to break it to you* when they're obviously gleeful about the news they're going to share?" Jenk asked.

"I'm not gleeful," Izzy said.

"Yeah, *dude*, you are."

"I'm actually depressed, because I really think I could have scored with her tonight."

God. "Yeah, I don't think so."

Instead of his fantasy with its meaningful eye contact and warm smiles, Tracy had been on the phone with Lyle, her scum-sucking ex-boyfriend. Jenk had walked into the reception area to find every other phone line ringing, as Tracy took a personal call—forgetting to switch on the voice mail system.

Lindsey was right behind him, and the two of them got the phones back under control. Of course, by then Tracy was focusing all of her energy on trying to hide the fact that talking to Lyle had made her cry.

The news that Jenk was babysitting for Tom tonight got absolutely zero reaction.

Nothing at all. Not even a blink in his direction.

"Tracy's got this ex who just won't leave her alone,"

Jenk told Izzy now. "He's trying to get them back together, and . . . She's pretty hung up on him. I have to figure out a way to—"

"Jenkins. Read my lips, okay? You're seriously deluded about this girl. And even if she was interested in you, I'd be advising you to hit and run. Did you check out her shoes? And her handbag? She's a shopper. Shag her, for sure, but then move on—before you're stuck paying her credit card bills for the rest of your life."

Shag her and move on. Jenk had done *shag her and move on*. His almost dying in Afghanistan had woken him up to a new reality. He didn't want *shag her and move on* anymore. He wanted the kind of closeness that Tom and his wife, Kelly, shared. He wanted the magic that the senior chief shared with his wife.

He wanted someone waiting for him when he came home at night.

Even crazy-assed Chief Karmody had found his soul mate. If *he* could do it, Jenk could too.

And why shouldn't it be Tracy Shapiro?

Sure, okay, she still didn't know he existed. She still saw him as Ginny Jenkins's annoying little brother. That was a perception he was going to have to change.

Was it going to be easy? No.

Was the fact that it wasn't going to be easy going to stop him?

No.

He was a Navy SEAL. He'd done difficult things in the past.

He *would* get Tracy to notice him, to fall in love with him, and yes, even to marry him, if that's what he decided he wanted.

It might take a while, but there was one thing he'd learned about himself over the past few years—he was a patient man.

"That Lindsey's pretty hot," Izzy said, as they took the turn onto Tommy's street. "I think she liked me, too."

"Lindsey?" Jenk couldn't keep the disbelief from his voice.

"You don't think she's hot?" Izzy misunderstood.

Oh, God. "Lookit, do me a favor," Jenk said. "And just . . . stay away from Lindsey, okay? She's—"

"Whoa," Izzy said. "Time out, Marky-Mark. You can't call dibs on everyone. One at a time, right? Fair's fair. So which is it, Tracy or Lindsey?"

Shit. "Tracy," Jenk said. "But seriously, Zanella, Lindsey's . . . different."

"Is she, you know, a friend of Ellen?" Izzy parked in front of the Paoletti's house. "That would be so cool. Do you think she's got a girlfriend, because I've always wanted to get with some lesbians." He laughed at the expression on Jenk's face. "Look at you. I'm kidding. That's the joke, right? Some asshole's all like, *Lesbians are so hot. Do you think they'll do me?* Only he's too stupid to know that they're lesbians because they're not into men and . . . never mind."

"No, I get it," Jenk said. "But Jesus, Izzy, sometimes you frighten me."

"So what do you think? *Is* she a dyke?"

Jenk exhaled his exasperation as he got out of Izzy's truck. "I don't know—it wasn't on the questionnaire I gave her about her sexual preferences. And frankly, I don't care. I like her, all right? As a friend. I don't want you to mess with her."

"You can call dibs on her if you want, but then you've gotta toss Tracy back. Otherwise, you've got no right."

Jenk followed Izzy up the path to the front door. "I don't know what I'm worried about. Lindsey's gonna break your balls."

"Perfect," Izzy said. "I'm into pain. Weeble."

Jenk stared at him. Had he just said . . .

"Tracy told me she used to call you that—right after she implied that she wanted to do me."

It was probably all true. Tracy had dreadful taste in men. Izzy was almost as big of an asshole as Lyle, so why shouldn't she be attracted to him?

This was going to be more difficult than he'd imagined.

Izzy grinned. "I'm guessing you were rounder when you were a kid, Wobble-Man."

"Fuck you."

"Fuck *you*," Izzy said cheerfully, as if it were some sort of blessing Jenk had bestowed on him, and that he was bestowing on Jenk in return.

From inside of the house, they could hear a baby crying. Ferociously. Izzy rang the doorbell. "Two Navy SEALS versus one angry nineteen-month-old," he mused. "The odds could go either way."

LOCATION: UNCERTAIN
DATE: UNKNOWN

She was cold. Always cold.

Hungry, too.

He kept the damp basement freezing, kept her carefully underfed.

And almost always in the dark. There were no windows. No way to tell the difference between night and day.

She tried to keep track of time, but it was impossible to do, especially during days like these, when she hadn't heard his footsteps in the kitchen overhead for what felt like weeks on end.

She couldn't remember the last time he'd brought her food. All she knew was that the supply she'd been hording was gone. She started to believe that she would starve to death, locked down here, cold and alone.

She tried to tell herself that that would be okay. It would be better than what he'd done to Number Four.

But then she heard it. Footsteps overhead.

His footsteps. She'd know them anywhere.

He was sliding something across the kitchen floor.

Someone.

She knew that he hadn't been shopping while he was gone all that time. She knew it wasn't a hundred-pound bag of potatoes that he'd dragged in from his car.

There was little she could be certain of in her life—in this nightmare that her life had become. But that he hadn't come home alone was definite.

And sure enough, he opened the door and came partly down the stairs. The glow from the kitchen spilled into the basement, lighting him from behind, making it hard for her to see his face.

"I'm back, Number Five. Did you miss me?"

She couldn't remember what he looked like. And she'd never really seen his eyes. Not without the sunglasses he'd worn when she'd gotten into his car. Time was a blur, but she knew it had been months since he'd first locked her down here. Maybe even years.

She'd had a name once—Beth. But now she was a number. Number Five.

He called her that, called her his champion, too, in his flat Yankee accent, when he opened the door to bring her food. Sometimes he brought fresh water, so she wouldn't have to drink the brackish liquid that seeped up in a pool in the corner of this prison.

God, how she hated him, how she feared him—yet how she looked forward to those dazzling moments of light.

This time, he threw something at her. She ducked, and it hit the wall before she realized what it was. A loaf of bread. A jar of peanut butter. She tore it open and ate it as quickly as she could. Because she'd learned that everything he gave her, he could easily take away.

She would have liked to save it, because she never knew if the food and water he'd brought was all she'd get for God knows how long. If he'd gone right back up the stairs, she would have rationed it, both dreading and praying for his swift return.

Sometimes he left food well out of range of her chains, with no way for her to reach it. She'd sit in the darkness, smelling it. Starving.

Sometimes he took and emptied the bucket he'd given her for her waste. Sometimes he wouldn't bring it back downstairs again for days on end. Sometimes he did. Sometimes he threw it at her, covering her with her own filth if she didn't move quickly enough out of the way.

All the while calling her Number Five. "You've been a good girl, Number Five."

"You've been a bad girl, Number Five."

It didn't matter what she did. God knows she tried being good, doing what she thought he wanted, but it soon became clear that the very thing she was praised for on one day would invoke his wrath on the next.

It was an awful way to live.

Only one thing was certain.

After he'd been gone for so long, he'd tell her it was time to get cleaned up. He'd get out his hose and spray her with water that stung and bruised her, that left her soaked and colder than ever. He'd toss her the key that would unlock the chain around her ankle.

But before that, he'd say the words she dreaded hearing, words she could count on hearing, words he spoke to her now.

"I've brought you a new friend."

More pulse-pounding suspense from
SUZANNE BROCKMANN

HOT TARGET

Cosmo Richter, suspended Navy SEAL and the newest member of the private-sector security firm Troubleshooters, Incorporated, finds himself in unfamiliar territory on his first case: a Hollywood movie set. Amid death threats from extremist groups, the film's controversial producer, Jane Chadwick, initially resists the Troubleshooters' protection—but soon she and Cosmo develop a bond more powerful than either could have anticipated. And when all hell erupts, desire and desperate choices will collide on a killing ground that may trap them both in the cross-fire.

"[An] intense thriller . . . an emotional banquet served with lots of taut adventure."
—*Romantic Times*

 Ballantine Books • www.suzannebrockmann.com